FINDING THE

"What did you want to talk about?" Sovilla asked as Snickers headed toward a tiny patch of grass and weeds.

Isaac stayed silent, trying to find the right way to reveal the truth.

Isaac jiggled Snickers's leash to move the puppy forward. He had to see Sovilla's face, but Snickers remained firmly planted.

"Sovilla?" Isaac breathed her name softly, reverently.

She turned when he called her, and their eyes met.

"You know h-how I feel about you, don't you?" he asked.

She shook her head.

Couldn't she tell? Or did she want him to put it into words?

He slipped the loop of Snickers's leash around his wrist so he could take both of her hands in his. This moment was too special and too sacred to make a mistake . . .

Books by Rachel J. Good

HIS UNEXPECTED AMISH TWINS

HIS PRETEND AMISH BRIDE

HIS ACCIDENTAL AMISH FAMILY

AN UNEXPECTED AMISH PROPOSAL

AN UNEXPECTED AMISH COURTSHIP

AMISH CHRISTMAS TWINS
(with Shelley Shepard Gray and Loree Lough)

Published by Kensington Publishing Corp.

An UNEXPECTED AMISH COURTSHIP

RACHEL J. GOOD

ZEBRA BOOKS
KENSINGTON PUBLISHING CORP.
www.kensingtonbooks.com

ZEBRA BOOKS are published by

Kensington Publishing Corp.
119 West 40th Street
New York, NY 10018

First Printing: August 2021
ISBN-13: 978-1-4201-5038-4
ISBN-10: 1-4201-5038-3

ISBN-13: 978-1-4201-5039-1 (eBook)
ISBN-10: 1-4201-5039-1 (eBook)

10 9 8 7 6 5 4 3 2 1

Printed in the United States of America

Chapter One

When a knock sounded on the front door, Sovilla Mast sloshed the mop back into the pail and hurried to answer. The mop handle clattered to the floor behind her, splashing dirty water onto the wall, the floor, and the back of her dress. Sovilla didn't care. She'd clean everything up later.

Perhaps Henry had been able to sneak away from work during his break after all. She flung open the door, her lips curved into a joyous welcome.

"O-Onkel Lloyd?" Her smile faltered along with her words.

"You look unhappy to see me."

"*Neh, neh.*" Not unhappy. Scared. Petrified. His visit signaled trouble.

"Aren't you going to let me in?" Nastiness oozed into his tone.

Sovilla loosened her white-knuckled grip on the door handle and stepped back. "S-sorry. Come in." Ignoring her roiling stomach, she pasted on a lopsided smile she hoped he'd mistake for friendliness. "You must be tired after your trip. Would you like something to eat?"

"Don't be ridiculous. A two-hour trip is not tiring, but

it is almost mealtime." He followed her down the hall to the kitchen.

Too late, Sovilla realized her mistake. Onkel had always chided her for untidiness.

He stopped short in the doorway. "What's this mess? At your age, you should do a better job with chores."

She withered under his critical stare. "I, um, had a little accident."

"So, you're still clumsy?" His expression reduced her to a pesky ant he'd be happy to crush under his boot.

Memories unspooled before her. All the times he'd scolded her as child for other accidents. Upsetting her glass of milk. Scorching the scrambled eggs. Shattering a plate. The list went on and on. For each infraction, he'd flayed her with his tongue.

Back then, whenever he'd thundered at her, she'd cowered. Now, at nineteen, she should be more courageous. But his contemptuous glance proved he could still make her shy and nervous.

To hide her edginess, she headed to the pantry. "Would you like spaghetti soup?"

He lowered himself into the chair at the head of the table. She assumed his grunt meant *jah*.

She bustled around, her muscles tense as she tried not to clank pots, bang the glass jar, or slop the sauce. Sovilla kept the flame low and stirred constantly as she heated the soup. She'd take care not to burn or spill the soup. She had no desire to hear more criticism.

For a brief moment, as they bowed their heads to pray, Sovilla exhaled a silent sigh at the temporary respite from her *onkel*'s glowers.

Lord, please help me to be kind and gracious.

She resisted the temptation to add, *Help me to survive until Mamm gets home.*

After they finished their meal, she washed the dishes and mopped under Lloyd's watchful gaze. Knowing he planned to pounce on any errors, she worked slowly and cautiously.

Her *onkel* blew out an exasperated breath. "If you moved faster, you wouldn't leave chores undone until afternoon."

Her back to him, Sovilla squeezed her eyes shut. No matter what she did, he'd find fault. And if she tried to explain, he'd reprimand her for back-talking. She bowed her head and swished the mop across the floor in rapid jerks.

"You missed a spot." Lloyd pointed to a place she hadn't yet reached.

Stretching her arms, she swiped the spot he'd indicated. If only Mamm would get home.

The battery-powered clock seemed to tick off the minutes in slow motion. Once she finished her chores, they sat in the living room. Positioning himself directly opposite her, Lloyd probed for information that Sovilla parried with neutral answers, attempting to give as little information as possible. Years ago, she'd adopted that defense to keep her privacy.

When he'd exhausted his questions, they sat in awkward silence. The click of the door broke the tension. Mamm had arrived. Sovilla wished she could warn her mother, give her a chance to compose herself.

"Whew. We had such a busy day. I'm—" Mamm stepped into the living room and froze, her face ashen. "Lloyd? What are you doing here?"

He rose. "Is that any way to greet your brother?"

"I—I just meant we weren't expecting you." Mamm

added a halfhearted greeting, then asked, "What brings you here?"

"You don't sound pleased to see me." The gloating expression on his face made it clear he enjoyed rattling her.

Without responding, Mamm sank into the closest chair as if sensing a disaster.

"I'm sure you know times are hard. Many businesses are closing." He steepled his fingers and pinned Mamm with a searching stare. "That means I can't afford to keep two households."

Mamm flinched and shut her eyes as if to ward off a threat.

"This house must be sold." Lloyd's words fell like a hammer blow.

"Mark gave it to me. Sovilla and I have been making payments." Mamm straightened her back and smoothed her apron over her black dress, which she still wore even though Daed had passed more than a year ago.

"But I've been taking care of the maintenance and taxes. Can you afford to take that on?"

Pain evident in her answer, Mamm said, "*Neh.*"

"Neither can I." Lloyd leaned forward. "I can stop paying, and after a while, the government will sell the house for back taxes. Or we can sell it now for a profit."

Mamm looked close to tears. "Mark and I moved in here when we married. We raised our children here. You can't—" Her voice shook. "Where would we live?"

"You'll move to Middlefield. My boys will move into one bedroom. You and your three girls can share the other bedroom."

"Leave Sugarcreek?" Before she could stop them, the words burst from Sovilla's lips. He couldn't be serious.

But Mamm's bowed head made it clear they had no choice.

Sovilla waited until Lloyd had gone to explode. "We can't move. I'll get another job."

"*Neh, dochder.*" Mamm spoke heavily, as if she'd borne the burdens of twenty years in one afternoon. "If Lloyd needs the money for his business, we can't be selfish."

"But—"

Mamm held up a hand to stop Sovilla's protest. "I'm going to lie down for a while and pray. Can you feed your sisters their supper?"

"You're not going to eat?"

"Not tonight. I have no appetite. Please don't say anything to the girls until I have our plans worked out."

Sovilla's heart plunged. Mamm looked so despondent.

The back door banged open, and her sisters' chatter washed over Sovilla, flowing around her like waves of sound with no meaning. By rote, she settled the girls at the table with a snack, but her thoughts had carried her far away, back to the summers and holidays they'd spent at her *onkel*'s farm.

Once, she'd caught her three cousins in the barn smoking. Older and taller, they'd ringed her in, threatening her until she agreed not to tattle.

Sovilla had shuffled back to the house, her head bowed, uncertain whether she'd keep her promise. If a careless spark ignited the straw, the whole barn would go up in flames. An inferno that burned in her nightmares.

Later that night, when she whimpered in the dark, Mamm and Daed rushed in to comfort her and keep her quiet. But they couldn't ease her conscience. What if keeping her cousins' secret destroyed property or killed animals?

Each time she started to confess, a picture of her cousins'

angry faces frightened her into silence. Even now, she sometimes startled awake, trembling in terror as fire spread uncontrolled in her dreams.

Seven-year-old Martha Mae tugged at Sovilla's apron. "What's wrong?"

"Nothing for you to worry about." At least not yet. Sovilla forced herself back to the kitchen, back to normality.

But life would never be normal again. Not if they moved to Middlefield.

A month later, Sovilla's footsteps echoed through the empty rooms. The house had sold quickly to another Amish family, and Lloyd had arranged for the sale of all their furniture at an auction. Mamm had remained stoic throughout, but as the auctioneers carted out the last of their possessions, tears trickled down her cheeks.

Sovilla wrapped an arm around Mamm's bowed shoulders. "I'm so sorry. I wish Lloyd had let you keep some of the furniture."

"*Ach*, *dochder*, I'm not crying over that. Furniture can be replaced. You're why my heart aches."

"Me?" Mamm made no sense.

"I've seen the way your cousins bully you. Now that you're nineteen, well, I worry—" She pinched her lips shut.

"I'll be all right." Sovilla's shaky response wouldn't lessen Mamm's fears.

"*Neh*. I don't trust them. I've made arrangements to send you to live with Wilma. She's been putting off her hip surgery, so I promised you'd take care of her and the house."

Wilma? Mamm wanted her to live with some stranger? "Who's Wilma?"

"My sister."

Sovilla stood there, stunned. "You have a sister named Wilma? Why haven't we ever met her?"

"It's a long story. She ran away during *rumspringa*. I never knew why. I'll let her tell you, if she's willing. But whatever you do, don't pry." Mamm opened her purse and held out an envelope.

"What's this?"

"Your tickets. Ardys at the quilt shop helped me print them."

"*Ach*, Mamm, no! Don't send me away. I'll do whatever you want, but not that."

Mamm's eyes overflowed with tears. "You have to do this, *dochder*. This move is hard enough. Please don't add to my burdens."

How could Sovilla fight that? With every ounce of love in her heart, she managed to say, "I'll do it for you, Mamm."

She'd go for now, but as soon as Wilma recovered, Sovilla intended to find a way back to her family.

In a tear-choked voice, she asked the question, but dreaded the answer. "When do I have to leave?"

"In about ten minutes."

"Ten minutes?" Sovilla practically screeched.

"Irene will be here to pick you up and take you to the station in New Philadelphia. The bus will take you to Harrisburg. Then you'll catch the train to Lancaster. Wilma will meet you."

Lancaster? Sovilla had never been farther from Sugarcreek than Middlefield. Those two-hour trips had been long and infrequent. To go all the way from Ohio to Pennsylvania? So far away she might never see her family again?

Sovilla blinked back tears. She didn't even have time to say goodbye.

Mamm hugged her tight. "I didn't want to tell you earlier and spoil our last few days together. I also want you out of here before Lloyd arrives in an hour. I'll not have him changing my plans."

"What about Henry?" They'd been courting for almost a year now, and Sovilla had been hoping he'd soon propose.

"You have a few minutes to write him a note. I'll run over and give it to his *mamm* before Lloyd gets here. I'll also give him Wilma's phone number. Maybe he can call you from work."

Sovilla didn't want to spend her last few minutes with Mamm and her sisters scribbling a letter, but what choice did she have? How would she ever explain to Henry why she'd left so suddenly? And even worse, that she might never be back? If she returned to Ohio, she'd have to head to Middlefield, not Sugarcreek.

Unless Henry offered to marry her.

Chapter Two

The scent of barbecuing chicken wafted through the air as Isaac Lantz stood in front of the baked goods counter at the Green Valley Farmers Market. He inhaled the aroma and almost tasted the crisp, crackling skin, the juicy meat. His stomach growled in anticipation, but he hadn't had breakfast yet.

He and his brothers had gotten here early with their lambs and chickens for the auction. Once they'd gotten set up, he'd sneaked off to get one of Fern's delicious cinnamon buns before her bakery sold out.

Isaac held Snickers's leash and waved away people who wanted to pet his puppy. Market regulars knew better than to touch his dogs, but strangers gave him nasty looks or huffed and turned away.

He sighed. If only he could explain. But it was too hard to keep struggling to repeat the same information over and over. That wasn't the worst part. He hated when people stared at him, their eyes filled with pity. Or, worse yet, got angry or impatient.

Keeping a close eye on Snickers, Isaac edged up to the counter when it was his turn. He didn't bother glancing up. Fern would bag up a cinnamon bun and hand it to him, saving Isaac from speaking.

"May I help you?" A woman's soft, sweet voice made him look up.

He blinked several times to clear his eyes. But this definitely wasn't Fern. Instead, a green-eyed brunette with a starched white *kapp* jutting straight out from the back of her head stared at him, a question shining in her eyes.

Tongue-tied, he could only gaze at this beautiful angel.

She repeated her question. "May I help you?"

Perhaps being unable to utter a word was a blessing. But she was waiting for an answer. He tapped on the glass, pointing to the two remaining cinnamon rolls.

"You want a cinnamon bun?"

His chest tight, he nodded. He longed to ask her name, to find out where she'd come from, to get to know her. But he kept his mouth closed, handed her his money, and accepted his change.

As he turned to go, she leaned over the counter. "Cute dog." Her gentle smile twisted his insides.

Isaac nodded his thanks, which must have appeared curt because hurt flared in her eyes. He longed to answer, but he wouldn't take that chance. He'd rather she thought him rude than face her pity.

He waved before he left, and his spirits rose when her expression softened into a smile.

Hurrying back to the auction, he pulled his brother aside and plied him with questions. Who was the new girl at Hartzler's barbecue stand? Did he know her name? When did she arrive? From where?

Judging by her *kapp*, she hailed from the Midwest. But Isaac wanted to know all the details.

Andrew laughed and shrugged. "Looks like someone's

interested in a girl," he said to his brother Zeke, who was walking past.

"Isaac?" Zeke laughed. "Really?"

Isaac wished he could stop the heat rising up his neck and splashing onto his cheeks. *I just asked a few simple questions, Andrew. You didn't have to turn it into such a big deal.*

Andrew clapped him on the shoulder. "Sorry, Isaac. I didn't mean to tease. Tell you what. I'll go over to the stand during our next break and see what I can find out. I'm curious about this girl myself."

Torn between wanting information and worrying the angel would prefer his brother, Isaac set his jaw and nodded. The girl wouldn't be interested in him anyway, not when she realized the truth.

If Sovilla hadn't been committed to Henry, she might have been interested in the strange young man who'd stopped at the stand. His blond hair and handsome features arrested her attention. But he'd been downright rude. Maybe girls fawned all over him, so he treated them with disdain.

He didn't even bother answering her questions. He just pointed at what he wanted and never thanked her for giving it to him. Yet something in his eyes called to her. A glint of loneliness.

She had no right to judge others.

The man who worked at the candy stand next to her laughed. "Wow, that kid has the hots for you."

Since they'd come in that morning, the man, who'd introduced himself as Nick, had made crude remarks as if he wanted to get a rise out of her. Although they bothered her, Sovilla ignored them. If she could stay calm through Onkel Lloyd's temper fits, she could handle Nick's comments. She hoped that if he didn't get a reaction from her, he'd soon stop.

"I noticed you eyeing him too. *Oh-ho*, we might just have another farmers market romance here."

Sovilla had no idea what other romance he was referring to, but she didn't want Nick to get the wrong impression. Keeping her tone polite and kind took some effort, but she managed to say, "I have a boyfriend in Ohio."

She hadn't heard from Henry yet, which had raised some doubts. What if he didn't want a long-distance relationship? What if he found someone else closer to home?

"Sorry. I'm just teasing."

Nick's apology startled her.

Sovilla handed her customer a bakery bag and some change, then she turned to face Nick. "That's all right. You didn't know."

He shook his head. "What's with all you Amish girls? You're so sickeningly sweet."

Sovilla could introduce him to a few sharp-tongued Amish girls or women who'd change his mind. "Not all of us are."

"Just my luck to get stuck with the ones who are, especially when I'm itching for a fight."

"Why?"

Her question had caught him off guard. He sputtered. "Well, because—because . . ."

"*Because* what, Nick?"

He shrugged. "I don't know. Pent-up anger and irritation, I guess. My son gets on my nerves. My wife, well, we had an argument this morning, and she got in the last word before she slammed the door."

Sovilla hid a smile. Nick seemed like the type who liked to dominate. Sort of like her *onkel*. It frustrated them if they didn't win an argument. Lloyd kept going until he did. Was Nick the same way?

She kept her tone gentle. "Maybe it's nice for your wife to get the last word in."

"Ya think? Now you sound like her." He peered at her suspiciously. "You been collaborating with her?"

"I've never met her." Then she added almost under her breath, "But I know what it's like to never win an argument."

Was that sympathy in Nick's eyes? Sovilla didn't have time to find out. She waited on another customer.

During their next lull, Nick sidled over. "Hey, I can understand you not wanting to get tromped on. That's what my wife says I do to her ideas. I imagine it's even worse with old battle-ax Wilma. People around here call her Pickle Lady."

Sovilla winced. She'd sensed a deep sadness under her *aenti*'s gruffness. Someone or something had hurt Wilma badly.

"Sorry," Nick said. "I guess with her being your relative and all, I shouldn't criticize."

"You're right." Sovilla didn't want to hurt his feelings, but she'd rather not hear negative things about her *aenti*.

"But you gotta admit, she can be one mean lady."

Nick had to get the last word in. Sovilla might have smiled if his words hadn't been so true. Still, she had to defend her *aenti*. "She's not as cruel as some people I know."

"Me?" Nick clapped both hands against his heart and fake swooned. "You wound me."

He was quite an actor and seemed to enjoy creating drama. "I didn't mean you, Nick."

"You didn't?" He looked almost disappointed. He obviously relished being the center of attention. Then his eyes widened. "Not your boyfriend, I hope."

"*Neh.*" She'd chosen Henry for his kindness and gentleness.

"Who, then?" Nick prodded.

Sovilla clammed up. She shouldn't be speaking negatively about her family this way.

"Oh, all right. Be that way." Nick lifted his nose in the air and strode off to wait on a customer.

How did Fern share her bakery stand space with such a temperamental man? It must be exhausting.

Speaking of temperamental men, here came that blond again. But as he neared, she changed her mind. He might be a mirror image of that previous customer, but he carried himself differently.

With a swagger and a confident smile, he leaned one elbow on the counter to study her. "You're not Fern."

Sovilla nodded. "May I help you?"

"I don't know. Can you? I'd like a little information."

"I'm brand-new here, but I'll to my best to help."

"Good. You answered my first question. I wondered why I hadn't seen you before."

Gideon glanced her way and cleared his throat. Sovilla jumped. He was paying her to wait on customers, not flirt with them. Not that she'd been flirting, but from a distance it might look that way.

"Did you want to order something?"

"I hadn't planned to, but I don't want you to get in trouble with your boss. Gideon can be vicious when he's cross."

Sovilla stared at him. So far, Gideon had only been kind.

The blond laughed. "You should see your eyes. You look scared. I was only kidding. I've never met anyone as easygoing as Gideon."

"Hey, Sovilla, is that kid bothering you?"

"I'm not bothering her, Nick. Am I, *Sovilla*?" He emphasized her name as if checking he'd gotten it correct.

"*Neh*, but some of the customers behind you might want to order."

With a sheepish grin, he stepped aside to let her fill the orders. He waited until everyone had gone and then stepped up to the counter again.

"Which Lantz are you?" Nick challenged.

"I'm Andrew. But you can tell us apart by now, Nick."

"Then that was your twin Isaac who was mooning over Sovilla this morning. Now you. It's her first day. Stop your pestering. Leave the poor girl alone."

"I'm just trying to get to know her."

"You and a dozen other Amish guys. Besides, she has a boyfriend."

Sovilla ducked her head. Nick sure knew how to embarrass people.

Andrew must have sensed her distress. "Sorry, Sovilla. I only wanted to be friendly and welcome you to the market."

"And snoop for details," Nick's voice boomed around the market, and customers turned to stare.

Sovilla wished she could sink into the floor and disappear.

"You're embarrassing her, Nick," Andrew said.

"I think the shoe's on the other foot. If I give you the gory details, will you go away and leave her alone?"

Andrew tapped his chin with one finger. "I'll think about it. Especially if you lower your voice."

"She's from Sugarcreek, Ohio. And she's living with her aunt Wilma, also known as the Pickle Lady."

Andrew's eyes popped open at that information.

"She's helping out this week while Fern's away. And she's probably around your age. Twenty or so?"

"Nineteen," Sovilla whispered. She didn't want all her personal details broadcast around the market.

"Perfect." Andrew smiled.

"She's already taken," Nick warned.

"Right. I heard you." Andrew turned to Sovilla. "Nice to meet you."

Just before he headed off, Nick said, "Watch out for those Lantz boys. There's a whole passel of them."

"Better be nice, Nick." Andrew's voice held a teasing note. "You wouldn't want to lose all twelve of your best customers."

"They have twelve boys?" Sovilla asked after Andrew had gone.

"Naw, only seven of the twelve are boys." Then he leaned close and said quietly, "They're all good kids, but don't let them know I said that."

Sovilla doubted she'd have the opportunity to tell them anything. Most likely Nick had scared them off. Not that it mattered. She already had a boyfriend. One she hadn't heard from since she'd arrived.

* * *

"So, Isaac, here's the good news," Andrew announced when he returned from his scouting trip. "She's nineteen. Her name's Sovilla. A pretty name for a pretty girl."

Isaac frowned. He hadn't intended for Andrew to get interested in the girl. If his twin decided to go after her, Isaac had no chance.

"Now for the bad news." Andrew lowered his voice. "She's Pickle Lady's niece."

No way. That sweet girl couldn't possibly be related to the meanest woman in the market.

Zeke rushed past. "I saw her getting out of Wilma's car this morning, so Andrew's right."

Poor Sovilla. Isaac wanted to rescue her. He couldn't even imagine how horrible it would be to live with Pickle Lady. She'd been awful to him from the time he was little. If she treated strangers and acquaintances so terribly, how did she treat her own relatives?

"Before you go charging off to save her . . ."

His brother had read his mind. That was the frustrating part of being a twin. Andrew always seemed to know what he was thinking. Caught up in pondering that, he almost missed the rest of Andrew's sentence.

". . . you should know she has a boyfriend."

Isaac's spirits plunged. Of course. Any girl that pretty and sweet would be taken.

Not that he had any chance with Sovilla—he rolled the name around in his mind, feeling the beauty and weight of it—but he wished she were free to date. He didn't feel right daydreaming about a girl who wasn't available. As hard as he tried to stop them, though, his thoughts kept straying.

Although he fought the temptation until midafternoon, Isaac couldn't stay away from the stand. He avoided the bakery counter at the end and instead got in line for chicken barbecue.

By craning his neck to the left, he had a perfect view of Sovilla's profile as she waited on customers. She had such a lovely smile—at least what he could see of it.

He'd been focusing so hard on glimpsing her full smile as she turned to get a bakery box, he missed the line moving forward.

"Yo, buddy," a man behind him groused, "you gonna move up, or should we move around you?"

Startled, Isaac glanced up to see no customers in front of him and Gideon waiting patiently for his order. Isaac jiggled Snickers's harness to move forward.

"Hey, Isaac," Gideon teased, "you want me to introduce you to our new worker?"

Isaac shook his head. "*N-neh.*"

"You seem interested."

Isaac froze. He'd only seen the girl once. Well, twice if you count now. Why would Gideon assume Isaac was interested?

Gideon put him out of his misery by asking, "Your usual?"

Relieved, Isaac nodded. They needed to get their conversation back to business. Still, he couldn't help sneaking peeks while Gideon filled his order. After he paid, he took one last look, then steered Snickers to a table where he had a perfect view.

Ten minutes later, Andrew strode over to the table. "I've been looking for you everywhere. What's taking so long? We have work to do."

Isaac lowered his gaze and crumpled his bag. “I’m coming.”

Andrew rotated to see what had caught Isaac’s attention. “I see why you chose to eat here.”

Ignoring his brother, Isaac tossed his trash in a nearby bin. He shouldn’t be wasting his time. Too pretty and too perfect, Sovilla would never consider him. Besides, he reminded himself for the millionth time, she had a boyfriend.

Chapter Three

Usually, Sovilla had energy to spare at the end of the workday, but her first day at the Pennsylvania farmers market had exhausted her. Part of it stemmed from missing Mamm and her sisters. She also had to get used to a new area, where her *kapp* stood out among the gauzy, heart-shaped *kapps* of Lancaster, and adjust to life with an *aenti* she had never known existed.

In fact, ever since she'd started for Lancaster on Saturday, she'd faced one shock after another. First, the crowded stations had bewildered her. She'd never seen so many people or heard so much noise.

If a kindly woman named Pearl hadn't come up to her and offered to help, Sovilla might still be paralyzed in the bus station, unsure of where to go or who to ask. Pearl was headed to Lancaster too, so she shepherded Sovilla through the stations and onto the bus and train.

The landscape whizzed by the windows so fast, Sovilla's stomach sloshed. By the time they pulled into the Lancaster station, she'd grown so dizzy, she swayed when she tried to stand. Pearl caught Sovilla's arm before she pitched forward into the man pushing his way out of the opposite seat.

"I'm sorry," she mumbled.

Giving her an impatient look, he brushed by, bumping her with his briefcase as he passed.

Pearl's grip on her arm tightened. "Just ignore him. I'm not in any hurry. Let's wait a minute to let those who are rushing to catch other trains get out."

When only a few stragglers remained, Pearl ushered Sovilla into the station.

A mannish-looking woman with short hair and saggy jowls approached them. "Sovilla?"

At the gruff tone, Sovilla backed away. How did this woman know her name?

"Oh, good," Pearl said. "Someone's here to meet you." She patted Sovilla's shoulder. "It was nice to meet you, dear. My husband's over there."

She wanted to grab Pearl's arm and beg her not to leave. Sovilla wanted to run from this frowning woman, who'd stuffed her blocky body into a floral-print dress that strained at the seams. The hem flowed down to bloated calves and ankles, which bulged over the tops of dirty, torn canvas sneakers. Although she appeared to be Mennonite, she wore no head covering.

"You are Sovilla, aren't you?" the woman demanded.

"*J-jah*, I mean yes." Sovilla should have been politer. Perhaps this woman was her *aenti*'s driver. She only wished Wilma had come with her.

"Thought so," the woman said with satisfaction. "You look like your *mamm*." Then she laughed. "Besides, right now, you're the only young one in the station wearing that Amish getup."

Sovilla had no answer to that. And when had this driver met her mother? She'd never known Mamm had traveled to Lancaster.

"Well, come along. I don't have all day." The woman marched out of the station.

Trailing behind, Sovilla ventured to ask, "Is Wilma all right?" Mamm had said Wilma would meet her, but maybe with her upcoming hip operation, she'd been confined to her bed.

The woman stopped so suddenly Sovilla almost ran into her. A loud bellow of laughter shook her body, and everyone around them stopped to stare.

"Mercy, child, who do you think I am?"

"I—I don't know. Wilma's driver?"

Pivoting to face Sovilla, the woman pointed her thumb at herself. "I'm Wilma."

Sovilla shook her head, trying to clear it. Maybe all that traveling had scrambled her brain or her hearing. "But—but . . ."

"What? I'm not Amish? You wouldn't be either if you'd gone through what I did."

"I'm sorry." Although Sovilla wasn't sure what she was apologizing for, the pain in Wilma's eyes called for some acknowledgment.

"I guess your *mamm* explained everything."

"*Neh*, she didn't. She said to ask you. If you want to tell me, that is."

For a moment, Wilma's face dissolved into sadness. Then her face hardened. "I don't." She whirled around and stomped toward the parking lot.

Sovilla had to race to keep up with Wilma's long strides. She hadn't meant to offend her *aenti*. Her *aenti*? Sovilla struggled to believe she and Wilma shared the same heritage.

On the way home from the train station, Wilma stopped at the market to be sure nobody had stolen any of her jars of pickles. That's when Sovilla discovered she'd be expected to take over her *aenti*'s market stand after the operation. Although Sovilla baked pies and cakes for the farmers market at home, here she'd make and sell pickles.

While her *aenti* went for what she called a quick *look-see*, Sovilla stayed in the car, her eyes closed, trying to make sense of her new life. Several times during the trip she'd caught the sharp side of Wilma's tongue. Not wanting to face Wilma's derision, Sovilla closed her eyes to hide the tears burning behind her eyes.

"Napping midday?" Wilma's critical tone matched Onkel Lloyd's. She blew out a loud breath. "Maybe it's for the best. Then I don't have to talk to you."

Sovilla bit the inside of her lip. Had Mamm known Sovilla would be such a terrible burden? How was this any different than staying at Lloyd's? Sovilla had been expecting an older version of her gentle *mamm*. Instead, she'd gotten a female copy of her *onkel*.

Even worse, Wilma had left the Amish, and her lip curled every time she looked at Sovilla's Plain dress. How would Sovilla live with her *Englisch aenti*? One who seemed mad at the world? How would she live in a house with electricity? How would she get around without a horse and buggy?

Please, Lord, help me to adjust and show Wilma your love.

Sovilla wished Wilma would hurry. After traveling all day, all Sovilla wanted to do was wash off the grime, eat supper, and curl into bed. The next thing she knew, though, her *aenti* had dragged her into the market to meet Gideon, who owned a chicken barbecue stand, and Fern, who sold baked goods at one end of his stand. They'd offered her a part-time job for the following week. Too tired to concoct a polite excuse, Sovilla found herself railroaded into agreeing to take Fern's place in the bakery and into baking a long list of pastries and cakes to sell.

Still reeling from the rapid changes in her life, Sovilla had fallen asleep that night in a strange bed uncertain about her future. What had Mamm been thinking to send her to another state to stay with an *aenti* who seemed to despise the Amish?

Wednesday, their day off from the market, passed in a blur. Isaac did most of his weekly kennel work, along with his farm chores. Today, though, he found himself longing for a cinnamon bun. He'd eaten plenty of Fern's light and airy rolls, but the one he'd had yesterday had been denser, with a chewier texture he preferred, and the perfect blend of sweetness to contrast with the tang of cinnamon.

Andrew's chuckle brought Isaac back to the barnyard with a thud. "Who are you thinking about?"

Although he hadn't been thinking of Sovilla, at least not that moment, he shook his head.

"Come on. You can't fool me."

Isaac managed to spit out the truth.

His brother's mocking laughter filled the air. "Cinnamon buns? You looked all"—Andrew lowered his lids halfway and assumed a dreamy expression.

"D-did not."

"*Jah*, you did." In a falsetto voice, Andrew warbled, "*Ach*, Sovilla, you are the most beautiful girl I've ever seen." He exhaled a long, shuddery breath.

For the first time in his life, Isaac longed to punch his brother in the stomach. How dare he make fun of Sovilla! And of the tender feelings Isaac held for her.

Andrew laughed. "You look like Mamm's teakettle."

Huh?

"All steamed." With a snicker, he danced out of Isaac's reach.

That was probably for the best. Isaac would never forgive himself if he hit his twin. But he needed to find a way to get these feelings under control. If even remembering her cinnamon rolls made him as dreamy eyed as his brother said, he had to erase Sovilla from his mind. Yet the harder he tried, the more it proved impossible.

In fact, he woke at dawn on Thursday hungering for cinnamon rolls and a glimpse of the angel who baked them. Her name replayed as a lilting melody. *Sovilla, Sovilla, Sovilla.* Had he ever heard a prettier name? Or seen a lovelier face?

At breakfast, he missed his plate when he dished out scrambled eggs and almost knocked over his glass of milk when he tried to scoop up the slippery mess.

"Goodness, Isaac, what's gotten into you this morning?" Mamm peered at him over the top of her glasses.

"Don't mind him, Mamm. He's in *love*." Andrew sang the last word.

Daed's stern glance sobered Andrew, but everyone else stared at Isaac.

He shook his head and lowered his gaze to his plate.

"Leave your brother alone." Mamm passed a bowl of applesauce. "Eat up so you won't be late to market."

To Isaac's relief, Daed turned the conversation to a new brand of chicken feed he'd heard about at the market. Mamm asked questions, and his brothers and sisters concentrated on eating. In his eagerness to see Sovilla again, Isaac practically inhaled his breakfast.

Once they reached the auction, he waited impatiently

for a chance. He intended to slip off without being noticed, but Andrew spied him and Snickers edging in the direction of the market.

"Bet you're going to get a cinnamon bun, right?" His brother waggled his eyebrows. "I'm hungry for one too."

Pinching his lips together as Andrew walked beside him, Isaac stewed. Now he couldn't stare at Sovilla. He focused on Snickers as they entered the market from the auction parking lot outside. The three of them headed for the bakery line.

"You do know she's only going to be there for a week while Fern's gone?"

She is? Isaac's gaze flew to his brother's face to see if Andrew was teasing.

No laugh lines crinkled around his brother's eyes. Andrew's face held the serious expression it always did when he told the truth. "That's what Nick said."

Isaac's spirits had been soaring like a kite zipping in the wind. His brother's words snipped the string. Down, down, down the kite tumbled to land with a crash. The kite—and Isaac's excitement—lay in a heap of torn cloth and broken sticks.

Only three more days to see her.

Andrew clapped him on the back. "I changed my mind. I'll skip the cinnamon roll today."

What? Isaac stared as his brother headed back outside to the auction. How odd. But it did mean he was free to stare at Sovilla. He turned around, but rather than Sovilla, Fern stood behind the counter.

She smiled at him, so he couldn't slip out of line. What had happened to Sovilla?

* * *

Sovilla reached her *aenti*'s stand. She'd rushed right over after getting the message. Wilma appeared to be in fine form as she traded insults with a customer.

"Don't buy it, then." Wilma turned her head away as if she couldn't care less.

Drawing in a relieved breath, Sovilla asked, "You needed to see me right away?"

"Is that what Margery told you?"

"Well, not exactly." But she had made it sound urgent. From Margery's breathless account, Sovilla had had mental pictures of Wilma collapsed on the floor.

"It figures. Can't trust people to take a simple message."

The customer broke in. "I'll take it."

"You'll regret not getting two jars if you're having company."

"Fine. Give me both." With a resigned look, the woman pulled out her wallet and handed over the money.

After Wilma gave the customer her change, she turned to Sovilla. "I heard Fern came back early. I only wanted to tell you that you can come help me if they don't need you."

Was her *aenti* being thoughtful? Or had she needed help but didn't know how to ask?

"Don't look so surprised," Wilma snapped. "I'm not going to have people talking about my niece being thrown out on her ear."

Sovilla doubted Gideon or Fern would toss anyone out. They seemed much too nice. "Nettie's out sick today, so Fern has been helping with the salads." Or she had been until Sovilla had to leave. "I should get back unless you need me."

"Does it look like I'm busy?"

Not really. But Sovilla didn't want to say that.

"Be honest, girl. You won't hurt my feelings."

Sovilla eyed the empty space in front of the counter. "*Neh*, but I'm sure you will be."

"Yeah, right. I'll be run off my feet." Wilma waved toward the bakery. "Go on back to work before you get fired."

"You can send someone for me if you need help," Sovilla said, reluctant to leave her *aenti* looking so despondent.

For a second, Wilma's expression softened, then she shooed Sovilla with a rapid hand flap. "Get out of here."

Sovilla scooted. Once again, though, she'd had a glimpse behind her *aenti*'s battle armor. Somewhere inside, Wilma seemed to be hiding a hurting heart.

Please, Lord, help me to break through that toughness with Your love.

When Sovilla returned to the stand, she had to brush past that blond guy to get inside. But before she did, she couldn't resist bending down to pet his cute puppy.

"*N-neh!*" The word exploded from his mouth.

She jumped back. To calm her jittery nerves, she took a deep breath and smoothed down her apron. *All right, then, be that way.* She whirled around and, head held high, entered the stand.

"You're back." Fern greeted Sovilla with a wide smile. "Can you take over here? Gideon needs help."

Without waiting for an answer, she started for the other end of the stand.

Sovilla turned to face the young man who'd just yelled at her. She put on her *be-kind-to-customers* face. She wasn't about to let him know he'd hurt her feelings.

"Oh, Isaac will have one cinnamon roll," Fern called over her shoulder.

"Is that right?" Sovilla asked him.

He stared at her as if she'd startled him. Then he nodded.

After she'd bagged it, he held out his payment, but his eyes seemed to be offering her an apology.

She tried never to hold grudges, but it was hard not to resent someone who was so selfish he wouldn't let anyone touch his dog. She'd thought him rude before, but now she added unkind.

When she handed him his change, he flicked his head in a nod that might have been thanks. And his eyes begged for understanding. Sovilla relented a little. Maybe he was just awkward around people. She'd give him the benefit of the doubt.

"Have a good day," she said as she gave him the bag.

His blinding smile dazzled her so much she could barely concentrate on the next customer.

Nick brought her down with a thud. "I'm warning you," he said, "those Lantz boys can be charmers. You don't want to get mixed up with them, especially if you already have a boyfriend."

"It never entered my mind," Sovilla retorted. But she had to admit Isaac's smile stayed with her. And somehow, even thoughts of Henry didn't erase it.

Isaac couldn't believe he'd yelled at Sovilla. Not yelled exactly, but snapped at her. Even scared her. He'd had to stop her before she petted Snickers.

He'd only seen a hand reaching out. If he'd glanced up and seen her, maybe he'd have softened his command. Or perhaps he'd have been too paralyzed to move or make a sound.

He owed her an apology. But how could he give her one?

Caught up in regrets, Isaac glanced over his shoulder at Sovilla one last time and almost ran into Mrs. Vandenberg.

The elderly woman waited at the end of Sovilla's line. "My, my. I've never seen anyone so smitten." She lifted her cane and almost poked Isaac in the stomach. "If you want my advice, you should speak up. Let her know you're interested."

Isaac glanced around, his cheeks burning. Mrs. Vandenberg's voice carried. He hoped Sovilla hadn't heard. Or if she did, that she wouldn't realize they'd been talking about her. Well, Mrs. Vandenberg had been speaking. As usual, he'd remained silent.

She set her cane down with a thump. "Better tell her soon before someone else does."

"I—I—I c-can't."

"Of course you can. Don't be shy."

"B-b-but—"

"You mean what will she think? She'll discover you're as wonderful as everyone else knows you are."

From the time he'd been small, Mrs. Vandenberg had encouraged him. She always knew what he needed and tried to help. He appreciated her advice, but in this case, she was wrong.

"I have a suggestion." Her *this-is-just-between-us* smile conveyed she was sharing something special. Something that could change his life. "Why don't you do what Demosthenes did?"

"D-d-dem who?"

"Demosthenes," she repeated. She fished around in her huge handbag and pulled out a small notepad with a pen attached. Then she jotted down a word, tore out the page, and handed it to him.

Isaac had no idea what Mrs. Vandenberg's word meant, but maybe he'd stop at the library to find out.

"I'll be praying," she called after him.

Although Isaac believed prayer worked wonders, he'd often begged God for a solution to his inability to speak to people and never received an answer.

Chapter Four

As Sovilla finished cleaning the bakery shelves, Wilma clomped over to the stand. Her *aenti* never walked; each footfall vibrated with displeasure. And a cloud of gloom enveloped her. Negativity radiated from her in waves that made people back away. Little children hid behind their parents or ducked behind the pillars when she passed.

Whatever pain Wilma had experienced, she had no intention of suffering in silence. She intended to make the rest of the world pay.

Sovilla sighed. The busy day had kept her from dwelling on missing Mamm, her sisters, and Henry. All of her customers had been friendly and welcoming—except for that blond guy with the puppy. But Wilma's grumpy face brought all the loneliness and sadness rushing back.

"Be ready to leave in ten minutes." Wilma barked out her order and marched off.

"Whew." Nick pretended to wipe his brow. "That woman would have made a great drill sergeant. I wouldn't even wish her on my worst enemy." He grinned. "Naw, maybe I would."

Sovilla didn't answer. She wouldn't criticize her family.

Nick chuckled. "I can't believe the two of you are related."

Neither could Sovilla. The idea that Wilma was her *aenti* still seemed unreal.

"Wait a minute." Nick wrinkled his brow. "How come you're Amish and she's not?"

"I don't know." Sovilla had wondered the same thing.

"How could you not know?" His narrowed eyes revealed his suspicion.

"I'd better finish up here before Wilma returns."

"Something fishy's going on. How come you call her *Wilma* instead of *aunt*?"

"It's the Amish way. We call people by their first names."

"Is that part of your silly beliefs like not letting people get high school degrees so they don't get uppity?"

"We're all the same in God's eyes."

Fern came up behind her. "Stop picking on her, Nick. She's only been here two days."

"Nothing wrong with being curious." He looked from Fern to Sovilla and then back again. "How come she has that barrel-shaped thingie sticking out of the back of her head? Everyone else has those flat see-through ones that look like hearts."

"They're called prayer coverings." Fern took out the cash drawer and said to Sovilla, "I'll take care of the rest of the cleaning after I close out, so you can leave with your *aenti*."

"*Danke.*" Sovilla appreciated Fern saving her from Wilma's tongue.

"OK, so prayer coverings, then," Nick persisted. "Why are they different?"

"Each Amish community has their own style of dress." Fern's practiced fingers riffled through the dollar bills. She tucked a few back into the drawer and stuffed the rest into a zippered pouch. "Sovilla's *kapp* is a style from the Midwest."

Nick stared at her, incredulous. "They have Amish in the Midwest? I thought only Pennsylvania had them."

Sovilla smiled. "Amish live in many different states all across the country. Ohio and Indiana have quite a few Amish. So do New York State and—"

"Wait a minute. You're saying they're all over?"

"That's right." Fern snapped a bill holder in place and moved on to the next divider.

"But how come I never knew that?"

Before either of them could answer him, Wilma's loud yell interrupted them. "Sovilla, what's taking so long?"

"I'd better go." Sovilla scurried around Fern. She'd been expecting Wilma to return for her.

When Sovilla rounded the corner, Wilma blew out an explosive breath. "It's about time. I said ten minutes."

"I'm sorry." Her excuse shriveled on her lips at Wilma's impatient expression. Wilma had already made it clear she wouldn't suffer fools or tardy nieces.

As they left the building, they passed Isaac holding his puppy in the air and rubbing noses with him. The puppy licked Isaac's face, and he laughed, a deep, mellow tone that strummed Sovilla's heartstrings. Once again, a dazzling smile lit his face, sparking deep delight that spread through her whole being.

"How disgusting." Wilma's harsh tones shattered Sovilla's joy. "Why would anyone want a filthy animal to slobber on them?"

"Some people enjoy their pets." Sovilla avoided saying *love*. Wilma had made it known she despised that word.

"I have no idea how he can stand it. And he takes that animal with him everywhere. I have a mind to complain to the market owner and forbid him to bring it inside."

"Please don't do that." Sovilla couldn't bear to think of the pain that would cause.

Isaac may have been rude to her, but he adored his puppy. Separating them would be cruel. He looked like a different person when he interacted with his dog. Maybe it was easier for him to communicate with animals than with people.

Sovilla wished she could wrap some of Isaac's happiness around her as a shield against Wilma's constant complaints. The rest of the way home her *aenti* whined about her day, detailing every real or imagined grievance. With her eyes closed, Sovilla could easily mistake Wilma's deep, low grumbling for her *onkel*'s. Not only did Wilma's tone mirror Lloyd's, they both oozed the same discontent.

At the house, Wilma stopped at the mailbox out front and pulled out circulars and a rolled-up newspaper. She tossed it all onto the back seat of her car without sorting through it. "Trash."

When she tromped on the gas, the pile slid to the floor and scattered. The corner of an envelope peeked out from under one of the ads. A letter? Maybe Mamm or Henry had written.

As soon as Wilma slammed the gearshift into park,

Sovilla hopped out. She had to prevent Wilma from scooping up the mail and tossing it in the garbage.

"Can't wait to get away from me?" Wilma sounded hurt.

"*Neh*, I only wanted to pick these up." Sovilla gathered everything on the floor, extracting the envelope.

"Let me see that." Wilma held out her hand for the letter.

"It's for me." Keeping a tight grip on it, Sovilla turned the address to face her aunt.

"Humph. Shoulda known. Nobody writes to me."

Sovilla would ask Mamm to mail Wilma a card or letter. Perhaps her *aenti* would also like to be included in the family's circle letter. Sovilla hoped Mamm would forward that.

When they got inside, Wilma dumped the circulars in the recycle bin, then sat at the kitchen table and stared at Sovilla, who was reading her letter. Feeling the intense gaze on her, Sovilla glanced up. Wilma focused on the newspaper she'd opened, but not before Sovilla had glimpsed the avid look in her *aenti*'s eyes. She looked like a small child hungrily watching someone eating an ice-cream cone.

Once again, Sovilla's heart went out to her *aenti*. What had happened to alienate Wilma from her family and cause her to leave the faith? To harden her heart and make her treat everyone around her as an enemy?

Wilma rattled the newspaper as if to indicate she had no interest in Sovilla's business. Yet she kept peeking over the top of the page.

Sovilla skimmed the details of family meals to dwell on the parts about her sisters struggling to adjust and Lloyd forbidding Mamm to get a job at the local quilt shop. Ardys, Mamm's employer in Sugarcreek, had recommended her to the Middlefield shop owner. In Sugarcreek, Mamm had taught quilting classes and done demonstrations in addition to making quilts to sell. Lloyd insisted that was *hochmut*, and he'd not have anyone in his household showing off and being prideful.

In the end, Lloyd worked out an arrangement for Mamm to sew quilts at home to be sold in the shop. Reading between the lines, Sovilla got the impression Lloyd planned to keep the money Mamm made.

At the end of the letter, Mamm had added a P.S.

Lloyd takes all the mail that comes in. I don't want him to know Wilma's address. If you write to us, please send it to the quilt shop. Melinda, the owner, promised to come during the day when Lloyd's not home to drop off any mail I get.

Sovilla's hands tightened on the letter. Her *onkel* had always been controlling, but something must have happened for Mamm not to trust him with her letters. Sovilla read on:

P.P.S. Not five minutes after you left for the bus, Lloyd arrived. I didn't have time to take your letter to Henry's mamm, but Lloyd agreed to mail it. I expect he sent it out on Monday after we arrived. I didn't want you to worry if you didn't hear from Henry right away.

Sovilla breathed out a soft sigh. She'd been wondering if Henry had decided he had no interest in a long-distance relationship. But judging from Mamm's letter, Henry should have gotten her letter by now. She'd hear from him soon. Maybe he'd left a message on the answering machine.

She headed to the table in the hallway that held the phone. Not sure how to check Wilma's machine, she bent closer to read the words. *Replay* caught her eye. If she pushed that button, would Henry's voice come out?

She'd extended her hand when Wilma came up behind her.

"What are you doing?"

Sovilla forced herself not to jump at Wilma's question.

"Ch-checking for messages." Perhaps she should have asked for permission first. And maybe Wilma had some private calls, and Sovilla shouldn't eavesdrop.

"Who would be calling you? Not your *mamm*. Not while she's staying at Lloyd's."

For some reason, Sovilla hesitated to tell Wilma the truth.

"That means it's some boy. Am I right?"

Unwilling to lie, Sovilla nodded.

"You gave him this number?" She didn't sound happy.

"*Jah.*"

"I don't give out this number to anyone. And especially not to strangers."

"I'm sorry. I didn't know."

"Well, if he planned to call, he would have done so by now. He hasn't, so that means he doesn't care. Typical man—out of sight, out of mind."

Sovilla bit her lip to hold back her protest. Henry wasn't like that. After all, he'd only have gotten her letter yesterday or today. A letter to Sugarcreek might arrive a little sooner than one to Pennsylvania.

"If he called, this light would be blinking." Wilma poked a gnarled finger at the clear round bump. "It's not. So forget him. He's forgotten you already."

"*Neh*, he hasn't. He'd only have gotten my letter today."

"Don't wait around for a call that most likely will never come."

Sovilla blinked back tears. Henry wouldn't forget her. He might be busy. Maybe he hadn't read her letter yet. Maybe he'd had no time at work. Maybe—

"You're wasting your time. Men, *pah*." Wilma brushed her hands together as if dusting away traces of dirt. "You're better off without them. They can't be trusted."

Sovilla disagreed but kept her opinion to herself. Wilma would see when Henry called. At least, Sovilla hoped he would.

Isaac lined up for a cinnamon bun the next morning, only to see Fern at the counter again. He glanced around, hoping to spot Sovilla somewhere else in the stand.

"Are you all right?" Fern asked.

He didn't know whether to nod or shake his head. Physically, he felt fine, but he'd counted on seeing Sovilla.

Andrew bumped into line beside him. "Isaac's pining for Sovilla."

Isaac elbowed his brother. Why did Andrew always try to embarrass him?

"I see." Fern's smile indicated she saw a lot more than Isaac intended.

He hoped she'd keep her mouth shut. What if she repeated that to Sovilla? Everyone in the stand would be laughing about him all day long. Why had he come to the bakery again? He'd only made a fool of himself.

"Well," Fern said as she pulled out a bag, "you'll be glad to know Sovilla will be working today. We're short-handed with Nettie out sick."

"It's your lucky day," Andrew crowed, elbowing him in the ribs.

Isaac elbowed him back and gave him a dirty look. *Be quiet*, he mouthed.

"Sorry I'm late," a breathless voice said behind them. Sovilla rushed past.

Isaac cringed. His brother had been so loud, she must have heard. If she didn't know about his interest before, she certainly did now. All Isaac wanted to do was escape. But with everyone hemming him in, he couldn't move and could barely breathe.

"Sovilla, have you met Isaac Lantz?" Fern asked as she moved out of the way to let Sovilla pass. "And his brother Andrew?"

Before Sovilla could answer, Nick called, "I introduced them and warned her those Lantz boys are trouble."

"What?" Andrew puffed up his chest. "Why would you tell her that?"

"He's only kidding." Fern's words smoothed Andrew's ruffled feelings, but did little to calm Isaac.

The less attention he got, the better.

"*Wie geht's?*" Chilliness edged Sovilla's polite question.

Andrew inched closer to the counter. "We're fine now that you're here."

Isaac swallowed. He couldn't believe his brother was doing this to him—first embarrassing him in front of Sovilla and now being overly friendly with her.

Fern's sympathetic look made it worse. She seemed to have sensed his distress. "Sovilla, have you met Snickers yet?" Fern pointed down to the puppy.

"I've seen her, but I've never met her."

Was that a jab because Isaac hadn't let Sovilla pet the

puppy? He studied her face, but she didn't seem to be holding a grudge.

"Ahem." The *Englischer* behind them leaned forward. "Were you two planning to buy anything, or did you only come to flirt?"

Isaac's face flamed. Embarrassment and shame kept him silent. But if his brother didn't give Sovilla their order soon, he'd have to do it. Then her kind expression would dissolve into pity.

"We'll take two sticky buns," Andrew announced, directing his words to the man behind them rather than to Sovilla.

Isaac wanted a cinnamon roll, but he wasn't about to correct his brother. He'd eat whatever Andrew ordered. Anything to get away from this uncomfortable situation.

Andrew smiled at Sovilla. "Don't mind my brother here. He doesn't talk much."

Her chilliness returned. "I expect that's better than yammering on about nothing."

Isaac grinned. He'd never seen anyone put Andrew in his place like that.

"*Jah*, well." Andrew tugged at his collar.

Isaac couldn't believe she'd discomfited his brother. Andrew usually had snappy comebacks. Instead, he backed up a bit, and Sovilla held the bag out to Isaac.

He'd been so enamored with her, he'd forgotten about paying. He fumbled for his money. She opened her palm to take the change, and Isaac dropped it in carefully so he wouldn't touch her. But when she handed him the bag, her fingers grazed his, and Isaac's skin tingled at her softness. He almost dropped the bag.

The man behind Isaac shouldered him out of the way.

"It's about time. Why don't you wait until she doesn't have a long line to chat with her?"

Heat rose from Isaac's neck to his face. Even the tips of his ears burned. He whirled around so fast, he startled Snickers. His puppy kept to his heels as Isaac darted to catch up with Andrew, who had his hands jammed into his pockets and his back to the stand.

"I guess she prefers you to me," his brother said sourly, looking dejected.

If only that were true. Isaac hardly dared hope. But what difference did it make? She already had a boyfriend.

Chapter Five

On Monday, Isaac headed for the library. He carried the paper from Mrs. Vandenberg and presented it to the librarian.

"You want information on Demosthenes?" She gestured toward a woman at a nearby desk. "Our reference librarian would be happy to help you."

Isaac crossed the floor and handed the note to the reference librarian. He shifted from foot to foot as she studied it, hoping she wouldn't ask him to explain why he wanted the information. Not only didn't he know what Mrs. Vandenberg's cryptic message meant, he also didn't want to be forced to speak to the librarian. Not when he was so nervous.

She smiled up at him. "Would you like books and articles?"

He released a pent-up breath and nodded.

She typed something into the computer, jotted down information, and led him to the shelves. "Here are some biographies." She pulled two off the shelves. "We also have some collections of his speeches. They're over here."

Isaac took the four books she'd selected and sat at the

nearest table. He opened a biography first and started to read. The more he read, the more confused he got. Why had Mrs. Vandenberg recommended he read about this great orator from ancient Athens? A famous speaker? When Isaac could barely get out a word?

He'd never known her to be cruel, but this seemed like an unkind joke. Maybe she had one of Demosthenes's speeches in mind? But how would he find it in these books? He was about to take all the books home with him, ready for long nights of reading, when the reference librarian came to his table.

She held out a few sheets of paper. "I printed out this article you might want to read before you begin your study. It highlights the most important parts of his life."

With a nod and smile to thank her, Isaac took the pages. He skimmed them. At age eighteen, Demosthenes sued his guardians for stealing his inheritance, and he won. Well, Isaac had no intention of taking anyone to court. Especially not his parents. But it surprised him that, more than two thousand years ago, a teen would challenge adults like that.

To train himself as a speaker, Demosthenes built an underground studio and shaved half his head to force himself to stay inside and study. Although Isaac wouldn't mind finding a way to avoid going out, he was pretty sure Mrs. Vandenberg hadn't intended for him to imitate that. He laughed to himself as he imagined his parents' reaction if he showed up at the dinner table with half of his hair missing.

He reached the next paragraph and stopped. This great speaker stammered as a child? He couldn't speak clearly, so he practiced talking with his mouth full of pebbles. That made him work hard to get the sounds out. He also ran along the ocean and yelled over the roar of the waves.

Doing those exercises made him one of the greatest speakers that ever lived.

Isaac didn't have an ocean nearby, but he did have a kennel full of barking dogs. Maybe he could try these exercises with them. They wouldn't laugh at him or judge him. And the path to the barn had plenty of gravel he could use instead of pebbles. He just had to be sure none of his brothers or sisters found out. They'd tease him mercilessly.

Picking up the two biographies, Isaac took them to the checkout counter, along with the article the librarian had given him. Maybe the books would have more tips on how Demosthenes had learned to speak well. Isaac didn't need the speeches for practice. He could use the Bible.

He left the library with hope in his heart. And gratitude for Mrs. Vandenberg's suggestion. Maybe someday he'd be able to share all the feelings and thoughts he kept trapped inside.

As the days passed with no word, Sovilla began to wonder if her *aenti* had been right. Had Henry forgotten her already? Or had he been hurt because she'd left suddenly without telling him? She'd explained why in the letter so he'd understand. Maybe she'd been foolish to hope he'd suggest they marry. The longer she waited, the less likely that seemed.

"Sovilla?" Wilma's shrill voice drew her away from the answering machine.

Every day after work, Sovilla waited until Wilma had gone into another room before hovering over the machine, praying to see a blinking light. And every day, she ended up disappointed.

"You're not checking that stupid machine again, are you?"

Sovilla didn't want to admit she had been or listen to another lecture on how awful and unfaithful men were, so she scurried into the kitchen.

"Stop torturing yourself," Wilma said when Sovilla walked through the doorway. "Give it up."

To distract her *aenti*, Sovilla interrupted, "Did you have something you wanted me to do?"

Before Wilma could answer, the phone rang. Sovilla wanted to bolt for it, but this was Wilma's house. Her *aenti* should be the one who answered the phone.

Please keep ringing, Sovilla begged as her aunt lumbered into the other room.

The phone stopped, and the answering machine kicked on.

Henry, please call.

Wilma lifted the receiver and barked a hello into it.

"This is the . . ." a tinny voice said.

Her *aenti*'s loud "I'm on here now" drowned out the rest of the words.

Other than a quiet *Yes*, Wilma didn't say another word. When she hung up, she sank into the chair beside the phone.

"Is everything all right?" Sovilla worried at her *aenti*'s pale face.

"Fine, fine." Wilma waved an impatient hand. "Just the hospital setting up the date for my hip surgery."

"You look upset."

"Would you want to have doctors cut you open?" Wilma challenged her.

"*Neh*, I guess not."

"You *guess* not? Why don't I let you take my place and see if you change your mind?"

"I'm sorry. I'm sure it's scary."

"Scary? You think I'm scared?" Her *aenti* glared at her. "I just don't trust those doctors. No telling what they'll do when you're sleeping."

Sovilla couldn't imagine what it would be like to distrust everyone the way Wilma did.

"And if they give me too much anesthesia, I might never wake up."

"I'm sure they'll be careful."

"That doesn't mean they don't make mistakes. With my luck, they'll make a fatal one."

"I hope not. I'll be praying."

"Praying? *Pah.* Like that'll help. Besides, even if it did work, God wouldn't do anything for me."

"He cares for everyone."

"You don't know what I've done."

"Whatever it is, God can forgive you."

"I doubt it." Wilma pushed herself to her feet.

Sovilla whispered a prayer for her *aenti* that God would heal her pain, both physical and spiritual. Perhaps Wilma believed turning *Englisch* had been unforgivable.

As her *aenti* started from the room, Sovilla suggested, "No matter what it is, you can ask for God's forgiveness. And if you got right with God, you could join the church." Sovilla assumed her *aenti* had left before she was baptized. Mamm wouldn't have sent Sovilla here if Wilma were under the *bann*, would she?

A cruel, hollow laugh burst from Wilma's chest. "I have no desire to be a part of the Amish church. That would mean I'd have to make peace with Lloyd, and I will never, ever do that. He destroyed my life."

"I'm so sorry." Her *onkel* had done many hurtful things, but Sovilla couldn't imagine anything that would make her turn her back on her faith. "What did Lloyd do?"

"Never mind. Forget I said that," Wilma growled. "That topic's off-limits. I never should have even let his name pass my lips." The pain etched into every line on Wilma's face indicated a deep heartbreak.

"Is there anything I can do to help?"

Wilma whirled around and glared at Sovilla. "If and when I ever decide to share my secrets with anyone, you'd be the last person I'd choose." Then she pivoted on her heel and stomped out of the room.

Sovilla grasped the nearest chair back to keep herself upright. If her *aenti* had stabbed her with a knife, the pain could not have been any more intense. They'd forged a tentative truce. Or at least Sovilla had believed they had. Now the truth had laid bare her *aenti*'s hatred.

How could Sovilla stay here knowing her *aenti*'s revulsion and distrust? But she didn't have enough money to leave. Besides, how could she abandon Wilma before her upcoming operation?

Chapter Six

The rest of the week, Isaac sneaked his books out to the kennel to read. He skimmed through most of the pages to find the chapters that revealed Demosthenes's secrets to becoming a good speaker. Once he'd finished reading those parts, he reread the article several times.

Because the market stayed closed on Mondays, Isaac usually did a deep cleaning of his kennels and prepared special foods and vitamins for his Labrador retrievers to last the rest of the week. He also had more time to play with his puppies than he did on market days.

Today, though, he tucked a Bible under his arm before he headed to the kennel. He'd rushed through his barn chores to dodge his siblings, who were still finishing up theirs. The last thing he needed was for one of them to spot him.

After scooping up a handful of gravel, he washed it at the outdoor pump near the building. Reluctant to put the stones into his mouth, he carried them into the building and, one-handed, let the puppies out of their cages.

Instead of sitting on the floor to cuddle them the way he usually did, he stood in the center aisle and popped in the handful of gravel. His cheeks bulged, and his mouth watered. How did you swallow the moisture without sucking down a stone? Very carefully.

If nothing else, he'd end up with stronger jaw muscles. Maybe that was part of the secret.

As the puppies tumbled over one another and his feet, yipping and yapping, Isaac opened the Bible. Taking a deep breath, he tried to read. "In the beginning . . ." He attempted to form words.

Glub, glub, glub.

His tongue stuck to the floor of his mouth, weighted down by the stones. He tried to clear his throat and almost choked. At a picture of his brothers discovering him collapsed on the floor, strangled to death by a mouthful of gravel, he spit it out.

Perhaps this wasn't such a good idea. After all, Demosthenes lived more than twenty centuries ago. Things might have been different. Or maybe using pebbles instead of gravel worked better. Pebbles would be smoother and not poke the insides of his cheeks. He debated about giving up altogether.

Then two images flitted through his mind: Mrs. Vandenberg. She'd always been kind and helpful. She wouldn't have recommended this if she didn't believe he'd succeed. And Sovilla. If he ever wanted to order a pastry without relying on his brother to speak for him, he had to try.

Focusing on Sovilla's face gave him courage. He practiced again. And again. And again.

He had to concentrate and work hard to make even one sound, and each one came out slow, painful, and mangled. After making it through one Bible verse, his brow dripped with sweat. He'd used more strength doing this than he did loading and unloading their animals for the auction. He prayed expending all this energy would be worthwhile.

At this rate, it might take years to put together one coherent sentence. By that time, his dream of speaking to Sovilla would have faded. She'd be married and have several children. After all, she already had a boyfriend. Maybe they already had a fall wedding planned. Isaac's stomach clenched. He had no right to be using Sovilla as an incentive. But as hard as he tried, he couldn't get her out of his mind.

Wilma had slipped out of the house early on Monday morning without mentioning where she was heading. Sovilla prayed for grace to put aside her hurt. She'd grown up in a house where everyone shared their plans and talked about their activities.

Her *aenti* had made it clear she'd been living alone since she'd left home at seventeen. All those years of having nobody to talk to or confide in must have made her self-sufficient. Trying to understand Wilma's viewpoint eased some of Sovilla's pique.

Sovilla had already grown used to silent meals. At first, she'd attempted to start conversations whenever they sat down to eat. But Wilma ignored her or snorted and shook her head. Even something as harmless as mentioning the weather elicited a glare or a nasty retort. Sovilla also tried not to mind her *aenti* slurping or scraping silverware during mealtime prayers. Sometimes, though, loneliness overwhelmed Sovilla.

Following the first letter from her mother, Sovilla had heard nothing. Nor had Henry written or called. After the first week of helping at the bakery stand, Wilma hadn't taken Sovilla to the market. Sovilla had cooked and cleaned, but Wilma never seemed to notice. As her second week in Lancaster passed, Sovilla grew more and more isolated.

When Wilma returned early that afternoon, she called Sovilla into the living room. "Sit," she ordered, motioning to the couch. She settled onto a stiff wingback chair across from Sovilla and pulled a thick sheaf of papers from a large manila envelope.

Wilma's eyes bored into Sovilla's as if trying to discern all her secrets. Sovilla squirmed.

"First of all," Wilma said finally, "I'll need you to take over my market stand when I go in for the operation the week after next. I've paid for the rent six months in advance."

"I see. Will you take me with you this week and show me what to do?"

Wilma pursed her lips and blew out a long breath. "I don't have any choice."

Like Lloyd's annoyed looks, Wilma's put-upon expression shriveled Sovilla's insides.

"We can talk about that later. Right now, I have more important items to discuss." She tapped a thick finger on the papers laying in her lap. "I spent this morning at my lawyer's office."

Sovilla gulped. From her *aenti*'s stern expression, Sovilla worried Wilma planned to drag her into court for something she'd done wrong.

"Because I don't have much faith in surgeons, I made out my will in case they kill me on the operating table."

Sovilla gasped. "I don't think—"

"Exactly. You don't think. The fact that you're still expecting that unfaithful boyfriend to call makes that clear."

Pinching her lips together, Sovilla held back a cry—of pain or rebuke, she wasn't quite sure. She'd been considering writing to Henry one last time to see if he'd respond.

He did owe her an explanation. Or did he? She'd been the one who'd left without a word.

"Are you listening to me? Or are you off into ridiculous fantasies?"

"I-I'm listening."

"I certainly hope so, because my life is at stake here."

Although Sovilla didn't believe that, she pulled her thoughts from Henry to concentrate on her *aenti*.

"I've turned everything over to you in my will." Wilma patted the papers. "The house and all its contents, my bank account, my investments—"

"Me?" Sovilla squeaked.

"Yes, you. Who else do I have?"

"But—but . . ."

"But what? You're my closest relative. Or at least the only one I can trust. I don't want this house sold. I've put too much blood, sweat, and tears into paying it off."

When Sovilla opened her mouth again to protest, Wilma cut her off. "If I don't give it to you, Lloyd will grab it. I know he'd sell it. I don't want him to get even one penny."

After the way Lloyd had sold their family house, Sovilla suspected he'd be eager to sell this one as well.

"Those are the two promises you have to make me. Not selling this house and not letting Lloyd get his greedy hands on my money. Do you agree?"

"Of course. But are you sure you don't want to leave it to someone else?"

"Absolutely not. I know I can trust you."

Wilma's certainty took Sovilla aback. The whole time she'd been here, her *aenti* had treated her with suspicion. Now suddenly, she planned to entrust Sovilla with all her possessions.

"I know you'll probably have no use for the car. You

can sell that or give it to that charity that buys cars. Again, if you sell it, don't let Lloyd touch the proceeds. Will you promise me that?"

I doubt that anything will happen to you. Sovilla kept that thought to herself. "I'll do whatever you ask."

Wilma's guttural laugh came out cynical. "It figures. Dangle money in front of someone and they'll grovel."

That stung. "I only meant I'd keep the terms you've asked of me."

"If I told you I had another condition for getting my fortune, would you do it?"

"First of all, I don't believe you're going to die. And second, I've agreed to what you've asked to ease your mind, not because I want your money. In fact, I'm not sure I do."

When Wilma's face crumpled, Sovilla regretted losing her temper.

"I thought maybe . . ." Wilma's jaw tightened, and she turned away. "I should have known nobody could ever care about me."

"I do care." Despite Wilma's snippiness, the frequent flashes of loneliness and longing in her eyes had touched Sovilla and allowed her to see past her *aenti*'s crusty exterior.

Wilma kept her face averted. "I bet."

The fact that her *aenti* planned to give all her possessions to someone she'd met only two weeks ago made Sovilla's heart ache. How isolated had Wilma been?

Sovilla longed to reach out, but would her *aenti* believe her? She had to try. "When I said I didn't want the money, I was trying to show you that I care about you, not about what I can get from you."

"*Humph.*" Head bowed, Wilma shoved the papers back into the envelope.

"And I'm praying the operation will go well. I'd much rather have you get better than have the money."

Wilma cleared her throat. "You almost sound convincing." She took a tissue from her dress sleeve and wiped her eyes and blew her nose. "My allergies always get bad this time of year."

Sovilla suspected her *aenti*'s sudden sniffles had a different cause. What had happened to make Wilma hide her soft heart behind a brittle shell? Would she ever feel comfortable enough to share her true feelings?

Last week, Isaac had missed seeing Sovilla in the market. Several times he'd been tempted to stop and ask Gideon or Fern if Sovilla would be back. But Isaac didn't want to start gossip. He could trust Gideon and Fern to keep his request private, but if Nick overheard, he'd trumpet it around the market.

Isaac had even strolled to a spot where he could see Pickle Lady's stand, pretending Snickers had pulled him in that direction. He hoped her niece would be helping her. But each time he'd passed, he'd come away disappointed. He'd never ask Wilma about Sovilla, not after the Pickle Lady had been so cruel to him when he was a boy. Since then, he'd avoided her.

He'd been tempted to drive by Wilma's house. He passed her lane on the way to and from work, but he always had his brothers in the buggy with him. Besides, if Wilma spotted him, she'd wonder why he'd turned down a back road that led to a dead end a half mile beyond her place.

So when he returned to the market on Tuesday morning, he avoided Wilma's stand. Once again, Fern stood behind the bakery counter. Isaac bought a cinnamon bun to hide his real reason for checking out the stand, but not even the sticky sweetness could cure his disappointment.

Head down, he shuffled back to the auction without looking where he was going. Snickers jerked back on the leash, startling him.

"Look out," a deep voice behind Isaac warned.

Isaac stopped just before he plowed into Mrs. Vandenberg. He reached out one hand to steady her. "S-s-sorry."

She smiled at him. "Thank you, Isaac. And thanks to Snickers for being so alert." Then she waved to the man behind the counter. "Thank you too, Gideon. God has sent many guardian angels to watch over me."

After Mrs. Vandenberg regained her balance, Isaac bent to pat his puppy. He rubbed her behind the ears. *Good job, Snickers.*

"Did you want your usual?" Fern called to Mrs. Vandenberg.

"Yes, please, but can you hold it for me? I want to speak to this young man." She stepped in front of Isaac so he couldn't take off.

Although he was always happy to spend time with her, he really needed to get back to the auction. Isaac glanced toward the doors, expecting to see his brother coming through to complain about Isaac being so slow. But Andrew was nowhere in sight.

"Did you have a chance to check out Demosthenes?" Mrs. Vandenberg studied him, her expression brimming with curiosity.

Isaac nodded. She deserved more than a head bob. "I-I'm d-doing it."

"You are? I'm so glad. I have something else for you." She dug into her large handbag and pulled out an article. "This speech therapist has some tips too, but keep on with the pebbles."

"*D-danke.*"

"By the way," she said, her eyes dancing with mischief, "you might want to walk back in that direction." She waved to her left.

He stared at her with puzzlement. The doors that led to the auction lay on the other side of the market. Isaac had delayed too long already.

But after her kindness, he didn't want to hurt her feelings, so he rushed off in the direction she'd indicated, planning to veer left at the end of the chicken barbecue counter, where she couldn't see him. Before he and Snickers reached the turn, though, a white, barrel-shaped *kapp* caught Isaac's attention.

He sucked in a breath. *Sovilla?* She was the only one he knew who wore a *kapp* like that. He continued heading straight, trying to act casual and disinterested. The pickle stand's location near the end of the aisle made it awkward. Beyond it, a stand held hanging planters and fresh-cut flowers, followed by a pretzel stand. If he didn't have a sticky bun in his hand, he could buy a pretzel.

If Wilma and Sovilla spotted him, they'd know he didn't intend to buy from any of the vendors around that corner—one with fabrics and supplies for quilting or bulk foods, which carried flour and other baking supplies.

Act like you're walking your dog, he told himself. Snickers needed to stretch her legs sometimes. This could be a perfectly innocent walk. *Keep your eyes straight ahead, and don't look at Sovilla.*

Pretending to be nonchalant while sneaking glances

from the corner of his eye almost tripped him up. Once again, Snickers pulled him to a stop. With a quick shuffle, he slid around a woman before they collided.

"You should watch where you're going," Wilma bellowed.

Isaac sighed. His near accident would have to happen in front of Pickle Lady's stand. Averting his eyes from Sovilla, he nodded politely to acknowledge her comment.

Before he could escape, Wilma buttonholed him. "Which brother are you?" She peered at him suspiciously.

She couldn't tell with his dog? Had she asked on purpose to humiliate him in front of Sovilla?

His lungs constricted, making it hard to suck in a breath. Could he walk on, pretending he hadn't heard her question?

As if guessing his intention, Wilma advanced on him threateningly. A low rumble in Snickers's chest warned Pickle Lady not to come closer.

"If that dog bites me, I'll call the authorities to have it destroyed."

"*Ach*, no!" Sovilla cried. "It's only a puppy."

Wilma turned on her. "If I want your opinion, I'll ask for it."

Sovilla shrank back, and Isaac's chest swelled at the injustice. "Sh-she h-has a r-right to t-talk." He always avoided talking when angry or nervous, because it made the stuttering worse. Now he'd shamed himself in front of Sovilla, but he couldn't let Wilma get away with bullying.

Sovilla couldn't believe Isaac, the short-tempered guy who'd snapped at her for petting his puppy, was defending her. She warmed to him, especially after his cheeks darkened to match the potted fuchsia geraniums in the next booth. His stuttering must embarrass him. Maybe that's why he didn't talk to her.

Also, now that she looked closer, she could read the printing on the side of the dog's harness: *Happy Helpers*. When she'd bent to pet the puppy before, she'd only seen the yellow padding from the front and assumed the puppy wore a coat or raincoat. Snickers must be a guide dog. No wonder Isaac hadn't wanted her to pet the puppy.

Wilma took a step back from the dog, but her frown drew her eyebrows so close together, they formed an angry V. Her tone cruel and mocking, she confronted Isaac. "Spit it out, why don't you?"

Sovilla gasped. "*Aenti*, I can't believe you said that." She stepped closer, trying to insert herself between Isaac and Wilma. Sovilla's face burned with rage and shame. "I'm sorry, Isaac. I'm sure she didn't mean that."

"I most certainly did."

"You didn't." Sovilla faced her *aenti* with a pleading expression, silently begging her not to contradict the comment.

To her surprise, Wilma subsided. She even appeared a little ashamed.

His back stiff and his jaw set, Isaac wove around Wilma. "I n-need to g-go."

Sovilla waited until he was out of earshot. "I wish you hadn't done that. I'm sure Isaac can't help his stuttering."

"You're defending a stranger over your own flesh and blood?" Then her eyes narrowed. "Or isn't he a stranger? You know his name and which twin he is."

"I've met him before." To Sovilla, the twins had distinct personalities that made it easy to tell them apart.

"Mm-hm. Sure." Wilma examined her with a critical eye.

"Just to be clear, I'm not picking sides—Isaac over you. I only meant that it isn't right to mock someone for something they have no control over. That's how God made him."

"*Pah.* If there really is a God, He's made a lot of mistakes."

"God doesn't make mistakes, and Isaac certainly isn't one of them. God's ways are perfect. He had a reason for how he created Isaac."

Wilma went into a diatribe about all the mistakes God had made with Isaac.

Finally, Sovilla interrupted her *aenti*'s ranting. "God knew what He was doing. He has a plan for Isaac's life." She softened her tone. "And He has a perfect plan for you too."

Wilma shook her head. "He really messed up badly with me."

"*Neh*, he didn't. God has a reason for everything that happens. But you need to give Him control of your life."

"That's easy for you to say. You haven't lived through what I've endured."

"Whatever it is, God can help."

Wilma turned her back and stalked away, shaking her head even more emphatically.

Sovilla bowed her head. *Dear Lord, please touch Wilma. Help her to accept You and Your love.*

When she lifted her head, Isaac came to mind. Her heart went out to him. Did other people treat him as badly as her *aenti*?

Please, Lord, be with Isaac. Give him your comfort and love.

* * *

Wilma might not realize it, but her voice carried. People at all the nearby stands could hear every word. And each one of her words stabbed Isaac. He wanted to cover his ears or hurry away. Instead, he slowed Snickers and strained to hear Sovilla's answers.

She hadn't mocked him. She'd championed him. And most of all, she'd reminded him that he should be grateful God had given him this challenge. Sovilla had said God had a purpose. Isaac had always believed that, but he'd never thought of his stuttering as part of God's plan.

He mulled that over the rest of the morning. Ever since he'd been a small boy, he'd been ashamed of his struggle to speak. He'd prayed God would fix his mouth and brain. And he'd harbored resentment toward the Lord when his prayers remained unanswered. Now Sovilla had caused him to rethink that.

His brother Andrew rushed toward him. "Where have you been? I've been looking everywhere for you."

Isaac gulped. How did he answer that? Before he could come up with a plan, Andrew raced on.

"You got a roll at Fern's?" He nodded toward the sticky bakery paper in Isaac's hands. "You weren't there when I looked."

"S-sorry."

"Never mind." Andrew pushed Isaac toward the door. "The auction's already started, and our chickens are next. Daed needs you to load them for the winning bidders."

Isaac scooted ahead of his brother and arrived in time to hear the auctioneer announce "Sold" and point to two *Englisch* women sitting in the front row.

They high-fived each other. Andrew clutched his arm. "I'll talk to them to explain the procedures in case they don't know them."

Englisch locals usually already understood how things worked, but many *Englischers* turned out to be tourists. Isaac had never seen the pretty blonde and her dark-haired companion before, so they'd probably need help.

Giggling together, the two women headed for the exit. Andrew waylaid them. "Just making sure you know what to do."

The blonde smiled. "This is the first time we've bid on chickens, but I'm a regular at the produce auction. We'll go pay for them."

"Great." Andrew gave them his own winning smile. "When you get back, my brother Isaac will help you load them."

Both women nodded at Isaac. "We won't be long." They headed for the office.

Andrew slipped back inside, leaving Isaac standing outside the building. He breathed in the familiar air, redolent of animals and people and overlaid with greasy funnel cakes and French fries.

As the market doors nearby swung open, a fishy odor seeped out. An employee from the fish stand carried a bucket of scraps to a covered tin pail outside the door. Birds cawed and swooped. He waved to shoo them off before he emptied his container and thumped the metal lid back into place.

Soon, the women returned with their receipt, and Isaac picked up one of the two chicken crates.

"The truck's in the parking lot over there." The woman pointed to an area across the street. "By the way, my name's Stacey, and this is Diana."

Isaac sucked in air and blasted out his name in one fast breath. He'd practiced for years to manage that.

"Nice to meet you, Isaac. Do you have a farm around here?"

He sighed inside. Of course he'd gotten stuck with chatty ones. Isaac scolded himself. Stacey was only trying to be friendly. He nodded.

She looked as if she were expecting more. He shifted the squawking chickens to distract her.

It worked. She leaned over and peeked in at the half dozen chickens flapping their wings. "Aren't they the cutest things?"

Again, Isaac nodded. He'd never considered chickens' looks before. Only their overall health and egg production. When he was younger, he'd gotten attached to some of the chickens, but he'd soon discovered they'd be sold and learned to hide his feelings.

"I think they're adorable." The brunette reached out a hand.

Before she could stick a finger between the mesh, Isaac twisted away. She might get pecked later, but he wouldn't allow it to happen on his watch.

"The blue truck over there is mine."

Isaac followed them to the pickup. The brunette lowered the tailgate and motioned to the pickup bed.

Isaac stared at her. She wanted him to let the chickens loose? Did she expect them to roam free in the back of the truck while they drove home? From the way they'd chattered about the chickens being cute, he'd guessed they'd never owned chickens before. But even complete newbies would know chickens fluttered off. They'd arrive home with an empty truck bed.

Then it dawned on him that they might think the cages came with their purchase. If Andrew were here, he could easily explain that they'd only bought the chickens, not the carriers.

Isaac didn't want to suffer through their pity. He set the container on the ground beside the truck and patted the top of the coop. "M-My c-crate."

"What?" The brunette's screech hurt his ears. "We can't put the chickens in the truck bed." She eyed the driver's door.

Was she thinking of putting them in the cab?

Isaac shook his head. They obviously had no idea what a dozen chickens would do in that enclosed space.

"I didn't know we'd need cages," the blonde said.

They stared at each other, their eyes wide and confused. Then they giggled nervously.

"You must think we're crazy."

He didn't want to agree with her, but he did wonder at their sanity. Who would purchase a dozen chickens on impulse? Did they even have anyplace to keep them? Or hadn't they thought about that either?

Although raising chickens was part of his family's business, he didn't want any of their chickens mistreated. He'd rather refund their money.

"Could we take the crates home with us? Diana has a nice chicken coop. We could let them out there and bring the containers back. I'm sure we can make it back before the market closes today."

She appeared trustworthy. Or was it only Isaac's reluctance to talk that made him give in? He should explain they couldn't do that. Instead, with a nod, he hefted the crate into the back of the pickup and returned for the other.

If these women didn't return the traveling crates, replacing them would be expensive. *Please, Lord, help them to bring the crates back*, he prayed as the blue pickup pulled out onto the road with two crates of chickens inside.

He dragged his feet heading back to the auction, dreading explaining the missing crates to Daed.

Andrew caught up with him first and stared at Isaac's empty hands. "Where are the crates?"

He stammered his way through an explanation.

"You did that because you were afraid to talk to them, didn't you?" Andrew glared at Isaac. "It's time you got over that."

Isaac lowered his eyes. *I'm trying.* But who knew how long it would take? Replaying Sovilla's words gave him hope. God had made him this way for a reason. Isaac just wished God had explained His purpose.

Chapter Seven

All morning long, the warm, yeasty smell of pretzels called to Sovilla. During a midafternoon lull, she turned to her *aenti*. "Is it all right if I take a quick break?"

"What for?"

Maybe Wilma never got hungry, but Sovilla had skipped lunch, and her stomach kept growling. "I want a pretzel."

"And just how do you plan to pay for it? You'd better not be stealing from my cash box."

Sovilla gasped. "Of course not. I have some money from my *mamm*."

Wilma winced at the word *mamm*. "Oh, go ahead. I'm used to dealing with customers all by myself." She made it sound as if they were swamped with buyers, but they hadn't had many people today, and nobody was in line now.

"I'll be right back." For heaven's sake, the pretzels were only two stands away. It wasn't like Sovilla planned to take off for another state.

At that thought, her heart clenched. It had been several weeks since she'd seen *mamm* and her sisters, and quite a while since she'd had a letter. She missed them all so much. Staying with Onkel Lloyd wouldn't have been much worse than being here with her *aenti*.

As Sovilla started to exit the stand, Isaac walked past with Snickers.

"Did you plan this?" Wilma demanded.

"Plan what?" Sovilla kept her expression neutral. Of course she hadn't planned anything.

"You're sneaking out to meet that boy."

Heat rushed to Sovilla's face. Why had she responded to Wilma's question? She'd given her *aenti* the perfect opportunity to make embarrassing remarks. Had Isaac heard?

Maybe she should wait until he turned the corner and headed down a different aisle. *Ach.* He'd just joined the line in front of the pretzel stand.

"What are you waiting for?" Wilma demanded.

"That line looks really long." But if Sovilla didn't go now, she might not get another chance.

"You're just upset because someone else got in line behind him."

"Behind who?" Sovilla tried to play innocent.

"Don't treat me like a fool. I saw the way you looked at him. And Isaac has never walked his dog past here until today." She muttered to herself, "Twice in one day, in fact."

Was she suggesting Isaac purposely walked past here? Sovilla found that hard to believe. "Maybe he needed a change of scenery."

"Yes, he did. And the only change of scenery around here is you."

Sovilla pressed her lips together so she didn't blurt out *Don't be ridiculous*. "I doubt he even noticed I'm here."

"No, but you wished he would."

It was getting harder to hold back an irritated comment. Sovilla forced herself to take a calming breath. "I have no interest in Isaac or any other man. I have a boyfriend back in Sugarcreek."

"One who's forgotten you already."

As much as Sovilla hated to admit her *aenti* might be right, Henry hadn't contacted her. Instead of letting doubts nag at her, she needed to sit down and write the letter she'd been putting off and ask him for the truth.

The only reason she'd delayed this long was because she didn't want to hear that her hope of moving back to Sugarcreek and marrying Henry had been only a dream. Even if he confirmed her mounting fears, Sovilla had no interest in Isaac. She had no desire to jump into another relationship.

From the corner of his eye, Isaac saw Sovilla head in his direction. He'd love to turn and watch her approach, but he'd already made the mistake of passing Pickle Lady's stand.

Wilma's voice carried, so he'd heard her accusing Sovilla of meeting him. He didn't want to confirm Wilma's suspicions or get Sovilla in trouble. Even though she'd barely noticed him, his eyes might betray his interest. He'd like to get to know her, but that would be impossible. Even friendship was out of the question when you couldn't carry on a conversation.

"Can I help you?" The young Amish girl's question startled him.

He'd been so busy keeping tabs on Sovilla, he hadn't noticed the line moving forward. And he hadn't rehearsed what he'd say when he reached the counter. The pretzel carousel rotated, so he couldn't point at the one he wanted.

"R-raisin."

"One?" she asked.

He nodded.

When she opened the warmer and extracted the pretzel with paper, he held out his hand to let her know he didn't want it bagged. Then he paid and turned.

His eyes met Sovilla's, and breath whooshed from his chest. He stood there mesmerized until the man behind him elbowed past.

"Do you mind?"

Isaac shot him an apologetic glance and tugged lightly on Snickers's leash to move her to one side. Sovilla stood three people behind the man. He'd have to pass her.

She smiled at him. "Is cinnamon raisin your favorite too?"

Isaac wished he could do more than nod. He wanted to have a real conversation. But he'd already humiliated himself once today.

Her cheeks pinkened. "I want to apologize for my *aenti*'s comments this morning. I'm so sorry."

"I-i-it's—" A rush of heat climbed from beneath his shirt collar and burned its way to the tips of his ears. Isaac wanted to tell her it wasn't her fault, but he couldn't get the words out.

Sovilla's sympathetic glance both melted and embarrassed him.

She spoke softly so that people around them couldn't hear. "It's all right. Just relax and take your time."

Relax? Isaac didn't only stutter when he was nervous or pressured. He did it all the time. But now that he was face-to-face with Sovilla, how could he help being on edge?

"Being tense can make it harder. When my cousin was little, he stuttered when he was nervous or rushed. My *onkel*, well, he was hard on Roy. That always made it worse."

If Sovilla's *onkel* was anything like her *aenti*, Isaac imagined the poor kid must have been terrified. Isaac struggled enough talking to his own loving family. "I-I'm s-sorry."

"You mean for Roy?"

Isaac nodded. He relaxed a little. Sovilla almost seemed to read his mind.

"You've met Wilma, but her older brother, my *onkel*, is worse. Much worse." Sovilla clapped a hand over her mouth. "I shouldn't be talking about my family that way."

Isaac laughed. "I-it's all r-right."

"*Neh*, I'll need to ask forgiveness for that." She turned her attention to the girl behind the counter. "I'll have one cinnamon raisin." She smiled at Isaac. "Yours looks delicious."

"I-it is."

"Maybe I should get a pretzel for Wilma. She probably won't like whatever I choose. What do you think?"

Me? You want me to choose a flavor for Wilma? Isaac shrugged. He had no idea what Wilma might want. But when Sovilla stared at him with pleading eyes, he gathered his courage. "P-plain?"

She laughed. "You're probably right. Best to play it safe. Besides, if she doesn't want it, I can eat it myself."

Isaac smiled. "G-good idea."

Sovilla ordered a plain one bagged and took the cinnamon raisin one wrapped in paper like his.

For some reason, that made Isaac's insides dance.

Although his whole body and mind were already whirling from talking to her. He'd done it. Carried on a conversation. A conversation with Sovilla.

Sovilla paid and took the pretzels. As she turned to talk to Isaac again, she caught Wilma's frantic wave. "*Ach*, I forgot all about helping my *aenti*. I promised I'd hurry."

"S-sorry I k-kept you."

"Not at all. I enjoyed talking to you, but I'd better get back now."

Wilma only had three customers, but that didn't mean she wouldn't berate Sovilla.

She'd enjoyed talking to Isaac and spending time together. Only as a friend. But Wilma had seen them chatting, which would only reinforce her belief that Sovilla had planned to meet Isaac.

"What took you so long?" Wilma frowned at the pretzel in Sovilla's hand.

She'd been so focused on Isaac, she hadn't taken a bite. To distract her *aenti*, Sovilla handed over the paper bag.

"Huh? What's this?" Wilma held the bag away from her with two fingers as if expecting a snake to emerge and bite her.

"A pretzel. I didn't know what kind you'd prefer, so I got plain. If you'd rather have cinnamon raisin, you can have mine." Sovilla extended hers.

Wilma batted it away. "What makes you think I want any pretzels? Did you even ask if I like them?"

"You don't?" Somehow, no matter what Sovilla did, it always seemed to be wrong.

"I didn't say that. Don't go putting words in my mouth."

Sovilla wanted to turn her back and walk away, but a small part of her remembered those glimpses of vulnerability. Besides, she should be showing Wilma God's love.

Swallowing her irritation and ignoring her growling stomach, Sovilla held out both pretzels. "If you like pretzels, why don't you take both?"

Wilma cocked her head to one side. "How do I know you haven't spit on both of them?"

Sovilla bit back the retort that popped into her mind. "I wouldn't do that to anyone, and especially not to you. You're my *aenti*."

A glimmer of surprise flickered in Wilma's eyes, but she flung her hand toward the shelf under the counter. "Just put the bag under there. We have customers."

Sovilla longed to take a bite of hers while it was hot, but she wrapped the tissue around it, set it on the shelf, and hurried over to wait on a customer. By the time they'd served everyone, her pretzel had cooled. Still, it tasted good.

Wilma acted indifferent as she picked up the bag, but when she thought she'd turned enough so nobody could see her, her face relaxed into enjoyment. It pained Sovilla to think about how much pleasure Wilma denied herself by being grouchy and negative. It was as if she were punishing herself by not allowing herself to like anything or anyone.

Wilma's gruff "Thank you for the pretzel" startled Sovilla.

Her *aenti* sounded more grudging than grateful, but Sovilla had seen Wilma savoring that first bite of pretzel.

That was thanks enough. And even reluctant appreciation could be counted as a step in the right direction.

Wilma followed this up by frowning at the shelf where the pretzels had been. "You'd better clean up that stickiness. Next thing you know, we'll have ants and cockroaches crawling everywhere."

Sovilla smiled to herself as she took out the spray bottle filled with disinfectant and wiped the wooden shelf. Every time Wilma softened a bit, she had to cover it up with a grumpy comment. Sovilla was growing used to her *aenti*'s ways but prayed God would touch Wilma's heart.

The excitement flooding Isaac's body made it hard for him to eat. By the time he returned to the auction, he'd only taken one bite of his pretzel.

Andrew confronted Isaac the minute he returned. "Where have you been?"

Isaac waved his pretzel in answer.

"What's with the pretzel? You've never bought one before."

Ever since the day when he'd been eight and Pickle Lady had shamed him for his stutter, Isaac had avoided that end of the market. He had no need for pickles or flowers. And he'd never wanted to risk running into Wilma ever again.

"We needed you here. What took so long?"

With a quick shrug, Isaac took a casual bite, although he was feeling very un-casual. He still tingled inside as he replayed his conversation with Sovilla.

"Wait a minute." Andrew's eyes narrowed. "You took

a long time getting a roll at breakfast too. Pickle Lady's stand is nearby. I don't suppose a certain girl is helping her *aenti*?"

Pretending not to hear, Isaac strolled past Andrew.

"You have a speaking problem, not a hearing problem," his brother said behind him.

Isaac whirled around. Andrew had never been deliberately cruel before.

His brother held up his hands. "Sorry. I shouldn't have said that. But you shouldn't have walked away without talking to me either."

"S-stop t-teasing me."

"I can't even ask a simple question?" Andrew acted hurt. "Don't you think when your brother gets interested in a girl he should share? Especially with his twin?"

"N-not if he l-likes the same g-girl."

"You think I like her? What gave you that idea?" Andrew's innocent look appeared fake.

Isaac answered with an eye roll.

"*Ach*, just because I talked to her and . . ." Andrew followed Isaac back to the auction building. "How else could we find out more about her?"

That wasn't all. What about him announcing Isaac was interested in Sovilla? Up until now, the two brothers had never had a rivalry over a girl, mainly because Isaac never felt comfortable approaching anyone at the singings.

Andrew talked to a lot of girls but never seemed serious. What if he settled on Sovilla? Isaac wouldn't stand a chance. Not when Andrew could charm girls and Isaac struggled to speak.

She'd been sweet to talk to him and to listen patiently.

That meant nothing. As a polite person, she'd be equally kind to a small child or an older person who needed special attention. That didn't mean they shared a connection. And Andrew couldn't be competition for Sovilla's affection anyway. She already had a boyfriend.

Chapter Eight

Sovilla waited until Wilma, an almost-contented smile on her face, settled on a stool to finish her pretzel. This was the calmest Sovilla had ever seen her *aenti*, so she chanced asking, "When will you teach me to make these pickles?"

Wilma sat bolt upright, almost tipping over the stool. "I've spent years getting my recipe just right. People come from miles around, even from other states sometimes, just to get my pickles."

Her *aenti* did have some very loyal customers, and Sovilla had to admit the pickles blended a vinegary tang with the perfect touch of sweetness.

"You'll never get your hands on my recipe. It's all up here." Wilma tapped her forehead. "And that's where it'll stay."

"What if I run out of pickles while you're in the hospital?"

"I have no choice but to trust you to sell what I have, but believe me, I'll count every jar, so if you have any plans to cheat me—" Wilma's ominous tone intensified her vague threat.

"I'd never do that." Sovilla couldn't believe her *aenti* suspected that. Although Sovilla tried to remind herself that Wilma didn't trust anyone, it still stung. "I asked about making pickles to help your stand earn more money."

"More for you to pilfer?"

Sovilla shook her head. No wonder Wilma had no friends, if she accused everyone of trying to hurt her.

Her *aenti tsk*ed loudly. "There they go again. I can't believe they're leaving their stand unattended." Wilma waved toward the pretzel stand.

Gideon and Fern stood waiting in line. They were the cutest couple, at least to Sovilla. Her *aenti* had a different opinion and mumbled to herself.

"Whoever thought it was a good idea to put such a young man—and even worse, an Amish one—in charge of the whole market?" Wilma sniffed. "What was the owner thinking?"

Having worked for Gideon, Sovilla could understand the owner's choice. Gideon seemed fair and upright and kind. He also must be a smart businessman, because he'd expanded his chicken barbecue stand to include two more businesses—candy and baked goods. And everyone seemed to like working for him.

"Seeing Fern reminds me," Wilma said, "I told them you'd sell baked goods while I'm in the hospital. That's what you did in Ohio, right?"

"*Jah*, I did, but I don't want to compete with Fern."

"Lots of stands in this market sell meat or crafts or other things. Competition is good. Besides, your baked goods will be so much better."

"I've never tasted Fern's cooking, so I don't know how mine compares." Sovilla doubted her products would be as tasty. Nick had mentioned that Fern's mother and grandmother had owned the stand. Fern must have recipes that had been perfected and passed down through the generations.

"I imagine we'll need Gideon's permission to change the products we sell at the stand." Wilma waved him over as he and Fern passed by.

Fern smiled at both of them. "So nice to see you again, Sovilla. And how are you doing, Wilma?"

Interestingly enough, Fern hadn't mentioned she was happy to see Wilma. But Wilma didn't seem to notice.

"I'm doing terrible. And I'll be in even worse shape in another week or so, if I'm even alive."

Fern's eyes widened. "I hope not."

"Well, you never know about doctors nowadays. They'd just as soon kill as heal."

"I don't think they'd do that," Fern said in a calming tone. "Most people do fine after hip operations. Better than ever, in fact."

"I'm not other people." Wilma shot Fern an indignant look. "My health has always been delicate."

It has? From everything Sovilla had seen, Wilma ate well, slept well, and worked long hours. She did limp a bit when she walked, and she winced if she had to stand for long hours. Other than that, she seemed quite healthy.

Gideon smiled at both of them. "We need to get back. It's good talking to you, and we'll be praying for you, Wilma." He took Fern's elbow to steer her away.

"Wait," Wilma commanded. "I need to talk to you."

Sovilla admired how patient Gideon acted. She'd watched other people's irritated reactions to her *aenti*.

"Sovilla will be working here while I'm in the hospital. Obviously, I can't trust her to make my pickles the way I do."

Fern's brows rose. Then she sent Sovilla a sympathetic glance.

Wilma pinned Gideon with a piercing gaze. "I assume I need to get your permission for her to sell something else. I'm sure you remember I told you Sovilla is a spectacular baker."

Behind Wilma's back, Sovilla shook her head. She opened her mouth to contradict her *aenti*, but Wilma bulldozed her way along.

"My niece is actually the best baker in Ohio, so I suggested she sell her cinnamon rolls, pastries, cookies, and cupcakes."

Gideon sent a tender, questioning look at Fern.

"That's nice." Fern smiled at Sovilla. "I'm sure people will appreciate your *wunderbar* baking."

You're sure? Gideon mouthed to Fern, and she nodded.

But Sovilla wasn't. Why had her *aenti* listed the exact same items that Fern had for sale? "I, um, don't want to compete—"

"Of course you do," Wilma broke in.

"*Neh*, I don't." Sovilla hated to argue, but she couldn't allow her *aenti* to hurt someone else today. She'd already done enough to humiliate Isaac.

Wilma glared at her. When she started to speak, Sovilla interrupted her *aenti* before she said anything more.

"You don't sell pies, do you? Or donuts? I could sell things you don't."

Fern's relieved smile conveyed her appreciation for Sovilla's idea. Fern probably had family members to support.

"That sounds like a fine plan." The frown lines on Gideon's forehead smoothed out. "I'll let Mrs. Vandenberg know. I'm sure she won't have any objection. When do you plan to switch?"

Wilma's disgruntled look made it clear she disliked Sovilla's plan. "My operation is in two weeks. Sovilla can sell my pickles this week and maybe next. Then she can start making her *pies*." At her sarcastic emphasis on the last word, Wilma seemed to indicate there'd be a change of plans.

Gideon stared at her sharply. He'd detected the undertone too, but he had nothing to worry about. Sovilla had no desire to take business away from Fern. She and Gideon had been so kind during Sovilla's first week in Pennsylvania. But Sovilla dreaded facing her *aenti*'s wrath once Gideon and Fern left.

On Wednesday morning, Isaac again practiced with his mouthful of gravel, trying to shout out Bible verses to his dogs as he went around feeding, grooming, and petting them after his morning chores. Then he let them out into their runs.

Despite doing this exercise every morning and evening for more than a week now, he could manage no more than incoherent mumbling. During that time, Isaac had read and reread the books about Demosthenes and memorized the passages about him learning to speak. The biographies didn't say how long it took Demosthenes to succeed. What if it took years and years?

After Isaac had cared for all the dogs and puppies, he spit out the gravel and washed it. Then he hid the small container of gravel in the cupboard with the dog food and brushes. His family would wonder what he was up to if he picked up a handful of gravel every day. To prevent his brothers from finding the biographies, he kept them in the cupboard too, along with the Bible.

Now that the puppies were playing and tumbling outside, peace descended on the kennel. The pups' joyful yips and playful growls filtered in through the open dog doors. The sound filled Isaac with contentment. He savored the glimpses of his sweet dogs running and wrestling with one another.

Isaac enjoyed his time away from the lively household with his eleven siblings. Having time alone was precious. Once his brothers noticed all the dogs had been let outside, they'd soon break his solitude.

He had one more thing to do before they found him. Reaching into his pocket, he pulled out the paper Mrs. Vandenberg had given him yesterday. *Tips from a Speech Therapist*, it said at the top.

> *Take a deep breath first and make sure you're filling your diaphragm with air. Then speak on the out breath. It may feel unnatural, but keep practicing. Shallow breathing, lack of air, and trying to force out words can be one cause of stuttering. Speak slowly. Your speech might sound a little halting, but it can reduce stuttering.*

Isaac sucked in some air and tried. Did most people talk this way? It felt odd, but not as strange as speaking with gravel in his mouth.

With all these techniques, maybe he'd be a great orator like Demosthenes someday. Isaac chuckled, imagining himself giving speeches to crowds of people. *Jah*, like that would happen in the Amish community.

Besides, all he wanted to do was to ask and answer questions without turning bright red, to carry on conversations with people, and to order food at the market without stumbling over his words. Just doing those things seemed impossible.

He'd stick with it until he conquered it, but he wished it didn't seem like such a lengthy project. He had someone he wanted to talk to now—a certain green-eyed brunette popped into his mind and distracted him from Mrs. Vandenberg's list.

He indulged in those pleasant thoughts as he refilled all the water dishes. The puppies would be thirsty after romping in the warm sunshine. He'd come back later to play with them, but right now, he needed to buy more dog food. It also might be a good time to return the library books.

He just had to get the books out to the buggy without any of his siblings spotting them. Isaac dug through the closet and unearthed an old canvas bag. He tucked the books inside and headed out to the barn to hitch up the horse.

"Isaac," his sister Leanne called, "come be on our team." She tossed a baseball in the air.

"*Neh,*" Andrew yelled, rushing out the back door. "Isaac's on my side. Right, Isaac?"

He shook his head. He couldn't be on anyone's team. Not right now. He had errands to run.

"What?"

At Andrew's shrill question, Isaac turned to explain. He took a deep breath and tried to push the words out along with the air. "D-dog food."

"*Ach*, but you're the only one who can strike out Leanne. Can't you wait until later?"

Isaac debated, but he wanted to play with the puppies before he had to do afternoon chores. The stop at the library would take time too.

When he shook his head, Leanne thrust her lower lip out in a fake pout. "Come on, Isaac. Mamm only gave us a little time to play. We have to go in to help her can in half an hour."

Leanne almost convinced Isaac, but he had the books in the canvas sack. If he set it on the ground, one of his curious siblings might peek inside.

He disliked letting everyone down. Without him, they'd have nobody who could strike out Leanne. But something seemed to be drawing him toward the town. It seemed urgent to go immediately, not later.

Isaac shot his sister an apologetic look. "N-not now."

"Aww, Isaac. We won't have time later. We'll be in the hot kitchen all morning and afternoon."

"S-sorry." Feeling guilty, he turned away and continued to the barn, leaving his siblings arguing over how to divide up the teams fairly without him.

Not sure why he'd been so adamant about going for dog food right away when he could have postponed it for a half hour, Isaac hitched up the horse. Twenty minutes later, he tied her up at the hitching post in the library parking lot and entered the air-conditioned building. Over near the checkout computers, he spotted a familiar barrel-shaped *kapp*.

Sovilla? His heart sped up. Joy filled him. If he'd stayed to play baseball, he might have missed her.

He walked closer. He tried filling his lungs with air before speaking. "Sovilla?" He didn't stutter, but the word blasted into the silent room like the crack of a bullet. People turned to stare.

Sovilla jumped. She turned with both hands pressed against her heart. "*Ach*, Isaac, you startled me."

"S-sorry."

"That's all right." She picked up her stack of books. Then she looked at him with delight. "When you called my name, you didn't stutter."

She'd noticed that? Isaac pulled the paper from his pocket to show her.

As she took the page he held out to her, her smile lit a flame inside him that even the air-conditioning couldn't cool.

"*Tips from a Speech Therapist*," she read aloud before skimming the page. "This is great. You were trying the first one? Pushing out words on your breath?"

He bobbed his head up and down. "T-too loud."

"If you keep practicing, you'll get it."

Isaac thanked her with a smile.

"Nice talking to you," she said. "I'd better hurry. Wilma's waiting in the parking lot, so I can't stay long."

Isaac wanted to spend more time with her. He breathed in and prayed he'd get the words out. "I could t-take you h-home." He spoke each word slowly, the way the paper suggested, but each beat between words seemed agonizing.

He expected Sovilla to look impatient or pained, but her smile never faltered.

"Thanks for offering, but I only needed to check out a few cookbooks."

He cocked his head as if asking why.

She got his unspoken question. "My *aenti* will be going

into the hospital in two weeks, so I'll be taking over the stand."

Isaac's spirits sparkled with colored fireworks. She'd be at the market every day without her *aenti*. He wanted to ask how long Wilma would be gone, but that would be rude and unkind.

Sovilla continued, "Wilma doesn't trust me to make her pickles."

Isaac's "Huh?" came out on an explosive breath. He was so upset for her, he hadn't even tried any techniques.

He wished he could erase the hurt in her eyes. Why in the world would Wilma not trust Sovilla? Anyone who met her could tell she was trustworthy.

"*Jah*, well, it's not only me she doesn't trust."

Had Sovilla read his mind? *Neh*, she'd been responding to his *huh*.

"I think something painful happened to her that's made her suspicious of everyone." Sovilla's laugh held a note of ruefulness. "She's probably wondering where I am right now and suspecting me of all kinds of wrongdoing. I'd better go."

Isaac sent her a look of sympathy. He couldn't even imagine how hard it must be to live with Wilma.

"I needed these cookbooks because my *aenti* wants me to sell baked goods while she's in the hospital."

Yum! Isaac wouldn't have to pretend to be interested in buying pickles. *Deep breath.* "Your sticky b-buns are g-good."

"*Danke.* Wilma wanted me to make those, but I don't want to compete with Fern, so I'm going to make something different. Maybe pies and donuts."

Plenty of people in the market opened competing stands. But it said a lot about Sovilla's kindness that she'd think of Fern's feelings. She'd done the same by patiently listening to him garble out his words.

As much as he wished she'd done that because she returned his interest, Isaac had to remind himself she'd have done the same for anyone. But it didn't stop him from rejoicing over spending time with her. And he saw plenty of pies and donuts in his future.

Chapter Nine

Sovilla headed for the exit, but she stopped as Isaac pulled books out of the canvas sack he was carrying. She strained to read the titles.

Demosthenes? It looked like both books were about the same thing. He sure had strange tastes in reading.

"What took you so long?" Wilma demanded the minute Sovilla opened the car door.

"Sorry. I had trouble finding the nonfiction section." She'd memorized the layout of the library in Sugarcreek, but she'd had to search for the 640s in this library.

"*Hmph.* That's what librarians are for. Why didn't you ask?"

Sovilla should have, but she wanted to learn the layout of the library here. Although she might not have any way to get there once her *aenti* went into the hospital.

Wilma started to back out of the parking space. Then she slammed on the brakes.

Sovilla pitched forward, and the seat belt cut into her. Books flew from her lap and crashed around her feet. "What . . . ?" Glancing around to see what they'd almost collided with, she spotted Isaac exiting the library.

Uh-oh.

"Is that Isaac Lantz?" Wilma asked through gritted teeth. "You came here to meet him, didn't you?"

"*Neh*, I had no idea he'd be here."

Her face almost purple, she glowered at Sovilla. "Don't lie to me."

"I'm telling the truth." But protests would be useless.

"Yesterday, you met him at the pretzel stand." Wilma spat out each word. "Today, it's the library. Where will it be next?"

"I don't have any plans to meet him." Sovilla could barely force words from her constricted throat. "I'm not interested in Isaac. I have a boyfriend in Sugarcreek."

"So not only is he cheating on you, you're cheating on him. I'd hoped my sister's *dochder* would have more morals than an alley cat."

Too stunned and hurt to respond, Sovilla twisted her fingers in the fabric of her apron. Although it might make her look guilty, she kept her eyes focused on her hands. If her *aenti* had slapped her, Sovilla couldn't have been more shocked.

"Speaking of cats, a cat got your tongue? You don't even have the decency to look me in the eye? Wait, what am I saying? You? Decent?"

Sovilla's chin shot up, and she stared directly into her *aenti*'s eyes. "I have never given you a reason to not trust me. And I've never done anything—*ever*—like that. I follow the Bible and the *Ordnung* and—"

Wilma cut her off. "You're not perfect."

"I never claimed to be." Close to tears, Sovilla tried to keep her voice from wobbling. "I try my best to stay away from sinning. And I would never cheat on my boyfriend or steal from you."

"Pretty speeches cover up plenty of sin."

Sovilla was tempted to retort that maybe Wilma saw evil everywhere because she'd turned her back on God. But Sovilla bit her tongue.

"Nothing to say to that, huh? How did you get to know Isaac? Never mind. I bet you met him when you worked at Gideon's stand." Wilma pushed on the gas so hard, they shot forward, and the books that had hit Sovilla's feet earlier smacked into her ankles. She'd have several bruises tomorrow.

The whole way home, Wilma harangued Sovilla. As they neared their road, her *aenti* moved from lecturing to threatening. "That boy nor any other had better not set foot in the house while I'm gone. If they do, you'll live to regret it, believe you me."

Sovilla sat hands and jaw clenched. *Please, Lord, open her eyes. Help her to see the truth.*

"I can imagine what trouble you and that boy will get up to."

Trying hard to keep her tone measured, Sovilla said in a quiet voice, "I barely know Isaac. I've said maybe four or five sentences to him when we've met. So far, we've talked about pretzels, books, and dogs."

"Oh, sure." Wilma wielded her sarcasm like a sharp sword, as if hoping to draw blood.

Her jerky driving revealed her agitation. As they came to a red light, she tromped on the brake. Sovilla had prepared for it by putting her feet on top of the cookbooks, so at least she didn't get hit by flying books. But the seat belt chafed each time she was thrown forward.

Wilma seared Sovilla with a fiery glare. "I know the kinds of things teenagers do."

"I've joined the church. I don't intend to do anything to

dishonor God or break any of the *Ordnung* rules." That didn't mean she always kept them, but she did her best.

And as for being around boys, Mamm had had no problem with Sovilla being alone with Henry. She knew they both could be trusted.

"All kinds of things can happen, even to those who plan to be good."

Evidently, Wilma believed—with no proof—that leaving Sovilla alone meant she'd do something bad. And Sovilla had no way to convince her differently.

They rode in silence the rest of the way home.

"Maybe I shouldn't go into the hospital," Wilma mused as she unlocked the front door.

Although Sovilla had tried to make allowances for Wilma's grumpiness, she wouldn't stay where she wasn't wanted. Wilma seemed to have had an abrupt change of heart. Not that long ago, she'd written Sovilla into her will. Now, she didn't even trust her alone in the house.

"If you're not having the operation, I can write to Mamm to see about going back."

Wilma whirled around. "You'd rather stay with Lloyd than with me?" Her accusatory tone didn't match the hurt in her eyes.

"I didn't say that. It just seems I'm trouble for you."

"Excuses, excuses. If you don't want to be here, be honest."

Sovilla couldn't help the sigh that escaped. "I came to help you. If you need me, then I belong here. But maybe you should tell me if you want me to stay or go."

Her *aenti* turned her back before saying grudgingly, "I want you to stay. After all, who'll take care of me if you don't?"

Sovilla was torn. She didn't know if she'd prefer to stay

here or return to Lloyd's. Neither seemed like a *gut* option. If she had her way, she'd return to Sugarcreek, but with every day that passed, that possibility seemed more and more remote.

While her *aenti* went into the kitchen to can more pickles, Sovilla sat on the couch, thumbing through the cookbooks. She tore up a piece of scrap paper to mark recipes that looked good. She picked organic recipes, both because they seemed to do well for Gideon and Fern and because the largest market stand sold organic meats and vegetables, including odd-colored ones. Sovilla couldn't figure out why people wanted to buy vegetables in such strange colors—orange or green cauliflower, purple asparagus, black carrots, and purple broccoli—but that stand did a brisk business. So it made sense to follow their lead.

One of the organic cookbooks had a section on other recipes. Their granolas looked good, and Sovilla hadn't seen any for sale at the market. Maybe instead of baked goods, she should do that instead. She read through all of the cereal recipes and then flipped the page.

She'd found it. The perfect recipe. And a totally different angle. This cookbook had a whole section on making organic pet food. Snickers came to mind. Would Isaac buy homemade dog treats?

Sovilla shook herself. What difference did that make? She wasn't looking for ways to lure him to her stand. The last thing Wilma needed to hear while she was in the hospital was gossip about Isaac visiting the stand every day. Still, she liked the idea of selling pet food.

As she added another marker to the cookbook, a loud knock echoed through the house.

"You'll have to get that," Wilma yelled. "The brine's ready to pour over the cucumbers."

Sovilla set the last cookbook on the stack and hurried to the door. An Amish man and his wife stood on the doorstep. Sovilla doubted they'd come to see Wilma, but she didn't know them.

"I'm Laban Troyer, and this is my wife, Mary."

"Nice to meet you." Sovilla wasn't sure if she should invite them in. If it were her own home, she'd have done so immediately. But she worried about Wilma's reaction.

"My husband's the bishop," Mary said.

Sovilla shifted nervously. Should she explain why she hadn't attended church since she'd arrived?

"We'd like to talk to you. Do you have time now?"

Though the bishop's smile and words were warm and friendly, Sovilla's failures made her feel judged.

Dreading having to be a buffer between Wilma and the bishop, Sovilla opened the door wide. "Please come in."

"*Danke.*" Mary followed Sovilla into the living room.

The bishop stood in the entryway frowning down the hall to where the phone plugged into an outlet.

"Laban," Mary called as Sovilla motioned to the couch. "What's keeping you?"

He entered the room and sat beside his wife. "You have electricity here? I assume you're planning to remove it."

"I most certainly am not," Wilma called from the kitchen.

The bishop's bushy eyebrows rose.

"I'm staying here with my *aenti* to take care of her after her hip replacement."

"I see." The bishop pulled on his lower lip for a second. "I didn't realize we had an Amish woman living here, or we'd have come sooner."

"No Amish live here except Sovilla." Wilma's annoyance spilled into her words. Though she was participating in the conversation, she hadn't appeared.

Sovilla had to explain. Keeping her voice low, she explained, "My *aenti* is *Englisch*."

"She's left the church?" Mary kept her words as quiet as Sovilla's.

Sovilla nodded, although she didn't really know if Wilma had ever joined.

"It's quiet in there. Are you talking about me?"

Laban cleared his throat. Instead of answering Wilma, he addressed Sovilla. "We received the letter of recommendation from your church in Sugarcreek."

"You—you did?" She hoped the bishop didn't pick up on her consternation. Inside, her mind raced, struggling to make sense of this.

Mamm wants me to join the church here? I thought she only meant for me to stay with Wilma for a few months.

Sovilla fought back tears. Had Mamm planned for this to be permanent? *I'm never going back to my family?*

"We noticed you didn't attend church last weekend." The bishop spoke kindly, but tiny frown lines formed between his brows.

Sovilla whispered in case Wilma was still listening. "I wasn't sure how to find out when and where you were meeting. Also, I don't have a buggy, so I can only attend services in walking distance."

Back in Sugarcreek, that would never be a problem. She knew all the families in the community, and several people would have offered her a ride. Here, she wouldn't mind walking several miles to church, but when Sovilla had asked her *aenti* about the Amish community in the area, Wilma had gone ballistic. Sovilla hadn't wanted to stir up trouble so soon after she'd arrived.

"Hmm." The bishop smoothed a hand down his beard and looked into the distance. "You do have neighbors not far from the intersection. I'm sure they wouldn't mind coming up the lane to get you."

"I don't want to be a bother."

Mary smiled. "They'd be happy to do it, I'm sure." Then she laughed. "That is, if you don't mind being squashed in with their many children."

"Not at all." Sovilla loved children, and she'd be grateful for a way to get to church.

"Some of them are old enough to drive buggies," Mary added, a mischievous twinkle in her eyes. "They might be happy to drive you in a separate buggy."

The bishop laughed. "What my wife means is that they have several boys around your age. Only one of them is courting."

"I have a boyfriend in Ohio." Sovilla's response came out with more stiffness than she'd intended.

"I'm sorry." Mary's repentant expression didn't reach her eyes, which still brimmed with merriment. "I was only teasing."

"Teasing or not"—Wilma burst into the living room—"the last thing I need is boys coming calling while I'm in the hospital."

Everyone turned startled eyes in her direction.

"I'm already fretting about her friendship with one boy at the market. I'm scared to death she'll get into trouble while I'm not here."

"*Ach*, I'm so sorry I worried you." Mary's eyes filled with compassion. "As a mother myself, I know how hard it can be sometimes to trust our children to the Lord."

Sovilla clenched her hands, dreading Wilma's reaction. Mary must have assumed Wilma was religious because she dressed like a Mennonite.

Her *aenti*'s face swelled, and she thundered, "First of

all, I'm NOT her *mother*. And, second, I'd never trust God for anything."

The bishop and his wife stared at her in shocked silence.

Then, in a gentle voice, Mary ventured, "I'm sorry you feel that way. I've found God to be *a very present help in trouble*."

Tears stung Sovilla's eyes. Mamm loved that verse. Many times since Daed had passed, she'd quoted it. She often repeated the beginning of that passage as well: *God is our refuge and strength*. And Sovilla had claimed it often since she'd been at Wilma's.

The bishop closed his eyes and seemed to be mumbling a prayer. Then he lifted his head and spoke gravely. "We'll all watch out for your niece to be sure nothing happens to her. In fact, we could see about having someone come to stay with her if that would ease your mind. And we'll keep both of you in prayer."

"You can keep your prayers."

"I'd appreciate them," Sovilla said.

Wilma glared at her.

"Also," the bishop added, "the boys we mentioned are good boys. You'd have nothing to fear from them."

"No boys can be trusted." Wilma turned her back and headed toward the kitchen. "But I would like you to watch Sovilla."

The bishop waited until Wilma had left the room before turning to Sovilla. "We'll make sure you have a ride to church. It's a bit of a walk this weekend."

His wife tugged on his arm. "We should go now. This might be a good time to catch John to ask him about picking up Sovilla." She smiled at Sovilla. "I'm sure he'd be happy to do it. He's one of the most generous men I know."

"*Danke.*" Sovilla disliked asking for help from a stranger. But if she didn't, she'd have no way to get to church.

After Sovilla stood to show them to the door, Mary embraced Sovilla. "It may seem difficult at times, but I believe God brought you here for a reason. Keep showing your *aenti* God's love, and we'll be praying."

Touched, Sovilla nodded. It had been so long since she'd hugged her *mamm* or sisters. And now she wondered if she'd ever get to see them again.

The bishop smiled at her. "We'll look forward to seeing you in church on Sunday."

After she closed the door behind them, tears trembled on Sovilla's eyelashes. She plodded into the living room and slumped onto the couch.

If she joined the church here, she'd have to change to the Lancaster-style dress and *kapp*. She had little money left from Mamm. Not enough to buy or make clothing. But that wasn't her main concern. She'd no longer belong to Sugarcreek. And she'd look different from the rest of her family.

Worst of all, though, had been discovering Mamm didn't intend for her to return. Sovilla had been able to endure life here because she'd been expecting to leave. Her spirits plummeted. Now it seemed she'd be stuck here forever.

Chapter Ten

Isaac had gotten through his pebble practice by reminding himself of his conversation with Sovilla in the library. It bothered him to answer her with nods, headshakes, and facial expressions. Daydreams of speaking in full sentences—the way he did in his mind—spurred him to work harder.

Then he went out to train Snickers. He'd soon have to give up his new puppies to puppy raisers, but he'd chosen to raise Snickers himself from the previous litters. Once she got a little older, she'd have to leave for her formal training. He'd really miss her.

A buggy pulled up to the barn. Isaac secured the other puppies in one of the play yards and hurried over.

The bishop? What was Laban doing here? Especially in the middle of the day?

Wishing he could ask the questions flooding his mind, Isaac waved and helped the bishop by tying his horse to a post. Snickers stood quietly beside the horse.

Isaac bent to pet her. "G-good dog."

"Hello, Isaac. We're here to see your *daed*."

Isaac motioned for them to follow him into the house.

Mamm came from the kitchen, wiping her hands on her black work apron.

"Laban, Mary, good to see you." She appeared as puzzled as Isaac. "Come sit down. Would you like some lemonade?"

Laban wiped a few beads of sweat from his brow. "It is warm out there. Lemonade would be nice. *Danke.*"

"I'll be right back." Mamm started to the kitchen.

"We're actually here to talk to you and John," Laban said.

She turned. "Everything's all right, I hope."

"*Jah, jah.* Just a chance to help someone in need."

"We'd be happy to do that." Mamm tilted her head in Isaac's direction. "Why don't you get your *daed*?"

Isaac went out to the small shed attached to the barn to collect his *daed*. "B-bishop."

"Laban's here? Did he say what he wanted?" Daed put down the sandpaper he was using to smooth the top of a small wooden box.

They sold the boxes to several area gift shops to make extra money. Isaac helped out whenever he could, but taking care of the puppies took much of his time. He helped the family by selling them, but he mainly did it because most of his litters went to be trained as guide dogs.

Although Isaac should be training Snickers, the two of them trailed Daed into the house. Daed did many charity projects, and the whole family helped, so they'd all hear about it at dinner. For some reason, though, Isaac felt drawn to listen.

He settled on the bench in the kitchen, close enough to see and hear, but not near enough to be included in the conversation in the living room. He'd rather not face friendly questions from the bishop or his wife.

Isaac patted the spot beside him, and Snickers jumped up. When he'd first started as a puppy raiser for Snickers, Mamm had objected to dogs on furniture. But guide dogs might need to sit next to their owners to help them, so sitting close to him was part of their training. After some hesitation, Mamm had gotten used to Snickers sitting next to Isaac at meals and sleeping on his bed.

In the other room, Daed greeted the bishop and sat in the chair beside Mamm's.

"I won't keep you long," Laban said. "We have a new member of the church who lives close to you, and she could use a ride to church. I told her I'd check with you."

"Happy to do it, Laban. Where does she live?"

"On the dead-end lane right beyond Myron Groff's barn."

Daed frowned. "Isn't that where Pickle Lady, um, I mean Wilma Mast lives?"

Laban raised his eyebrows. "Pickle Lady?"

Daed gave an embarrassed chuckle. "Sorry. That's what my kids call her. She sells pickles at the market."

"I wonder if that's why she earned that nickname," the bishop said drily.

"Laban, that's not nice." Mary tapped him on the arm. "I knew her face looked familiar. I've seen her at the farmers market. I can my own pickles, so I've never bought from her, but I sometimes pass her stand."

"Wilma's coming to our church?" Daed sounded surprised.

Isaac would have been too, but he suspected someone other than Wilma would be attending church. At least he hoped he was right.

Mamm's brow wrinkled into a puzzled frown. "I thought she was Mennonite."

"*Neh*, she's not," Mary corrected. "But it's not Wilma who's joined the church."

I knew it! Isaac leaned forward eagerly.

"She has a niece, Sovilla Mast, from Sugarcreek staying with her." Laban confirmed Isaac's suspicion. "I'm guessing she's about the same age as your *dochder* Leanne."

And we'll get to take her to church every Sunday? Isaac had to find a way to drive her or be in the buggy with her. He couldn't believe he'd get to be with her on Sundays too.

Daed stroked his beard. "So, Wilma's *Englisch* and this Sovilla's Amish?"

"*Jah*, curious, isn't it?" Mary answered. "Sovilla's here to take care of Wilma, who's having surgery."

Isaac hadn't thought about it before, mainly because he'd been too enamored of Sovilla. But now he wondered if Wilma was an *aenti* by marriage or if she'd left the Amish church. He'd never heard about her being married. If she had been, Sovilla's *onkel* must have left the church. Such a sad thing to happen in a family.

The bishop rose. "We need to do some errands, and plenty of work awaits me at home. *Danke* for taking care of Sovilla."

"We're happy to," Mamm assured him. "We can see that she gets to youth group too. We have plenty of drivers."

Laban hesitated. "Wilma seems very concerned about Sovilla being around boys, especially when she's in the hospital. Could she ride with you or your *dochders*?"

"Of course." Mamm smiled brightly while Isaac's hopes crumbled. "Leanne usually drives the older girls. Sovilla might like to have some friends her age."

What about me? Isaac pictured taking Sovilla home after a singing. But many obstacles stood in the way. First of all, he couldn't ask her. No matter how many times he practiced with pebbles or took deep breaths, he'd get so nervous, he'd stutter like crazy. Maybe she wouldn't even be able to understand him.

But he had two other roadblocks: an *aenti* who didn't want Sovilla around boys, and Sovilla's boyfriend back in Sugarcreek. He should forget her, but how did you rein in your heart?

After the bishop left, Wilma banged around in the kitchen, crashing pots, slamming kitchen equipment, and muttering to herself.

Sovilla mirrored Wilma's mumbling, only silently. The idea of changing the clothing she'd worn since childhood upset her. Wilma had taken Sovilla's pay for working at Gideon's, and she only had a little money left from Mamm. Not enough for fabric.

She also wasn't sure Wilma had a sewing machine. Several of the bedroom doors remained closed, and Sovilla had never dared to peek inside.

And she certainly couldn't ask Wilma for money. Sovilla pictured Wilma's reaction to the request. Like an erupting volcano, hot, angry words would spew from her *aenti*'s mouth. She'd never give a penny of her hard-earned money for anything to do with God or the Amish.

Sovilla sighed. Every day, she questioned why Mamm had sent her here. She struggled to accept this as God's will for her life, but many days, it was difficult.

Bowing her head, she pleaded, *Dear Lord, forgive me for doubting You. Please remind me to be grateful that You've brought me here. And show me how to get a dress and* kapp. *And, Lord, please give me patience with Wilma so I can reach her with Your love.*

Her heart lighter, Sovilla lifted her head. She'd left three of her most pressing problems with the Lord.

One more minor concern nagged at her. She hoped she'd like the family who'd drive her to church. What if they didn't like her? Or what if they resented going out of their way to pick her up?

Sovilla shook herself. She'd been spending too much time around Wilma. Some of her *aenti*'s negativity and suspicion had rubbed off. Most Amish families looked for opportunities to help one another.

Trying to find other positives, Sovilla recalled the bishop mentioning the family had some youngsters. Little ones at church had always clustered around her. She'd probably get along fine with the younger children in this family.

What about the boys who were her age, though? Sovilla would explain that she had a boyfriend. She'd have no trouble staying away from any boys. Wilma had nothing to worry about.

Although as each day passed without any word from Henry, their relationship seemed more a fantasy than a reality. Still, unless she and Henry officially broke up, Sovilla intended to remain faithful.

For some odd reason, Isaac's face supplanted Henry's. Sovilla shook her head. She only wanted to help Isaac. Her heart went out to him as he struggled to speak. That was all there was to their friendship. So why was she having so much trouble banishing him from her thoughts?

At the supper table that night, Daed looked at Leanne. "The bishop stopped by today. He wants someone to pick up a young girl who's staying with Wilma Mast and take her to church and youth group."

"Sovilla?" Andrew asked with a sly grin at Isaac.

Even hearing Sovilla's name made Isaac's heart flutter, but he'd rather it hadn't been his brother who said her name.

Dad turned to Andrew. "You know her?"

Andrew chewed slowly, his eyes on Isaac, as if waiting for him to answer.

"She works at the market. We"—he waved in Isaac's direction—"met her when she was working at Hartzler's Chicken Barbecue. Well, actually, she was filling in for Fern at the bakery counter."

"I see." Daed returned his attention to Leanne. "I'd like you to get her on Sunday."

Andrew broke in. "Why are you asking Leanne when someone else at this table is dying to pick up Sovilla?" He threw a pointed glance at Isaac.

Everyone turned to stare. Isaac struggled to maintain an *I-don't-know-what-he's-talking-about* expression, but blood rushed to his face, ruining his efforts to look disinterested.

"Ooo, Isaac," his older brother, Zeke, teased. "You sweet on this girl?"

Isaac glared at Andrew, who shrugged and added another jab. "You haven't noticed how many cinnamon rolls and sticky buns and pretzels he's been eating lately?"

"Come to think of it," Zeke said, "he has been missing a lot lately when we have jobs to do."

Isaac sucked in a deep breath, hoping he could make Mrs. Vandenberg's technique work. Before he could form words, Leanne interrupted.

"Stop being mean. Leave Isaac alone."

Danke, *Leanne.* His younger sister often came to his rescue. He smiled to let her know he appreciated her kindness.

Daed tapped a fork on his plate to get their attention. "Sovilla's *aenti* doesn't want her around boys. So, we'll be honoring Wilma's wishes."

Andrew groaned. "Aww."

Leanne studied Andrew. "You're interested in her too? Is that why you were teasing Isaac?"

Zeke rolled his eyes. "What girl isn't Andrew interested in? At singings, they all flock around him like hens around a rooster."

"Can I help it they all like me?" Andrew tried to act nonchalant, but a proud smile spoiled the effect.

Daed cleared his throat. "Don't be prideful, *sohn*. Perhaps you also need to consider how you're acting to attract so much attention. That might be something you need to pray about."

Andrew squirmed under Daed's stern look, and his show-offy expression wilted.

"As I was saying," Daed continued, "Sovilla will ride with you girls, Leanne." He glanced from Andrew to Isaac and even included Zeke, pinning each of them with a piercing gaze. "And I expect you boys to honor Wilma's request to stay away from her."

Isaac's spirits sank. Not spend time with Sovilla?

Did that mean he couldn't talk to her at the market? If he met her in the library, did he turn and go the other way? Did he stop buying pretzels? Stop taking Snickers for a walk down her aisle?

What had sounded like the ideal opportunity to spend more time with her at singings, maybe even get up the courage to ask her to ride home with him, had turned into a nightmare. Instead of getting to know her better, he'd need to avoid her.

The next morning, a girl came rushing up to the stand as Sovilla helped her *aenti* remove the tablecloths covering the pickle jars.

"Are you Sovilla?"

When Sovilla nodded, the girl rushed on. "I'm Leanne, and we'll be taking you to church on Sunday. I hope you'll want to go to the singing with us too."

Sovilla ignored Wilma's frown. "I'd like that."

"I wouldn't."

Her *aenti*'s flat declaration doused Sovilla's enthusiasm with a deluge of ice-cold reality. Would Wilma refuse to let her attend?

"I'd like to go to the singings." Sovilla kept her tone respectful, but firm.

"Much too dangerous. Lots of boys there. Too easy to get in trouble."

Leanne favored Wilma with a sunny smile. "Daed mentioned you were worried about that. He told my brothers to stay away. And I can let the other boys know you don't want Sovilla dating."

"I already have a boyfriend back in Sugarcreek," Sovilla said.

Wilma snorted, but Leanne's smile grew wider. "Perfect. I'll make sure everyone knows she's dating someone. That'll keep the boys away."

"I doubt it. They're not to be trusted."

"I think if you met the boys in our buddy bunch, you'd see they're trustworthy."

"No male is trustworthy."

Leanne raised her eyebrows, but then pasted on a neutral expression. Keeping her tone polite, she said, "I'm sure you don't mean that."

"I'm sure I do." Wilma turned her back and stomped over to count the money.

"Do you think she'll let you go to the singings?" Leanne whispered.

Sovilla shrugged. "I'm not sure." Since she'd arrived, she'd never rebelled against anything Wilma had asked her to do or not do. This might be her first time.

"I hope you can come. We have a really nice group. But I'll plan to get you for church at seven thirty on Sunday morning."

"*Danke.* I'm looking forward to it." This girl seemed sweet, and it would be nice to have a friend.

Leanne took in Sovilla's clothes. "Are you planning to change your *kapp* and dress?"

"I'll have to, won't I?" Thinking about it again brought up a deep ache. "In my church, they gave people a few weeks."

"We do here too, but wouldn't you be more comfortable if you dressed the same as everyone else?"

Sovilla bit her lip. Comfortable? *Neh.* She'd never be comfortable in the Lancaster Plain clothes, not when she looked so different from her family. But she'd stand out if she wore her Sugarcreek *kapp*. "I guess I would. I'll have to figure out something for next time."

"Sovilla!" Wilma's voice cracked through the air. "Are you here to help, or do you plan to socialize all day?"

"I'm sorry," Leanne whispered. "I didn't mean to get you in trouble."

"It's not your fault." If Leanne hadn't been here, Wilma would have found some other reason to complain.

"I'll see you Sunday." Leanne scooted off.

Wilma had scared off Sovilla's first chance at friendship. And she'd hurt Isaac's feelings too. Would Sovilla be able to have any friends?

Wilma had made it clear Sovilla wasn't to have any male friends, but it seemed as if she might not be allowed have female friends either. Or perhaps Wilma only objected to Amish friends.

Chapter Eleven

"Hey, Isaac," Leanne called as she raced across the parking lot from the market to the auction building.

He stopped and waited for his sister to catch up.

She huffed a little. "Whew! I'm out of breath. Not as young as I used to be, I guess."

Isaac laughed. Leanne was seventeen. He still thought of her as his baby sister.

He'd been six when she was born, so he'd spent a lot of time taking care of her. He'd found comfort in being around a little girl who could only speak baby talk and mis-pronounced many of her words. He'd already reached the age when people no longer considered that cute. They frowned at his problems talking, but no matter how hard he tried, he couldn't make his words come out like Andrew's or Zeke's.

"You r-run in b-baseball."

She ran faster than anyone in the family. And hit better too. That's why everyone always wanted her on their team.

Leanne waved a hand. "That's sprinting, not speeding

after someone. I'm glad I caught you before you went inside."

Isaac tilted his head. She wanted to talk to him privately. Was something wrong? Leanne often confided her problems in him, probably because Isaac couldn't talk well enough to gossip.

"I went over to Pickle Lady's stand to meet Sovilla. I can see why you have a crush on her."

He wanted to protest that he didn't, but would that be lying? Before he could decide, Leanne hurried on.

"Sovilla seems really sweet and kind. Not at all like her *aenti*."

Isaac agreed with that. He nodded, hoping Leanne would say more.

"I think Wilma wanted to toss me out. She's not happy Sovilla's going to church. I'm not sure if she'll forbid her to go to singings. It sounds like she might."

Neh. Isaac had been counting on seeing her there even if he couldn't talk to her.

"*Jah*, I'm d-disappointed too."

Leanne read more than his face. She seemed to see into his heart too. Sovilla also had that gift. Conversations with both of them were much easier than with anyone else. When they'd been younger, Andrew had done this too. But laterly, his twin had gotten more self-absorbed and stopped listening or understanding.

Turning down her lips, Leanne said, "It's not fair for Wilma to keep Sovilla from having fun. Maybe Daed or Laban can convince Pickle Lady."

Isaac wiggled his brows at the nickname.

"I know, I know. Mamm doesn't want us to call her that, but she is sour."

Although he should have discouraged Leanne from criticizing Wilma, Isaac nodded.

"Can you imagine living with Wilma all day long? I have trouble being nice to her for ten minutes."

Isaac's heart went out to Sovilla. It had to be a trial to be cooped up in the house with an old woman who always griped.

"Anyway, I thought you'd like to know she'll be coming. I'd better go. Mamm'll be wondering where I am. I was only supposed to drop off the canned goods at Wolgemuth's stand, but I couldn't resist checking out Sovilla."

Mamm and the girls canned their extra garden produce—beans, tomatoes, corn, peas, and whatever else was in season and also made chow chow—for a stand at the market. Everyone did small jobs to bring in extra money. Even so, they'd barely scrape by if it weren't for the money Isaac made by selling his puppies for guide dogs.

He waved as Leanne headed for the buggy. Being with his sister always made Isaac's heart lighter. Today, though, it soared. Sovilla would be coming to church! Even though he couldn't talk to her or ride in the same buggy, he'd get to stare at her across the room during the service.

That night after dinner, Leanne beckoned to Isaac as he headed out to check the dogs before bed. He slipped out of the living room to join her in the hallway.

Andrew came galloping after them. "What are you two up to?"

Leanne waved him away. "Nothing that'd interest you."

Isaac followed her upstairs to her bedroom. Andrew stayed on their tail. After Leanne opened her door, she motioned for Isaac and Snickers to go in first, then she shut the door before Andrew could enter.

He yelped. "You almost cut off my nose."

"Your nose wouldn't be in danger if you didn't keep sticking it into other people's business."

"Hey!" Andrew pounded on the door.

Daed yelled upstairs. "What's going on up there? Stop that banging."

Andrew stopped knocking and started wheedling, "Aww, Leanne, let me in." When she ignored him, he asked, "Don't you need to help Mamm with the canning?"

"Not until the younger ones are done with the dishes. If you're so worried about Mamm, you could help."

Grumbling, Andrew clomped downstairs.

"I didn't want Andrew to see this because I know he'll tease." Leanne went over to the closet she shared with three of her sisters and opened the door. "I already checked this out with Mamm."

Leanne pulled out three dresses and laid them on the bed. "I thought Sovilla might feel more comfortable if she could dress like everyone else."

Leave it to Leanne to think of that. To Isaac, Sovilla looked beautiful the way she was, but he could understand her not wanting to stand out.

"You know Sovilla better than I do. Which colors do you think she'd like best?"

Isaac had no idea. He tried to picture her glossy brown hair and green eyes. She'd look lovely in any of these colors, but she'd look pretty in the bright rosy pink. He tapped that one.

"Sovilla will be lovely in that color."

She'd also be easier to spot. Not that he'd need any help with that. His eyes automatically picked her out in a crowd.

"Which other one?" Leanne asked. "She should have at least two."

Isaac fingered the yellowish one. "This?" That color would emphasize her green eyes. It would also stand out among the darker colors.

Leanne put away the other dress. Then she came back to the bed and slipped the pink and yellow dresses off their hangers, folded them neatly, and placed them inside a canvas drawstring bag. "I have a white church apron in there already. And a black half apron and a work apron."

Isaac smiled broadly to show her how much he appreciated her helping Sovilla, but one thing worried him. They usually passed dresses down to the next sisters in line. "M-Mamm's all r-right with it?"

"I already said she was. She agreed as soon as I suggested it. One dress is mine and one belongs to Mary Grace, so we'll be fine."

"*G-gut.*"

"And Mamm offered to make Sovilla a *kapp*, but we'll need her measurements to be sure it fits properly. There's a pattern in there for her to mark, but you'll need to bring it with you."

"M-me?"

"Don't worry. I wrote out the instructions, and you can fold the paper and put it in your pocket."

Isaac gulped. He'd have to take a pattern from Sovilla and keep it with him?

"She'll feel more comfortable if she has a Lancaster *kapp*. I expect it's hard enough being a newcomer without wearing clothes that make you stand out."

Isaac often had that stomach-sinking feeling of standing out in a crowd. He never wanted Sovilla to experience it.

Leanne slid the drawstring bag closed and held it out to Isaac.

He gave her a questioning look.

"I won't get to the market tomorrow or Saturday. If Sovilla's going to get this before Sunday, you'll need to give it to her."

"M-me?" He'd be the laughingstock of his brothers if he went around with a drawstring bag containing two dresses.

"Should I ask Andrew?"

"*Neh.*" Isaac snatched the bag from her fingers. No way would he let his brother deliver these dresses. He'd have to find a way to keep the bag hidden and to sneak it to Sovilla. Wilma didn't want Sovilla around boys, which made it even more difficult.

Lord, help me to find a way to give the clothing to Sovilla so she doesn't get in trouble.

First, though, he had to get it out of the house without Andrew or his brothers noticing.

Leanne sensed his plight. "Here. Give the things to me. I'll take them into the kitchen and set them out in the mudroom by the door. You can get them when you go out to check the puppies."

"*D-danke.*"

His sister waited until he'd gone downstairs, then she descended, swinging the canvas bag casually. Andrew eyed both of them, but lost interest when Leanne entered the kitchen.

Isaac spent ten minutes reading, but he was too antsy to concentrate. He kept turning pages, because if he went out too soon, Andrew might follow him. But Snickers sensed Isaac's restlessness and kept nosing him. He rubbed the puppy's ears and tried to figure out how to get outside without anyone paying attention.

He didn't want his brother to see the bag. If Andrew discovered the contents, he'd mock Isaac. Even worse, if his brother found out who the bag was for, he'd insist on going along to deliver it.

Finally, Isaac rose and sauntered through the kitchen, Snickers at his side.

"Don't stay out in the kennel too late," Mamm said as he passed. "You've been out there much longer than usual the past week or so."

He'd been using the extra time to read aloud. Most mornings were too busy to allow much practice. "All r-right."

As he walked through the mudroom, he picked up the drawstring bag. He hunched over it and turned his back to the kitchen window as he strode out the door. If anyone looked out, he hoped they couldn't see him carrying anything.

He hurried into the kennel and stowed the bag in the feed closet. After the girls and Mamm finished in the kitchen, he'd hide it in the back of the buggy and toss an old blanket over it.

Isaac opened his Bible and slipped the handful of gravel from the container. As he kicked the closet door shut, the kennel door banged open. He froze.

Andrew burst into the building. "What did you sneak out here? What were you and Leanne up to? I saw you carrying something."

Isaac tried to turn so his brother couldn't see the Bible. He slid his hand in his pocket and dropped in the pebbles. Thank goodness, Andrew had come now before Isaac filled his mouth with gravel.

"What are you hiding?" Andrew moved closer and pulled on Isaac's arm to reveal the book in his hand. He stopped and stared. "A Bible?"

Isaac prayed his brother wouldn't ask him why he had a Bible in the kennel.

Andrew chuckled. "Are you out here preaching to the puppies?"

Could you keep your face from turning red? Isaac tried, but didn't succeed.

"You are, aren't you?"

Not exactly. "*N-neh.*"

"You want to be a preacher." Andrew doubled over with laughter. "You? I can just see you up there." He stood up straight, assumed a serious expression, and cupped his hands as if he held a book. "G-G-G-God s-s-says-s-s . . ."

Isaac's eyes burned. Why was Andrew being so cruel? Turning his back on his brother, Isaac set the Bible on a shelf. Then he headed blindly for one of the pens, lifted the latch, and sank to the floor.

Snickers hunkered beside him as the pups climbed and tumbled over Isaac's legs. He picked up the nearest pup to cuddle. The puppies didn't care if he couldn't speak.

"*Ach*, Isaac, I'm sorry. I was angry because you and Leanne wouldn't let me in, but I shouldn't have done that. Will you forgive me?"

Isaac bobbed his head up and down, but he didn't face Andrew. Deep down, Isaac ached, but not because of his brother's teasing. Inadequacy twisted Isaac's insides. So many things he couldn't do or be.

"Can I help you with the dogs?" Andrew sounded regretful.

"All d-done. J-Just p-playing now."

"All right. I'll go back to the house, but I really am sorry."

Isaac nodded, and his brother left, closing the door softly behind him.

Andrew hadn't hurt Isaac's feelings by saying he could

never be a preacher. God chose their preachers when the men drew lots. Isaac's name would never be entered in the first place. Not that he cared. The last thing he wanted was to speak in front of the church. But that represented one more option closed off to him.

Nor could he be an auctioneer like Zeke. Or a salesperson. Or a husband. Who'd want a husband who couldn't speak? He'd never even be able to ask a girl on a date.

Although he'd talked to Sovilla twice now and she'd been incredibly patient, each of those conversations had only lasted a short time. Even she'd grow irritated after a while. Most people did.

He'd content himself with loving her from afar. Was it even right to do that when she had a boyfriend?

God, if my feelings for Sovilla are wrong, please take away these longings.

The next morning, Sovilla headed out to the car to bring in another crate of pickles. After the bishop had left the other day, Wilma had worked feverishly, canning batch after batch of pickles. She hadn't spoken to Sovilla the rest of that day.

Sovilla had opened the trunk and leaned in to grasp the wooden box when someone touched her arm. She gasped and jerked away, almost clunking her head on the open trunk.

"S-sorry."

Isaac looked so upset, Sovilla wanted to reach out to comfort him.

"It's all right. I didn't hear you come up. Hi, Isaac." She smiled down at the puppy. "Good morning, Snickers."

He glanced over his shoulder, then thrust a drawstring bag into her hands.

"Is this for me?"

Once again, he looked all around, then nodded.

As Sovilla undid the drawstring, Isaac gave the leash a gentle tug, and he and Snickers turned to go.

"Wait. What is this?" Sovilla pulled a bright pink dress from the bag. Then she lifted out a yellowish dress. Under it, three aprons lay neatly folded: a white one that she assumed was a church apron, one black half apron, and a full black work apron. "Where did these come from?"

"L-Lee-a-anne."

Leanne? The girl I met yesterday? "You know Leanne? She sent these for me?"

Isaac nodded. Then his eyes widened, and he backed away.

"What's wrong?"

Without answering, he and Snickers took off.

Sovilla opened her mouth to call after him, but Wilma's strident tones echoed across the parking lot.

"I sent you out here to get pickles. You took so long, I came to see what was keeping you."

Ach! Could she have any worse timing? Keeping her back to Wilma, Sovilla tucked everything back in the bag. Seeing Plain clothing would upset her *aenti*.

Wilma stomped over. "And what do I find? You canoodling with that boy again."

Sovilla had no idea what *canoodling* meant, but from Wilma's inflection, it sounded bad.

"I can't even trust you for five minutes."

Sovilla tugged on the drawstring to close the canvas bag. She wished she'd put it straight into the car without opening it.

"What's that in your hand?"

"Some, um, clo—"

Wilma's screech interrupted her. "You're getting presents from that boy?"

"*Neh*, it's not from him. He only delivered it for Leanne, the girl who stopped by yesterday."

Wilma's eyes narrowed. "She couldn't give it to you herself?"

"I don't think she works here. At least, I've never seen her, have you?"

"Stop changing the subject. Why didn't she give it to you? And what's in it?" Wilma snatched the bag from Sovilla's hands and tugged at the drawstring.

A sickish look crossed her face. After a quick glance at the clothing, her jaw clenched. She yanked open the car door and tossed the bag onto the back seat.

"Keep that thing away from me." Wilma slammed the door. "Now, explain to me, why is a complete stranger giving you clothes?"

"I don't know. She's being kind, I guess. She did ask if I had Lancaster clothing."

"And she just did it out of the goodness of her heart? So why was that boy delivering it?"

"I didn't get to ask him. He was only here for a few seconds."

"Yeah, right."

"I imagine Leanne asked him to drop off the clothes." Sovilla had wondered the same thing. Perhaps Leanne was his neighbor, but Sovilla kept circling back to the explanation that made the most sense—Leanne was his girlfriend.

Leanne seemed like a nice, caring girl. Sovilla should be happy for Isaac. So why did she feel depressed?

To banish those thoughts, Sovilla reached into the trunk

and lifted a crate of pickles. "We'd better hurry before the market opens."

"Whose fault is it that we're late?"

"I'm sorry." Sovilla moved around her *aenti* and rushed to the market door as fast as she could with the heavy box. She set it down on the floor of the stand and hurried out for another, passing Wilma on the way.

Sovilla took the last crate, set it on the ground to slam the trunk, and returned to the stand as Gideon made his rounds to unlock the doors.

"Watch where you put that." Wilma pointed to a small red spot on her ankle, then to the crate Sovilla had carried in first. "Were you trying to trip me? I could have been badly hurt."

Once again, Sovilla clamped her lips together to avoid an unkind retort. She longed to snap back, *Why didn't you look where you were going?* And she wanted to defend herself. She'd placed that crate in the far corner of the stand out of the way.

To release some of her pent-up energy, Sovilla rapidly filled any empty spots on the shelves with pickles. Clanking the jars together or plunking them down a bit too hard dispelled some of her irritation. A brief prayer helped too.

Sovilla reminded herself of the bishop's words. She needed to show her *aenti* God's love. It seemed impossible.

Lord, I want to do Your will, but I can't do this without Your help. Fill me with love for Wilma and touch her soul.

Chapter Twelve

Soon after they arrived home after work on Saturday, someone knocked on the front door. Wilma had gone up to bed early complaining about her legs, so Sovilla answered it. Leanne stood on the porch.

"I hope the dresses fit."

Sovilla had planned to wait until Wilma fell asleep before trying them on. "*Danke* for lending them to me."

"*Neh*, they're yours. Alter or hem them so they fit."

"I can't take them."

"You can and you will. I've come to take you *kapp* shopping. We'd give you one of ours, but they have to fit properly, since Isaac didn't explain about the pattern."

"My *aenti* . . ." Although she didn't want to disturb Wilma, Sovilla needed a Lancaster *kapp*. She couldn't ask her *aenti* to take her. Not after the way Wilma recoiled at seeing the dresses and aprons. "Let me leave a note."

If Wilma woke and discovered Sovilla gone, would she get in trouble?

As she shut the front door quietly, Sovilla let out a breath. "I can't stay long."

"Don't worry. The stores will close soon, so we'll hurry."

Leanne chattered the whole way, making Sovilla feel comfortable and relaxed. At the store, Leanne picked a box with a # 2 on it. "Let's see if this one works."

Feeling guilty, Sovilla removed her *kapp*. They were in a back aisle of the store with nobody around, but she'd never taken her *kapp* off in public before.

Leanne set the *kapp* on Sovilla's head and tugged at it. "That one doesn't cover enough of your ears. Let's try a different one."

They tried a second one, and Leanne checked the sides and back. "That one fits properly. Let's get it. In addition to the white one, you'll also need a black one." She selected another box with the same number from a different section of the shelves.

While Sovilla put her own *kapp* back on, Leanne picked up *kapp* strings, and then they headed for the checkout counter. As they passed rows of clothing, Leanne pointed out a nearby rack. "They have used clothes here, and the prices are good if you want more dresses and don't have time to make your own."

If Sovilla had more money, she might have selected a few and given back the dresses. But she barely had enough to pay for the *kapps*. For now, she'd have to use Leanne's dresses. Later, Sovilla intended to find a way to pay Leanne back.

On the way home, Leanne explained the proper way to pin on the *kapp*. Sovilla thanked Leanne several times for the shopping trip. It had been a blessing. And Sovilla tried not to think about the changes she'd be making tomorrow.

She entered the house quietly, relieved to find her note where she'd left it and her *aenti* snoring upstairs.

She tiptoed to her room with the *kapp*. Because she was a little more petite than Leanne, she spent several hours taking in the side seams of both dresses and turning up the hems.

When she finally went to bed, Sovilla tossed and turned most of the night. She couldn't wait to go to church, but she dreaded meeting new people and being under scrutiny. That wasn't the main thing keeping her awake, though. Each time she drifted off into sleep, Isaac's face appeared. She'd sit up, startled and guilty.

Before dawn, she gave up trying to sleep and slipped downstairs for breakfast. She'd rather not wake Wilma. Anxiety and anticipation warred in her stomach, so she could barely eat. She didn't need the added stress of Wilma's criticism.

Although Sovilla tried not to use the electricity, after she put on the pink dress, she slipped into the bathroom and turned on the light. Sovilla followed Leanne's instructions for the *kapp.* Light as a feather, the gauzy, heart-shaped *kapp* barely seemed to be there. Unlike her stiff pleated *kapp,* she kept reaching up to reassure herself it was still on her head.

After Wilma's fury at the market yesterday, Sovilla stayed away from her *aenti*, who'd embarked on another pickle marathon. They'd filled all the shelves at the market, so Wilma stored the extras in the basement. Sovilla would have plenty to sell during Wilma's hospitalization. She had to admit, she looked forward to having the house to herself for a brief time.

Sovilla's conscience nagged at her. She'd prayed to love her *aenti*, but since then she'd spent most of her time wishing Wilma were gone.

One other thing weighed on Sovilla. Yesterday, she'd

peeked into the bedrooms to find a needle and thread. One room held a sewing cabinet, and Sovilla sneaked inside. Not only did she take the sewing supplies without asking, but she opened the closet door, which stood slightly ajar.

Inside, Wilma's Amish dresses hung next to a black cloak. Most of the Midwest-style dresses would fit a slim young girl. A few of them appeared larger and baggier. When had Wilma decided to become *Englisch*? If she lived here, why hadn't she changed into Lancaster Amish clothing?

That brought up additional questions. Had Wilma been baptized? If so, she'd be under the *bann*. Mamm wouldn't have sent Sovilla here if that were the case, would she? But if Wilma had left before she'd joined the church, she must have continued to live Amish for a while. When and why had she become *Englisch*?

Sovilla wished she could ask her *aenti* all these questions, but Wilma's rage over anything Amish made that impossible. And Mamm would provide no answers. She'd said to talk to Wilma.

After one last check of the unfamiliar *kapp* and dress in the bathroom mirror, Sovilla flicked out the light and eased open the door. She tiptoed downstairs and out onto the front porch so she could catch Leanne before the buggy pulled into the driveway.

Several horses clip-clopped by before Leann arrived. She stopped out front, and a buggy full of young men swerved off the road behind her. Sovilla didn't glance their way in case Wilma was staring out the window. If only that buggy had traveled on.

Why had they stopped too? Were they following their girlfriends? Or maybe those were Leanne's brothers. The bishop had mentioned several boys. Either way, if Wilma saw a buggy of boys chasing after Sovilla, she'd be furious.

Conscious of all the eyes on her, Sovilla stared at the ground so she wouldn't have to see everyone examining her. She walked stiffly up the driveway and rounded the buggy, watching for oncoming cars zooming past. She breathed a sigh of relief when she reached the passenger side.

When Sovilla slid open the door, Leanne brightened. "That color does look pretty on you." She seemed pleased to see Sovilla in her dress. "It fits all right?"

Sovilla nodded. "I took up the hem so it's the right length."

"Great." Leanne's cheery disposition poured sunshine over Sovilla after the thunderstorms of negativity she'd endured over the past few weeks. "You can sit beside me." Leanne waved behind her. "These are my sisters."

Three teen girls sat squished together in the cramped space. One of them would normally be sitting in the seat Sovilla occupied. "I'm sorry. I can sit back there so one of you can come up front."

They shook their heads in unison. "You stay up there," one said.

Leanne introduced them, but the names jumbled in Sovilla's head. She'd be bombarded with names and faces soon. How would she remember them all?

"Some of my older brothers are behind us. My parents are bringing the younger five."

Sovilla hoped Leanne wouldn't tell her all of their names too.

But Leanne glanced over at Sovilla's dress and *kapp*. "Does it feel funny to wear different clothes?" Leanne asked as she flicked the reins to get the horse to move onto the road.

"*Jah.*" Sovilla patted the *kapp*. "This is so light, I keep checking to be sure I put it on."

"I guess after the larger and stiffer ones you're used to wearing, it would be strange. Looks like you got it on right."

"*Danke.* Your instructions helped a lot."

"I'm glad." Leanne urged the horse to move faster. "If you're joining the church, that means you'll be staying with Wilma permanently?"

Sovilla's stomach churned. "I guess so." She needed to write to Mamm to find out the plans, but she dreaded hearing the answer.

"I suppose it's not easy staying with Wilma."

Leanne's sympathetic glance made Sovilla feel bad. Her reluctance to answer made it seem as if she agreed with the comment about her *aenti*. "I'm sure God has me here for a purpose. I miss my *mamm* and sisters, though."

The horse stopped for a red light, and Leanne questioned Sovilla about life in Sugarcreek. Talking about everything she'd left behind caused both pain and pleasure.

When Leanne asked why Sovilla had come to Lancaster, she sidestepped Mamm's concerns about her *onkel* and cousins. "I'm here to help Wilma after her operation."

"I heard she's getting hip replacements," one of the girls in the back seat said. "But that won't take long until she recovers. Will you go back home after that?"

"I don't know." Sovilla wished she did. To change the subject, she waved at the cornfields they passed. "I always love seeing the corn shooting up."

"Me too," Leanne said. She took Sovilla's cue to stop

talking about her life and started pointing out landmarks and crossroads that led to other towns.

Places Sovilla would probably never see. Wilma rarely drove anywhere except the farmers market, the bulk foods store, and the grocery store. Most of the time, she didn't invite Sovilla to accompany her. The only other places Sovilla would visit were the library and the hospital. Going to church on Sundays would be her only chance to see more of the area.

Leanne pulled into a wide driveway. "This is the Fishers' house. Why don't you four get out here, and I'll take the horse out back?"

Sovilla smoothed down her borrowed white church apron and tried to calm her roiling stomach. The buggy of boys halted behind them, and several hopped out. She avoided looking in that direction as she climbed down and pulled the seat forward so Leanne's sisters could squeeze out.

"Hey, Sovilla," one of the boys called.

Her head jerked up. Who here knew her name?

She turned her head in the direction of the greeting. Andrew had jumped from the buggy behind them.

Sovilla stood there stunned. He was Leanne's brother? That meant Isaac was too. Her gaze moved up to the driver of the buggy.

Isaac had been more excited than usual about attending church, and his pulse raced as Sovilla climbed into Leanne's buggy. The pink dress looked as lovely on Sovilla as he'd imagined. And now that she wore familiar clothing, she seemed even more desirable.

After Leanne picked up Sovilla, Isaac could hardly wait

to get to church. He *rutsched* with impatience at every stop sign and light until they finally pulled into the Fishers' driveway. When Sovilla stepped out of the buggy, Isaac stopped breathing. Then their eyes met, and he was lost, drowning in a flood of emotions.

He might have sat there frozen if Zeke hadn't hooted with laughter.

"You planning to sit here all day and stare at her?"

Isaac pulled his gaze away. Leanne had already driven down into the yard, and several buggies had lined up behind him. He flicked the reins to move their horse down the driveway.

Had everyone seen how besotted he'd been?

Isaac's face was still burning after he'd taken care of the buggy and horse. As he and Snickers strode toward the group of men gathered to chat before the service, he greeted everyone by rote. But his mind stayed fixed on a pretty brunette in a rose-colored dress.

After what seemed like hours, although only ten minutes had passed, the men filtered into the house and settled on the benches. When the girls filed in, Leanne must have ushered Sovilla ahead of her. She sat with Mamm and his younger sisters. Isaac took a seat directly across from them. After he'd settled in his seat, Leanne smiled and raised a conspiratorial eyebrow as if to confirm she'd done a good job.

Isaac tried to control his grin, but he had a feeling his attempt wasn't successful. His sister covered her mouth, the way she did when she giggled. He hoped Sovilla didn't realize why his sister was laughing. So far, Sovilla had been so busy staring around and getting situated, she hadn't glanced at the men's side of the room.

A sharp elbow dug into Isaac's side.

"Stop staring," Andrew said loudly enough for everyone around them to hear.

Zeke snorted. "Will you listen to any of the sermons today?" He kept his voice lower than Andrew's. "In case you've forgotten, the preacher stands in the middle, not in the women's section."

Isaac lowered his eyes until the singing began. Although he held a hymnal, he didn't need to read the words in the *Ausbund*. He knew the songs by heart. During the second hymn, Isaac chanced a quick look across the room and couldn't look away.

Mamm had passed two-year-old Rose to Sovilla, who cuddled his baby sister close and bent to whisper something in her ear. Then Sovilla resumed singing. She reminded him of an angel. His little sister stared up at Sovilla with adoration. Isaac worried his expression might be the same, but Sovilla mesmerized him.

Some Sundays, Isaac railed inwardly at the length and draggy pace of *Das Loblied*. Today, they finished much too fast.

All during the sermons, he had to keep tugging his attention back to the message. If only Sovilla didn't look so sweet with Rose asleep in her arms and her cheek resting on his sister's short blond curls.

His brothers, who sat one on each side, frequently poked him. Snickers lay by his feet. Each time, Isaac returned to the sermon, only to find himself drawn back to the lovely picture directly in front of him.

"Are you dreaming of being a preacher?"

Andrew's whispered comment jerked Isaac from a daydream. Sovilla had been holding their daughter, an adorable girl with tiny brunette braids, who resembled her beautiful mother.

"Wh-what?" Isaac said, a bit too loud.

Several people turned to stare. Heat rose from his neck to his hairline. That, plus the warm day and closely packed room, dotted his forehead with beads of sweat.

Andrew's unkind comment focused Isaac's concentration on the sermon. Each time he was tempted to stray, his brother's remark flitted through his mind, reminding Isaac he had no chance with Sovilla.

Sovilla cradled the baby close. It had been so long since her sisters were this small. She missed holding them. An ache started in her chest and grew until she had to swallow back a lump in her throat.

Being separated from her family, wearing unfamiliar clothing, worshipping in a strange home, surrounded by people she didn't know . . . She forced herself to listen to the sermon and sing the well-known hymns, but that only increased her loneliness.

Whenever she could, she stole glances at Isaac. Often, he seemed to be staring at her, but more likely, he was checking on his little sister. She excused her frequent looks in that direction, because seeing a face she recognized in this crowd of strangers comforted her. Yet, for some reason, she never found her attention straying to Andrew.

Usually, Sovilla loved being at church, but relief flooded through her when the service ended. Now she just needed to get through the meal. Still holding Rose, Sovilla followed Leanne to the kitchen.

"Could you carry Rose to the back bedroom upstairs?" Isaac's *mamm* asked. "She can nap up there while we set out the meal."

"Of course." Sovilla searched for the stairs and found her way to the bedroom.

In Sugarcreek, she never stumbled around like this. She knew the layout of everyone's homes. Staying here in Lancaster meant learning all new houses, faces, and names. The whole idea left Sovilla overwhelmed.

For a few minutes after she lowered Rose onto the bed, Sovilla rested a hand on Rose's soft curls. The small girl didn't yet have enough hair for braids or a bob. Sovilla wrapped a tiny ringlet around her finger and watched Rose's chest rise and fall with gentle, rhythmic breaths.

Sovilla preferred to remain upstairs and avoid the meal. Maybe if she stayed here, no one would notice her missing.

Footsteps tapped up the stairs, and Sovilla wished she'd closed the bedroom door. She hoped the person planned to use the bathroom down the hall. Her heart sank when the footfalls neared.

Leanne poked her head into the room. "There you are. We wondered if you'd gotten lost."

Sovilla untangled her finger from Rose's curl. "She's so darling, it's hard to leave her."

"I know. Mamm never expected to have another baby after most of us were grown. My youngest brother is nine. But God sent Rose as a special gift." Leanne gazed fondly at her sleeping sister.

Tears burned behind Sovilla's eyes. She'd been overjoyed when her sisters had been born. When would she ever see them again?

Leanne smoothed down her apron. "We'd better get downstairs to help with the food."

Suppressing a sigh, Sovilla rose and accompanied Leanne

to the kitchen, where meal preparation swirled into a blur of introductions. Isaac's *mamm* stayed close by, mothering Sovilla like a hen protecting a chick.

After the men finished, Leanne beckoned to Sovilla to sit on a nearby bench. Isaac's *mamm* settled beside them.

She slipped an arm around Sovilla's shoulders and gave her a brief hug. "I'm so glad God gave us the privilege of bringing you to church."

Sovilla had believed she was a burden. Her eyes filled with tears to be considered a blessing. And the warmth of the hug made her long to be with Mamm.

Before they bowed their heads for prayer, Isaac's *mamm* patted Sovilla's hand. "*Danke* for taking such good care of Rose. You'll be a *wunderbar* mother someday."

That praise reminded Sovilla of Henry. She'd always thought they'd marry and start a family. Now, as each day passed, that hope grew more distant. Did he care for her? Think of her? Would he ever write? Although she'd sat down several times to a compose a letter, she'd been unable to find the words to ask her questions. Tomorrow, though, she'd do it. She couldn't live with this uncertainty.

When Sovilla lifted her head after the silent prayer, all the women around her peppered her with questions.

"Wilma Mast is your aunt?"

When Sovilla nodded, the woman persisted. "Is she your real aunt?"

As opposed to a fake one? But Sovilla answered politely, "*Jah*, she's real."

"She's Mennonite, isn't she?" someone else butted in. "She doesn't talk like any Mennonites I know. They don't swear or scream at people."

Sovilla often cringed at Wilma's salty language. "She's not Mennonite."

"Well, thank the good Lord for that. She'd give Mennonites a bad reputation."

"Isn't it hard living with her?" another woman asked.

"I'm not used to her *Englisch* ways, if that's what you meant." Although Sovilla had no doubt that had not been what the woman wanted to know, Sovilla refused to disparage Wilma.

"Not exactly," the woman admitted.

Isaac's *mamm* intervened. "Better not to invite gossip."

Sovilla hissed out a quick breath and stuffed a slice of bread and peanut butter spread into her mouth. The stickiness would give her an excuse for not talking for a while.

An older lady at the table behind them tapped Isaac's *mamm* on the shoulder and held out a newspaper article. "I thought your son should read this. It sounds as if this group is getting dangerous."

"Is that about the protestors?" another woman asked. "My brother said they picketed at two kennels in Ephrata."

"*Jah*, the article mentioned that. They also destroyed a kennel in Bird-in-Hand. It says they're rabid. They label all Amish kennels as puppy mills."

"It's a shame they can't tell the difference between well-run kennels and puppy mills," someone else chimed in.

"We'll be careful," Leanne promised. "So far, no one's bothered us. I wish these groups would stop labeling all Amish dog breeders as puppy mills. They should come and see how well-run Isaac's kennel is. He loves and cares for his puppies."

"Instead of picketing and damaging businesses, why don't they report the badly run kennels?" A woman feeding her baby milk bread looked indignant. "They could ask someone to come out to investigate. The government will close the bad ones."

A teenage girl across the table leaned toward Leanne. "Tell Isaac to be careful."

"I will, Ruthie."

"*Gut*, I wouldn't want anything to happen to him."

Sovilla took a bite of her pie. Ruthie seemed awfully concerned. Was she Isaac's girlfriend? A twinge of irritation shot through Sovilla.

Why do I care? Isaac's only a friend. And I have Henry. At least, she hoped she did.

To avoid these bothersome thoughts, she tapped a fork on her plate to get Leanne's attention. "What kind of pie is this?"

Ruthie stared at her, but Leanne answered in a matter-of-fact voice. "It's *schnitz* pie. We make it from dried apples."

In a snooty tone, Ruthie asked, "You've never had *schnitz* pie before?"

Before Sovilla could answer, Leanne explained, "Sovilla's from Ohio. I'm guessing they have different desserts."

"Rhubarb, peach, blueberry, and pecan pies are more popular where I live." *Or lived*. A heavy ache in her chest made her want to cry. She blinked to hold back tears.

"I see." Ruthie made it sound as if those pies weren't acceptable. "We always have *schnitz* pie."

"I can see why. It's delicious." Sovilla tried to be friendly.

"You've probably never tried some of our other specialties," Leanne said. "You'll have to try shoofly pie and Lebanon bologna."

"I wonder if that tastes anything like Trail bologna."

Mentioning it made Sovilla miss home and the delicious baby Swiss cheese and Trail bologna sandwiches Mamm made. She could almost taste them.

"You'll have to find out." Leanne laughed. "Too bad you didn't bring any with you. We could have a bologna-tasting contest."

Isaac's *mamm* smiled at Sovilla. "If you can't tell, my *dochder* loves to eat."

"And cook," Leanne added.

"*Jah*, she's a good cook. You'll have to ask Isaac to bring you to the house for supper one night after the market closes. Leanne can make a shoofly pie."

Picturing Wilma's expression if Isaac ever came to get her, Sovilla almost choked on her last mouthful of pie. Ruthie's horrified expression mirrored Wilma's reaction.

To her credit, Ruthie quickly masked her response and smiled sweetly at Sovilla. "You work at the market too?"

"I help my *aenti*."

Isaac's *mamm* interrupted. "Haven't you girls met? Ruthie, this is our neighbor, Sovilla. We'll be bringing her to church on Sundays."

Ruthie's faint "I see" sounded less than enthusiastic. But she added, "Nice to meet you."

Although Ruthie's response had been tepid, Sovilla infused her greeting with warmth. *Poor Ruthie must see me as competition.* Sovilla didn't know how to reassure Ruthie she had no reason to worry.

"You're from Ohio, then?" Ruthie asked, her tone polite, but disinterested.

"*Jah*, Sugarcreek. I miss it and want to go back to Ohio as soon as my *aenti* is well enough to get around."

Ruthie thawed a little. "I hope she gets better fast." She stood. "I'm going to get some *schnitz* pie."

After she left, Leanne stared at Sovilla. "I thought you were joining the church here."

"I said I want to go back." Wanting was not the same as going.

"I noticed that." Isaac's *mamm* hugged Sovilla again. "That was kind. You sensed Ruthie was getting upset and went out of your way to calm her concerns."

"What do you mean?" Leanne demanded. "Are you going back or not?"

Sovilla traced small circles on the tabletop with her finger. "I don't know. I want to, but I can't go to Sugarcreek unless . . ." She didn't want to confess she hadn't heard from her boyfriend in weeks. "We don't have a house there anymore. Mamm and my sisters moved to my *onkel*'s house in Middlefield."

"I'm sorry." Isaac's mother looked troubled. "I didn't realize . . ."

"I think Mamm intends for me to stay here"—she forced out words around the lump in her throat—"permanently."

"We're glad to have you." Leanne gathered her plate and Sovilla's, then reached for her *mamm*'s. "I hope you'll stay. I'll take these into the kitchen and be right back."

When Leanne had moved far enough away, Isaac's *mamm* lowered her voice so no one at the table could hear. "I expect it's hard having your family so far away. Maybe I'm wrong, but I expect Wilma isn't very soft or motherly. So if you ever need someone to listen, to pray with you, or even give you a hug, I'd be happy to act as a substitute mother."

Sovilla choked up. A perfect stranger offering to take

her *mamm*'s place? No one could ever replace Mamm. But having someone to confide in and depend on—something Sovilla didn't have with Wilma—meant a lot to her.

"*Danke.*" If only she could tell Isaac's *mamm* how much that offer meant to her. But she might burst into tears.

"We're not that far away if you cross the fields behind the houses. You're up on the hill, and we're in the valley below. It's much farther on the roads."

Maybe next Sunday, Sovilla could walk to their house and save them the trouble of turning down the narrow dead-end lane. Right now, she couldn't speak, but she'd suggest it later.

Leanne came back with Rose, who was eating bread with peanut butter spread. She held out her arms to Sovilla. Despite the stickiness around the little girl's mouth, Sovilla took Rose and cuddled her close. Messy hands smeared peanut butter and soggy bread on Sovilla's pink dress.

"We should get going," Leanne said. "Can you go to the singing here tonight, Sovilla?"

She'd love to, but Wilma had objected. "I'm not sure. I'll have to check with my *aenti*."

"We're meeting for a volleyball game at four thirty. I'll stop by to pick you up."

"Your *mamm* said I could walk down the hill to your house. If I can go, I'll get to your place by four." That would prevent Wilma from seeing the boys' buggy behind Leanne's—something else she hoped she could avoid when she reached home this afternoon. Wilma hadn't looked out the window this morning, but this time, they might not be as lucky.

"All right. That sounds like a good plan." Leanne called to her *mamm*, who was chatting with one of the women at another table. “Should we take Rose? She seems to be clinging to Sovilla.”

“That would be nice.” Isaac’s *mamm* smiled at Sovilla.

As they walked to the buggy, Sovilla lowered her voice. “My *aenti* doesn’t want me around boys. Do you think your brothers would mind going home at a different time?”

“They’ll be disappointed.” Leanne hurried over and had a quick conversation with Isaac.

Although Sovilla was positive it wouldn’t matter to the boys, she wished she could see Isaac’s face. He had his back to her, so she had no way to judge his reaction, but his shoulders did seem to slump.

Andrew glanced over his shoulder, and Sovilla pretended she’d been watching a small boy running through the grass. She didn’t want Andrew to know she’d been staring at Isaac. Andrew might call attention to it.

Why did she care so much what Isaac thought?

Chapter Thirteen

Hearing that Sovilla didn't want them to follow her home crushed Isaac. He fought to keep his face neutral, but inside questions bubbled up one after the other. Had he made her uncomfortable by gazing at her in church? Had she realized his feelings for her?

Andrew elbowed him in the ribs. "Aww, look. Isaac's sad."

Isaac frowned at his brother. "C-cut i-itt out."

His twin had always been his ally and best friend, but lately Andrew went out of his way to tease. And not just to tease, but to hurt.

"We could leave now and go home a different way," Zeke suggested.

If they did that, they might pass Sovilla at the intersection.

Isaac walked briskly to the barn to hitch up the team.

Andrew's mocking laughter followed him as he hurried toward the barn. "Wonder why you're in such a hurry?"

Isaac's ears burned. Had Sovilla heard? He'd purposely turned his back to her so he wouldn't be tempted to stare at her, but she'd been close enough to hear.

Andrew's remarks reminded Isaac he needed to talk

to his brother. Andrew had changed, and Isaac wanted to find out why. As his hands automatically hitched up the horse, he rummaged through all his recent memories. Had he done something to bother or hurt his brother? Isaac couldn't think of anything, but maybe Andrew had taken something the wrong way.

Once Isaac had the buggy in the driveway, he positioned it well for a good view of Leanne's. As his brothers headed over, Isaac stole glances at Sovilla as she accompanied his sister.

"Hmm." Andrew threw a pointed glance at Leanne's buggy. "Wonder why you parked here."

"Th-this s-spot was open." Although Isaac spoke the truth, not admitting his main motivation turned his statement into a fib.

"*Jah*, I'm sure that happened to be the only reason."

Isaac's jaw clenched as he waited for Leanne's buggy to pull out. Why couldn't Andrew stop with his jabs?

"What are you waiting for?" His brother laughed. "Too busy watching a certain buggy?"

Blowing out a slow breath and praying for patience, Isaac waited until Leanne started up the driveway. Then he motioned for another buggy to go ahead of him. He didn't want it to be obvious he wanted to follow Sovilla.

When they reached the road, Leanne turned left, but the other buggy turned right. Isaac had expected that buggy to stay between him and Leanne. He hoped Sovilla didn't notice him trailing her. He slowed to allow a large gap between them.

Andrew sighed loudly. "How long is it going to take to get home? We'll be going the long way as it is."

At the crossroads, Leanne went straight ahead, but Isaac turned to take the winding street to the right. He calculated how long it might take Leanne to get to the major intersection. If he timed it right, she'd pass by while he waited at the stop sign.

He clucked to the horse to speed up. He had farther to go than Leanne.

"First you crawl along," Andrew grumbled. "Now you're driving like you're in a race."

Isaac clenched his teeth. *You complained I was driving too slow.* "Y-you s-said g-go fast."

"Well, I didn't mean I want to hit my head on the roof every time we go over a bump."

"M-make up your m-mind," Isaac snapped.

Then he regretted losing his temper. His desire to see Sovilla shouldn't take precedence over his brother's comfort. He slowed the horse.

"Now what?" Andrew muttered. "I do have some things I'd like to do before we have to leave for the singing."

Zeke turned around. "What's with you today, Andrew? It's not like you to be so *mürrisch*."

Timing no longer mattered. Leanne would reach the intersection before them.

When they reached the crossroads, Isaac looked both ways before pulling out. In the distance, Leanne headed toward them. If he waited for a while, she'd drive by and he could wave. And get to see Sovilla.

"You have plenty of room to get across before that buggy gets here." Andrew pointed in the opposite direction than the one Isaac had focused on.

"Andrew," Zeke said in a *big-brother-to-little-brother* tone, "it's not your turn to drive. We don't nag at you when you're in the driver's seat."

"Maybe that's because I don't drive like a maniac."

Zeke shook his head.

The three oldest brothers alternated driving, each taking a day, and the unspoken rule had always been "no criticism." Andrew drove more recklessly and much faster than Zeke and Isaac, yet they'd never bugged him to slow down and be careful.

His brothers' sparring had kept Isaac from moving, and now the buggy coming from the opposite direction had gotten too close. He had to wait for it to pass. By then, Leanne would be headed through the intersection. The timing had worked out perfectly.

As soon as she spotted them, Leanne slowed and waved. Isaac waved back, but he focused his attention on Sovilla. A look of surprise crossed her face, but then she smiled broadly.

Was she looking directly at him? Isaac wanted to think so, but he couldn't be sure.

A car zoomed up behind Leanne. Instead of speeding up, she pulled onto the shoulder to let it pass, giving Isaac more time to admire Sovilla.

Danke. Isaac flashed his sister a quick grin.

She pinched her lips together, but didn't succeed in holding back her smile. She seemed quite pleased with herself. Maybe she'd driven slower than usual so they'd arrive at the same time.

Leanne glanced behind her to check if she could pull out, and Isaac waited until she'd driven past before he crossed the intersection. He couldn't stop his lips from curving upward. The joy of seeing Sovilla filled him with happiness the rest of the afternoon.

* * *

Sovilla was still glowing from the chance encounter with Isaac. His eyes had lit up when he saw her, giving her a little thrill. She told herself her excitement stemmed from having a friend. But deep inside, Sovilla's conscience warned her those feelings signaled something more.

As Leanne pulled in front of Wilma's house, Sovilla wiped away her smile. If she looked like she'd had too much fun, her *aenti* might suspect Sovilla had done something other than attend church.

She thanked Leanne and slid open the door.

As she stepped from the buggy, Leanne asked, "Should we expect you tonight?"

That question sobered Sovilla. "Probably not. If I'm not there by four, go ahead without me. Wilma doesn't want me to socialize with boys." Truth be told, Sovilla had a suspicion her *aenti* would rather Sovilla have no pleasure at all.

Leanne sighed. "I wish you could come. We always have lots of fun."

"I'll try to convince Wilma." But Sovilla held out little hope she'd succeed. At least she had Sunday services to look forward to every other week.

Dreading the cloud of gloom awaiting her in the house made it easy for Sovilla to don a somber expression. Her steps dragged as she approached the porch.

If only she could go home with Leanne and be a part of her large, lively family. Isaac's *mamm* made her feel so warm and welcomed. And Isaac . . .

Sovilla jerked her thoughts away from him. Wilma would sense what Sovilla was thinking if her mouth curved into a secret smile. Then there'd be no chance of getting permission to go to the singing. Not that being serious gave her more hope.

Wilma was still banging around the kitchen. She must be canning even more pickles. Maybe her canning frenzy served to distract her from the fear of the upcoming surgery.

Sovilla debated easing the door shut and sneaking up to her bedroom without speaking to Wilma. But that would be impolite. And the longer she took to greet her *aenti*, the more likely Wilma would assume Sovilla had spent her time doing something wrong.

With a small sigh, she shut the door and headed for the kitchen. All the joy she'd stored up from the service and meal leaked out.

"Hi, Wilma, I'm back."

"It's about time. What were you doing all that time? If you even went to church."

"I went to church. You can check with the bishop if you don't believe me. And he and his wife were getting ready to leave the Fishers' when Leanne pulled out. They can tell you we came straight home."

"Like I could trust the bishop. No Amish man can be trusted. Or woman, for that matter."

Does that include me? Sovilla almost asked the question aloud, but she already knew the answer. She didn't want to hear Wilma confirm it.

"Do you need anything before I go up to change?"

"It would be nice to have some help with the pickles."

Sovilla stared at her. Wilma had refused to teach Sovilla how to make them. How did she expect her to help?

"My hips are killing me." Wilma ran her hands down her sides and winced. "I shouldn't be on my feet like this."

"But I don't know how—"

"Figures you'd refuse to help. You couldn't care less how much pain I'm in."

"I do care. Tell me what to do, and I'll do it." Sovilla

expected Wilma to give her an impatient look and criticize her for trying to find out the recipe.

Wilma groaned. "I can't do this." Her eyes filled with moisture. She dashed the back of her hand over her eyes and pressed her lips together. Then, in an almost-pleading voice, she asked, "You do know how to can pickles, don't you?"

"Of course. We always can our pickles. Do you want me to use Mamm's recipe?"

"Don't be ridiculous. I doubt her recipe is as good as mine."

"*Neh*, it's not," Sovilla admitted. She wished she knew what her aunt added that made her pickles taste so good.

A triumphant smile lit Wilma's features, but then she winced. "My brine's on the stove. Fill the jars and seal them. I'm going up to take a pain pill and a nap."

As Wilma hobbled out of the kitchen, Sovilla mused about her *aenti*'s constant irritation. Could her *aenti*'s short temper be connected with her pain? Until today, Wilma had concealed her pain. Only her limp gave the slightest clue. Maybe once she'd recovered from her operation, she'd be less nasty. Somehow, though, Sovilla doubted it.

Sovilla waited until Wilma's door had slammed shut before tiptoeing upstairs to exchange her white church apron for her black work apron. Her conscience gave her a sharp twinge. She shouldn't be working on Sunday. But she needed to pour Wilma's brine while it was still hot. And shouldn't she help anyone who asked?

As she slipped down the stairs, though, she wondered about Wilma's timing. Her *aenti* had never asked her to help with pickles before. Had she done it on a Sunday on purpose?

Sovilla shook her head. *Neh*, Wilma had been in pain.

It took more than an hour to finish all the jars. Sovilla had promised to be at Leanne's by four if she planned to go to youth group, and the clock hands had almost reached three thirty.

Wilma still hadn't come out of her room, so Sovilla couldn't ask. She went upstairs and stood outside her *aenti*'s door. Loud snoring showed Wilma was asleep. Would it be right to slip out now?

Part of Sovilla wanted to take advantage of her *aenti*'s nap, but her conscience chided her. Wilma would be furious if she woke and Sovilla had left. Images of Isaac overshadowed the voice of reason.

Sovilla hurried downstairs. She carted all the hot pickle jars down the basement steps. They could cool in the cellar as well as on the kitchen tables and counters. That way, Wilma couldn't complain that Sovilla had left her the hard work.

Then she rushed upstairs, checked one last time to be sure her *aenti* was still sleeping, and got ready to leave. She jotted a note and left it in the kitchen. Wilma would go there first to check that Sovilla had done what she'd asked. Then she inched open the back door and slipped outside.

Sovilla stood in the backyard unsure of where to go. She should have asked for better directions. Isaac's *mamm* had said to head down the hill. She could do that, but beyond the small patch of woods below, several farms lay scattered in the valley. Maybe once she got down there, she'd be able to tell.

Now that she'd decided to defy Wilma and go to the singing, she gathered her courage and plunged down the hill. Several times she stumbled and almost turned around. First working, then disobeying, on a Sunday, no less.

Only the thought of seeing Isaac—and Leanne, of

course—kept her going. At the foot of the hill, she walked through a thick grove of trees. Disoriented, she emerged on the left side of the wooded area. Had she gotten off track and wandered around instead of heading straight out?

She tried to look up the hill, but down here the trees blocked her view. She had no idea which direction to head, and even worse, she didn't know her way back home.

Please, Lord, help me.

As soon as she prayed, guilt over ignoring Wilma's wishes rose. This might be her punishment. She'd go to the closest house and ask for directions back to her *aenti*'s house. She trudged that way.

Someone came out of the house and ran toward her. "Sovilla! You came! I hoped you would!"

Leanne! Sovilla forgot her plan to find her way home. Had God directed her here? Maybe she was supposed to go to the singing after all.

Isaac's heart lifted as Leanne called Sovilla's name. The bright pink dress had caught his attention fifteen minutes ago. He stood in the shadow of the kennel's eaves to watch Sovilla's descent. When she didn't emerge from the woods, he almost dashed into the trees to find her. But then she emerged, far from where she'd gone in but much closer to their house.

He could breathe again, but his rapid heartbeat never slowed. The closer she came, the more his heart picked up its pace. And knowing he'd sit across from her all evening made it pound even more.

"We'll be leaving soon," Leanne said, and Sovilla followed her to the barn.

Maybe Isaac should hitch up his team too. Then he'd be near the girls.

Andrew cocked an eyebrow. "You have to go to the barn right now?"

Isaac took a deep breath but decided against answering. "C-come on, Snickers." Isaac headed off after Leanne and Sovilla.

Once Leanne and Isaac had their buggies ready and waiting in the driveway, Andrew headed over to Sovilla.

Isaac tried to tamp down the jealousy flickering inside. If only he could talk as smoothly as his brother. Sovilla would be drawn to Andrew rather than to someone who could barely speak.

"Would you like to ride with us?" Andrew asked her.

Isaac held his breath. Part of him hoped she'd agree, but he worried Andrew wanted to invite her to sit in the back with him, where they'd be crowded together.

Sovilla didn't look at Andrew. Instead, she turned to Leanne. "There won't be enough room with you?"

"Of course there is. I'd love to have you ride with me." She glanced at Isaac and bit her lip. "I mean, you'd probably rather go with my brothers."

Sovilla's eyes widened. "*Neh, neh.* I'll go with you if that's all right."

Leanne shot Isaac a helpless look. He shrugged and turned away so she couldn't read the hurt in his eyes. Sovilla didn't want to go with him.

He tried to tell himself she wanted to follow her *aenti*'s directions about not being around boys, but he'd seen the desperation in her eyes, as if begging Leanne to save her. That cut him deeply.

He wished he could believe she'd been rejecting Andrew, but Sovilla probably assumed Zeke would be polite and sit in the back with Andrew. That would leave Sovilla beside him.

"C-come," Isaac called to Snickers. His puppy jumped into the passenger side.

"I suppose she'll be on my feet the whole ride," Zeke grumped. Then he smiled. "Just kidding. She's such a good dog." He let Andrew into the back, then he climbed in. "You're a good dog, Snickers."

Isaac hadn't asked if they could follow Leanne to the singing. They might be late if he took the back roads, so he stayed behind his sister the whole way to the Fishers'.

When they arrived, Ruthie was sitting at a picnic table in the backyard holding a volleyball. A net stretched across the grass. She jumped up and hurried toward them.

"*Gut!* You're here. You'll be on my team, won't you, Isaac?"

Andrew glowered. "What about me?"

Ruthie blushed. "I planned to ask Leanne too. She's so good at spiking."

"I see." Andrew sounded miffed.

"I'm sorry. I didn't mean to leave you out." She looked down and brushed off her apron. "I, um, don't think it's fair to take all the best players. Maybe you could play opposite me." Her tentative smile begged him to understand.

"*Jah.* I suppose."

"Will you promise not to spike the ball at me?" Ruthie fluttered her eyelashes at him. "You're so strong. I don't want to get hurt."

Andrew brightened. "I'll be careful."

"*Danke.*" She smiled prettily. "I knew I could count on you."

"Of course you can." Andrew's chest puffed up, and he strode to the opposite side of the net.

Ruthie sat on the bench beside Isaac, who was petting Snickers. "Don't tell Andrew," she whispered, "but he's not as good as you. Or Leanne."

Isaac bobbed his head. Even if Ruthie hadn't asked, he had no intention of telling Andrew. "S-stay, S-Snickers." Isaac signaled to the puppy.

Then he rose and headed to the opposite side of the net from Andrew. Ruthie trailed behind him. Andrew glared at him. What was wrong with his brother now?

Ruthie waved Leanne over. "You're on my team," she announced. Then she waved to the opposite side of the net. "You two can be on Andrew's team."

Isaac cringed. Surely Ruthie hadn't meant to sound so unwelcoming. He tried to make up for her tone by giving Sovilla and his younger sister a big smile.

Ruthie's tone had been dismissive, but Sovilla tried not to let her hurt show. Isaac's sixteen-year-old sister, Mary Grace, didn't hide her feelings. She looked like she was about to cry. Isaac's special smile and thumbs-up softened the blow.

Ruthie frowned as she studied him.

On the bright side, if Sovilla played opposite Isaac, she'd be able to observe him.

A girl emerged from the house. "Oh, I didn't know so many people were here already. Sorry."

"It's just our family, Katie. We got here a little early. Oh, and Ruthie's here, and our friend Sovilla. I introduced you to each other this morning after church."

Sovilla had met so many people that their faces had all blurred together. She only recalled meeting Ruthie.

Perhaps because Ruthie had been so unkind. Still, she wanted to be polite. "Nice to see you again, Katie."

"I'm glad you came, Sovilla. It'll be fun getting to know you."

"Katie," Ruthie called, "I've been dividing up the teams."

"I see." Katie glanced from one side to the other and frowned.

Ruthie beckoned her over. "You can be on this side."

"We should make sure the teams are even." Katie headed over to Sovilla's side. She leaned close and whispered, "I hope you know how to play. Leanne and Isaac are the best players. We usually put them on opposite sides."

"I've played back in Ohio, so I hope I can help." Sovilla had been a good player in Sugarcreek, but she had no idea about Isaac and Leanne's skill level. Maybe she wouldn't be close.

"I'll try to make sure the rest of the players are more evenly matched." Katie turned her back to the other team and lowered her voice. "Ruthie's their weakest player, and she jumps back from spikes, so aim them toward her."

"What are you two whispering about?" Andrew strode over to them.

"Plotting how to win," Katie said with a smile. "Sovilla needs some tips." She smiled at Sovilla. "Whatever you do, try not to hit any balls toward Isaac or Leanne."

Andrew frowned. "I can handle anything they send over the net."

Katie's slight eye roll clued Sovilla in that Andrew liked to brag.

Mary Grace spoke, her voice so quiet Sovilla could hardly hear her. "Not always, Andrew." Ignoring his narrowed eyes, she added, "Besides, they'll probably return the ball to the weaker players like me."

As other buggies pulled in and friends exchanged greetings, Sovilla tried not to feel left out. If she'd been back in Sugarcreek, she'd be chatting with everyone and looking to spend time with Henry. She missed her youth group.

Her loneliness increased at the reminder that Henry hadn't written. Tomorrow, she'd make time to write the letter she kept putting off.

Leanne did her best to include Sovilla and Mary Grace in all her conversations. Sovilla appreciated Leanne's kindness, even though she remembered few of the names and faces.

When Mary Grace moved out of hearing distance, Leanne confided, "My sister only started coming recently. She's shy, so I try to stay close. I hope she'll be more talkative once she gets comfortable."

Ruthie interrupted them by clapping. "We should get started."

"Good idea." Katie took over and directed people to different teams. "We'll need some stronger players over here if both Isaac and Leanne are on the same side."

Because they had more players than they needed for each side, Katie asked for volunteers to sit at the picnic table and rotate in as subs. Mary Grace rushed to the bench. Sovilla offered, but Katie took her arm.

"*Neh*, stay here. I want you to play for my team."

"I might not be as good as the rest of you."

"Don't worry about it."

But after several exhausting games, Katie smiled at Sovilla. "You were worried about not being good enough?" She wiped her forehead. "I never expected to lose to Leanne and Isaac by only two points. You really know how to spike."

Sovilla felt a bit guilty, but she'd taken Katie's advice and spiked the ball to Ruthie, who squealed and jumped back. Once Andrew and Sovilla had jumped up for the ball at the same time. Andrew glanced down at Ruthie and hesitated. Sovilla reached in and smashed a spike right in front of Ruthie's feet.

Ruthie leapt away. When Ruthie's eyes filled with tears, Sovilla wished she hadn't been so aggressive. She had no right to be jealous of Ruthie's interest in Isaac.

Chapter Fourteen

Isaac stared at Sovilla in amazement. Her skills matched Leanne's, and she quickly figured out the weakest players and sent the ball sailing to them. Playing across from her had been a pleasure, and when they went inside for the singing, Leanne snagged two seats across from him, and Isaac rejoiced. Now he could watch her the whole evening.

Before Sovilla could sit, Ruthie nudged Sovilla over one space.

"You don't mind if I sit beside Leanne, do you?" Ruthie plopped into that place before Sovilla could respond.

Sovilla appeared startled, but she sat beside Ruthie. Leanne sent Isaac an apologetic look, and Mary Grace slid in beside Sovilla.

Isaac inched his chair over a little and angled his body slightly. That way, when he looked up from the *Ausbund*, he'd see Sovilla rather than Ruthie. Andrew bumped him over a little more so he sat across from Ruthie instead of Isaac. She didn't look pleased.

After the singing, Isaac tried to keep a surreptitious eye on Leanne as she introduced Sovilla to some of the girls who'd come after the volleyball game ended.

"Isaac, I need a ride home."

He nodded and Ruthie beamed. He held up a finger to ask her to wait.

Although he suspected Ruthie wanted to go with him, Isaac hurried over to Leanne. "R-Ruthie asked f-for a r-ride."

With you? Leanne mouthed. When he nodded, she pinched back a grin. "We can take her."

Isaac gave his sister a relieved smile. "*D-danke.*"

"Of course. I'll let her know."

He trailed behind Leanne as she crossed the room to where Andrew stood joking with a bevy of girls. His brother had edged close to Ruthie.

Leanne tapped Ruthie on the shoulder. "Come on, Ruthie. We're almost ready to leave."

A puzzled look crossed Ruthie's face. "I, um, thought I was going with Isaac."

"She can go with us, Leanne," Andrew said. "It doesn't seem like she's quite ready to go yet, are you, Ruthie?"

"*Neh*, I wanted to talk to Katie first."

Isaac cringed. Leave it to Andrew to mess up the plans.

"That's all right," Leanne said. "I don't mind waiting. Isaac's ready to leave now. Zeke's already outside."

Bless you, Leanne. Zeke had only gone out to talk to two of his friends on the porch, but Isaac didn't correct her.

Ruthie shifted from one foot to the other. "I could talk to Katie some other time."

"*Neh, neh,* go ahead." Leanne waved her toward the food table, where Katie was clearing dishes. "Maybe we could both help with the cleanup."

Brilliant. His sister was a genius. Ruthie couldn't refuse to assist Katie.

"T-time to g-go," Isaac said to Andrew and nodded toward the door.

His brother didn't move. "I don't mind waiting for Ruthie."

Ruthie flashed him a grateful smile, and he reddened.

Isaac couldn't believe it. Andrew never blushed. At least, not around girls.

"Don't be silly," Leanne said. "Ruthie wouldn't want to be squashed into the buggy with three boys and Snickers. I have more room." The challenging look she shot Ruthie dared her to disagree.

Isaac owed his sister a huge *danke*.

"Let's go help Katie." Leanne steered Ruthie toward the other side of the room.

Isaac rushed for the door. He needed to get out of here now while Leanne had Ruthie distracted. Andrew said goodbyes to all the girls gathered around him and stomped after Isaac.

"What's the hurry?" he griped. "It's not like we have to rush home for anything. We could have waited for Ruthie."

Isaac stopped so suddenly, Andrew almost plowed into him. "You w-want to t-take Ruthie?"

"*Jah. Neh.*" He looked uncertain. "I was only being polite."

Hmm. Andrew had never seemed too worried about any girl's feelings or well-being. He loved being the center of attention. Until now, he'd never shown a special interest in anyone. Had Ruthie caught his eye? Or was he intrigued because she didn't pay as much attention to him as she did to Isaac?

If only Sovilla didn't have a boyfriend, Isaac could discourage Ruthie. Perhaps if she turned her attention to

Andrew, he'd start seeing her as one of the admiring crowd. That might be the fastest way to make him lose interest.

"You don't mind waiting, do you, Sovilla?" Leanne asked quietly behind Ruthie's back.

"Not at all." Sovilla would be happy to do anything to keep Isaac out of Ruthie's clutches. "I can help too."

Mary Grace joined them. With all five of them working, they had the table and kitchen cleaned in no time.

Sovilla, Leanne, and Mary Grace hung back to give Katie and Ruthie private time in the kitchen, but the other two girls talked about the food, the upcoming baseball game the youth group had planned, and the restaurant where Ruthie worked.

When they finished, Leanne looked at Ruthie. "Did you need some time alone to talk to Katie? We can wait for you in the buggy."

Katie tilted her head, her eyes filled with surprise. "You need to talk to me?"

"*Neh,* it's all right." Pink spots appeared on Ruthie's cheeks. "I didn't have a chance to talk to you much today. I'm glad we chatted now."

Her awkward excuse made it clear she'd been angling to ride with Isaac. Leanne turned away to hide her smile, but Sovilla caught it.

When they got in the buggy, Sovilla climbed into the back with Mary Grace. Ruthie glanced around as if to see whether Isaac had left yet. Then she got into the passenger seat, a glum expression on her face.

Leanne attempted to start a conversation several times before Ruthie responded. Although Leanne tried to include everyone, Sovilla didn't remember most of the people they mentioned. She soon subsided into silence.

With each mile closer to home they got, the more Sovilla's dread increased. She'd managed to put Wilma out of her mind and enjoy youth group. But she'd pay for her disobedience. Nausea rose in her. What would her *aenti* do?

After they pulled over at Ruthie's house, Leanne invited Sovilla to sit in the front seat. "I hope you enjoyed the singing."

"I did. Everyone's so nice."

"Even Ruthie?"

When Sovilla didn't respond, Leanne laughed. "You don't have to answer that."

"Sorry I haven't been talking much. I'm anxious about going home."

"You think Wilma will be upset?"

"*Jah.* She'll be furious. I slipped out while she napped. I didn't ask her permission. I left a note."

Leanne sucked in a breath. "*Ach*, Sovilla. Can we do anything to help?"

Sovilla had only one answer. "Pray."

As soon as he arrived home after the singing, Isaac headed out to the kennel with Snickers. He checked all his pups, made sure they had fresh water, and then pulled out his Bible.

Sitting across from Sovilla tonight made him determined to conquer his stuttering. Actually, Ruthie had also encouraged him. He needed to be able to say *neh* forcefully or to suggest she ride with someone else.

Isaac removed the gravel from the container and shoved it into his mouth. He almost gagged. But he had to do this.

Sometimes he could only manage a few verses, but tonight he read a complete chapter. He'd started on the next chapter when, behind him, the door creaked.

Not Andrew again. Isaac spit the gravel into his hand and slid it into his pocket.

"What are you doing?" Leanne asked.

Still holding the Bible, he turned to face her.

She stared at the book in his hands. "You're reading the Bible out here?" Leanne sounded curious but not judgmental.

Isaac could trust her with his secrets. Trying to explain Demosthenes would be a challenge. He motioned for her to follow him to the closet, where he took out the library article and pointed to the underlined parts.

His sister bent her head to read. Her puzzled frown changed to a look of delight. "Oh, Isaac, you're doing this?"

He nodded and pulled the damp gravel from his pocket.

"I'm so proud of you. I hope this works."

"Me t-too."

"I'll let you get back to practicing, but first I wanted to talk about Sovilla."

Isaac worried his face might reveal his eagerness. He struggled to act casual, but Leanne would never tease him. She'd saved him from taking Ruthie home.

He grimaced. "*D-danke.*"

Once again, his sister read his mind. "You mean about Ruthie? No problem. I couldn't believe she asked you for a ride home."

Neither could Isaac. A smile tugged at his lips at the way Leanne had outfoxed Ruthie.

She guessed what he was thinking and burst into laughter. He joined her.

Then he sobered. "And-drew?"

"I wondered about that." Leanne raised an eyebrow. "Do you think he likes her?"

Isaac nodded. He was pretty sure Andrew did. He'd tried to work out a way for Ruthie to ride home with them. And he seemed annoyed at Isaac.

"Do you think he really cares about her? Or does it bother him that she doesn't pay attention to him?"

The same thing had occurred to Isaac. His brother's recent barbs might be a sign of his interest. "An-d-drew's mad at me."

"Then maybe he'd like to date her." Leanne tapped her lip. "We need to find a way to get her interested in Andrew instead of you."

Isaac mimed wiping his forehead. That would be a major relief.

Leanne laughed. "You could get rid of her by asking Sovilla to ride home after a singing."

"Sh-she has a b-boyfriend."

"*Ach*, Isaac. I'm so sorry."

He'd rather not think of that. Leanne had come to tell him something about Sovilla. He needed to get her back on track. "S-Sovilla?"

For a moment, Leanne's brows pinched together. She hadn't figured out his message. Before he could form another painful sentence, his sister's face cleared.

"That's what I came in to tell you."

Is something wrong? She's not ill or—

A worried look crossed Leanne's face. "Wilma was napping when Sovilla slipped out for the singing. Sovilla hadn't asked for permission."

Ach! Knowing Wilma, she'd be livid. How much trouble would Sovilla be in? Isaac wished he could protect her.

"Sovilla asked if we could pray for her."

Of course. Isaac bobbed his head up and down.

"I figured you'd want to know. I'll be praying too."

"*D-Danke.*"

After Leanne closed the door behind her, Isaac sank to his knees on the cold cement floor. Snickers whined.

"It's all r-right, g-girl." Isaac rubbed the puppy's head to reassure her.

Tucking the handful of gravel into his mouth, Isaac poured out his heart. If anyone came through the door and heard him, they'd never understand his garbled words. But God could.

Swallowing hard, Sovilla dragged her feet as she headed for the door. Maybe she could slip in without Wilma noticing.

She eased the doorknob and pushed. The door didn't open. Had Wilma locked her out?

Sovilla stumbled around to the back door. She'd left that open.

That knob didn't turn. No doubt about it. Her *aenti* had locked her out.

What should she do now? Knock and disturb Wilma? Sleep on the porch? Go down the hill and ask to stay with the Lantzes?

Isaac's *mamm* had issued an invitation, but what would she think if Sovilla showed up on the doorstep at this time of night?

From the back porch, Sovilla could see their house in the valley below. Dark windows stared back at her from every room. The only light burning on their property came from a long, narrow building with rows of fencing surrounding it.

Isaac's kennels.

Suddenly, the back porch light flicked on, and Wilma's leering face appeared in the glass.

Sovilla gulped in air and leapt back. She flailed her arms as she teetered on the edge of the porch steps. Catching her balance, she inched forward until she could plant her feet firmly on the wooden boards. But her heart battered her ribs.

Please help me, Lord.

The door lock clicked open. "Hoping to sneak in? The way you sneaked out?"

"*N-neh.*" That wasn't entirely true. Sovilla had been hoping to avoid Wilma.

How could she expect God's assistance if she didn't tell the truth?

She hung her head. "Actually, I was."

Wilma looked taken aback. "Well, at least you're honest about that. Even if you're dishonest about other things. You knew I didn't want you to go, yet you waited until my back was turned to defy me."

"I'm sorry. I went upstairs to ask you, but you were asleep."

"You're trying to blame your defiance on *me*?"

Sovilla shook her head. "*Neh.* It's not your fault. I shouldn't have left without getting permission. I did it anyway."

"You admit you did wrong?" Wilma sounded incredulous.

What else could she do?

By telling the truth, Sovilla seemed to have drained

some of Wilma's firepower. Her *aenti* must have prepared for a shouting match. She appeared almost disappointed.

Wilma winced. "I can't be on my feet this long. I'm going to bed. We'll finish this tomorrow."

Thank you, Lord! Maybe by tomorrow Wilma would have simmered down enough to let the whole incident blow over.

Isaac prayed long into the night. He asked the Lord to heal Wilma's soul and for her to be kind to Sovilla. He also unburdened his own soul, begging for God to show him the path for his life. If falling for Sovilla was wrong, he pleaded to have his desires taken away. He wanted to do the Lord's will, no matter how difficult and painful.

When he finally fell into bed, worn out and uncertain of his future, he drifted off into lovely dreams of being with Sovilla, and he didn't awaken until Andrew poked him.

Isaac groaned. He didn't want to get up. He never wanted to let go of Sovilla's soft hand.

"What's the matter with you?" Andrew nudged him again. "You're usually the first one up. Don't you need to take care of the puppies?"

Puppies? Isaac's eyes flew open. As much as he desired staying in dreamland with Sovilla, he had animals to tend.

As he dressed, Isaac's mind wandered to Sovilla. How had last night gone for her? He hoped his prayers had helped.

His sore knees reminded him throughout the day to lift her to the Lord. If only the market were open today, he could check on her. All the hours until tomorrow seemed so far away.

In the afternoon, when he and his siblings took a break for a quick baseball game between chores, Leanne sidled up next to him. She whispered so that only he could hear, "I wonder what happened to Sovilla last night. I'd love to go up and ask, but I don't want her to get in any more trouble."

"*J-jah.*" The same thought had crossed Isaac's mind too.

"What are you two whispering about?" Andrew leaned close as if hoping to hear.

"N-nothing."

Andrew glared at Isaac. "That's a lie."

"He meant it was nothing that concerned you. Why don't you mind your business?"

"You are my business." From Andrew's gloating grin, he thought he'd gotten the best of Leanne.

"Really? You think it's your duty to take care of me?" Leanne acted innocent. Isaac could tell she had a zinger planned.

"Of course. All of us older ones have to take care of you little ones."

"Good." Leanne smiled sweetly. "My back's been hurting. I'm sure you won't mind mucking out the stables for me this week."

"Whoa." Andrew held up a hand. "I didn't say that."

"Yes, you did. You promised to care for me. Didn't he, Isaac?"

Isaac nodded.

"That's not—"

"Are you breaking a promise? You know what the Bible says about that."

Turning to hide his smile, Isaac headed for the kennels. Once again, Leanne had saved him. He needed to find a way to thank her. Knowing Andrew, he'd find a way out of the chore, so it looked like Isaac would be mucking out the stables for the rest of the week.

Chapter Fifteen

When Sovilla went downstairs for breakfast on Monday morning, she passed Wilma's door. Her *aenti* was groaning. Sovilla debated knocking on the door, then decided against it. Wilma didn't appreciate intrusions, but Sovilla could use breakfast as an excuse to check on her *aenti*.

She prepared Wilma's favorite meal—scrapple and scrambled eggs with ketchup. After Sovilla loaded a tray with the plate, silverware, orange juice, and milk, she headed upstairs and knocked on her *aenti*'s door.

"What?" Wilma barked.

"I brought you breakfast."

"Come in." Wilma sounded grudging.

When Sovilla entered, Wilma, her face tight and drawn, wriggled into a sitting position. She truly was hurting. Sovilla carried the tray to the bed and set it on her *aenti*'s lap.

Wilma stared down at the tray, her eyes damp. Was it from the pain and exertion of sitting or because she was touched by Sovilla bringing her breakfast in bed?

Wilma picked up the fork. "You forgot a napkin."

"I'll go get one." Sovilla started for the door.

"Never mind. I don't need it."

Sovilla cleaned the downstairs and then went upstairs to collect her *aenti*'s dishes. Wilma had gotten out of bed and was sitting in a chair staring out the window, sadness etched into every feature.

She didn't thank Sovilla for the meal, but Sovilla hadn't been expecting that, so she wasn't disappointed.

As she walked out of the room, Wilma said, "Fawning over me won't make me forget your disobedience."

That hadn't entered Sovilla's mind, so it stung.

After Sovilla washed and dried the dishes, she went into her room to write a letter to Henry. She agonized over each word, writing and rewriting, crossing out sentences. Once she'd decided on the final phrasing, she took out a fresh sheet of paper and recopied it. She read through it again, deleted a paragraph, and jotted a replacement. Now she'd need to recopy it again.

Was she ready to send this? What if Henry dashed her hopes?

Before she could rewrite it, Wilma screamed up the stairs.

"I need help."

Her *aenti*'s bellow sounded as if she were in pain. Had she fallen? Or burned herself?

Sovilla dropped the letter and dashed downstairs. When she reached the kitchen, Wilma was standing at the stove stirring another huge vat of brine. Jars filled with bread and butter pickles covered every surface.

"Are you all right?"

"Of course not. My joints ache." Wilma nodded toward the jars. "You finished the canning yesterday. I need you to do it again. I'm going upstairs."

Another rest? In the short while Sovilla had been living

here, she'd never seen Wilma give up so easily. Her *aenti* had bullied her way through her aches, grimacing and grousing. She'd never pampered herself. If anything, the more she hurt, the harder she worked.

Had she discovered letting someone else help her made life easier? Or had her hips grown worse? She'd been working nonstop for the past two weeks.

Sovilla didn't mind finishing the canning, but she'd hoped to get the letter out to Henry today. She wouldn't finish the canning before the mail arrived. Now that she'd finally written to Henry, she wanted to send the message on its way before she changed her mind. Maybe if she hurried, she could finish the pickles and complete the letter.

As she filled the last batch of pickle jars, the mail dropped through the slot in the front door. She'd almost made it.

She sighed. One day would not make a difference.

As she headed for the stairway, she passed the mail scattered on the floor by the front door. She bent and gathered the circulars and junk mail. An envelope peeked out from under the pile. Sovilla set the rest of the mail on the hall table for Wilma, then rushed upstairs, clutching the envelope to her chest. A letter from Mamm!

Sovilla shut herself in the bedroom to read it. She savored each word of the first few newsy paragraphs about Mamm and her sisters. Then the letter took a darker turn. Mamm never complained, but she recounted a few hardships in an offhand way.

Sovilla read between the lines. Lloyd constantly scolded her sisters, and his sons tormented them. He kept a close watch on all of them and had forbidden Mamm to walk to the quilt shop. She could only go if he accompanied her.

Melinda had started coming to the house in secret to collect Mamm's mail and to drop off materials for quillows, the cute quilts that tucked into pillows Mamm had made for the Sugarcreek quilt store. She made them for babies, and she could slip that work in between the larger quilts that Lloyd collected the money for. Melinda secretly paid Mamm in cash.

It sounded like Melinda had become an ally. Sovilla was grateful for the woman's kindness to Mamm.

Sovilla returned to the letter:

I wish we could move back to Sugarcreek. I could make enough for a small apartment if I went back to the quilt shop there. And Melinda said if I moved away, she'd send someone to pick up my quilts and quillows once a month. So I'd have that work too. I'd like to have all my girls together again.

After Sovilla took over the stand, any pickle money would go to Wilma. But she could keep the money she made for her baked goods, at least until Wilma healed enough to go back to the market. Once Sovilla started earning a profit, she'd send it all to Melinda.

Mamm didn't say it, but Sovilla sensed Mamm also wanted her freedom. Lloyd had always been controlling. He seemed to have gotten worse over the years. Sovilla had to help them start a new life.

She dreaded reading the last paragraph of Mamm's letter. What she'd heard so far had made her heart ache for Mamm and her sisters. She wasn't ready for more sad news, but she traced her fingers under the words, wishing she could hear Mamm speaking them.

I received a letter from Betty Zook. She caught me up on all the news in Sugarcreek. Maybe you already know, but Henry's dating Nancy Hershberger. I'm so sorry. I wish I didn't have to write such sad news. If only I could be there with you to comfort you. I pray for you many times a day, my darling dochder. *I hope Wilma is as kind and loving to you as she was to me when we were growing up. I cried so hard when she ran away, and I've missed her every day since.*

Sovilla sat at the desk, stunned and unable to take in the news. Henry and Nancy? It didn't seem possible.

Tears stung Sovilla's eyes. She tried to block out the picture of Henry taking Nancy for picnics, strolling down the lane, riding home from singings. Each memory she'd shared with him drove another knifepoint into her heart.

At least she hadn't sent her letter to Henry. She picked up the pages and ripped them to shreds.

Not until she fell into bed that night did Mamm's last two sentences pop into Sovilla's mind. Wilma, kind and loving?

Sovilla had never seen her *aenti* act that way. Why had she run away from the family?

Mamm had cautioned Sovilla not to ask Wilma about the past, but Sovilla wanted to discover the reason her *aenti* had changed so much.

Andrew's poke in the ribs jolted Isaac awake on Tuesday morning. Two days in a row, Isaac had to struggle to rouse himself from dreams of Sovilla. He'd better not make this a habit.

Reluctantly, he rolled out of bed, dressed, and hurried out to help with chores and then take care of the pups. Most days, he spent time playing with them, but today he wanted to get to the market to check on Sovilla. He hoped his prayers had helped.

"L-let's g-go," he said to his brothers as soon as they'd herded the lambs onto the truck.

Andrew smirked. "You were the one who couldn't get out of bed this morning. Now you want us to hurry. I wonder why."

Isaac pointed to Daed, who'd climbed into the livestock transport truck beside Myron Groff, their Mennonite neighbor who drove their animals to the auction on market days.

"I'm sure you're not worried about getting there to unload." Andrew's laugh held a touch of spite. "Is your eagerness because of a certain Sovilla?" He dragged out Sovilla's name and batted his eyelashes.

Zeke burst out laughing. "You look ridiculous, Andrew."

"Not any worse than my lovesick brother."

Isaac ignored them and hurried to the passenger side of the buggy with Snickers. Andrew cut in front of him, opened the door, and moved the seat forward. Instead of getting in, he waited for Isaac.

Today was Zeke's turn to drive, and Andrew should sit in the back.

"B-back seat?" Isaac sent Andrew a questioning glance.

"So nice of you to offer." Andrew waved to the back seat with a flourish.

Because Isaac didn't want to waste time, he signaled for Snickers to get in. No point in arguing.

Zeke untied the reins and climbed into the driver's seat.

As the horse trotted down the driveway, he asked Andrew, "Why are you teasing Isaac this morning?"

"Didn't you see him at the singing?" Andrew put on an exaggerated dreamy-eyed expression.

At least, Isaac hoped it was exaggerated.

"He couldn't keep his eyes off Sovilla." Andrew accompanied her name with a breathless sigh.

"Sounds to me," Zeke said wryly, "like you're jealous."

"Me? Jealous of Isaac? I have plenty of girls interested in me."

"But none of that counts if the girl you want to date likes someone else."

So, Zeke had noticed Andrew's ploys to get Ruthie's attention.

"I haven't picked anyone special yet." Andrew acted indifferent. "I have too many choices."

"Really?" Zeke shot Andrew an *I-don't-believe-you* smile, and Andrew lapsed into sullen silence.

They reached the auction parking lot an hour before the market opened. It'd be a long wait until Sovilla arrived.

Once they'd unloaded the lambs, Daed turned to Isaac. "Could you ride back with Myron to pick up the chickens? I can't do it, because I have to pay Gideon this month's rent, and he just pulled in." Dad motioned to a buggy near the market entrance.

Why not Zeke or Andrew? What if Sovilla arrived while he was gone? Then he'd have to wait until they had a break to see her.

Isaac formed the questions in his mind, but before he could stutter them out, Daed had already started jogging across the parking lot. He obviously hadn't expected Isaac to protest.

Resigned about not seeing Sovilla until later that morning, Isaac rushed over to Myron's truck. Maybe if he hurried, they'd make it back in time.

"You're eager this morning," Myron teased as Isaac patted the seat to get Snickers to jump into the truck before he hopped in after his puppy.

Isaac smiled and nodded, hoping it'd persuade Myron to increase his usual poky pace.

After they arrived at the house, the girls came out to help load the crates, and when Leanne noticed Isaac's impatience, she mouthed, *You want to get back to see Sovilla?*

His lips curved into a huge answering smile.

"Come on," Leanne encouraged her sisters. "Let's see who can put in the most crates."

Isaac and Leanne won the race, but with everyone competing, they'd loaded the truck in record time.

"*D-danke.*" Isaac sent Leanne a grateful glance before he rounded the truck.

"Wow, that was fast. I'm impressed." Myron shifted the truck into gear.

Please hurry, Isaac begged silently as the old man meandered along the back roads.

When they reached the market, Isaac leaned forward, scanning the parking lot for Wilma's big, old-fashioned Oldsmobile.

Myron chuckled. "You looking for someone? No wonder you've been in such a rush today." He studied Isaac. "A girl, I bet."

Isaac forced himself to relax back against the seat. But as Myron turned toward the auction building, Isaac glimpsed a light green car with white tail fins. Without thinking, he twisted in his seat to follow its progress into the parking lot.

"You like antique cars?" Myron asked. "I'm sure you aren't that eager to see Wilma Mast."

Isaac mumbled a *neh*. He'd given himself away.

"I did hear a rumor that Wilma has a niece visiting from Ohio. We were all surprised to find out the girl's Amish."

If Myron expected Isaac to admit anything, he was sorely mistaken. No way would Isaac reveal his interest in Sovilla. Except . . . he already had.

Chapter Sixteen

Right before they reached the market, Wilma's loud sniff roused Sovilla from her unhappiness.

Since she'd awoken that morning, pictures of Nancy and Henry—smiling at each other, walking together, attending singings—flooded her mind. Sovilla had kept hope alive that Henry would propose and she'd return to Sugarcreek. An impossible dream.

"What are you moping about?" Wilma demanded. "You haven't said a word the whole trip."

"I, um, had some bad news in a letter from home." The last thing she wanted to do was reveal that Henry had a new girlfriend. Wilma would gloat that she'd been right: men couldn't be trusted.

Her *aenti*'s eyes widened. "Is your *mamm* all right?"

Wilma's concerned face startled Sovilla. Would she care if something happened to Mamm?

"*Neh*, the news was about someone in Sugarcreek."

"You're more worried about that than you are about me? I might be dead in two days."

"I hope not." Sovilla dreaded Wilma's operation on

Thursday too, but although hip replacements might be painful, they most likely would not be fatal.

"A lot you'd care. You'll probably rejoice. After all, you'll be an heiress."

"There are more important things than money." They'd already been over this. What would it take to get her *aenti* to see the truth? "I've already told you, I'd rather you lived than to have all the money in the world."

"*Humph.* I doubt that."

Before Sovilla could answer, Wilma turned into the parking lot. Nearby, an old truck rumbled toward the auction. The passenger craned his neck to stare right at Sovilla. *Isaac!*

She turned her attention away and prayed her *aenti* didn't notice. Sovilla hoped Isaac wouldn't come to the stand today. With only two days until Wilma's operation, Sovilla didn't want to stir doubts and worries in her *aenti*'s mind.

Wilma parked close to the building instead of finding a distant and secluded space to keep the car safe. Another clue her hips hurt. Sovilla had loaded the car this morning, and her *aenti* hadn't helped at all.

"I can carry in the pickles while you set up," Sovilla offered.

To her amazement, Wilma agreed. She unlocked the trunk, and Sovilla carried in the first box. When she returned for the next one, Isaac was standing by the car with Snickers seated by his feet.

"A-are you all r-right?"

"How did you know?" She hadn't told anyone about Henry, not even her *aenti*.

"L-Leanne."

Sovilla's brain had been whirling since yesterday's letter,

and Isaac's words made no sense. She'd seen Leanne Sunday, not yesterday. *Oh, right. Sunday night. Did Leanne tell him about my fears?*

Isaac appeared upset, like he'd trespassed into something private.

"I'm sorry. So much has happened the past few days." Actually, it had only been one day and a few hours this morning. "Did Leanne say I was worried about Wilma being angry because I'd sneaked out for the singing?"

He nodded. "I p-prayed."

"*Danke.* It must have helped. Her anger didn't last long. She seems to be more focused on her surgery this Thursday."

"S-sorry."

"I'm sorry for her too. She's scared she's going to die. I keep trying to reassure her, but it hasn't worked."

The sympathy in Isaac's eyes told her he cared. "I'll p-pray."

Sovilla smiled to let him know how much she appreciated that. "*Danke.* She'll need a lot of prayer." Wilma might not believe prayer worked, but Sovilla depended on God's help and trusted His power.

Sovilla waved toward the auction building. "I think your brother's looking for you." Andrew headed in their direction.

With a goodbye nod and one last reluctant glance at her, Isaac took off across the parking lot, with Snickers trotting beside him.

"Isaac," she called after him, "please don't come to the stand today."

He halted and turned around, his eyes filled with hurt.

She hadn't meant she didn't want him to visit. Although she wanted to tell him that, she'd rather not give him the wrong idea. Sovilla tried to soften the blow. "I don't want to upset Wilma."

He nodded to let her know he understood, but the sadness in his expression didn't change.

The last thing Sovilla wanted to do was to be unkind. She'd just experienced a painful rejection herself. She didn't want to snub Isaac.

With Andrew so close, she couldn't risk telling Isaac she liked his visits. She'd seen his brother tease him.

Before she could say any more, Isaac and Snickers sprinted toward Andrew, leaving Sovilla staring after him, wishing she could talk to him. Being around Isaac always calmed her. And she desperately needed that peace.

Andrew planted his hands on his hips as Isaac ran toward him. "Do you plan on doing any work today?"

Isaac wished he could snap at his brother. *I've done the same amount as you. I even helped load and unload the chickens.* He'd also checked the schedule to see when their livestock would be auctioned. He had twenty minutes.

It didn't matter, though. He'd been hoping to help Sovilla unload and talk to her a bit more, but she'd dismissed him and told him not to come to the stand. No pretzels for him today.

Andrew studied him. "What's the matter with you? Did I hear her tell you to stay away from her?"

"*Neh.*" Isaac regretted the denial as soon as it passed his lips. No amount of justifying it to himself—she'd said to stay away from the stand, not her—didn't change the fact that he'd lied.

Staying away from the stand meant staying away from

her, didn't it? Had she meant it'd be all right after today? Or had she hoped he'd take the hint and not return at all?

The questions tumbled around in his mind most of the day. Had she brushed him off or only warned him away because of Wilma?

Although Sovilla received a scolding for taking so long to bring in the second carton, Wilma didn't question her. Sovilla hoped Isaac listened and didn't come for a pretzel. She'd like to keep everything peaceful for Wilma before her operation.

Her eyes focused on the distance, Wilma lumbered through the morning. Several times, she sat on the stool behind the counter and ignored the customers. She didn't even have the energy to make sharp, critical remarks. Twice she gave customers the wrong change.

The first time Sovilla pointed it out to her *aenti* and then cringed, expecting an explosion. But Wilma only recounted the money and handed over the correct amount.

The second time, a sweet Mennonite lady returned the extra five dollars Wilma had given her. Instead of making excuses, Wilma stared at the bill blankly. Then she nodded and put it in the cash register.

Sovilla had little time to worry over her *aenti*'s uncharacteristic behavior, because business stayed brisk until almost lunchtime. Sometimes, they experienced a brief lull as shoppers flocked to the food counters to eat. To Sovilla's relief, business slowed, and Wilma sank onto the stool.

Sovilla was filling the empty spots on the shelves with more jars of pickles when an elderly woman hobbled up to the counter. She leaned on her cane and appeared shaky. Wilma didn't seem to notice her, so Sovilla rushed over.

"Good morning, Wilma," the woman said, and when she received no answer, she turned to Sovilla with a smile, "You must be her niece Sovilla. I'm Liesl Vandenberg."

"Nice to meet you." Sovilla had heard that last name mentioned before, but she couldn't place it.

"I understand you'll be going into the hospital on Thursday, Wilma. With Sovilla being Amish, I thought you might need a driver. I'm sure you won't want to bump along in a buggy."

When her *aenti* didn't look up or answer, Sovilla responded. "I don't have a buggy, so thank you for your offer."

Liesl Vandenberg didn't look like any of the drivers in Sugarcreek. Everything about her screamed wealth. And, not to be unkind, but the woman appeared ancient. Was she even capable of driving?

"No buggy? My goodness. How do you plan to get to work?"

Sovilla hadn't even thought about that. Her mind had been too filled with being in a strange place, adjusting to her temperamental *aenti*, missing her family, and fretting over Henry. Thinking of him brought a fresh wave of sorrow.

Pushing aside those feelings before they swamped her, Sovilla admitted, "I don't know."

"Well, we'll have to remedy that." A secretive smile crossed her face. "And I have the perfect solution. I'll make the arrangements."

What? A stranger just waltzed up and started to tell them what to do with their lives? Sovilla waited for her *aenti* to blast the woman, but Wilma stayed silent.

"You'll also need rides to the hospital, Sovilla. That's quite a distance from the house. A car would be more comfortable for that. I'll take care of it."

Sovilla stood there dumbfounded. Drivers in Sugarcreek

waited for you to call them. They didn't come around and insist they'd be taking you somewhere. Is this how it worked in Lancaster?

Liesl Vandenberg didn't give Sovilla time to explain that she couldn't afford to pay a driver. Instead, she plunged ahead. "I understand you plan to sell baked goods here while Wilma's recovering. What did you plan to sell?"

With a quick glance at her *aenti*, Sovilla said, "Pies, donuts, granola." She hesitated. Should she mention her other product idea? This woman looked like the type to pamper a dog. Maybe she'd be a customer. "Also, organic dog biscuits and pet foods."

Mrs. Vandenberg's face lit up. "What a brilliant idea. I'm so glad you won't be competing with Fern. I worried about that."

"I don't want to do that. I like Fern."

Once again, Wilma didn't contradict Sovilla to insist she make the same baked goods as Fern or tell her making organic dog biscuits was crazy. What had happened to her *aenti*? Was she even listening to this conversation?

Sovilla glanced over. Wilma was slumped on the stool, head in hands. Mrs. Vandenberg turned her attention in that direction while Sovilla waited on the occasional customers. But she couldn't help listening to the nearby conversation.

"Wilma," Mrs. Vandenberg said in a crisp, no-nonsense voice, "stop feeling sorry for yourself. You're not the first person to have hip replacement surgery. I had this hip replaced ten years ago when I was in my eighties." Teetering on her cane, she patted her other side.

Sucking in a breath, Sovilla started to make a dash toward Mrs. Vandenberg to catch her before she fell. But the elderly woman grasped the counter to steady herself.

"I broke my other hip recently. I'm not going to lie—both operations were painful. But you'll survive."

"You don't know that." Wilma glared, but her expression didn't hold its normal venom.

"I do know that few patients die, and you're much younger and healthier than I was either time."

"That doesn't mean I won't—"

"Are you ready to meet your Maker?" Mrs. Vandenberg's voice vibrated with sympathy. "People who are right with God can be at peace whatever the outcome."

"I don't believe in that stuff."

Mrs. Vandenberg trained a piercing gaze on Wilma. "Don't you?"

Wilma didn't answer. She stared down at the floor and twisted her gnarled hands in her lap.

"I suspect you once believed it." Mrs. Vandenberg spoke with confidence

"Maybe I did, but things change." Wilma glared at Mrs. Vandenberg. "You don't understand. Nobody does."

"Why don't you tell us?" Her tone came across as a warm, caring invitation.

"I—I can't." Wilma covered her face with her hands.

"Sometimes keeping old pain bottled up inside makes us hit out at others. But those people aren't responsible. You've hidden a great sorrow under all that anger."

Sovilla marveled at Mrs. Vandenberg's insight. Sovilla, too, had often sensed that softer, wounded part of her *aenti*.

Wilma moaned and shook her head, shielding her face with her hands.

"When you're ready to let it go, trust it to God. He'll forgive anything. And He's the only one who can heal old hurts."

Sovilla braced for her *aenti*'s bitter answer, her usual response to any mention of God. Yet it never came.

"What time do you need to be at the hospital on Thursday?" Mrs. Vandenberg asked.

When Wilma kept her head bowed, Sovilla answered, "Eight o'clock."

"The car will be out in front of your house by seven fifteen. That'll give you time to get to the hospital, find your way around, and do the paperwork."

"*D-danke.*"

"Happy to help." She started to shuffle away, but then she turned. "Although I like the idea of selling pet food, I am concerned about it being sold with human food. I'd suggest using this side of the counter for pies and donuts. This shorter leg of the counter around the corner would be best for pet treats. That way, people won't get mixed up."

Sovilla hadn't planned to intermingle her dog biscuits with her other baked goods, but she didn't contradict the elderly woman. "That's a good idea."

"Oh, and why don't you close the stand until next Tuesday? You'll want to spend the first few days after Wilma's operation with her. And she'll be glad for company. Believe me, I know."

"If she's not planning my funeral," Wilma said darkly.

Mrs. Vandenberg wagged a finger. "Positive thinking works wonders. And I'll be praying."

Although Sovilla had answered all the woman's questions out of politeness, Mrs. Vandenberg's take-charge attitude made Sovilla uncomfortable. She kept waiting for Wilma to jump in and attack the elderly woman for being so intrusive. Yet her *aenti* never did. Even when she contradicted Mrs. Vandenberg, Wilma lacked her usual fire.

After Mrs. Vandenberg left, Sovilla ventured a quick comment. "She's very sure of herself."

Before Sovilla could ask if the older woman's behavior had bothered her *aenti*, Wilma retorted, "That's why she ended up as the owner of the market."

"She owns the market?" Now the expensive clothes and handbag made sense. "I thought she was a driver for the Amish."

Wilma snorted. Then rusty peals of laughter erupted from her mouth. "Mrs. Vandenberg—a driver?" She said it again several times as if she couldn't believe anyone could make that mistake. She accompanied each repetition with snickers.

Sovilla didn't find it as humorous as her *aenti* did, but from the sounds of it, Wilma hadn't laughed in years. Humor might be healing.

By the time her *aenti* got control of herself, she had to wipe her streaming eyes. "Mrs. Vandenberg turned the market over to Gideon."

"Gideon? The one from Hartzler's Chicken Barbecue?"

"That's the one."

He also hadn't come across as the boss—not of the whole market—when Sovilla had worked in his stand. Now she remembered, he'd been the one who'd mentioned Mrs. Vandenberg. He'd said he had to run something by her.

"Gideon's the real owner, but she holds the mortgage, so that gives her say over what happens here. She believes in being hands-on."

"I see." Sovilla hoped she hadn't said anything to offend Mrs. Vandenberg.

Wilma chuckled again. "The only car you'll see on

Thursday will be the limo with her driver. And don't worry about paying her. She won't let you. She also runs a charity and is known for her generosity."

Sovilla would still offer to pay. She didn't feel right taking something without doing anything in return.

Chapter Seventeen

Isaac looked up from loading chickens into a customer's truck to see Mrs. Vandenberg beckoning him. He held up a hand to let her know he'd be right there. She nodded and made her way to a picnic table.

Gut. He wouldn't have to worry about her toppling over.

As soon as he was done, he and Snickers hurried to the table. He always enjoyed talking to Mrs. Vandenberg.

"Do you have a few minutes?" she asked.

With a smile, Isaac sat across from her. He patted the bench beside him, and Snickers hopped up.

"First of all," she said, "have you had a chance to practice Demosthenes's technique and the other information I gave you?"

Isaac wanted to prove it to her, so he closed his eyes, inhaled deeply, and pushed out a loud "*Jah.*" He'd done it. Gotten out an answer without stuttering.

"Wonderful." She beamed. "Once you learn to modulate it a little, it'll be perfect."

He nodded to let her know that had been his plan. Unfortunately, he hadn't learned how to do that for whole sentences. And the effort it took him to speak on the outbreath meant he had little control of his volume—yet.

"Don't look so discouraged. It's a big change, and you're coming along nicely."

He drew in a breath and managed an explosive "*Danke.*"

"What about Demosthenes? Are you still working with the pebbles?"

"G-gravel."

"That'll help too. I want you to invite me to your first speech."

Isaac laughed. He'd like to invite her to hear one full sentence. He'd be thrilled to get to that point.

"Don't laugh," she said, leaning forward with a serious glance. "I have no doubt you'll be able to give a speech someday."

He couldn't help smiling at her earnestness, but it did give him encouragement. Knowing she believed in him made him want to prove her right. If he got to that point, his first speech would be a sincere *danke* for her kindness and inspiration.

"I have a favor to ask."

He'd do anything for her.

"I know a young lady who'll need a ride to market starting next Tuesday. I'm not sure how long she'll need transportation, but I'm hoping you can take her."

Isaac tried to keep his expression cheerful. He imagined driving a strange *Englischer* every day and struggling to speak. Was this Mrs. Vandenberg's way of making sure he practiced?

"You don't look too happy. Should I ask someone else?"

His too-loud "*Neh*" startled them both. Mrs. Vandenberg even jumped a bit. Isaac regretted that, but he'd gotten out another whole word.

"Are you sure?"

Mrs. Vandenberg had done so much for him. The least he could do for her was drive her friend. He nodded.

"One of our stand owners will be going into the hospital this week, and her niece—"

"S-Sovilla?" Did Mrs. Vandenberg want him to drive Sovilla? *Jah, jah, jah!*

She laughed. "Perhaps I shouldn't have teased you, but it was worth it to see the joy on your face. I promised her I'd find her a ride starting next week."

Isaac tried to control the smile stretching his lips until they ached, but he had little success.

"I don't know how long Wilma will be in the hospital, but if you wouldn't mind doing it until she's well, I'd appreciate it."

Mind? Of course I don't mind. I'm thrilled.

What if she didn't want to go with him? "D-does S-Sovilla know?"

"About you being her ride? Not yet, but I'm sure she'll be as delighted as you."

He wasn't so sure about that, but still, he couldn't wait. With a quick breath, he popped out a "*Danke!*" Its volume reflected the deafening decibels of his heart.

Just before closing, Mrs. Vandenberg showed up at the pickle stand and handed Sovilla two professionally lettered signs: *Closed until Tuesday*.

"You can put one on each side of the stand." Mrs. Vandenberg handed her a roll of tape.

Wilma sat on a stool, counting the money. She paid no attention to Sovilla hanging the signs.

Mrs. Vandenberg smiled her approval. "Would you

have a little time to talk to me"—she glanced at Wilma—"privately?"

"I need to take the empty crates out to the car." Sovilla took Wilma's car key from its under-the-counter hook and picked up two of the wooden boxes.

Used to making several brisk walks to the car and back, Sovilla slowed to Mrs. Vandenberg's limping pace. Sovilla wished she'd suggested a different place to talk. She hadn't considered Mrs. Vandenberg's difficulties with walking.

"You're very thoughtful to move at my snail's pace." Mrs. Vandenberg sounded winded. "I'm sorry for slowing you down."

"It's not a problem. We won't be leaving soon. Wilma has a lot to do before we go." Her *aenti* had made it clear she intended to count every pickle jar on each shelf to be sure Sovilla didn't cheat her.

"Perhaps we could sit at one of the tables outside or one of the café tables in here."

"Let's pick one in here." Sovilla steered the elderly lady to the nearest table.

"Thank you, dear." She sank onto a chair and sighed. "It's been a busy day." Pulling a list and a pen from her large handbag, she crossed off an item.

Across the table from her, Sovilla recognized her name. She tried to read some of the other tiny, upside-down handwritten items, but Mrs. Vandenberg's hand blocked most of the words. Quite a few had been scribbled out.

"First of all, you'll have a ride to the market starting Tuesday. Isaac Lantz has agreed to pick you up. You know him, don't you?" A smile played on Mrs. Vandenberg's lips as she examined Sovilla's face.

"*Jah*, I mean yes. We're in the same youth group at church."

"And he lives near you, so that works out well."

"It does." Although Sovilla's spirits had been weighed down all day by Henry's jilting her, it gave her a lift to think about riding with Isaac.

"He's a wonderful young man." Mrs. Vandenberg continued to study Sovilla's face. "Too bad you have a boyfriend."

A sharp pain pierced Sovilla's heart. "How did you know?" How did Mrs. Vandenberg discover so much about people? Who could have told her about Henry?

"I have my ways, dear. People often tell me things, and luckily, I still have a good memory." She tapped her forehead. "More importantly, many years of living have taught me to look beyond people's words and actions to their motives and hearts."

Sovilla wished she had Mrs. Vandenberg's gift. Maybe she could unravel the reason for Henry's change of heart.

Mrs. Vandenberg sighed. "If only you weren't tied to this boy in Ohio."

"I'm not." Sovilla couldn't believe she'd blurted that out.

"You aren't?" Mrs. Vandenberg looked intrigued. "Is that recent?"

Sovilla ducked her head so Mrs. Vandenberg couldn't see the tears stinging her eyes. "I'd rather not talk about it."

"Very recent, then."

The woman was uncanny. How had she sensed Wilma's deepest fears? And here she was, analyzing Sovilla's.

Reaching across the table, Mrs. Vandenberg laid a hand on Sovilla's. "You'll find I'm a good listener."

Sovilla shook her head. She'd never be able to discuss Henry's betrayal.

"Well, if you ever want to talk, I'm here. I'm sure it must be hard to be so far away from your family."

"It is." Sovilla bit her lip. "I miss them terribly."

"I expect Wilma isn't much comfort there." Mrs. Vandenberg squeezed Sovilla's hand. "Your aunt has a good heart deep down, but she's been badly hurt."

"You know what happened?" Had Wilma confided in Mrs. Vandenberg?

"No, I don't. Wilma keeps her pain locked inside. And she's walled off her feelings and erected a *No Trespassing* sign."

"I know," Sovilla agreed, her eyes focused on the warm, wrinkled hand covering hers. The kindness and caring flowing from the woman, this stranger, made Sovilla want to cry. Would she ever see Mamm again?

"What is it, dear?"

Sovilla blinked back the wetness in her eyes. "I thought I was coming here for a few months to care for Wilma. But now I'm not sure if or when I'll see my family again."

"You won't be going back home afterward?"

"I don't know." Changing churches made this move seem permanent. And neither Sovilla nor Mamm had enough money for a visit.

Mrs. Vandenberg's caring and sympathy soon had Sovilla pouring out the whole story of Lloyd and the family's move to Middlefield. And even her heartbreak over Henry.

Gideon walked past to lock the market doors, jolting Sovilla back to the market. Wilma would be furious. Sovilla should be helping to close down the stand.

Shakily, she got to her feet, emotions swirling through her, drowning her. No wonder Mrs. Vandenberg knew so much about people. She sweet-talked them into spilling all their secrets. Yet she also gave the impression she'd keep your confidences private.

"I'd better get back. Wilma will be wondering where I am."

"I'm sorry for keeping you so long." Mrs. Vandenberg looked regretful.

Sovilla gave a trembling laugh. "You didn't keep me. I kept you."

"No, you didn't. I have plenty of time on my hands, and helping others is the best use of whatever time the good Lord gives me." Her loving smile touched Sovilla. "And you needed to release everything bottled up inside."

Sovilla's spirits had lightened now that she'd unburdened her soul. "*Danke* for listening."

"Anytime." Mrs. Vandenberg fumbled in her purse and extracted a business card. "Here's my number. Call anytime. You do have a phone at Wilma's, don't you?"

"Yes."

"Also use this number to call for rides to and from the hospital."

Sovilla shook her head. She couldn't expect Mrs. Vandenberg's driver to pick her up and drop her off.

Mrs. Vandenberg pressed the card in Sovilla's hand. "This is for Wilma. She won't let me help her, but I can give her the gift of your presence. Please let me do that."

Somehow Mrs. Vandenberg had turned the situation around so Sovilla would be letting two people down if she didn't take the rides. The woman was a miracle worker.

"Meanwhile, I'll be praying for both of you. I believe God has brought you here for a special reason." Mrs. Vandenberg's mysterious smile made it seem as if she had an inkling of that purpose.

Sovilla had lost sight of that truth. She'd been so

focused on all the negatives of being in Lancaster, so far from her family. She'd forgotten to seek God's will. He had led her here. She needed to trust Him in all things, including about Henry.

On Thursday morning, Sovilla woke before dawn. Despite working until almost midnight yesterday canning batch after batch of pickles, Wilma was already banging around in her room. Maybe she'd never gone to bed.

Sovilla prayed for her *aenti* and for the doctors. She dressed and headed down to the kitchen. First she moved the final batch of pickles to the basement shelves. Then she spread apple butter on a slice of bread. She didn't want to cook breakfast and waft tantalizing smells into the air when her *aenti* had been forbidden to eat.

True to her word, Mrs. Vandenberg had her car outside the door at exactly seven fifteen. Sovilla ignored Wilma's protests and carried her suitcase. She only made it to the front porch before the driver took it from her. He helped them both into the car and stowed the suitcase in the trunk.

As he rounded the car to get in, Wilma sniffed. "Not the limo. Only the Bentley."

Sovilla settled back on the cushy leather seats. She'd never been in such an elegant, roomy car. If they hadn't been headed to the hospital, she'd have enjoyed the ride more.

When they arrived, the driver escorted them into the lobby, deposited Wilma's suitcase, and handed Sovilla the large zippered canvas tote he'd also carried.

"Mrs. Vandenberg said to open this after your aunt goes into surgery," he told her. "And call whenever you're ready to go."

"Wait," Wilma called after him. "You need to take Sovilla to the market. We can't leave the stand untended."

Sovilla shook her head and shouldered the heavy bag. "I'm staying with you. Didn't you see the signs Mrs. Vandenberg brought on Tuesday?" Wilma had been distracted and spacey, but surely she'd seen the large signs Sovilla had hung.

"You are not staying with me. I don't need anyone. People could steal from the stand if nobody's there to supervise."

"I apologize," the driver said. "Mrs. Vandenberg asked me to let you know the neighboring stands agreed to keep an eye on yours. And the maintenance staff will make regular rounds."

When her *aenti* opened her mouth to protest, Sovilla cut her off. "I'm not letting you go through this alone."

Wilma huffed. "I've done everything alone most of my life."

"You aren't this time."

Her *aenti*'s eyes glittered with moisture. She turned abruptly and marched toward the elevator. Sovilla stayed beside her *aenti* as she got out on the second floor and made her way to the check-in desk. After Wilma filled out her paperwork, shielding all her answers from Sovilla with her hand, they waited together until a nurse called for Ms. Mast.

A while later, they led Sovilla to the pre-op bay, where Wilma lay in a hospital bed with an IV in her arm. Her *aenti* had her eyes closed, and Sovilla wasn't sure if Wilma had already drifted off under the anesthesia.

"I'll be praying," she whispered.

Wilma's eyes snapped open. "What are you doing here?"

"They said I could come back to this room."

"They did that because they know I'm not going to make it."

"They do this for everyone. You'll be fine." Sovilla hoped that was true. But she didn't know the day or the hour God had chosen for Wilma to leave this earth.

"If I die, find my son," Wilma begged, "and share the inheritance."

"Your son?" Sovilla'd had no idea her *aenti* had a son. Of course, until recently, she hadn't known she had an *aenti*. Had Wilma had a husband she'd never mentioned? Was she widowed? Or divorced?

Wilma squeezed her eyes shut. Tears trickled down her cheeks.

"What's your son's name?" He could have all of Sovilla's inheritance.

"I don't know."

"You don't know?" Had he changed his name? How could Sovilla find him if he had? "Are there a lot of Masts around here?"

"His last name won't be Mast."

What? Maybe the anesthesia had taken effect, because Wilma made no sense.

"I don't understand," Sovilla said softly, "but I'll do whatever you want."

Wilma turned her face away. "No, of course, you wouldn't," she mumbled. "Our parents died when your *mamm* was fourteen, and I was seventeen. Lloyd took over the farm and our lives."

Mamm had never mentioned that, but maybe that was why she still did whatever Lloyd asked. He must have been like a parent to her.

"At twenty-four," Wilma went on, "Lloyd had been planning to marry, but he postponed his wedding to take care of the two of us. Until then, our brother had been gentle and caring, but he grew more and more rigid, and soon became a tyrant."

Lloyd, kind and nice? Sovilla had trouble imagining it. She'd also had the same problem with Mamm's comment about Wilma.

"I fell in love, and I rebelled against Lloyd's strict rules. Eli and I did things we shouldn't. Then . . ." Wilma choked and went silent.

When she continued, her voice shook. "Lloyd found out. That was the worst day of my life. He went to see Eli." Wilma hunched her shoulders as if to ward off a blow.

Sovilla wanted to reach out, but her *aenti* had always rebuffed touching. Sovilla kept her hands in her lap and did the only thing she could—pray.

"Lloyd said Eli wanted nothing to do with me or the baby. My brother went out to the neighbor's phone shanty and made several calls. Next thing I knew, he'd bundled me into a car, tossed my suitcase in the trunk, and wouldn't let me say goodbye to your *mamm*. I had no idea where the driver planned to take me, and I was crying too hard to ask."

Poor Wilma. No wonder she wants me to avoid boys. No wonder she worries about me being alone with a boy. No wonder she believes men can't be trusted.

"After hours and hours in the car, we pulled up in front of a house in Pennsylvania. It turned out to be a home for unwed mothers. All of us—Amish, Mennonite, and *Englisch*—had been sent away to hide our shame."

Sovilla's heart ached for her *aenti*. To be so alone, so frightened, and so far from home.

"The owners of New Beginnings were kind and helpful, but they followed Lloyd's directives. He insisted the baby be given up for adoption. I only held my son for a short while, then they took him away."

That explained Wilma's animosity toward Lloyd.

"Lloyd didn't want me to come back to Ohio. He feared I'd influence your *mamm* to live a life of sin."

"I'm so sorry you went through that." Sovilla couldn't imagine being left in Pennsylvania as a teenager, all alone and so far from home.

Her *aenti* rolled over and grasped Sovilla's hand. "Promise me you'll find him."

"I'll do my best."

Anguish and desperation etched deep lines into Wilma's face. "Your best isn't good enough." Her grip tightened until Sovilla feared her bones might be crushed.

"I promise."

Wilma fell back onto the pillow with a loud sigh. Then, a short while later, she murmured sleepily, "If you're Amish, a promise is your bond."

Sovilla had only meant to comfort her *aenti*. What had she gotten into? How would she find a baby born so long ago when she didn't even know his name?

Chapter Eighteen

After they took Wilma into the operating room, the nurse handed Sovilla a pager. She clutched it and the heavy canvas bag as she made her way to the waiting room. While waiting for Wilma's updated information to appear on the electronic information board, Sovilla mulled over what her *aenti* had confessed.

Her heart ached for Wilma. Lloyd had basically kicked her *aenti* out of the family. What a terrible thing to go through alone! And then to have to give up her baby.

Not that Wilma could have cared for a child. How did she take care of herself at seventeen, even without a baby? In a strange town where she knew no one. And where did she live? Sovilla planned to ask her *aenti* all these questions and more once she'd recovered.

For now, Sovilla had to figure out how to find Wilma's son. Her *aenti* had mentioned New Beginnings. That might be a start, but Sovilla had no way to get there even if she could find an address. She'd made a promise, though, and she intended to keep it, no matter how difficult.

After considering various strategies, Sovilla bowed her head and asked God to direct her search. Then she spent time praying for her *aenti* and for the surgeon and medical team.

The hours ticked by slowly. Because she'd been blindsided by Wilma's news, Sovilla hadn't opened the canvas bag Mrs. Vandenberg's driver had given her. Now she turned her attention to that, hoping it would provide a distraction.

She unzipped it to find books, magazines, snacks, and a note from Mrs. Vandenberg:

Dear Sovilla,

I know waiting can seem long, so I've put a few things in here to help you pass the time. In the outer pocket, you'll find a cell phone. Please use it to call my driver. It's preprogrammed, so all you need to do is push the phone icon and then the number two. If you'd like to talk to me, hit number one.

Be sure to encourage your aunt to do her physical therapy exercises. They hurt, but they're essential for recovery.

Please know I'll be praying for both of you.

In God's love,
Mrs. V

With tears in her eyes, Sovilla lifted out the gifts—two Christian novels, a book about finding God's peace in difficult circumstances, and a Bible crossword puzzle book. The multiple inside pockets held juice boxes, soda, chips, candy bars, granola bars, and an apple. Below the books, a small, thin cooler bag held a sandwich and some cheese sticks.

Until she'd opened the bag, Sovilla hadn't realized she was hungry. Bless Mrs. Vandenberg. After eating the sandwich and several snacks, Sovilla settled back with the book about God's peace. Perhaps when she finished, she could leave it on her *aenti*'s bedside table. Maybe if Wilma got bored enough, she'd read it.

Reading helped the last two hours to pass quickly. Sovilla had almost reached the end of the slim book when the information board announced Wilma was in the recovery room. That meant she'd be moved to her room in about forty-five minutes to an hour. Sovilla finished the book before they paged her and gave her Wilma's room number.

When they wheeled Wilma into the room, she barely lifted her lids. "Go to work," she commanded, although her words were slightly slurred.

"It's too late," Sovilla told her. "The market will soon be closing."

"If anyone stole my pickles . . ."

"Don't worry. Lots of people are watching the stand." Sovilla hoped a soothing, confident voice might reassure her *aenti*, but Wilma tossed her head from side to side and plucked at the sheet.

"Try not to agitate her," the aide whispered to Sovilla. "She seems distressed. Do your best to calm her."

Wilma peered at them, her eyes narrowed. "What are you two plotting?" She tried to lift her upper body but fell back on the pillow and groaned.

"You need to be still for a while, Ms. Mast." The aide raised the back of the bed slightly so Wilma had a better view of Sovilla. "Relax a bit and let your body heal."

"Easy for you to say. Nobody's robbing you blind while you're stuck in bed." Although Wilma's words came out slowly, they hadn't lost any of their tartness.

The aide picked up the water cup with a straw and held it out. “I’m sure the police will take care of it.”

Wilma batted the cup away. “Police? A lot of good that’ll do me.”

“It’s a market stand,” Sovilla explained.

“Oh.” The aide put the water back on the bedside stand. “Try to get her to drink a bit.” She pointed out the various buttons and headed for the door. “Someone will be in later to help you with your exercises.”

“I don’t want do to exercises.” Wilma’s declaration ended in a whine. “I’m tired and want to sleep.”

“The exercises are important to keep the mobility in your joints.”

Sovilla remembered Mrs. Vandenberg’s note. “You need them to help you recover properly.”

Her *aenti* glared at her.

The aide smiled at Sovilla. “It’s so nice you have your daughter here as a coach.”

“She is not my daughter.” Wilma spat out each word. “I don’t have a daughter.” Her face twisted, and she slumped back onto the pillow with her eyes squeezed shut.

“I’m her niece,” Sovilla told the puzzled aide.

“If she’s in pain, she can use the button.” The nurse frowned. “She shouldn’t need it already, though.”

A few tears trickled down Wilma’s face.

Sovilla moved closer to the aide to whisper, “I don’t think she’s hurting from the operation. She’s upset about something.”

The aide nodded. *Good luck*, she mouthed. With one last *I-don’t-envy-you* expression, she closed the door behind her.

Once the door shut, Wilma swiped at her eyes with her fist.

Sovilla hurried over to the bedside table and plucked a tissue from the small box. "Would you like this?"

"I wouldn't need one," Wilma said savagely as she snatched the tissue from Sovilla's hand, "if they didn't give you medications that make your eyes water."

Sovilla hid a smile. Her *aenti* went to great lengths to avoid appearing soft or vulnerable. Then Sovilla sobered. Now that she'd learned some of her *aenti*'s history, she understood Wilma's need to appear strong.

"I wanted to ask you about what you said before your operation," Sovilla said.

Wilma glared. "Forget everything I said. Consider all of it the ravings of a sedated lunatic."

"It didn't really happen?"

"None of your business." Wilma pinched her lips together.

"Do you want to find your son?"

"Drop it. No use pining for what you can't have."

"I could check at New Beginnings."

"They closed. Now don't mention it again."

Wilma shut her eyes, but the tears leaking out from under her lids revealed she wasn't sleeping. Sovilla set the inspirational book on the bedside table and prayed.

After a while, a bouncy, bubbly woman knocked and entered the room with a walker and a cheery smile. "You must be Wilma. I'm Jen." She turned to Sovilla. "And you're her coach?"

"Yes, I'm her niece Sovilla." She didn't want Jen to mistake her for Wilma's daughter. They didn't need another meltdown. Her *aenti* would provide enough of a trial.

Jen glanced at the bed, and her eyebrows rose. Wilma lay back on the pillow, and light snoring sounds came from her mouth. "I could have sworn she was awake when I walked in."

Evidently, her *aenti* had no intention of cooperating.

With a loud sigh, Jen asked, "Which do you think would wake her up fastest—a dousing with ice water or a mild electrical shock?" She winked at Sovilla.

Wilma opened one eye. "Don't you dare."

Jen smiled at her. "I'm so glad you're awake. I hate disturbing people when they're sleeping."

Sovilla suspected her *aenti* had met her match.

"Let's get you up and into the reclining chair to start." Jen leaned over to help Wilma into a sitting position.

"I can do it myself."

To Jen's credit, she waited patiently while Wilma struggled. Then she reached in right before Wilma admitted defeat. "You did very well."

"No, I didn't. I needed help."

"We want you do as much as you can on your own, but you might need a little assistance here and there. Don't be afraid to ask."

"I'm not afraid. I don't want any help." That statement, along with Wilma's resistance to exercising, set the tone for the rest of the session.

By the time her *aenti* had returned to bed, both she and Jen looked exhausted. Sovilla's jaw ached from clenching her teeth.

Jen turned to Sovilla. "You saw what we did, right? She'll need to repeat the exercises she practiced today. And then we'll add more."

"I will not endure any more of your torture," Wilma announced.

"Don't worry. It won't always be me." Jen looked relieved.

When she left the room, Wilma pointed at Sovilla. "You get out of here too. I don't need a babysitter."

"I'm not—"

"I said go," Wilma thundered. "I don't want anyone sitting here watching me sleep. Besides, the house could get robbed along with the stand. I can't rest thinking about that."

Her *aenti*'s ashen face revealed she needed sleep. Sovilla was torn. She knew how much Wilma worried, but she didn't want to leave her alone.

Wilma sagged back against the pillow, and her eyelids drooped. "I didn't sleep at all last night. And I want to be alone."

Sovilla rose. "I'll go, then."

Before she made it to the door, intermittent snores—not fake ones this time—lifted her *aenti*'s chest in gentle waves. Sovilla eased the door closed behind her and called for the driver.

When he arrived, she sank into the cushiony seat, grateful for Mrs. Vandenberg's kindness. After he pulled in front of the house, she thanked him multiple times and asked him to tell Mrs. Vandenberg how much both she and her *aenti* had appreciated everything.

"I'll do that," he said. "She also sent this." He handed her a large, warm insulated bag. "She figured you'd be too tired to fix a meal when you returned."

After another round of thanks, Sovilla entered the house with gratitude in her heart. Like her *aenti*, Sovilla couldn't wait to drop into bed. The meal was a heaven-sent blessing. She wondered if Mrs. Vandenberg was an angel on earth.

After eating the delicious hot meal and storing the leftovers, Sovilla sank into bed. She prayed for her *aenti*'s recovery and for the staff who cared for her. They had difficult jobs already. Her *aenti* wouldn't make it any easier.

Before she fell asleep, Wilma's request gnawed at her. Should Sovilla search for her *aenti*'s son? Although Wilma had said to drop it, she'd longed for Sovilla to give him the inheritance. An inheritance that rightfully belonged to him. If they found him, Wilma could rewrite her will.

Sovilla prayed again for God's direction. As she drifted off, one last thought came to her. She'd been so busy all day, she'd had no time to think about Henry. Maybe the stress of caring for Wilma would be a blessing.

Since he'd be driving Sovilla, Isaac wanted to be able to talk to her. Slipping into the kennel as often as he could, he worked hard on his speech. He needed to improve on releasing his first word on the outbreath, so he didn't blast the first syllable in people's faces. He wanted to sound natural.

When he took Snickers to obedience class on Wednesday, Isaac inhaled before each command. Some came out too loud, but other people in the class used strong tones. No one seemed to notice anything different. Maybe it wasn't as noticeable as he thought.

On Thursday, he stayed away from Wilma's stand, assuming it would be empty. But Friday, he and Snickers took off for the stand as soon as they'd unloaded the lambs and chickens. He only had a short break before the auction began, but he wanted to spend it with Sovilla. Without

Wilma to stop him, he could ask Sovilla how her *aenti*'s operation had gone and discuss the plans for picking her up next week.

A few stands away, he stopped and stared. The stand was empty. He'd been expecting Wilma to be missing, but not Sovilla.

A sign said, CLOSED UNTIL TUESDAY.

Tuesday? He wouldn't see her until then? That seemed so far off.

The sign meant she wouldn't be here tomorrow. He should have expected that she'd stay with Wilma in the hospital, but her *aenti* didn't seem to like attention. And she'd never left her stand untended. Not in all the years he'd come here with his family.

"Are you looking for Sovilla?" a soft voice behind him asked.

Isaac spun around. He couldn't lie to Mrs. Vandenberg, so he nodded.

"A reasonable assumption. Wilma has never taken a vacation or stayed out sick. Seeing her stand closed is like a sudden gap from a missing tooth. A gigantic, uncomfortable hole."

A huge empty space. Isaac hoped he didn't look as gloomy as he felt.

"As you can see, Sovilla won't be back to the market until Tuesday. You're still willing to pick her up, right?"

He bobbed his head up and down so vigorously, she laughed.

"Good. But Tuesday is a long wait for someone in love."

Love? He barely knew Sovilla. *Jah*, he was attracted to her, interested in her, but love took time to grow.

"I planned to invite Sovilla for dinner on Saturday

night. Would you like to be my guest?" She smiled. Before he answered, she said, "I take it the answer is yes."

Had his face glowing with eagerness given him away? Try as he might, he couldn't erase his excited grin.

Mrs. Vandenberg handed him a card. "This is my home address. Be there at six. If you'd prefer to be picked up, I can send a car for you."

Too excited to practice his techniques, he answered, "*N-neh. D-danke!*"

After she hobbled away with a contented smile, he wanted to leap in the air the way his little sister did whenever she was waiting for a special treat. Instead, he strolled casually to the pretzel stand and ordered extras for his brothers and Daed. He'd share his happiness.

That day and the next passed in a slow, tedious drip. Saturday seemed to be nonending. Isaac watched the clock tick off minute after minute. Finally, they piled into the buggy to head home.

Normally, Isaac dreaded the days Andrew drove. His brother, a fast and reckless driver, often took chances. Most of the time, Isaac prayed they'd make it home without an accident. But today, instead of silently begging Andrew to slow down, Isaac mentally urged him to hurry.

He hadn't told anyone about Mrs. Vandenberg's invitation except for his *mamm*. And he never mentioned the other guest. Now he needed to get cleaned up and change his clothes. He hoped he could slip out without anyone, especially Andrew, noticing. But he'd need help with the dogs.

Isaac went into the kitchen, caught Leanne's eye, and signaled for her to meet him in the kennel. He headed outside and tended to the dogs while she finished the dishes and cleaned the kitchen.

She came through the door with a puzzled frown. "What's going on?"

He kept practicing his speaking techniques as he explained about Wilma's operation and Mrs. Vandenberg's dinner. "Could you t-take care of the d-dogs tonight?"

"Sure. I guess I have to since you've been mucking out the stables for me."

"*Danke.*"

"If you're going to Mrs. Vandenberg's house, do you want me to watch Snickers? I'm guessing her house is too fancy for a dog to be sitting on the furniture."

"*Gut* idea." He smiled to let her know how much he appreciated her thoughtfulness.

"You know, Isaac, you're doing great with the stuttering. You started your sentences without any problems."

Talking to Leanne didn't make him nervous. He did much better when he could relax. And trying to speak on the outbreath seemed to help. Too bad he couldn't keep up the momentum through the whole sentence.

"Why did Mrs. Vandenberg ask you to supper?" she asked.

This time, he couldn't help stammering, "S-Sovilla."

"She's going to be there too?"

He tried to act casual as he nodded.

Leanne laughed. "People say Mrs. Vandenberg's a good matchmaker. She helped Fern and Gideon get together."

Isaac hoped Mrs. Vandenberg's skills extended to him. Except . . . did she know Sovilla had a boyfriend?

Chapter Nineteen

Since Wilma's operation, she'd balked at doing the exercises and remained uncooperative. As her coach, Sovilla's job included learning how to do the exercises and encouraging her *aenti* during sessions.

By the time they finished, Sovilla felt like a limp rag, wrung out and drained. Dealing with her *aenti* was difficult during the best of times, and this proved to be worse.

Wilma crossed her arms and ignored the therapist's instructions. She closed her eyes and refused to respond to questions.

The therapist turned to Sovilla. "Can you do anything with her?"

Before Sovilla could admit defeat, the cell phone in her bag rang. For the first time in her life, she was thrilled to answer. Mrs. Vandenberg's kind voice on the other end almost caused Sovilla to burst into tears.

"Are you all right, dear?" Mrs. Vandenberg's concern vibrated through the phone.

"Well . . ." Sovilla couldn't complain with her *aenti* listening in. "Not exactly," she admitted.

"Is Wilma giving you trouble?"

"You could say that." All the tears Sovilla had been holding back threatened to overflow.

"I rather expected that. Is she refusing to do her therapy?"

"Yes."

"Put her on."

Sovilla carried the phone over to her *aenti*, but Wilma ignored it and kept her eyes shut. "I'm sorry," Sovilla said to Mrs. Vandenberg. "She won't take the phone."

"Just put it near her ear. I'm going to give her a talking-to."

Sovilla held the phone close to her *aenti*'s ear.

"Wilma Mast," Mrs. Vandenberg's voice blasted from the phone.

Her *aenti* jumped but didn't open her eyes. Sovilla moved the phone to her *aenti*'s new position.

"Now, you listen to me, Wilma. You do those exercises."

Wilma moved her head away, but Sovilla followed her movements, keeping the phone close.

"Do you know what will happen if you don't do your therapy? You'll lose your mobility. Do you want to spend the rest of your life limping around? Or stuck in a wheelchair or using a walker?"

With a noise deep in her throat, Wilma tilted her head. Once again, Sovilla held the phone to her *aenti*'s ear.

"Are you being fair to Sovilla? You shouldn't expect her to care for an invalid."

"Leave me alone," Wilma shouted. Then she glowered at Sovilla. "And get that thing away from me." She flung an impatient hand in the direction of the phone.

"It's all right." Mrs. Vandenberg's soothing voice echoed from the speaker. "I'd like to talk to you, Sovilla."

Sovilla moved away from her *aenti*, who was grumbling.

"I got a reaction from her," Mrs. Vandenberg said. "Sometimes getting a person angry will give them the energy they need when they want to quit. I hope that's the case with Wilma."

It would be *wunderbar* if Mrs. Vandenberg was right, but Sovilla couldn't see her *aenti*'s anger as productive. Mrs. Vandenberg had been right about other things, so maybe she'd be right about this. Sovilla hoped so.

"I imagine you're exhausted, aren't you, dear?"

The word *dear* wrapped Sovilla in a warm hug. She closed her eyes and relaxed into the love.

"Would you be able to come to dinner tonight? I could have my driver pick you up in an hour."

More than anything Sovilla wanted to go. "I'd like that, but I'll be staying here until eight."

"I don't want you here." Wilma spoke loudly enough for Mrs. Vandenberg to hear. "I already told you to go home."

"You know," Mrs. Vandenberg said, "sometimes giving people what they ask for makes them realize they didn't mean it. Why don't you come for dinner? I suspect Wilma will regret getting her way tonight."

"I don't think—"

"I'll send the driver. He'll be there at five thirty. Please be downstairs waiting."

The phone cut off before Sovilla could protest.

"I suppose you're leaving me." Wilma looked peeved. "It figures."

Sovilla sighed. No matter what she did, she upset her *aenti*. "I'll be back tomorrow morning."

"Don't bother."

Even though Wilma stubbornly refused to cooperate for the rest of the session, Sovilla finished the usual therapy tussle with a lighter heart. She waved goodbye to her *aenti* and headed toward the door, feeling as if a great weight had lifted.

"Don't look so happy about leaving," Wilma called after her.

With difficulty, Sovilla held back her smile until she'd left the room. But it blossomed as soon as she reached the hallway. And even her *aenti*'s carping couldn't deflate her buoyant spirits.

The driver was waiting near the entrance as she exited, and Sovilla hurried to the car. Although she shouldn't feel so relieved to get away from the hospital, she perked up. And when she slid into the Bentley, all her stored-up tension dissolved.

As they pulled through the wrought iron gates and drove down the tree-lined driveway, Sovilla sucked in her breath. A marble fountain stood in the center of the plush green lawn. Reflecting the sunlight in rainbow sparkles, water cascaded over several levels of shell-shaped stone bowls, forming the perfect introduction to the stone mansion.

"It's gorgeous." And massive. Four or five houses the size of Wilma's could fit inside. All this space for one person?

They wound their way around back. A smaller stone cottage nestled in the trees beside a four-car garage. The driver stopped beside a covered porch.

Mrs. Vandenberg emerged from the back door. She greeted Sovilla and led her past an enormous kitchen. A woman bustled around the huge room, and delicious smells wafted from the stove. Sovilla inhaled, and her mouth watered.

"Would you like to freshen up?" Mrs. Vandenberg asked. "The powder room is off to the left."

"*Danke.*" If Sovilla looked as frazzled as she felt, no wonder Mrs. Vandenberg had suggested fixing herself up.

Despite wearing the Lancaster *kapp* for more than a week, Sovilla still startled herself each time she looked in the mirror. A quick glance revealed strands of hair escaping in several places. She didn't have time to redo her bob, so she removed her *kapp*, wet her hands, smoothed down the strands, and tucked them in. Then she pinned her *kapp* back in place.

After washing her face and hands, she straightened her dress. Feeling a little tidier, she exited to find Mrs. Vandenberg waiting for her.

"It's such a lovely evening, I thought we could eat out by the pool. The dining room is too formal for a relaxed, friendly conversation." She led Sovilla out French doors onto a stone terrace.

A waterfall flowed over stones at one end of a freeform stone-lined pool. The soothing sound of rippling water soothed Sovilla as she settled into one of the cushioned chairs. "It's so beautiful."

"I sit out here when I need peace amid my hectic life." Mrs. Vandenberg lowered herself unsteadily into a chair across from Sovilla. "I enjoy having my morning devotions out here."

"I can see why." Sovilla leaned back and let some of the tensions from the past few days drain away. All around her, birds chirped, and a breeze stirred the trees that surrounded them on all sides. The scent of pine drifted toward her. "Thank you for having me and for the canvas tote and your kindness and . . ."

Mrs. Vandenberg held up a hand. “Don’t thank me. Thank God.” She smiled at Sovilla. “And I’m grateful God sent you into my life. You’re a blessing.”

Sovilla couldn’t see why. She’d done nothing to help Mrs. Vandenberg.

“Do you know how lonely I’d be without a purpose in life and the chance to make a difference, however small, in other people’s lives?”

Melodic chimes rang through the air.

Mrs. Vandenberg struggled to her feet using her cane to aid her. “That must be our other guest. I’ll be right back.”

Another guest? Sovilla’s spirits plummeted. She’d been expecting to have time alone with Mrs. Vandenberg. Now instead of a relaxed conversation, she’d be on edge around a stranger.

Mrs. Vandenberg started for the house, but turned as a woman came through the doors carrying a large tray. “Thank you, Amelia.” She turned to Sovilla. “Help yourself to some hors d’oeuvres.”

All the tiny tidbits looked too pretty to touch, so Sovilla sat, hands clenched in her lap, trying to enjoy the beauty around her. But her body tensed at the thought of conversing with one of Mrs. Vandenberg’s *Englisch* friends.

As the footsteps drew closer, Sovilla turned toward the French doors. Isaac stepped out and held the door open for Mrs. Vandenberg to totter onto the patio.

Isaac? What’s he doing here?

Isaac had imagined this moment for days, but nothing could have prepared him for this vision by the pool. With water rippling in the background and trees forming a secluded area on the terrace, Sovilla sat illuminated by sunlight filtering through the leaves behind her.

If only he could imprint this scene in his memory forever.

Mrs. Vandenberg cleared her throat behind him, making him realize he'd been staring. Sovilla seemed stunned. Hadn't she known he was coming?

"Why don't you sit there?" Mrs. Vandenberg motioned to the chair beside Sovilla. "That way you'll both be facing the waterfall. It's especially lovely at sunset."

Isaac would rather admire Sovilla than a sunset, but sitting beside her would be thrilling. A soft gasp escaped Sovilla's lips as he sank into the chair Mrs. Vandenberg had indicated.

His chest ached, and he realized he hadn't taken a deep breath since he'd walked out through the door and onto the patio. In fact, his chest had been constricted since he'd driven up to the house—if you could even call it that. Mansion or castle, maybe? He'd never seen such an elegant home.

After a man had directed him to the garages behind the house and assured Isaac they'd care for his horse, he'd rounded the massive stone building and mounted the curved stone steps to the imposing front door with its lion head knocker. He stood for several minutes vacillating between ringing the bell or heading home to eat supper with his family.

Gathering his courage, he reached over to the gold plate embossed with flowers and leaves, took a deep breath, and pressed the button. Loud gongs like church bells echoed inside the house. Isaac shuffled his feet and waited.

He was about to turn to go when a shadow appeared behind the stained glass sidelight next to the front door.

The ornate brass doorknob rattled, and Mrs. Vandenberg opened the door and greeted him. For a moment, Isaac's nervousness disappeared.

But as she'd led him through the house, he could barely breathe. And now, being here with Sovilla tied his insides into tight knots. What if he made a fool of himself?

Mrs. Vandenberg settled shakily into the chair across from them. "It's such a lovely evening. I'm so glad both of you could come. I know you pray silently. I usually do the same." She bowed her head.

When they lifted their heads, she waved toward the platters of food in the center of the table. "Help yourselves."

Isaac hesitated. Some of the foods arranged on the tray he'd never seen before. He'd wait for Sovilla and Mrs. Vandenberg to start. When Mrs. Vandenberg spread her white linen napkin in her lap, Isaac did the same. Sovilla followed their lead.

They both exhaled slight sighs when Mrs. Vandenberg selected a few items and set them on the small plate in front of her. Isaac chose the same things she had.

As he drew his hand back with his final choice, he brushed Sovilla's arm. Shocks coursed through his body, and he almost dropped the stuffed mushroom onto the pristine white tablecloth. He hoped Sovilla hadn't noticed his reaction, but Mrs. Vandenberg's face crinkled in a knowing smile.

Isaac's face flamed. If she'd seen it, Sovilla must have too. He cut his eyes to the side, where Sovilla was struggling to pick up a tiny squash adorned with a swirl of cheese and a tiny slice of red pepper using silver tongs. Maybe she'd been too busy to pay attention to him.

Mrs. Vandenberg picked up one of the hors d'oeuvres, bit into it, and closed her eyes. "Mmm. Have you tried these figs yet? Amelia uses the best creamy cheese in them. Or, if you like garlic cheese, you'll enjoy that pattypan squash, Sovilla."

Figs. Those were the ones with the walnuts on top. The cheese had been squirted into them so they looked like fancy bakery cupcakes. Isaac tried that first. The sweet, salty, and savory flavors blended on his tongue. Unexpected, but delicious.

Beside him, Sovilla murmured with delight. His heart rate increased at her soft sighs.

They ate in silence until Amelia cleared the table and returned with dinner plates.

"I wasn't sure what you prefer to eat, so I asked Amelia to make chicken cordon bleu, risotto, and braised asparagus. I hope you'll like it."

"It smells wonderful," Sovilla said.

Isaac cut into the chicken breast smothered in sauce, and cheese squirted out. The first bite combined a tangy mustard sauce, smoky ham, and Swiss cheese. He savored the combination. His *mamm* would love this, but she'd never have time to prepare it for twelve children.

Mrs. Vandenberg turned to Sovilla. "How is everything going?"

At Sovilla's long exhale, Isaac sent her a sympathetic glance. It sounded as if she'd been through a rough time. "The operation w-went w-well?"

She nodded. "Very well, but Wilma's fighting the therapy."

Knowing Wilma, Isaac could imagine the tussles.

"I have some ideas that might help. We can talk about it later. It must be hard dealing with all this. You didn't need all this extra stress so soon after your breakup."

Beside him, Sovilla froze.

Breakup? Had she broken up with her boyfriend? Was it permanent or a soon-to-be-repaired disagreement?

Sovilla sat there stunned. Why had Mrs. Vandenberg brought that up? Was she trying to humiliate her? And how did she answer?

If Isaac weren't sitting beside her, she could spill out her shock and heartache to Mrs. Vandenberg. Maybe Sovilla could pretend Isaac wasn't there and answer honestly. Except for the fact that she'd been aware of his every movement, his every breath since the moment he sat next to her. It would be impossible to forget he was listening.

She had to say something. Both of them were staring at her. She hung her head and gazed at the linen napkin on her lap. "It isn't easy," she admitted.

"Being jilted never is."

If Mrs. Vandenberg understood that, why did she have to broadcast that fact to Isaac? It hurt enough to have your boyfriend move on to someone else in only a few weeks. Sovilla would rather not give her new community fodder for gossip.

Not that Isaac would spread rumors, but still . . . He might mention it to his sister, and she might tell a few girlfriends, and then if Ruthie heard, she'd be sure to announce it to everyone.

"I've always found that when God closes a window," Mrs. Vandenberg said, "He opens a door. I'm positive He has someone much better in mind."

Sovilla glanced up in time to catch Mrs. Vandenberg glance at Isaac and flick her head in Sovilla's direction. Was Mrs. Vandenberg trying to encourage him to say something sympathetic? That's the last thing she needed or wanted right now.

"Actually," Sovilla said, "I haven't had much time to think about it. I spend most of my day at the hospital, and yesterday, I spent the whole evening baking dog biscuits."

"Dog b-biscuits?" Isaac's forehead furrowed.

"*Jah.* I wanted recipes that wouldn't compete with what Fern's selling. I found some recipes for organic pet food. I'll be making that along with other baked goods."

"S-Snickers would l-like them."

"I hope so. I'd rather make my own creations than copy someone else's recipes, so I've been experimenting. Would Snickers be willing to test them?"

"You could c-come to the k-kennel."

Mrs. Vandenberg gazed at Isaac fondly. "Did you know Isaac raises Labrador retrievers to work as service dogs?"

A few dogs had been barking in the building behind his house when Sovilla had gone down the hill for the singing. "I didn't know you had dogs. I mean, I knew you had Snickers." Warmth crept up her neck. She lowered her head and pretended to concentrate on cutting her chicken. "I meant when I heard the dogs in the kennel, I didn't realize they were yours."

"I think it's wonderful he does that." Mrs. Vandenberg sounded like a proud parent. "And he also works as a puppy raiser. It takes a special person to do that. Not everyone can bond with a puppy, take it everywhere with them, take it to obedience classes, and then give it up."

Isaac blushed deeper than Sovilla had. Mrs. Vandenberg seemed intent on embarrassing both of them.

"You have to give them up?"

"*J-jah.*"

If Sovilla could sink into the seat cushion, she would.

She'd made a fool of herself again. If he raised service dogs, they'd go to the people who needed them. "Is it hard?"

He nodded. "I g-get attached."

Mrs. Vandenberg was right. Isaac was special. And until now, she hadn't noticed how handsome he was. Probably because she'd been so focused on Henry. She swallowed the lump in her throat. She had to forget about him.

"Are you all right?" Mrs. Vandenberg's question penetrated the fog of sadness closing over Sovilla.

She couldn't answer. She didn't want to lie. Yet she couldn't admit the truth.

Chapter Twenty

The sorrow on Sovilla's face made Isaac long to comfort her. What could he do or say to help? If only he had the right to hold her hand. By shifting his chair a bit, he'd be close enough that her fingers would be only inches from his.

He tightened his grip on his fork. *Neh.* For the first time that night, he yearned to have Snickers sitting between them. He had no business even thinking things like that.

She didn't have a boyfriend, though. Now he didn't need to feel so guilty. Still, if she'd just broken up—*jilted*, Mrs. Vandenberg had said—Sovilla had to be hurting. She wouldn't be ready for another relationship. Maybe not for a long time. Even if she did get over her heartbreak, he doubted she'd want to date him.

He'd been so lost in his thoughts, he'd missed what she and Mrs. Vandenberg were discussing. The word *Tuesday* caught his attention. Mrs. Vandenberg had asked something about the market.

"*Neh*, I can't go in to work on Tuesday," Sovilla said. "Wilma won't be out of the hospital by then. With her refusing to do her therapy, she's progressing more slowly than she should."

Isaac's heart dropped. He'd been counting on driving her. More than counting on it, he'd been longing to, yearning to . . .

"I'll take your place at the hospital for the day so you can go to work as usual." Mrs. Vandenberg didn't sound as if she'd take no for an answer. "I think I can get Wilma to do those exercises."

As swiftly as his heart had plummeted, it soared.

"I don't think anyone can get her to cooperate." Sovilla lifted a forkful of risotto to her mouth.

"I have my ways." Mrs. Vandenberg swirled an asparagus tip through the sauce on her plate.

Isaac silently cheered her on. *Please, convince Sovilla to go to the market.*

Sovilla chewed slowly, and he waited for her response.

"If you really think you can convince her, I'd appreciate your help."

"Good, then it's settled." Mrs. Vandenberg dabbed at the corner of her mouth with her napkin. "You'll go to the market on Tuesday. I'm sure Isaac will be happy to take you, right?" She looked at Isaac.

He'd thought of little else ever since she'd first asked him. He nodded enthusiastically.

Sovilla shook her head. "Wilma will expect me to be there."

Neh, Isaac wanted to say. From what he'd seen of her *aenti*, he suspected she'd prefer Sovilla to keep an eye on the stand.

"I doubt that. Wilma would much rather have you selling pickles." Mrs. Vandenberg had echoed Isaac's thoughts.

"She probably would," Sovilla agreed, "but I wouldn't feel right leaving her alone."

Would he lose his chance altogether?

"I heard Wilma telling you"—Mrs. Vandenberg winced—"she didn't want you around. I'm positive she doesn't mean that. I believe, though, if you skip spending some time with her, you'll find she'll miss you. And maybe she'll even look forward to your visit on Wednesday."

"You might be right," Sovilla conceded as Amelia cleared their dinner plates. "I'll do the market on Tuesday only if you promise to tell me the truth about your visit. If Wilma is upset, I won't do any more market days until she's better."

Isaac hoped Mrs. Vandenberg was right. She usually was. *Dear Lord, please help Sovilla's* aenti *to heal well and quickly.*

"I'm sure it'll be fine." Mrs. Vandenberg's conspiratorial smile at Isaac made it appear as if he'd been the one behind the insistence. He hoped she'd clear up the misunderstanding.

Instead she said, "You've made Isaac very happy. Just look at his smile."

Isaac tried to drag the corners of his lips into a straight line, but they curved up—totally out of his control.

Sovilla had been keenly aware of Isaac beside her, so she didn't follow Mrs. Vandenberg's direction. She focused instead on the hills and trees in the distance, where the setting sun splashed a rainbow of colors across the sky. Blue faded into streaks of salmon, lavender, and apricot. "It's so pretty."

Mrs. Vandenberg craned her neck. "Yes, it is, isn't it? When I gaze at that beauty, I can't understand how anyone could doubt God is real."

A reverent hush fell over them as the sun slid below the horizon and the sky slowly darkened and filled with stars. A deep peace descended like balm on Sovilla's soul. She'd been fighting God's will, refusing to accept that He'd brought her to Lancaster, possibly permanently. She placed Henry and the hurt he'd caused in the Lord's hands. Even Wilma had been brought into her life for a reason. She only needed to trust His leading.

Amelia came out bearing a silver tray edged with flickering votive candles. The center held a cake swirled with chocolate frosting and topped with raspberries. She set it in the center of the table.

A fancy dinner, a candlelit table, a gorgeous sunset, the rippling water, a man close beside her—all hinted at romance. The dreamy atmosphere enveloped Sovilla in its enchantment. And the creaminess of chocolate melting on her tongue added to her bliss. She wished the evening never had to end.

After Amelia cleared the plates, they all sat, quiet and contented, gazing at the stars. The expansiveness of the heavens, the stars sparkling in the blackness, flowed over Sovilla, washing away old hurts and replacing them with new beginnings.

She sat upright in her chair. *New Beginnings.*

Mrs. Vandenberg gazed at her in concern. "Are you all right, dear?"

"I just remembered something." Should she share her *aenti*'s personal secret? Maybe she could ask about New

Beginnings without giving anything away. "Have you ever heard of a place called New Beginnings?"

"Certainly. My charity helped them with construction funds for their new building. And we continue to help various girls. They take in teens who—" Mrs. Vandenberg peered at her across the table. "You don't need their services, do you?"

Beside her, Isaac sucked in a breath.

Grateful for the darkness hiding her burning cheeks, Sovilla managed a strangled "*Neh*, of course not."

The worry lines in Mrs. Vandenberg's face relaxed. "That's a relief."

"So it's still around?" Sovilla persisted.

Wilma had said it closed. Maybe Sovilla could visit and get information.

"Still? It opened rather recently."

Sovilla slumped back in her chair. This must not be the same place. "I thought it had been around for a while."

"The mission itself has been. I believe the present owner's grandmother took girls into her home. Later, Elvira's mother took over and expanded the house. Elvira and her husband built a much larger facility outside of Lancaster."

"Would Elvira have kept the older records?" Sovilla pressed a hand to her mouth. She hadn't intended to ask that question aloud.

"Most likely, I would think. I imagine government agencies would require that." Her eyebrows raised, Mrs. Vandenberg studied Sovilla. "Any special year you were thinking of?"

Staring down at her lap, Sovilla mumbled the year

Wilma had mentioned. Her *aenti* would be furious at her for sharing a closely guarded secret.

"I'm guessing this is for a certain person." The compassion and understanding in Mrs. Vandenberg's eyes made it clear she could be trusted. "Would you like me to make inquiries?"

Sovilla hesitated. She'd prefer to keep it a family matter, but she didn't want to hurt Mrs. Vandenberg's feelings.

"On second thought," Mrs. Vandenberg said, "perhaps it would be better for you to handle the matter yourself." She turned to Isaac. "You know where New Beginnings is, don't you?"

When he nodded, she smiled. "Perfect. I'm sure you wouldn't mind driving Sovilla there on Wednesday."

"S-Sure."

"But Wilma   " Although Sovilla appreciated Mrs. Vandenberg's thoughtfulness, she did have a habit of arranging people's lives.

Mrs. Vandenberg held up a hand. "I'll take care of Wilma. And you can visit her later in the day. Besides, it'll give you an opportunity to test your organic dog biscuits with Isaac's puppies."

Sovilla shook her head. Leave it to Mrs. Vandenberg to connect so many different threads.

Candlelight reflected the hurt look in Isaac's eyes. Did he think she'd been rejecting Mrs. Vandenberg's idea? Maybe he thought she'd shaken her head because she didn't want to spend time with him.

"I'd like to go with you, Isaac." Sovilla cringed inside. In trying to soothe his feelings, her statement bubbled with enthusiasm. She didn't want to give him the wrong idea.

And no one had asked him if he wanted to take her. "If you want to, that is."

"I d-do." Isaac would accept any chance to be around her. He'd love to have her test her dog biscuits at his kennel.

"That's settled." Mrs. Vandenberg dusted her hands together. "Isaac, I'd like to ask one more favor, if I may."

He'd be happy to do whatever she asked. She'd done so much for him.

"I'd rather not bother my driver at this time of night. Would you be willing to drop Sovilla off?"

A favor? Mrs. Vandenberg was doing him a favor. She'd planned this to give him more time with Sovilla. Leanne had been right. Mrs. Vandenberg was a skilled matchmaker.

"I'd b-be happy t-to."

She leaned on her cane and pulled herself to her feet. "I'd love to sit out here longer and talk, but I find I'm rather weary."

Isaac stood. "We should g-go."

"Thank you for having us." Sovilla rose from her chair. "Do you need help?"

"No, thank you, dear. I'll be fine."

They followed her into the house and waited while she locked up. Then she escorted them toward the front door. As they passed a carved wooden panel, she pressed a button. A whooshing noise came from behind the wall. Just before she closed the front door behind them, the panel slid open to reveal an elevator.

Sovilla stopped on the porch. Isaac smiled as she examined

the carved door, the lanterns glowing overhead, the perfectly manicured lawn with its illuminated fountain.

"It's all so beautiful," she said in an awestruck voice.

"I was t-too nervous t-to knock," he admitted.

"I can see why. The driver took me around to the back door. Even that stunned me."

Sovilla stayed beside him as he rounded the mansion and headed for the garages. To his surprise, the buggy waited for them. His horse had been hitched up, and the reins were looped around a decorative metal fence post.

"Do you think she's lonely?" Sovilla asked as she climbed into the buggy.

"P-probably." Mrs. Vandenberg had a cook and a driver and other people who worked for her, but he assumed they all went home at night.

Having Sovilla so close to him left him exhilarated but edgy. If only they were courting. He could barely draw in a breath.

"Can you imagine being all alone at night in a place like that?" she asked.

Isaac shook his head. His mind couldn't stretch that far. With twelve children, their large farmhouse always seemed to be bursting at the seams. You couldn't walk through any room in the house without encountering a family member, a puppy, or visiting friends.

"I guess not," Sovilla said. "Your house must be busy."

"It is." He'd done it. Two words in a row.

Sovilla smiled at him but didn't call attention to it. He liked that she acted as if it were an everyday happening.

With a little thrill in his chest, he flicked the reins to start the horse down the driveway.

"I imagine you always have people around." Sovilla sounded wistful. "I miss being with my family."

Isaac couldn't even fathom what it would be like to be so far from his parents and siblings. And with Wilma in the hospital, she'd be alone. No wonder she'd mentioned Mrs. Vandenberg's loneliness.

He couldn't bear the idea that Sovilla would be lonely. Although he'd like to invite her to stay at his house, he shouldn't do that without checking with Mamm and Daed. Leanne often squeezed a friend or two into the bedroom she shared with three of the younger girls. She'd be happy to have Sovilla as company.

Mamm never minded them inviting friends for meals. Tomorrow was an off-Sunday. Maybe Sovilla would like to spend most of the day with his family. Is that what she'd been hinting?

"Would you l-like to come for d-dinner t-tomorrow?"

She looked startled.

His invitation must have sounded abrupt.

A look of regret crossed her face. "That sounds nice, but the hospital brings Wilma a lunch tray, and I eat with her."

"S-supper, maybe?" Was that being pushy?

"I usually stay with her until bedtime."

Was that a brush-off? He hesitated. "C-come anytime. Mamm l-loves c-company." *And so would I. If it's you.*

"I'd like that." Her words seemed warm and grateful. Or was he reading more into her politeness?

"I'm p-praying for Wilma."

"*Danke.* She could use it. I wish I could get her to do her exercises."

"Mrs. V m-might help."

"True. If anyone can get people to do things, it's Mrs. Vandenberg."

Isaac smiled to himself. She had managed to orchestrate many things, including a romantic dinner, several chances to drive Sovilla, and this ride home under the stars.

Chapter Twenty-One

After the magical night with Mrs. Vandenberg, Sovilla dreaded facing her *aenti*. Wilma would puncture the dreamy bubble Sovilla had floated in ever since. She longed to be headed to Isaac's house for Sunday dinner.

As soon as she entered the room, her *aenti*'s grumpy face drove all thoughts of last night from Sovilla's mind.

"Breakfast here is inedible."

"I can bring food when I come."

"Anything would be better than the slop they serve."

Maybe Wilma's displeasure with the hospital would motivate her. "If you did your exercises, you could go home much sooner," Sovilla pointed out.

"Don't start with the therapy stuff again. I get enough from that girl."

"You need to do it to heal."

"What I need is for you and everyone else to leave me alone."

"Hello." A cheery voice interrupted their squabble.

Mrs. Vandenberg limped toward them carrying a large picnic basket.

"Let me get that for you." Sovilla rushed over and took the basket.

"Thank you, dear." Somehow, by the time Sovilla set the basket on the wide windowsill, Mrs. Vandenberg had managed to maneuver into Sovilla's spot by the bed.

"Good morning, Wilma." Mrs. Vandenberg exuded optimism and determination. "I'm taking over as your coach. You won't bully me the way you do Sovilla."

Wilma crossed her arms and set her jaw. "Nobody's telling me what to do."

"I didn't expect to. I'm hoping your better nature will assert itself."

Wilma's cynical laughter echoed around the room. "My better nature?" she said when she could speak again. "I don't have one."

"Everyone has one. It just requires chipping away at the crusty exterior and"—she paused dramatically—"unlocking the steel door you've put in place to hide your heartache from the world."

"What do you know about that?" Wilma muttered.

"You might be surprised." Mrs. Vandenberg pressed on. "There's one more step to bringing out your better nature, the most important one. But knowing how you feel about talk of God, we'll save that until we've made some inroads on the first two."

"If you think you can come in here and chip away at anything, you're sadly mistaken."

"We'll see about that. But for now, we'll concentrate on getting you walking again."

"You're the perfect coach for that," Wilma mocked. "You can barely hobble."

"I do quite well for a ninety-two-year-old who's recovering from a broken hip." Mrs. Vandenberg's calm reply showed Wilma's barb had no sting. "Is this what you want to walk like at your age?"

Wilma rolled her eyes.

"I'm still determined to coach you, although you might prefer your niece not to be a witness." Mrs. Vandenberg turned to Sovilla. "My driver is waiting for you outside the front door."

"*Neh*, I should stay here."

Her *aenti* pinned her with a *you'd-better-not-leave-me* stare. "Yes, you should."

"*Should?* Do you hear that, Wilma? You both used the word." Mrs. Vandenberg's steely stare outdid Wilma's. "Do you want your niece to stay out of obligation or because she wants to be with you?"

"I want to stay with her." The weakness of Sovilla's words belied her protest.

Wilma's lower lip quivered. Then her face hardened. "Go on, Sovilla. Get out of here. You don't want to be around me. Nobody does."

"I do." Mrs. Vandenberg's crisp words sliced through Wilma's self-pity. "In fact, I'm looking forward to it."

Her *aenti* scowled. She obviously didn't return the sentiment.

"Please don't keep my driver waiting. He'll bring you back later. After Wilma and I have come to an understanding. No telling how long that will take."

Mrs. Vandenberg cut off Wilma's protest and shooed Sovilla from the room. Dazed, Sovilla headed out to the car. What had just happened in there? Mrs. Vandenberg had come in like a whirlwind and turned everything upside down.

Sovilla relaxed back against the seat, her head still spinning. She closed her eyes and prayed Mrs. Vandenberg could convince her *aenti* to cooperate. When she opened them again fifteen minutes later, the car had pulled into the Lantzes' driveway.

"I live on the lane back there." Sovilla didn't understand the driver's mistake. He'd picked her up at the house before.

"I know. My instructions were to bring you here. I understand they're expecting you for Sunday dinner. I'll be back later this afternoon to pick you up and take you to the hospital."

With a hesitant *danke*, Sovilla climbed out of the car.

Before she could head up the hill to her house, the front door banged open, and Leanne rushed toward her. "I'm so glad you're here. So's the rest of the family. We've been waiting for you."

"How did you know I was coming?"

"Mrs. Vandenberg called the phone in the kennel and talked to Isaac." As she chattered, Leanne led Sovilla into the house. "Of course, Isaac said yes to her request. He wanted to have you." Her smile implied a closer relationship than Sovilla had with Isaac. "And we're all happy you could come."

The family had already gathered around the table. Mary Grace smiled shyly as Leanne indicated that Sovilla should slip in beside her sister. Leanne sat on her other side.

"Welcome, Sovilla." The warmth of their *mamm*'s smile included Sovilla as one of their family.

They all prayed and passed around fried chicken, mashed potatoes, green beans, applesauce, and gravy. Although this meal didn't match the elegance of last night's, the food tasted equally delicious.

Everyone made her feel welcome, and soon she was joining in the bantering and teasing. Once, when she smiled over a joke, her gaze met Isaac's. Andrew dug his elbow into Isaac's side, and Sovilla forced herself to look away.

She liked Isaac a lot, but she didn't want his family, especially his brothers, to get the wrong impression. She tried to limit her glances in his direction, but with him sitting almost directly opposite from her, that proved to be difficult.

After the meal, as she helped in the kitchen, Sovilla almost felt as if she were at home with her sisters and Mamm. Oh, how she longed for those family times. Since she'd been at Wilma's, Sovilla had not only missed being with her loved ones, she'd also missed the friendly conversation and laughter. She loved being a part of this large, boisterous family.

Isaac, with Snickers beside him, stood in the kitchen doorway when she finished. "Would you l-like to see the k-kennel?"

Sovilla responded with a smile. She couldn't wait to see it, but if she expressed too much enthusiasm, she worried his brothers would tease him.

Isaac assumed that was a yes. He didn't want to force her if she'd rather stay here.

"You'll love the puppies," Leanne said from behind her. "They're the sweetest things."

"I can't wait to see them."

So she was excited about the dogs, not about spending time with him. Once they left the house, Sovilla's smile blossomed and tugged at Isaac's heart. If only she'd turn that sunshine in his direction.

"*Danke* for letting me see the puppies. I always wanted

a dog, but with Daed being ill, Mamm had too many worries. After he died, we both went to work, so we didn't have time or money for a pet."

"I'm s-sorry."

"That's all right. It's made me appreciate dogs more."

Isaac had intended his *sorry* to be because she'd lost her *daed*. And for all she'd missed. Trying to explain required too many words, so he only bobbed his head and opened the door to the kennel.

He motioned for her to go inside first. Most of the dogs were outside in their runs, but he wanted Sovilla to see the building.

She stared around her, taking everything in. "It's so clean and neat. I'm sure your dogs are happy here."

When he opened the gates to a few of the cages, some of the pups and their mothers scampered in. Sovilla *ooh*ed and *aah*ed, which filled his heart with joy. Not everyone enjoyed being around dogs the way he did.

"How many dogs do you have?" She bent to scratch the mother dog under its chin.

Could he get out a full answer? "Four mamas, thirty p-pups." He'd almost done it.

"That's a lot to care for."

"It is, but I l-love them." If Isaac wanted this to be a real conversation, he needed to speak, not only answer questions. "Most go to b-be guide d-dogs."

Too late, Isaac realized he'd wasted his energy and breath on something she already knew.

"I think that's *wunderbar.*"

His ear tips burning, he lowered himself to the floor and opened his arms to the puppies. Snickers hunkered down beside him.

Sovilla sat next to him and, cooing and sweet-talking,

let the puppies climb and tumble over her lap. He'd dreamed of a day like this. Now that his dream had come true, his heart hammered a delighted song in his chest. He couldn't stop smiling.

"I wish I'd known I was coming to your house. I could have brought them dog biscuits."

"You d-didn't know?"

"*Neh*, Mrs. Vandenberg's driver brought me here instead of to my house. I thought he'd made a mistake." At Isaac's frown, she added, "It was a delightful surprise. Your family is so much fun to be around. And you are too."

Had that last part been an afterthought to avoid hurting his feelings? Isaac weighed her words and tone to see if she'd said it from politeness or interest. Politeness won.

Sovilla asked question after question about the dogs and seemed not to mind his halting or stuttering.

Isaac relaxed enough to practice his techniques, and the conversation flowed even more smoothly. He enjoyed her company, and she even encouraged him to talk about himself.

He hoped she wanted to know more about him because she'd like to get to know him better. He wanted to do the same with her. Taking a deep breath for courage, he asked her a few questions.

They got sidetracked on Mrs. Vandenberg. Sovilla had just begun recounting Mrs. Vandenberg's visit to Wilma's hospital room this morning when Andrew banged open the door.

"Why are you keeping Sovilla all to yourself? The rest of us want a turn to spend time with her."

"Isaac's showing me the puppies. They're so adorable."

Andrew rolled his eyes. "Wouldn't you rather be outside playing baseball? My sisters have been waiting for you."

"I'm sorry. I didn't know . . ." Sovilla appeared torn.

"We can play b-baseball if you want." Isaac would prefer staying here alone with her, but maybe her hesitation had only been good manners. Or perhaps she preferred to stay with the dogs. She did seem to enjoy his puppies.

"Come on, Sovilla," Andrew said. "Let's see if you're as good at baseball as you are at volleyball," he challenged.

"D-do you—"

Andrew butted in before Isaac could ask what she'd prefer. Ignoring Isaac's irritated glare, Andrew beckoned her. "You can be on my team. We'll beat Isaac and Leanne."

Sovilla glanced at Isaac as if asking permission. He shrugged.

"Do you want to play?" she asked him.

"Sure he does," Andrew said. "If he doesn't, he can sit in here with his dogs for company. Everyone's waiting for you, Sovilla."

Rather than responding to Andrew, she turned to Isaac. "The puppies have to go back, don't they?"

"*Jah.*"

"I'll help you."

"Isaac's used to handling the puppies alone." Impatience edged Andrew's tone. "We can start warming up."

"In a minute. First, I'll help Isaac."

"Hurry." Andrew banged out the door.

Sovilla helped Isaac put the puppies back in their pens and refill their water dishes. She didn't seem to be in any hurry to join Andrew. That eased a little of Isaac's disappointment at losing his time alone with her.

"*Danke,*" he said when they finished. He'd been glad for her help, and he especially appreciated that she'd made Andrew wait.

"It was fun. When I have time, I'll bring some dog biscuits over to test them."

"The p-pups would l-like that." And so would he.

Before they could start playing, Mrs. Vandenberg's car pulled into the driveway. Sovilla had been looking forward to the game. She wanted to watch Isaac bat and pitch. He'd been a standout in volleyball. She expected he'd be the same in baseball.

Andrew groaned. "I was planning on winning with you on my team. You'll have to visit us again, Sovilla." With a sly look at Isaac, he said, "Don't forget, next time you come, you're on my team."

Isaac's sad expression as she left stayed with her the whole way back to the hospital. Having had a break for fun and relaxation made it doubly hard to return to her *aenti*'s room.

To her surprise, Wilma's red, sweaty face revealed she'd done her exercises—or at least tried.

"You did your therapy?" Sovilla directed her question more to Mrs. Vandenberg than to her *aenti*.

"You mean the torture sessions?" Wilma's words dripped with sarcasm.

"You survived. That's what counts." Mrs. Vandenberg studied Sovilla. "You look rested. We need to be sure to send you home for a break like that every day." With her back to Wilma, Mrs. Vandenberg winked at Sovilla.

"*We?*" Wilma's voice rose to a screech. "Who put you in charge of ordering my niece around?"

"Calm down. No need for a heart attack." Mrs. Vandenberg spoke in the calm, superior tone of a mother to a two-year-old having a tantrum. "Although if you choose to have a heart attack, this is the best place to do it."

Wilma sat there sputtering.

"Now that you're back, dear," Mrs. Vandenberg said to Sovilla, "I'll head home. I haven't had this much exercise in years."

Sovilla walked her to the door. In a low voice, so her *aenti* wouldn't hear, she confided, "I had a lot of fun. *Dank*—thank you for doing that. And I appreciate you getting my *aenti* to do her exercises."

"You deserve it. Plan for another break tomorrow." Raising her voice, Mrs. Vandenberg said, "I'll see you both tomorrow at ten."

"You don't have to do that."

"I believe God has called me to do this." She leaned close so she could whisper, "I'll make arrangements for Isaac to take you to—" She motioned in Wilma's direction with a slight head tilt.

Sovilla couldn't leave Wilma two days in row. Before she could protest, Mrs. Vandenberg hurried away.

Chapter Twenty-Two

As she'd promised, Mrs. Vandenberg showed up at ten. "Time for you to go, Sovilla." Mrs. Vandenberg waved toward the door so vigorously, she almost lost her balance. Grabbing the doorjamb, she righted herself and leaned heavily on her cane.

"What gives you the right to tell my niece what to do?" Wilma demanded. "You're bossy."

Mrs. Vandenberg nodded as if unperturbed. "Some people have called me that, including you at least three times yesterday. On the bright side, I get things done."

Wilma's low growl didn't bode well for the exercise session.

Sovilla was torn between staying to keep the peace or leaving Isaac waiting. She decided both women could stand up for themselves, although Mrs. Vandenberg seemed to have the advantage. Sovilla hurried to the elevator.

Instead of Isaac's buggy, Mrs. Vandenberg's driver waited. Sovilla couldn't help being disappointed. She'd looked forward to spending time with Isaac. But when the door opened, she saw that Isaac and Snickers were sitting in the back seat.

The driver smiled. "Mrs. Vandenberg asked me to pick up your young man. She thought you might want company."

Her young man? Sovilla didn't dare to look at Isaac. She hoped he didn't think she'd told Mrs. Vandenberg that. Riding home in a man's buggy after a singing usually signaled you were dating, but Isaac had been forced to take her home last night. That didn't count.

"I—I hope you d-don't mind." Isaac's red face must match hers.

"*Neh*, I'm glad you're along."

He exhaled a breath. Had he been expecting her to be upset? For some reason, that made her heart rejoice.

During the ride, she described the confrontation between her *aenti* and Mrs. Vandenberg. Isaac and she laughed so much that her stomach ached. Having fun together took her mind off the errand she'd soon face.

When they arrived at New Beginnings, Sovilla sobered. She stood on the sidewalk outside the building and whispered a prayer.

Please help me to find out the truth for Wilma.

"Nervous?" Isaac asked.

"A little. I'm glad I didn't tell Wilma about this, in case we can't find out information."

"I've b-been praying."

"Me too." Sovilla tried to calm her nerves, although being so close to Isaac made her pulse unsteady. "All right. Let's go in."

He accompanied her to the front desk, but then he and

Snickers stepped back. He remained near enough to be supportive, but in a way that let her take the lead.

All around them, pregnant girls—Amish, Mennonite, and *Englisch*—sat in a living room to the left, chatting with one another or texting on their phones. A Mennonite girl had curled up on the window seat to read a book, and an Amish girl sat in a rocker cradling a newborn.

Sovilla tried to picture a young Wilma among these girls. Had she been tense and anxious like the brunette on the couch or downcast like the blonde staring at the baby across from her? Had she been fearful? Nervous? Uncertain?

Her heart went out to these girls, separated from their families. Poor Wilma. She'd gone through all this alone.

"Hello." A cheerful Mennonite woman entered and slid behind the desk. "I'm Elvira Hess." She looked from Sovilla to Isaac and back again. "How can I help you?"

Ach, did she think Sovilla and Isaac were in trouble? Sovilla wished she'd come alone. For a moment, embarrassment kept her silent.

Elvira Hess waited with a kind and patient welcoming expression. Sovilla hoped Elvira's mother and grandmother had appeared this nice and caring.

"I, um, I'm hoping you can help me."

"We'd be happy to." She picked up a pen and bent to unlock a file drawer.

"*Neh.*" Sovilla had to stop Elvira before she tried to register them. "I'm here about my *aenti*."

Elvira blinked. "Your aunt?" She appeared thoroughly confused.

"My *aenti* had a baby at New Beginnings. She's in the hospital now, and I wanted her son to get her inheritance." The words had come out in a jumble.

Elvira looked troubled. "She gave her baby up for adoption and would like to find him before she dies?"

"*Jah*, but—"

Before Sovilla could explain her *aenti* wasn't dying, Elvira started into a long explanation of the legal rights of children and their adoptive parents. Too concerned about her mistake, Sovilla barely took it all in.

When Elvira finished her long speech, she asked, "Do you understand?"

The only thing Sovilla had gotten was that it sounded almost impossible to find a child's identity once he'd been adopted. "Is there any way we can find out about her little boy?"

"We guarantee confidentiality to adoptive parents and their children. Some have been told they're adopted. Others have not. We don't want to disrupt the child's life."

"He's an adult." Sovilla gave her the birth date.

"So he'd be thirty. In Pennsylvania, adoptees over eighteen are allowed to access their birth records. Perhaps he's done so."

"Wouldn't he have found my *aenti* by now?"

"Some children never contact their birth parents. They just want to solve the mystery of their heritage."

"Is there a way to find out if he got his records?"

"There are many online forums now where people can search for and meet their birth families." Elvira glanced at Sovilla's *kapp* and dress. "I guess you wouldn't be doing a computer search."

"*Neh*."

Isaac spoke up. "Mrs. V."

Of course. What a brilliant idea!

* * *

Sovilla turned to him with shining eyes. "*Gut* idea."

He didn't want to interrupt her conversation, but he wished she'd keep looking at him like that.

Elvira Hess attracted Sovilla's attention again. "Now that I think about it, an Internet search might not work. My mother ran the home then. She always tried to place Amish children with Amish adoptive parents and Mennonite babies with Mennonite families."

"He'd be Amish?"

Isaac suspected that might upset Wilma. She'd left the Amish herself.

"Unless my mom couldn't find an Amish family to take him."

"If he went to an Amish family, I doubt we'll find him online," Sovilla pointed out. "Is there a way we can get his name?"

"You might try a search angel."

"What?"

"They're people who help adoptees find their birth families. They might be able to locate an adopted child."

This was sounding more and more complicated. Isaac wanted to simplify it for Sovilla. He'd remained silent most of the time, but he had to speak up. "C-could we ask your m-mother?"

"Like I said, we abide by strict rules so as not to interfere in an adoptee's life."

"My *aenti* wouldn't interfere in his life," Sovilla said. "I only want to make sure he inherits her property."

"Tell you what," Elvira said. "Why don't you give me your aunt's name and the child's birth date? My mother only took in a few teens at a time and often placed them in the community. If she knows who adopted this baby, she might be able to tell you if he and his parents would want any contact with his birth mother."

She removed a tablet from a drawer and slid it over to Sovilla. After Sovilla printed the information on it, she started to slide it back.

"Phone n-number," Isaac suggested.

That earned him another bright smile before she turned back around and jotted down her name. Then she faced him again and whispered, "I wish I knew Mrs. Vandenberg's number. If the answer's no, I don't want Wilma to get the call."

He took the pen from her and wrote his number. "That's my k-kennel."

Her grateful look provided more than enough reward.

Elvira Hess took the paper. "Either my mother or I will call to let you know whether or not the boy—or I suppose I should say *man*—should be contacted."

"*Danke.*" Sovilla turned to go, but stopped and faced Elvira again. "I don't know if it'll help, but my *aenti* came from Ohio."

"It might. I'll make a note of it."

Sovilla waited until Elvira had added that to the note.

As they walked to the car, she added, "I'm so glad you were there. *Danke*. The kennel number was a great idea."

"I'm happy it h-helped."

"I should have asked for Elvira's mother's name. Maybe we could have contacted her ourselves. Do you think she'll be able to help?"

"I h-hope so." If her mother only took in a few girls, maybe she'd remember Wilma. "We c-could pray."

"Another *gut* idea."

Making Sovilla happy filled him with joy. He hoped she'd like their next destination.

When they pulled in front of his house, the driver said to Sovilla, "I'll be back in two hours to take you to the hospital."

Her eyebrows rose. "I planned to go back now."

"I have my instructions."

Noticing Isaac's grin, she asked the driver, "Who asked you to do this?"

He inclined his head in Isaac's direction before he drove off. Snickers stood patiently waiting as they talked.

"We n-never played b-baseball."

"You got me over here to play baseball when I should be visiting my *aenti*?"

"Mrs. V and I w-want you to have f-fun."

"I feel guilty enjoying myself when Wilma's in the hospital."

"Mrs. V n-needs more t-time."

"And she asked you to keep me busy?"

He nodded. "I v-volunteered. And Mamm w-wants to f-feed you."

Sovilla planted her hands on her hips. "I can't eat at your house again"—a mischievous smile crossed her lips at his disappointment—"unless you do something for me."

He'd do anything, anything at all. "What?"

"Help me find my way back home. I don't want to get lost in the trees again."

"You're g-going home?" He'd been counting on enjoying the next two hours together. And she wanted to leave.

* * *

Sovilla had only planned to tease Isaac, but he seemed so upset, she gave him a hint. "I need to get something from the house."

He perked up a little, but he still seemed a bit glum.

Maybe when he saw what she was getting, he'd be a little happier. And she wanted to thank him for coming with her this morning.

As they headed into the backyard and past the kennel, his dogs started barking. "I'll be b-back," he called to them.

With Isaac and Snickers to guide her, the trip through the woods only took a short while.

"Maybe I should mark this path," she said when they emerged on the other side.

He looked pleased. "*Gut* idea. I'll d-do it on the way b-back."

Sovilla stared at the steep incline. Coming down this slope was a lot easier than going up. Snickers started up the hill with Isaac, but she searched for an easier path.

Isaac turned around. He took a deep breath. "Are you coming?"

He'd said a whole sentence. Did he even realize it? Maybe she shouldn't call attention to it.

"I'm worried I might fall."

"Look for r-rocks." He pointed to the narrow outcroppings he'd used. When she still hesitated, he climbed back down and took her hand.

The warmth of his fingers wrapped around hers sent tingles through her. This had been a mistake. In addition to struggling for breath, she might not be able to keep her balance with her senses whirling. Only the thought of tumbling down the hill kept her upright.

I can't fall. I won't fall, she chanted to herself the whole way up.

As soon as they were on level ground, she drew in a breath and disengaged her hand. But she missed the gentle pressure of his hand and the protection it provided.

His breathing was as ragged as hers. Pulling her up behind him must have winded him.

"The rest of the way is flat," she said with both relief and regret.

Was it her wishful thinking, or did he look disappointed?

When they got to the house, she led him into the kitchen. She smiled when his eyes widened.

"When d-did you have t-time to do this?"

She'd gotten up at four this morning and baked one pie after another. The granola and dog treats she'd made in the evenings or before going into the hospital in the mornings. "In my spare time."

She picked up a few plastic bags. "These are the dog biscuits that broke. I've labeled them so we can see which ones your dogs prefer."

Snickers whined and nosed Isaac's leg.

Sovilla laughed. "Is it all right to give her one?"

"I need to d-do it."

She held out two pieces. Their hands brushed, and sparks sizzled through her. Sovilla almost jerked back, but she forced herself to drop them into his open palm. She only hoped Isaac hadn't sensed her reaction.

A jolt zinged through Isaac as her fingers grazed his palm. He'd struggled to breathe coming up the hill while holding her hand, but the intensity of this touch, of being so near her, constricted his chest.

Sovilla was speaking, but her words didn't make sense to his jumbled mind.

"Huh?"

She repeated herself, "Can you see which one Snickers takes first?"

Her words sounded a little shaky, but maybe that was only his own unsteadiness. He held the pieces out, one on each hand.

Snickers sniffed both, then went for the hand Sovilla had touched. He didn't blame his dog. Definitely the most desirable. Snickers's rough, moist tongue lapped up the broken biscuit. Isaac regretted holding the treat in that hand.

"Looks like she prefers this one." Sovilla marked the label on the bag.

Snickers snapped up the other one.

"She l-likes both." Isaac needed to get out of the kitchen. They should get back so they'd have time to play baseball.

Sovilla picked up a pie. "You can carry this one. I'll take that one."

"What for?"

"Dessert. I hope everyone likes blueberry."

"You d-don't have to d-do that."

"I want to. Your *mamm* will be feeding me twice. The least I can do is bring something."

"But your m-market stand?" If she gave away the pies, she wouldn't have them to sell.

"I can make more. Let's hurry. I don't want to make your family wait for their dinner again."

Isaac wouldn't mind them waiting all day if it meant

spending more time alone with her. With regret, he shut the door behind him and followed her to the hill. He also had one more regret—he couldn't hold her hand on the way down while they both were carrying pies.

Chapter Twenty-Three

The next week passed with almost the same daily schedule. On the days the market was closed, Mrs. Vandenberg arrived at the hospital at ten and sent Sovilla off to spend time with Isaac and his family. Sovilla always brought the Lantzes one of the treats she'd baked. And she enjoyed helping Isaac in the kennels.

On market days, Isaac arrived early, helped her pack the baked goods into the back of his buggy, and assisted her with unloading and setting up when the auction schedule permitted.

They had such good conversations on the way to work that Sovilla never wanted the trip to end. And she loved being around Isaac's family too. His *mamm* treated Sovilla like one of her children. She especially appreciated the hugs, because she'd missed those from Mamm.

"Are you all r-right?" Isaac stared at Sovilla with concern in his eyes as she headed for the Bentley.

"I always hate leaving here. It feels so much like home. That makes me miss Mamm and my sisters so much." The ache increased every time she left Isaac's house.

"I'm sorry. It must b-be hard."

Sovilla tried to smile, but her lips twisted.

With a sigh, she climbed into the car. She hadn't told Isaac, because she'd been trying not to dwell on it, but the doctor had announced that Wilma would be going home in a day or two. She'd still ride to work with him, because Wilma couldn't drive for four weeks. But once her *aenti* came home, the visits to his house would end.

When Sovilla reached Wilma's room, Mrs. Vandenberg and her *aenti* were sparring.

"You're not going to blame me for your slow recovery, Wilma Mast. If you'd listened to Sovilla and done what she said, you'd be home already."

Wilma's crossed arms and pouty lips showed they'd reached an impasse.

Sovilla hoped her happy "Hello" might thaw the chilly atmosphere.

"Did you have a good time?" Mrs. Vandenberg asked.

Seeing her *aenti*'s scowl, Sovilla tempered the smile that longed to break free. "It was nice." She hoped Mrs. Vandenberg could tell it had been much more than that.

"I'm glad." Mrs. Vandenberg winked and gathered her huge handbag. "I hope you'll have just as much fun the rest of the day."

She shuffled to the door. "Oh, in case Wilma forgets to tell you, the doctor says she can go home on Wednesday."

"I'm perfectly capable of making my own announcements, Liesl Vandenberg."

"Then maybe you should explain to your niece why you didn't go home in a week the way you should have, Wilma Mast." With that parting shot, Mrs. Vandenberg shut the door behind her.

Sovilla didn't need her *aenti*'s explanation. Wilma had not healed as well or as quickly as she should mainly because refusing to do her therapy had prolonged her stay.

"That woman," Wilma fumed.

"She's been kind enough to come in and serve as your coach." If Mrs. Vandenberg hadn't taken over, Wilma most likely would be heading to rehab this week rather than going home.

"*Humph.* I'd rather have you. She's the bossiest person ever."

"At least you only have one more day here."

"Thank heavens for that."

Wilma might be grateful, but Sovilla wasn't. Although she was glad Wilma had healed well, her *aenti*'s homecoming meant no Wednesday dinner and baseball game with Isaac's family.

"Well, that news made you glum," Wilma said. "I guess I'll be putting an end to your fun and games and whatever else you had going on."

Jah, that was for sure. With Wilma around, Sovilla'd have no time for fun and games. No time for Isaac.

When Isaac picked up Sovilla the next morning, he missed her bright smile and bouncy steps. As they loaded up her baked goods, she looked miserable.

"Are you all r-right?" he asked.

Sovilla fiddled with stacking the containers of pies and didn't answer. Usually she responded to every question. Had something happened with Wilma?

"How's your *aenti*?" He couldn't take any joy in the full sentence. Not when Sovilla was unhappy.

"She's doing well. Mrs. Vandenberg got Wilma to do her therapy, so she'll be discharged tomorrow."

That sounded great. Why wasn't Sovilla excited? "What's wrong?" Another triumph of speech he couldn't celebrate. Not while he worried about her.

With a heavy sigh, she said, "I won't be able to come to your house on our days off anymore."

No wonder she was upset. Now he was too. He hadn't thought about that. But her reaction offered a ray of hope. She'd miss being with him—or at least with his family.

"You'll still n-need a ride?"

"Until Wilma can drive. The doctor said four weeks."

At least they'd have that. Once Wilma returned to work, Isaac wouldn't be able to stop by the stand several times a day.

"Isaac?" Sovilla squeezed in the last container. "I hope you don't mind me saying this, but you haven't been stuttering as much. You even had two sentences where you didn't do it at all."

She'd noticed. "I d-don't mind." He wished he'd tried harder with that one, but he'd been so elated she'd been paying attention. "I'm practicing a l-lot." Every spare minute when he wasn't with her or with his family he'd been reading aloud with the gravel in his mouth or working on his breathing.

"I'm sure it's not easy."

Deep breath. "It's not." But it was worth it. She was his inspiration.

Several nights later, as Isaac hugged the last pup and put him back in the pen, the phone rang. He hurried to answer it.

"Is Sovilla Mast there?" a woman asked.

Sovilla? Only one person would be calling for her on this phone. Elvira Hess.

"She's not here. Could I take a message?"

"I'm afraid not. I need to speak to her or her *aenti*."

He was too startled to take a breath. "C-can she c-call you back?"

"Of course." Elvira rattled off her phone number. "I'll be up for another hour or so."

Isaac had nothing to write on, so he committed the number to memory. This time he tried harder to control his breath and his words. "I'll have her c-call you."

The minute he hung up, Isaac checked all the pens to be sure he'd secured the locks. "C-come, Snickers," he said as he shut the door and raced up the hill.

Sovilla wouldn't mind him coming so late, would she? She'd probably want to return the call as soon as she could.

Sovilla had just doused the propane lamp in the kitchen when someone pounded on the door. All the surfaces in the dining room and kitchen were covered with pies or baked goods either packaged or cooling.

Should she answer at this time of night?

The banging came again. "Sovilla!"

Isaac?

She raced to the back door and pulled it open.

"H-hurry! Elvira Hess c-called."

"She did?"

Isaac beckoned for her to come, and she stepped out onto the porch and closed the door. Then he reached for her hand and tucked it into his before dashing down the hill, Snickers on his other side. Sovilla managed to keep up with them, and they reached the kennel breathless and laughing.

He turned on the large flashlight he used at night and led her to the phone. He still hadn't let go of her hand. Sovilla's heart banged against her ribs, and not only from the exertion. She regretted that she'd need both hands for the phone.

With puppies yipping in the background, he recited the numbers as she dialed and then stood silently beside her. He tensed when she did, and his breathing mirrored hers. And after the call ended, she turned to him with tears in her eyes.

"Elvira's mother remembered Wilma, and they placed her baby with an Amish schoolteacher who couldn't have children. That mother has adopted several other children since then."

"They know her n-name."

Sovilla nodded. "And she said her son wants to meet Wilma."

"That's g-great!"

"I guess." Sovilla had been waiting and praying for this call. Now that it had come, nausea rose inside.

Wilma had told her to forget it. What if she'd really meant that? What if she got angry about people going behind her back? What if she refused to meet her son?

"What's wrong?" Isaac's quiet question enveloped Sovilla in sympathy.

"Wilma might say no."

"She c-could, but—"

"I'd feel terrible if her son has gotten his hopes up. I can't even imagine how it would hurt him."

"But you p-prayed."

"You're right. God helped us find him for a reason.

We'll have to trust Him." Peace flooded through Sovilla. This was part of God's plan, no matter how it turned out. "I dread telling Wilma."

"I d-don't blame you."

Isaac's rueful expression comforted her a little. If only she could have him there for support when she broke the news to her *aenti.* Unfortunately, Isaac's presence would only make the situation worse.

As Sovilla stared into his eyes, her pulse picked up its beat. All thoughts of Wilma fled, and only the two of them existed within the small circle of light from the flashlight. Darkness surrounded them. Except for the soft snuffling and shuffling of sleeping puppies, they were alone.

Isaac inhaled. "Sovilla?" He fought the urge to lean in and touch his lips to hers. As much as he desired it, he shouldn't. But he couldn't step back, step away from her.

"I should go." Sovilla's words, harsh and abrupt, hung in the air between them. She stepped back into the shadows.

His spirits sank. She must have read the feelings in his eyes. He'd scared her with his intensity. They weren't courting. He'd never asked her on a date. How could he?

As hard as he tried, he'd never be able to complete a full sentence without stuttering. He'd be much too nervous. Even if he could, how could he marry? His family needed all the money he made. Dating implied a commitment. One he couldn't make. He had no way to buy a house or support a wife and a family.

"Isaac?"

Her small, frightened voice made him long to take her

hand. To protect her, to care for her. He had no right do any of those.

"The hill's n-not safe at n-night." He didn't want anything to happen to her. "I'll h-hitch up the team."

"I don't want you to do that. I can go alone."

"*NEH!*" exploded from his lips.

She leapt back and stared at him with wide, wary eyes.

"I d-didn't mean t-to scare you." An explanation of his concern and need to keep her safe seemed impossible. Putting together the words without stuttering . . .

"I appreciate you worrying about me, but I don't want you to hitch up the team to drive less than a mile. Now that I've been up and down twice, I think I can do it."

He shook his head. "Too d-dangerous."

Motioning for her to follow him, he exited the building. A crescent moon hung in the sky overhead, illuminating her with watery light. Sovilla looked even more beautiful out here than she had in the flashlight beam.

As he drove her home, he had no control over the galloping hoofbeats of his heart.

Chapter Twenty-Four

All day long, Sovilla wrestled her mind back to her customers, but that evening's meeting loomed large. It had been more than a week since they'd found out about Wilma's son. Mrs. Vandenberg had made the arrangements to drive David to Wilma's house that evening.

Sovilla questioned Mrs. Vandenberg's advice to wait to tell her *aenti*. Mrs. Vandenberg's wisdom had been valuable in so many ways, but not letting Wilma know until David was already on his way seemed unfair—to her *aenti* and to David. What if her *aenti* balked or refused to see her son?

She didn't want to dash David's expectations. If he'd gotten his hopes up and Wilma turned her back on him, it would be horrible.

"Are you all r-right?" Isaac asked when he came to take her home from the market.

"*Neh.* I still haven't told Wilma yet. I have to do that when I get home. Mrs. Vandenberg plans to pick up David in two hours."

"Do you want c-company?"

"Would you come with me?" Maybe having another

person there would make Wilma less volatile. "You can stay for supper."

"I'd be g-glad to."

Sovilla could have hugged him. She fidgeted during the whole ride and looked up in surprise when Isaac pulled into his driveway.

"I'll t-tell Mamm."

"Not about Wilma."

"*Neh.* About s-supper."

Snickers lifted her head from the back seat and whined.

"Stay," Isaac commanded.

A few minutes later, Leanne rushed out and greeted her. "I'll take care of the horse and Isaac's chores and the puppies."

"I didn't mean to keep him from all his work."

"Don't worry about it. Isaac's so excited to be going with you." Leanne laughed. "Looks like you are too. You make a *gut* couple."

A couple? Isaac had never said anything to indicate that, although he had stared at her from time to time and made her wonder.

Leanne leaned in and patted Sovilla's hand. "Don't worry. He's shy, but he likes you."

Isaac came up behind his sister in time to hear the end of her sentence. *Likes you?* Who had she been referring to? Him? Or someone else?

He shot his sister a warning side-eye.

She giggled. "Sorry, Isaac, but you know it's true."

"What is?" His face on fire, he spoke stiffly, shooting her a *don't-give-away-my secrets* stare. "Are you r-ready to g-go, Sovilla?"

She climbed out and headed into the trees with him. When they reached the hill, he hesitated. He wanted to take her hand, but if Leanne had said what he suspected . . .

Sovilla, her cheeks pink, held out her hand. "Would you help me?"

He reached for her hand, a song in his heart. She wanted him to guide her. The warmth of her small, delicate hand in his did strange things to his insides. Stepping carefully, he led her up one outcropping at a time, grateful for this opportunity to protect her.

When they neared the flat ground, she pulled her hand from his. "I don't want Wilma to worry."

He nodded but had trouble concealing his disappointment. Of course, they couldn't go into the house holding hands. Even dating couples shouldn't do that. But Isaac reveled in the memory of her hand in his.

After they climbed the stairs to the back porch, Sovilla halted and stood on the top step with her eyes closed, drawing in deep breaths. "This won't be easy."

"Should we p-pray?"

"*Gut* idea."

They both bowed their heads, and Isaac asked the Lord to give Sovilla courage and to help Wilma to accept the news. He also prayed for David. This had to be hard for him too.

When he lifted his head, Sovilla had a slight smile. "Thanks for praying. It helps to have you here with me."

If his heart had been full before when she'd offered him her hand, it now overflowed.

"I guess I should go in and get this over with." As she turned the doorknob, her hand shook a little.

He wished he had the right to close his hand over hers. Staying as close to her as he dared, he followed her into the kitchen, through the dining room, and out to the living room, where Wilma was reclined in a chair with her feet propped up.

"How did everything go today?" Sovilla injected a cheery note into her strained voice.

Isaac again prayed for God's peace and calm, for Sovilla as well as Wilma.

Wilma grumbled something. As Sovilla crossed the living room and invited Isaac to sit beside her on the sofa, Wilma's eyes narrowed. "What's he doing here?"

Isaac stopped. Should he go or stay? He didn't want to make things worse for Sovilla.

Isaac looked ready to flee, and Sovilla silently pleaded with him to stay. Having him here would give her added strength.

"We, um, I have something to tell you." Sovilla twisted her hands in her lap.

Isaac shifted uneasily under Wilma's hostile glare.

"I knew it." Wilma's tone rose triumphantly. "Didn't I warn you about this? I never should have left you alone while I was in the hospital." She rubbed her forehead.

"*Neh, neh.*" Sovilla was horrified. Her face blazing, she couldn't bear to look at Isaac. Wilma had shamed both of them.

With a skeptical expression, Wilma examined their faces. "You're both blushing, so you must be guilty."

More than anything, Sovilla wished she'd never invited Isaac to accompany her. He didn't deserve to be humiliated. Embarrassment kept her tongue-tied. She had to say something to stop her *aenti*'s accusations. But what?

Please, Lord, give me the courage and strength to do this.

Wilma opened her mouth, but before she could speak, Sovilla cut her off. "This is about you."

"Me?" Wilma scoffed. "Trying to change the subject from your wrongdoing?"

Sovilla prayed she'd be able to do this in a gentle way. She regretted asking Isaac to come along. At the time, her only concern had been to have an ally. She should have thought about Wilma's privacy.

It was too late now to change that.

Beside her, Isaac shifted uneasily. "Maybe I should g-go."

Had he sensed her unspoken concern? She hoped her weak smile expressed her gratitude.

"Yes, you certainly should." Wilma sounded as if she'd push him out the door if he didn't.

"Come back later," she whispered.

"You'll come back at your peril. Sovilla will not be going anywhere tonight."

Sovilla tried to convey with her eyes that she wanted him to return with Mrs. Vandenberg. His nod and supportive smile told her he'd gotten her message.

"Good riddance," Wilma said loudly enough to be heard just before Isaac closed the door behind himself. "Now what is this little drama all about?"

Her voice trembling, Sovilla began haltingly, "Remember in the hospital . . . right before surgery? You said, well . . . you wanted me to share the . . . house, you know, the will."

Wilma's face purpled and swelled until Sovilla feared she'd have a heart attack. "I told you to forget that," she thundered. "Don't you ever dare to talk about that again."

Sovilla bit her lower lip. "I have to."

"No, you don't. Erase it from your memory. I never said anything."

"I can't forget it. Because we found your son."

The swollen purple balloon of Wilma's face deflated into ashen, saggy flesh. "You what?" Her words, low and unbelieving, came out shaky. In her eyes, fear fought with longing.

"His name is David Riehl."

Wilma's chins wobbled. "David?" Her eyes damp, she stared off into the distance. Then her voice melted into tenderness. "That was one of the names I picked for him."

Sovilla blinked back tears. "He lives in Honeybrook, and—" Sovilla paused, hoping this wouldn't come as too much of a shock. "Mrs. Vandenberg will be picking him up and bringing him here in about an hour."

"No, no. He can't come here. I don't want him to see me like this."

"I'm sure Mrs. Vandenberg will tell him you had an operation."

"Not that. My clothes. My dress," she wailed.

"You look fine." Yesterday, Wilma had started putting on regular dresses rather than loose housedresses. "Smooth down the skirt. That's a pretty color on you."

Wilma brushed at the wrinkles on her dress, then ran a hand over her head. "My hair's a mess."

"I'll run up and get your brush and mirror."

When Sovilla returned, Wilma was dabbing at her eyes. "You shouldn't have done this. I told you not to."

"You don't want to meet him?"

"No. Yes. I don't know." She tilted the mirror with one hand and tugged the brush through her short hair with the other. Both hands trembled. "I can't do this. Why didn't you give me more time?"

Sovilla took the brush from her *aenti* and smoothed the hair around her face. Then Sovilla slipped behind the chair to brush the rest. Plucking the mirror from Wilma's hand so she didn't have time to examine and criticize the results, Sovilla said, "I'll run these upstairs and then straighten the living room."

"Ack! The house is a mess."

Sovilla ignored the yelps. She'd cleaned the downstairs thoroughly before she'd left for the market this morning, so the only things out of place were a few items Wilma had disturbed. Since her *aenti* rarely left her chair, *redding* up wouldn't take long.

"Why did you do this to me?" Wilma moaned.

"I can call Mrs. Vandenberg and tell her not to come."

"Don't you dare." Then her tone softened. "What if if David was counting on meeting me? We can't disappoint him."

When Sovilla reached the bottom of the stairs, Wilma was muttering, "Why would he want to meet an old hag like me?" Her face crumpled. "He won't want anything to do with a mother who abandoned him."

Sovilla wasn't sure if she should be eavesdropping, but she wanted to ease some of her *aenti*'s fears. "Mrs. Vandenberg said David is eager to meet you."

"Probably to scream at me for messing up his life."

"He's not upset at you." Sovilla picked up two crossword puzzle books, a novel, a deck of cards, and the channel changer and slid them into a drawer.

"You don't know that. He has to be harboring lots of unresolved anger."

"For what? Once he hears your story, he'll understand you had no choice."

Wilma twisted her hands in her lap. “I can’t tell him that. I won’t be able to speak.”

“You’ve never had any trouble with talking.”

“Sincc when did you become such a smart mouth?”

Since a few minutes ago. Sovilla had to do something to distract her *aenti* from her defeated attitude. She straightened the doilies on the backs of chairs, fluffed the sofa pillows, and took an empty water glass to the kitchen.

“Why, oh, why did you do this?” Wilma’s cry trailed off as the doorbell rang. “He’s here. What am I going to do?”

“Just be yourself.” Maybe that wasn’t the wisest advice.

Sovilla headed for the door.

Chapter Twenty-Five

Sovilla's gaze went first to Isaac, standing on the stoop with Snickers beside him. "*Danke,*" she murmured before turning to greet Mrs. Vandenberg and the tall, thin Amish man standing beside her.

"This is David," Mrs. Vandenberg said. "David, this is your cousin, Sovilla."

When he turned toward her, a genuine smile replaced the nervous tic by his mouth. "Nice to meet you."

"Don't keep everyone standing on the doorstep, Sovilla," Wilma called from behind her.

"Welcome. Come in." Sovilla opened the door wider.

Then tension in Wilma's face dissolved into amazement. "Eli," she said in a soft, tender voice as David took off his straw hat.

Crushing his hat against his chest, he cleared his throat. "I'm David."

"I know. You look just like . . ." The tears brimming in her eyes flowed down her cheeks. She clenched her hands in her lap. "I never dreamed . . ."

"It's nice to meet you," David said in a husky voice.

Wilma nodded, obviously too overcome to speak.

Sovilla waved Mrs. Vandenberg to a sturdier, more upright chair that would support her. Isaac sat where Sovilla indicated and patted the cushion beside him. Snickers leapt up and snuggled close to him.

"Get that beast off—" Wilma's screech dropped into a lower register, but the tension in her words revealed she could barely control her fury. "I mean, please don't let the dog sit on the sofa."

She glanced toward David, but he didn't appear to notice. He was helping Mrs. Vandenberg into the chair.

"I'm s-sorry." Isaac patted the floor beside his feet. "D-down, Snickers."

Sovilla sank onto the cushion beside him. "I'm sorry too," she whispered.

Her *aenti* glared at her, but she held her peace as David settled into the seat opposite her. Her eyes brimmed with tears. "I never thought I'd see you again," she choked out.

"I wish I'd known you worked at the Green Valley market. My, um, *mammi* sometimes took me there in the summertime."

"We might have crossed paths millions of times and never known." Anguish twisted Wilma's face. "I lost all your childhood."

She gulped.

"I couldn't keep you." She squeezed her eyes shut, and in a low, quivering voice, she recounted the story she'd told Sovilla. Taking a deep breath, she continued, "I bawled the day they took you from my arms, and there's not a day since I haven't cried." She hung her head. "I know you can never forgive me, but I loved you and wanted only the best for you."

"I forgive you." David's quiet words were heartfelt and genuine.

Without looking up, Wilma shook her head. "I don't see how. Even God can't forgive me for that."

"God forgives you." David waited until she looked up. Then, in a serious voice, he added, "You need to forgive yourself."

Sovilla waited for Wilma to rail against any talk of God. Instead, her *aenti* bowed her head and wept.

"I didn't mean to make you cry." David's faced creased with distress.

Wilma shook her head and held up her hand. When she could talk again, she said in a tear-choked voice, "God and I have a lot of unfinished business."

He looked puzzled.

"I've been angry at God since the day I had to give you up. More than anything in the world, I wanted to keep you. But I was seventeen, alone in an unfamiliar state, and had no job."

Tears formed in David's eyes. "I don't blame you."

"But I blamed me. Every day since then, I've lived with the guilt. Of my rebelliousness. Of my sins. And most of all, of giving you up."

"You did what you had to do. I grew up with loving parents and adopted brothers and sisters. My *mamm* . . ." He hesitated. "I mean my adoptive *mamm*. You're my real *mamm*."

Wilma covered her face with her hands and burst into tears.

"I didn't mean to upset you more."

She lifted her head, her eyes wet, but shining. She could barely speak. "They're . . . they're happy tears. I never thought . . . I'd see you again. To hear you call me *mamm* . . ." Her voice shook.

David sounded choked up. "I prayed for you, even though I didn't know anything about you or who you were."

Wilma stared at him. "You prayed for me?"

"I had a loving family, but I thought"—he cleared his throat—"well, I thought if you hadn't married, maybe you didn't have a loving family. I worried you might be all alone."

"I was," she whispered.

"I wish I'd known. I'm glad I prayed."

Wilma shook her head. "I can't believe you prayed for me." She lowered her head into her hands again, muffling her voice. "I should have prayed for you. I only prayed to have you back. And every day that didn't happen, I grew angrier at God. I didn't deserve—"

"None of us are deserving," David interrupted, his voice gentle. "That's why God sent Jesus."

Sovilla waited for her *aenti* to explode. But she didn't. Her shoulders shook, and her head remained down.

He seemed to sense the need for silence. Wilma had decades of pent-up pain to process. They needed to give her time.

While they waited, Sovilla smiled at David to thank him for being so patient. His serene smile in return showed he understood what his birth *mamm* was going through.

What a wonderful son Wilma had. With his deep faith, he might help to bring her back to the Lord.

Sovilla prayed that would be the case. Beside her, Isaac seemed to be praying as well, and across the room, Mrs. Vandenberg's eyes were closed, and her lips moved. They'd surrounded Wilma with prayer.

When Wilma finally lifted her head, David stared down

at his clasped hands. "I also prayed for my dad. I don't know why he didn't marry you."

Wilma's whole body slumped, and the lines etched into her face revealed the deep pain of rejection. "I don't either." She stayed silent for a moment. "I thought he loved me as much as I loved him." A trace of bitterness seeped into her tone.

"I don't understand. Even so, I'd like to know who he is."

The pain in her eyes magnified, and she pressed her lips together. After a moment, she spoke. "Eli Hochstetler in Middlefield, Ohio. You look just like him."

"I'm glad to know that. I don't look anything like my brothers." David stared at his birth *mamm* with sympathetic eyes before saying hesitantly, "I'd like to meet him. Do you think it might be possible?"

Wilma's lower lip quivered. "I . . . I don't know. I'm sure he has a family now." She winced. "What if he didn't tell them? It wouldn't be right to disrupt his life."

"Maybe I could go to Ohio and just see him, meet him without telling him who I am. Although that would feel dishonest."

Mrs. Vandenberg lifted her head. "If you look like him, I don't think you could keep your identity a secret. I have a better idea. I'll ask a detective who works for me to find out more about Eli Hochstetler before you approach him."

David turned to her with eagerness. "Would you? It would mean a lot to me. I still can't believe I've met my *mamm*."

Wilma pressed her hands to her heart, and tears flooded down her cheeks. "I'd like to know too." Almost under her breath, she mumbled, "I never stopped loving him."

Sovilla wished she could hug her prickly *aenti*. What pain and loneliness Wilma had endured all these years.

Sovilla couldn't imagine losing two people she most loved in the world.

And she had no idea why that thought made her turn toward Isaac.

Isaac found his attention straying to Sovilla more and more often as the evening progressed. Her tenderhearted sympathy for her *aenti* wreathed her face in a heavenly beauty that took his breath away. When their gazes met, her shining eyes touched a place deep in his soul, and he couldn't look away.

Everything about this evening had been sacred. Perhaps Sovilla's eyes only reflected the spiritual awakening unfolding before them. This meeting between mother and son had transformed the room into holy ground. Isaac's heart directed him to pray for Wilma, and everyone else seemed to be doing the same.

When she lifted her bowed head, Wilma had eyes only for David. Moisture sparkled on her lashes, and her face held a new softness. The tense, angry lines in her expression had smoothed. Openness and vulnerability radiated from her. Isaac prayed this change would be permanent and that she'd turn her life over to the Lord.

"We should go," David said. "You need your rest, and I'm sure Mrs. Vandenberg does too. I'm so glad I finally got to meet you, Mamm."

When he said the word *Mamm*, Wilma collapsed into a fresh spate of tears. Mrs. Vandenberg swayed as she stood, and David rose to help her. After she'd steadied herself on her cane, he crossed the room to Wilma, who'd started struggling to her feet.

"*Neh.*" He pressed a gentle hand on her shoulder. "You don't need to get up for us." Then he leaned over and gave her a side hug. "I wish you hadn't been in such pain for so long, but God has a purpose for everything."

In a broken voice, she said, "I'm not sure about that, but if I hadn't made a mistake as a teen, you wouldn't be here. I can be thankful for . . . my—my son."

"And I'm thankful for you." He straightened. "You gave me life and sacrificed to give me a loving family. I hope we can stay a part of each other's lives."

Wilma's face glowed. "I'd like that," she said softly.

Isaac swallowed hard at the tenderness between the two of them. He'd never seen Wilma so gentle, so calm, so happy. God had worked a miracle.

He looked over at Sovilla to share his joy, and the love-light shining in her eyes set his pulse on fire. Was that radiance for him or for her *aenti*'s reunion with her son?

Chapter Twenty-Six

While they waited to hear about Eli from Mrs. Vandenberg, Wilma did her exercises without prodding. She gritted her teeth and didn't complain. Mrs. Vandenberg offered to continue acting as Wilma's coach, but Sovilla, grateful for her *aenti*'s cooperation, took over the task.

When the call finally came, Wilma hung up the phone, shuffled from the hall table to the living room with her walker, and collapsed into her chair. Sovilla hurried from the kitchen to hear the news.

"Eli still lives in the same house, but both his parents have passed. And Mrs. Vandenberg insists Eli is a bachelor." Wilma shook her head. "I find that hard to believe. He was the handsomest boy in our district. And the nicest."

"Does David know?"

"*Jah.* He wants me to come with him to visit Eli, so Mrs. Vandenberg is making arrangements for all of us. David enjoyed meeting you and Isaac, so he asked if you could join us."

"When would we go?" Sovilla needed to take pies out soon, but she was eager to learn the details.

"The driver will pick you and Isaac up after work at the

market on Saturday. David has off on Saturday, so we'll already be in the car. He'd like to go sooner, but I didn't want you to close the stand again."

The pies were cooling on the counter when Mrs. Vandenberg called back. Wilma covered the phone to say Isaac planned to go. Then she turned on the speakerphone so Sovilla could hear the plans.

"I've made arrangements with Keturah Esch," Mrs. Vandenberg explained. "Sovilla, she'll take over for you at noon on Saturday. She's the petite strawberry blonde who works at the pretzel stand near you. The oldest sister in that family."

"I know which one she is." Sovilla had taken to Keturah after she'd been so kind to Isaac. "That's very nice of her."

"She's a sweet girl," Mrs. Vandenberg said. "Her family's owned that stand for a decade. And she's very trustworthy."

Sovilla assumed that last statement had been made for Wilma's benefit.

"I've made arrangements at a lovely hotel in the area," Mrs. Vandenberg continued. "It'll be my treat."

Wilma's face hardened into mutinous lines. "You don't have to do that. I can pay my own way."

"I'm sure you can," Mrs. Vandenberg's crisp, no-nonsense voice vibrated over the phone lines. "I'll hear no arguments about this. It's my gift to David."

As soon as she said David's name, Wilma's face softened. "I want to give him something too."

"You can give him the gift no one else can." She paused and then added, "A mother's love."

Wilma stayed silent for a few moments, her eyes damp. Then she said, "I don't know about showing up in Ohio with you. You definitely don't look Plain."

"Can't you tell them I'm your driver?"

Wilma guffawed. "With a car like yours? And dressing that ritzy? You don't look like any driver of the Amish I've ever seen."

"What would they look like?"

"They'd have an older, serviceable car or van and plain, ordinary clothes. Stuff you buy off the rack at one of the big chain stores."

Mrs. Vandenberg chuckled. "Thanks for the tips. I'll see what I can do."

Wilma bit her lip. "This will be hard enough. I don't want to stand out or call attention to myself. If people see a fancy car, they're sure to gossip."

"I understand. I'll do my best to be discreet."

After she hung up the phone, Wilma grumbled, "I don't think that woman knows the meaning of *discreet*."

But Wilma's griping couldn't take the edge off Sovilla's excitement. Mrs. Vandenberg was not only giving David a gift—she'd given Sovilla one too. She'd get to spend three days with Mamm and her sisters. And best of all, she'd also be with Isaac. Sovilla could hardly wait.

On Friday, following Wilma's orders, Sovilla completely emptied the cash register and zippered all the bills and rolls of change into the bank deposit bag. The pouch bulged so much, she worried the seams might split. Then she re-counted to be sure she'd left exactly thirty dollars' worth of change in the register.

Isaac arrived as she was spreading cloths over the tables, and Sovilla slipped a dog biscuit shaped like a bone from the display jar she was covering and handed it to him. He reached into his pocket to pay.

"*Neh*, it's my gift to Snickers." She'd received a huge gift from Mrs. Vandenberg, so she could give a small one. And Snickers wagging her tail and gnawing on her treat delighted her.

"*Danke.*" Isaac's admiring smile tripped her pulse.

Sovilla's heart flooded with gratitude. She had so many blessings. "I'm so excited about tomorrow."

"Me too." The joy on Isaac's face lifted her spirits even higher.

"I've never b-been to Ohio."

Disappointment snaked through her. Maybe his enthusiasm was because he'd be traveling somewhere new. But the gleam in his eye seemed to be directed toward her.

She broke their gaze to pick up the money pouch.

"W-wow! You made a fortune t-today," he said as they headed for the exit.

Sovilla laughed. "*Neh.* Wilma's worried Keturah might rob us, so she wants all the coin rolls and bills we keep for extra change emptied out. I'm sure she also wants to be sure I haven't been stealing from her."

Isaac stopped and stared at her. "You?"

"*Jah*, me. Wilma doesn't trust anyone." Remorse filled Sovilla. "Knowing what she's been through, I can understand that."

"She's had a r-rough time."

"I hope this trip will go well for her. And for David." If only Mrs. Vandenberg could check to see if Eli wanted to meet his son—but she had no way to do that. Their visit would be a complete surprise.

As soon as she entered the house, Sovilla kicked off her sneakers and collapsed onto the sofa. She hadn't gotten much sleep since Mrs. Vandenberg had confirmed they'd be going to Ohio. Sovilla let her mind drift to the coming weekend with Isaac.

Wilma clicked her walker down the hall. "Where's my money?"

The demand roused Sovilla from her daydreams. *Ach!* Sick to her stomach, she opened her eyes. "I left it on the back seat of Isaac's buggy."

"You what?" Wilma's eyes bulged. She looked about to have a heart attack.

Sovilla jumped to her feet and shoved her feet into her sneakers. "I'll go get it now."

Wilma's *Acckk!* almost drowned out the knock on the front door.

That must be Isaac. He'd discovered the money pouch.

Sovilla opened the door with a huge smile. Her *danke* faltered on her lips.

"Who were you expecting?" Lloyd's barb punctured Sovilla's happiness. "I'm sure that welcome wasn't for me."

Neh, it definitely wasn't. What was her *onkel* doing here?

Lloyd pushed his way past her into the living room, then stopped and stared at the overhead lights. "You have electricity?" His glance strayed to the hall table. "And a telephone?"

Until her *onkel*'s arrival, Sovilla had pushed down her guilt over enjoying modern conveniences. Now, it returned in full force.

Lloyd's gaze fell on Wilma, and his mouth fell open. His expression grew stormy. "You—you—" For a moment, he seemed at a loss for words. "You're not fit to be around Sovilla."

Wilma shrank back against the couch. Lloyd came in like a tornado, flattening everything in its path. Sovilla had never seen her *aenti* cowed.

He scowled at Sovilla. "Why are you staying with her? She's been shunned."

"No, I'm not, Lloyd." Wilma, her chin jutting out, sat up straighter. "I can't be shunned. I never joined the church."

"You're not Amish?" Lloyd asked, horrified.

"Not since you dumped me in Pennsylvania and stole my child."

He blinked and took a step back at the vehemence in her tone.

Wilma leaned forward and stayed on the attack. "How did you expect me to survive at seventeen knowing nobody here, having no job or money?"

"I assumed they'd help you."

"You thought wrong. That wasn't their responsibility."

"Don't try to blame me for your sins." Lloyd's posture and words became defensive.

"My sins?" Wilma's voice rose in a screech. "Dying alone in the streets should be the punishment for a teenage mistake?"

"You obviously didn't die."

"What would you know about that? I've died inside every single day since I was separated from my son."

"I'm sure he had a better life." Lloyd started backing toward the door. "And you'll be glad to know I'm saving Sovilla from that fate." He turned to her. "I'll give you fifteen minutes to pack. You can't stay in this house of sin."

"But Wilma needs me."

"Your *mamm* needs you more right now."

"Mamm? Is something wrong with her?" Is that why Lloyd had come all this way?

"Don't believe him, Sovilla," Wilma begged. "He's a liar."

Lloyd's malevolent glare silenced her.

Sovilla didn't trust him, but if something was wrong with Mamm, she'd never forgive herself for not going.

"Fifteen minutes, Sovilla. I'll be waiting in the car."

He'd hired a driver to come here? Hadn't that been expensive? He wouldn't have done that if it weren't an emergency.

She ran up the stairs and pulled out the small suitcase she'd brought to Pennsylvania.

"I'm warning you, Sovilla," Wilma yelled after her. "You're going to be sorry."

Sovilla would never regret doing something for Mamm. She hated to leave Wilma, but her *aenti* got around well with her walker. She even fixed herself meals while Sovilla was at work.

Sovilla didn't need the full fifteen minutes. She only had two Lancaster dresses, and she was wearing one. Sovilla folded her aprons and tucked her undergarments and nightgowns into the small suitcase. At the last minute, she added her Ohio clothing in case her sisters could use any of it.

Only one more thing to pack—the cell phone Mrs. Vandenberg had given her. Luckily, it was fully charged. She couldn't charge it in Ohio, but once she got there, she'd contact Wilma, Isaac, and Mrs. Vandenberg to let them know about Mamm. She turned off the ringer so Lloyd wouldn't know she had it and slid it between her clothing. Then she closed the suitcase and hurried out to the car, with Wilma's "You're making a big mistake" ringing in her ears.

How could it be a mistake when Mamm needed her?

As the car pulled away from the curb, the automatic locks clicked, startling Sovilla and making her feel trapped.

A buggy headed toward them. Isaac. He must have come to return the money pouch. She waved frantically to get his attention, but he didn't see her until he'd almost passed the car.

Once he did, his mouth moved, but she couldn't make out what he was saying. She craned her neck as the driver sped up and shot by the buggy. The car moved so fast, Isaac turned into a blur.

Chapter Twenty-Seven

Isaac pulled his buggy into Sovilla's driveway. Where had she been headed? Who were those men? She'd tried so hard to get his attention. They'd whizzed past so quickly, Isaac hadn't been able to read her expression, but had she thrown him a *help-me* plea?

"Stay here," he told Snickers as he picked up the money pouch. He rushed to the front door, hoping Wilma could answer his questions. If Sovilla needed help, he'd go after her.

When he reached the doorstep, he heard loud sobbing coming from the living room. The door hadn't been shut properly, and through the crack, Isaac glimpsed Wilma weeping on the couch. He didn't want to push the door open any farther, so he knocked on the doorjamb.

Wilma lifted her head, her eyes red and swollen. "What are you doing here?" Her words held a sharp edge.

"I b-brought your money." Isaac held up the money pouch.

"Bring it here," she commanded. "I hope you didn't take any."

"It's still full." He indicated the bulging sides. "Sovilla couldn't have fit anything more in there."

With a sniffle, Wilma took the bag.

"What's wr-wrong?" Isaac asked. "And where's Sovilla g-going?"

Wilma pinched her lips together, and he expected her to snap at him to mind his own business.

Instead, she choked out, "My brother took Sovilla."

"T-took?"

"He came in here and dragged her away, just like he did to me when he sent me to Pennsylvania. Seeing him again . . ." Wilma swallowed hard and clenched her hands. "Seeing him brought back all the pain. Now he has Sovilla in his clutches."

Clutches? She's a prisoner? "Will he h-hurt her?"

"Lloyd hurts everyone."

The thought of anyone harming Sovilla cut off Isaac's breath. "He's abusive?"

"You don't think sending me here alone and taking David away is abusive?" Her harshness had a bitter edge.

Jah, Lloyd had inflicted a lot of pain. Isaac's hands curled into fists. He'd meant physical abuse, but he didn't want Sovilla to endure any cruelty. "We have t-to rescue her."

"And how do you propose doing that?"

"G-go after her." He wanted to gallop after her, but his buggy would do little good. "Let's c-call Mrs. Vandenberg." They'd already made plans to leave for Ohio. Maybe they could leave now.

Distraught about Sovilla and nervous about Wilma listening as he used her hall phone, Isaac stuttered so much, he could barely get his message across. But when he finished, he begged, "C-can we l-leave t-tonight?"

"David has to work until nine this evening, but let's leave at dawn tomorrow. Can you skip work and be ready at five?"

"*Jah.*" Because it was an emergency, surely Daed would agree.

"I'll contact David, and you tell Wilma. Bring your suitcase to her house by five a.m. I'll check with Keturah to see if she can work at the stand all day."

Isaac had already packed his suitcase. He was ready to leave now. "What about S-Sovilla?"

"If she has the phone I gave her, you can call her and tell her we're coming." As Mrs. Vandenberg recited Sovilla's phone number, Isaac memorized it.

The minute he hung up, he dialed Sovilla and did his best to speak clearly and calmly. He needed to set aside his fears and worries so he didn't add to her distress. But with Wilma listening from the living room, Isaac had to watch his words.

He left a brief message telling her they'd be there tomorrow. He estimated they'd arrive by midday or early afternoon. He ended, "We'll b-be praying."

"Speak for yourself," Wilma said in the background as he hung up.

Isaac hoped the phone hadn't picked up Wilma's comment. He returned to the living room and stumbled through an explanation of Mrs. Vandenberg's plans. Then he hurried home.

Several more times that evening, he tried contacting Sovilla from the kennel phone, but each time it went to voice mail. Although he needed to get up early, he stayed in the kennel until late, hoping to hear back from her. He practiced his speaking with gravel, but as hour after hour passed with no return call, his fears for Sovilla increased. Powerless to help her himself, he surrounded her with prayer.

"What's wrong with Mamm?" Sovilla asked her *onkel* as the car picked up speed.

"Nothing," he said carelessly. "If I'd known you were living with Wilma"—he spat out her name as if it were a curse—"and that you were living as if you were *Englisch*, I'd have come for you sooner."

"But you said Mamm needed me."

"All *mamms* need their daughters."

Sovilla's heart sank. Wilma had been right. "You lied?"

Laughter rumbled in Lloyd's chest. "I didn't say anything untrue. You're the one who misunderstood."

Anger burned hot inside Sovilla. She never should have ignored Wilma's warning. Sovilla had spent enough time around her *onkel*. She should have known better.

Wilma needed her, and Sovilla had left her alone. As good as it might be to see her mother, Sovilla suspected that Lloyd intended to keep her in Ohio.

Months ago, she'd have been delighted. Now, though, she'd miss Isaac. The thought of staying in Ohio permanently made her realize how much she cared.

"How did you know where I was?" Sovilla hoped he hadn't done anything mean to Mamm to get her to reveal Sovilla's location.

"I found some letters your *mamm* had hidden."

He'd rooted through Mamm's things? "But that's—"

"It's necessary when someone in the family is sneaking

around behind my back. My responsibility is to keep everyone safe."

Sovilla bit back an uncharitable retort. Although he didn't go about it in a loving way, Lloyd did take his responsibility seriously. He had helped Mamm by paying bills after Daed died. And when he couldn't afford to do that, he'd offered to take them into his home. But that didn't excuse his other actions.

They finished the trip in uncomfortable silence.

Mamm's tears of joy and tight hug made the long ride worthwhile.

"But what are you doing here?" she asked as she embraced Sovilla.

Under Lloyd's watchful gaze, Sovilla swallowed back the answer she longed to give. She'd tell Mamm later, when they were alone. "I heard you missed me."

Evidently, Mamm understood Sovilla's desire for privacy. "You must be tired. Let's go up to bed." Mamm ushered Sovilla up the stairs and into the bedroom, where both of her sisters were sound asleep.

Conscious of her cousins' room on the other side of the wall, Sovilla whispered a brief explanation. Then she fumbled through her suitcase in the dark to find her nightgown. Her hand hit the phone.

Isaac had left several messages, each one more frantic than the last. She had to call him back, but not here in the house. Not with her cousins in the room next door.

When she'd visited as a girl, she'd found a spot to hide away from her cousins' teasing. She might be too big to fit now, but she had to try. Her *onkel* and *aenti* went to bed early. She only had to worry about the boys. They might hear and follow her.

"*Mamm,*" she whispered, "I need to . . ." She held up the phone.

Her mother's eyes widened, but she asked no questions. She pressed a finger to her lips and pointed to the wall they shared with her cousins as if warning her to be extra quiet. Sovilla nodded. She had no intention of staying in the room.

She eased the door open an inch at a time. At the halfway point, it squeaked, and she stopped, waiting and listening. The conversation in the boys' room continued, and she let out a pent-up breath. Turning sideways, she squeezed through the opening.

She remembered which steps creaked and hoped no new ones would give her away. The back door groaned as she opened it.

She scurried out onto the porch, shut it, and dashed off toward the barn. Right before she reached it, she veered off into the trees on the left.

Too late it occurred to her that the tree with the opening might be occupied by woodland creatures and spiders. She stopped where she stood, concealed by the trees and too far from the house to be heard.

"Isaac?" Relief washed over her at the sound of his voice. "I'm in Ohio at my *onkel*'s. I can't talk long, but when you come with Mrs. Vandenberg tomorrow evening, please come to get me." She gave him the address. Wilma might not remember the directions, because it had been thirty years since she'd lived here. "I have to go. I'll explain when you get here."

"Wait," Isaac begged. "We'll b-be there around n-noon. We'll c-call."

"I'll keep the phone with me and turned to vibrate. I can't wait until you get here."

He promised to pray, and she said a quick *danke* and goodbye. Then she shut off the phone, concealed it in her pocket, and rushed back toward the house. This time the door creaked louder. Before she could shut it, angry footfalls stomped toward her.

"What do you think you're doing?" Lloyd growled. "Shut that door. If you had plans to meet someone after dark, you're mistaken."

Sovilla gladly shut the door. "I don't know anyone here." She tried to sound reasonable and convincing, but Lloyd only puffed up more.

"I'm supposed to believe that?" He waved a hand toward the stairs. "Get up to bed. And don't you dare leave this house again without permission."

Bowing her head, she acted chastened as she hurried past him and up the stairs, thanking God Lloyd hadn't caught her before she went outside.

Isaac held the dead phone in his hand. What was going on? Sovilla had rattled on, barely letting him speak. She'd sounded breathless and nervous. The fact that she couldn't talk long worried him.

But she had said she couldn't wait until he got there. His insides danced—until his mind replayed her words. She had said, *I can't wait until you get here*. She'd said *you*. Most likely, she'd meant all of them. His high spirits drooped.

* * *

He slept fitfully. Dreams of Sovilla calling for help kept waking him. At four, he hopped out of bed and got ready. Snickers's claws clicked across the floor as she accompanied Isaac to take care of the puppies.

Leanne had agreed to care for the dogs while he was gone. He left her a note to let her know he had to leave earlier than expected. Then he collected his suitcase and headed for Wilma's.

The lights were on downstairs, so he didn't hesitate to knock. When she yelled, "Come in," he entered, hoping she wouldn't be upset Snickers had come with him.

She didn't notice as she dithered. After packing one thing, she second-guessed herself and pulled it out, only to return it to the suitcase again. By the time Mrs. Vandenberg pulled up out front, everything had been returned to the suitcase.

While Wilma locked the door, Isaac carried her luggage out with his.

When she turned around and saw the van waiting for them, she pretended to smack her forehead. "You have to do everything large, don't you, Liesl? When I said a van, I meant a minivan, not a fifteen-seater."

"You never know when you might need extra room. We already have five passengers going out, plus Snickers. And Sovilla will be coming back."

"Hopefully," Wilma muttered. "You don't know Lloyd."

Wilma's words added to Isaac's anxiety. Would Sovilla's *onkel* forbid her to return to Pennsylvania? What if she chose to stay there? Maybe she'd get back together with her old boyfriend.

Wilma was still sniping at Mrs. Vandenberg.

"Does my outfit pass muster?" Mrs. Vandenberg asked Wilma with a touch of humor in her tone.

"Hmm . . . Where'd you buy it?"

"Everything I packed is from the thrift shop."

"I guess that'll do." Wilma's sigh seemed to come from deep within. "Even when you buy used clothes, they look more expensive and better quality than most people run around in. Maybe nobody will notice." She rolled her eyes. "I doubt it, though."

Isaac didn't care what people thought of them. He wanted to get on the road now. "Sovilla," he burst out. With that one word, he ended the sparring and got everyone hustling.

The driver loaded the luggage while David helped Wilma into the van. He patted the seat beside where he'd been seated. "Sit here beside me, please, Mamm."

Wilma beamed and settled near the door. Isaac stowed her walker and climbed into a back seat with Snickers. *Hurry, hurry.* He leaned as far forward as he could with his seat belt on, as if that would make them move faster.

They'd organized for their trip as quickly as they could, but they still lagged behind their expected starting time. Then they made three stops, including for some fast food they could eat in the car. Isaac would have gladly given up eating to get to Ohio sooner, but he couldn't deny the older women a meal.

Wilma and Mrs. Vandenberg napped, but Isaac stayed on high alert, willing the driver to speed up. Mrs. Vandenberg handed Isaac her cell phone, and he left a phone message for Sovilla each time they stopped so she'd be updated on their arrival time.

When they reached Middlefield, Mrs. Vandenberg insisted on stopping at the hotel. "Wilma and I need to freshen up."

All Isaac wanted to do was get to Sovilla.

Mrs. Vandenberg's sympathetic glance made it clear she understood his impatience. "It would be best if David stayed here with us, don't you think, Wilma?"

"Definitely. If Lloyd takes one look at him, he'll know."

"And I'm sure you'd prefer to go alone, wouldn't you, Isaac?" Mrs. Vandenberg kept her voice low so the others couldn't overhear.

He nodded, wishing they'd hurry and unload the car.

"You can be the white knight riding in to rescue the damsel in distress." As a gentleman in a uniform piled the luggage onto a cart, Mrs. Vandenberg asked her driver to take Isaac to pick up Sovilla. Finally.

Just before they reached the driveway of the house, Isaac asked the driver to pull over. Using Mrs. Vandenberg's phone, Isaac called Sovilla. "We're here. I-turn left p-past the c-cornfields." Concern for her made it hard to keep from stuttering.

Waiting for her to appear was agonizing. What if she couldn't come? She seemed to be afraid to talk on the phone, but maybe her *onkel* didn't approve of phones. Isaac hoped her family wouldn't object to her leaving. He'd almost given up on seeing her when she slipped around the rustling cornstalks.

She kept glancing over her shoulder. Once she saw the van, her face lit up, and she dashed toward them. Isaac opened the van door for her.

She climbed inside and ducked low. "Hurry, before anyone notices I'm gone. I told Mamm, but . . ." She bit her lip.

The driver gunned the engine and peeled away. When they were out of view of the house, Sovilla sat up.

She giggled. "I didn't know you were a race car driver."

He only smiled.

Her laughter faded. "I hope Lloyd doesn't blame Mamm for my disappearance." She hated leaving her mother to face his wrath.

Isaac thanked God she seemed all right, but he still worried about her. What was she trying to escape? "What's g-going on?"

"Lloyd told me Mamm wanted me to come back home. I assumed it must be an emergency, so I went with him. But when I asked what was wrong with Mamm, he said, *Nothing*. He lied about it to get me away from Wilma's. He called her place a *house of sin*. He was also upset about me living *Englisch*."

Isaac still didn't understand the first part of her story. "He l-lied to g-get you to c-come home?"

"*Jah*. And now he doesn't want me to leave."

"He's k-keeping you p-prisoner."

"I guess you could call it that. He told me not to go out without permission. He has a terrible temper when you don't listen."

"Like Wilma?"

"Ten times worse."

"He d-doesn't hit you, d-does he?"

"*Neh*, but his rages can be as painful as beatings." Her face squinched up as if she were remembering one. Then she relaxed back against the seat. "Getting outside the house is such a relief. And I didn't want to miss a chance to be with you."

Isaac's spirits soared. Maybe last night she *had* meant she couldn't wait to see him.

Then she continued, “I want to be there when David and Wilma meet Eli. I’m so grateful to Mrs. Vandenberg.”

Isaac bit back a sigh. It hadn’t been only about him.

“Aren’t you excited too?”

Sovilla must have noticed his dejected expression. Isaac forced his thoughts away from his selfishness and let his happiness for her and her family show in his smile. “I’m p-praying for Eli.”

“Me too. Meeting David will be a shock.”

As soon as they pulled up outside of the hotel, Sovilla hopped out of the van. Isaac and Snickers followed more slowly. Now that he had her back with him, his urgency to hurry things along faded. Mrs. Vandenberg and David stood in the lobby, waiting.

“Wilma said she’d be right down,” Mrs. Vandenberg informed them.

When the elevator door opened, Wilma surprised everyone by stepping out wearing Ohio Amish clothes. She’d slicked back her short hair, and from the front it looked almost like it should. Sovilla guessed she had a lot of hairpins under her *kapp* to hold the ends in place.

David smiled. “That’s how I always pictured you, Mamm.”

Wilma’s watery smile showed he’d touched her heart. “I couldn’t do much with my hair, though.”

“It looks fine,” Sovilla assured her.

“I thought Eli, I mean your *daed*, would be more likely to recognize me like this. Although with the ravages of time”—sadness filled her eyes—“I’ve probably changed too much.”

“I doubt it,” David said.

Sovilla sent him thanks with her eyes.

"Well, let's go." Despite her walker, Wilma hustled out ahead of everyone and headed to the van, where the driver waited.

As Sovilla got in, she moved the seat forward so Snickers could get into the back with Isaac. Thoughtful little gestures like that made him appreciate her even more than he already did. He turned to thank her for her kindness, but the deeper feelings he meant to keep hidden spilled out into his expression.

Chapter Twenty-Eight

Isaac's eyes, gleaming as if lit from within, startled Sovilla and held her in place. Unsure if she was reading his emotions correctly, she couldn't look away.

"What's taking so long back there?" Wilma grumped.

Her *aenti*'s complaint broke the spell, and Sovilla tore her gaze from Isaac's. She slid into the seat beside him, wary of the churning he'd started inside her. She sat frozen in place, conscious of him next to her. His breathing. His movement. His presence.

On the way to Ohio, she'd discovered she cared for him, but this connection was deeper, stronger, truer. She'd never experienced this pull, this attraction before.

Throughout the ride, she tried to make sense of what had happened between them, but she couldn't put it into words.

In front of them, Wilma's perky expression drooped as they drove down country lanes, and when they turned at a crossroads, her shoulders slumped.

"What if he doesn't want to see me?" she mumbled.

Sovilla prayed that he'd not only be willing to see her *aenti* but that he'd also open his heart to David.

As they pulled in front of Eli's house, Wilma emitted a strange sound, like the cry of a trapped animal.

"Are you all right?" David asked.

"*Neh.*" Her voice shook. "It's been so long, yet it looks the same. Exactly the way I remembered it."

He craned his neck to study his *daed*'s house.

She buried her face in her hands. "I can't do this. I can't face him after all these years."

"You can do anything with God's help." Mrs. Vandenberg's crisp words seemed intended to brace Wilma.

Without acknowledging the statement about God, Wilma squared her shoulders. "I have to do this. For David's sake." She stared at the house for a moment. "Maybe I should go in alone."

"It's up to you," Mrs. Vandenberg said. "We're here to support you. We'll do whatever you want."

"I want to break the news gradually. If he sees David, he'll know right away."

David reached for the door handle. "Why don't I go for a walk around the grounds? I can look at the horses in the pasture."

Sovilla's heart went out to him. Meeting his *daed* after thirty years had to be as difficult for him as it was for Wilma. Maybe he needed time to compose himself. Or maybe he was doing it for Wilma's sake. He'd proved to be skilled at reading other people's needs.

Very like Isaac.

Sovilla couldn't help glancing at him. His hand rested on his leg, so close she could reach out and entwine her fingers in his. She wished he'd reach over and—*Neh*, she shouldn't be longing to hold his hand.

As she looked up, Isaac's smile made her feel accepted and understood. Almost as if he'd read her thoughts. And shared them.

Wilma unclicked her seat belt. "I'll go alone." She got out of the car and braced herself with her walker. But she didn't close the door behind her.

Maybe preparing for a fast escape? As her *aenti* marched toward the front door, Sovilla prayed all would go well.

When Wilma neared the porch, her steps faltered. She stopped and tilted her head to take in the whole house. Then, straightening her shoulders, she set her walker down firmly and climbed the steps one by one. She hesitated again before knocking on the door.

Following a brief wait, the front door opened, and the man in the doorway stepped back, shock on his face. "Wilma?"

Her words floated through the air. "You recognize me after all these years?"

"How could I forget? You look almost the same."

Her laugh was tinged with disbelief.

"Who's in the car with you? Have them come in." He beckoned to all of them.

"Do you think we should go?" Sovilla asked. "Wilma would probably prefer her privacy."

Isaac nodded. "We should s-stay."

But when Eli called out, "Come in, come in," they all got out of the car and entered the house. All except David, who stood by the pasture fence out of sight.

After Wilma had introduced everyone and they'd all

settled into chairs, she and Eli gazed into each other's eyes as if everyone else in the room had disappeared.

Eli finally broke the silence. "What brings you here?"

"I have something to tell you." Although Mrs. Vandenberg had told them Eli was a bachelor, Wilma stared at his clean shaven chin. "You—you never married?" Her words came out low and shaky, but also surprised.

"The only girl I ever loved broke my heart."

"So you did find someone else?" She gazed down at her hands as she pleated a section of her apron between her fingers.

"*Neh.* Even though you urged me to do that, I stayed faithful to the only woman I ever loved."

"What?" Wilma's eyes flew to his face. "I never told you that."

"Not to my face," he said heavily. "Your brother told me that. It hurt twice as much that you couldn't even tell me in person."

Wilma shook her head back and forth the whole time he was speaking. "You were the one who rejected me. I never—"

"How can you say that? The last time we were together"—Eli lowered his head as shame washed across his features—"every time we were together, I told you I loved you. That never changed."

In an anguished voice, she said, "Lloyd." Her mouth worked, but no sound came out. She closed her eyes. Then, her face a mask of agony, she asked, "What did he tell you?"

"He said you wanted to break up but were too ashamed to face me because you'd fallen in love with someone else. You were moving out of state to marry him." Eli's voice trembled. "I barely heard the rest. I could hardly believe you'd done that. Not after we—"

Wilma let out a pitiful cry. "*Neh.*"

Eli raised his head and stared into her eyes. "I didn't want to believe it. I went to your house to talk to you, to beg you to stay, to ask you to marry me." He drew in a shuddery breath. "But you were gone."

"That was a lie."

"A lie?"

"I never married. Lloyd sent me to Pennsylvania. I didn't have any choice. I couldn't come back."

"I don't understand."

Wilma put her head into her hands and wept. "Lloyd told me," she said between sobs, "you didn't want anything more to do with me. You wanted me out of your life. He had a driver waiting. I didn't even know where I was going."

"That makes no sense. Why would he do that?"

"Because he'd found out about us." Her words muffled, she added, "What we were doing."

"*Ach.* All of this is my fault. Your brother wanted to protect you."

"*Neh.* He wanted to protect himself. If he'd cared about me, he'd have let me stay. I would have faced the shame." Tears trickled down her cheeks. "We could have married, if you'd have had me."

"Of course I would. Nothing ever changed that."

"But Lloyd didn't tell you the truth. He sent me to Pennsylvania to have the baby. Our baby."

Eli sat bolt upright in his chair. "You had our baby and never told me? Why? You knew I loved you."

"Lloyd forbade me to talk to you. He went to tell you

instead of letting me do it. But he lied to you. And to me." Wilma dashed at the tears coursing down her cheeks.

"You thought I rejected you because of the baby? I never would have done that."

"I wish I'd known," she said, each word infused with bitterness. "For thirty years, I've lived alone and heart-broken from the pain of losing you and our baby."

"*Ach*, Wilma. I can't bear to think of you going through all that alone. We could have married. What happened to the baby?"

"They made me give him up for adoption."

"Him? We had a little boy?"

"He's not so little anymore." Wilma smiled through her tears. "He's thirty. And—" She paused. "I just met him a few weeks ago. Now he wants to meet you."

"Me?"

"*Jah*, you." Wilma's tender smile held so much love.

Sovilla could hardly bear to watch. What if Eli said he didn't want to meet his son?

"After all these years? It's too much to take in. I don't know . . ."

Wilma's face crumpled. She pushed on the chair arms as if to stand.

"Wait, wait." Eli motioned for her to stay seated. "I'm a crusty old bachelor."

A sardonic laugh burst from Wilma's lips. "Someone recently called me *crusty*." She sent a pointed look in Mrs. Vandenberg's direction.

"You? *Neh*, you must have misheard. You were always the sweetest, kindest, gentlest girl I ever knew."

Sovilla stared at him. He must be viewing her *aenti* through dreams of what he wished she'd been. Or maybe not. Maybe Wilma had once been that way. Hadn't Mamm said something similar?

"I've changed, Eli. I'm no longer any of those things."

"I don't believe that." His piercing stare seemed to see straight into her heart. "You're also brave. Coming here to tell me this after all these years? You're an amazing woman."

Wilma blinked as if she didn't believe him. "And you're as smooth-talking as you always were." She made a sweeping motion with her hand, as if she were brushing away his compliments.

"But you do know one thing about me, Wilma. I always tell the truth."

Wilma sat silently, her teeth digging into her lower lip. Then a wobbly smile tilted her lips. "*Jah*, that's so."

"When did our son want to meet me?"

"Um, now?"

Eli's bushy eyebrows rose. "Now?" He looked around the room, and his gaze fell on Isaac.

"*Neh*, not Isaac." Wilma waved toward the door. "He's outside near the pasture. Maybe Isaac could go and get him—if you're ready, that is."

Sovilla had never heard Wilma be so deferential.

"Are you sure he wants to meet me? A father who never had anything to do with him growing up?"

"How could you?" Wilma defended Eli like a mother tiger protecting her young. "You didn't know he existed."

Sorrow descended over Eli's face. "I wish I had."

Grief swirled through Sovilla. So many lives destroyed. Lloyd had torn apart couples—Wilma and Eli, Sovilla and Henry—and now that Lloyd had dragged her here to

Ohio, he might break apart her budding relationship with Isaac.

If Mrs. Vandenberg hadn't arrived, Sovilla would have been stuck in Ohio permanently. Lloyd would have taken any money she earned at the bake shop, just like he did with Mamm's paychecks. She'd never have seen Isaac again.

She turned toward him with all her longing never to be separated ever again, and Isaac's eyes opened wide when they met hers. Had he read the message she sent?

Isaac's chest constricted at the look in Sovilla's eyes. Was he misreading the intensity as longing and love? Perhaps she was only reflecting Wilma and Eli's romance. Or maybe not? Maybe she truly did intend it for him?

"Isaac," Wilma said with a touch of impatience, "if you could tear your gaze from Sovilla's, I'd like you to get David."

"Aw, Wilma, don't be so hard on the boy." Eli chuckled. "I once stared at you that way."

"You did?"

"You don't remember?" He sounded hurt.

"I guess I was too busy admiring your gorgeous blue eyes."

Eli's smile was tender. "Some things never change."

Wilma sucked in a breath. Then her tartness returned. "You think I've been admiring your eyes all this time."

He sighed and shook his head. "You can't blame a man for wishing."

"Actually, I was." Wilma ducked her head, then mumbled, "I've never seen anyone with that exact shade of blue."

"Not as pretty as your green ones."

Mrs. Vandenberg cleared her throat and tilted her head

toward the door, indicating Isaac should get David. Isaac had been so caught up in the love story unfolding before his eyes and wondering about the meaning behind Sovilla's gaze, he'd forgotten Wilma's request.

He stood and, with one last glance at Sovilla, started for the door.

Mrs. Vandenberg also rose and tottered after him. "Maybe we should leave you two alone while you meet David."

Sovilla jumped to her feet. Isaac held the door for both of them and the driver.

Once they all exited, he jogged toward the pasture. David saw him coming and met him halfway.

"He wants to meet me?" he asked, half-nervous and half-hopeful.

Isaac nodded, and then Sovilla distracted him.

"David, before you go in, there are a few things you should know." Sovilla recounted the story of Wilma and Eli's breakup.

Creases formed on David's forehead. "Your *onkel* lied to break them up?" He sounded as if he couldn't believe it. "Then he sent my *mamm* away?"

"*Jah,*" Sovilla confirmed. "I think they still love each other. Neither of them ever married anyone else."

"I can't believe anyone would separate a courting couple." David stared at Sovilla. "Could they have misunderstood?"

"*Neh,*" Sovilla answered, her voice flat and sad.

David checked with Isaac for confirmation. After a brief glance at Sovilla, he backed up her story.

David accompanied them to the house. "I'm so sorry for both of them."

"So are we."

It thrilled Isaac that Sovilla had included him in that *we*.

"Mrs. Vandenberg suggested we leave the three of you alone," Sovilla said when they reached the front door. "We'll be praying."

She'd done it again. Isaac conveyed his gratitude with a smile, and she returned it with one so brilliant it set his heart ablaze.

"Want to g-go for a w-walk?" He hoped she'd realize his true intent—time alone with her and his first hesitant overture toward a relationship.

Chapter Twenty-Nine

Sitting in the air-conditioned van, Mrs. Vandenberg nodded her approval as Sovilla and Isaac headed for the pasture together. Now the meal at Mrs. Vandenberg's house made more sense to Sovilla. Mrs. Vandenberg had also suggested Isaac drive Sovilla to work. And Mrs. Vandenberg had coached Wilma in the hospital so Sovilla could visit Isaac's family.

Mrs. Vandenberg had been playing matchmaker all along. Did Isaac know? Or had it been his idea in the first place? Sovilla didn't care who'd come up with the idea. She only knew that whoever had planned it, they'd made the perfect choice.

Perhaps this hadn't been arranged by people, after all, but by God. Sovilla and Isaac shared a heart-to-heart connection. Everything about it seemed right and holy.

"I can't even imagine how Eli and Wilma endured being separated when they were so in love." Sovilla ached for all the pain her *aenti* had endured.

Isaac's face filled with compassion. "And then t-to meet again."

"After all those years apart. When they looked at each

other, didn't it look like they were seeing each other as teenagers?"

"*Jah.* When you l-love someone, you see their soul."

Love? Is that what she'd been feeling for Isaac? She'd thought she loved Henry, but she'd never been this in tune with him. That infatuation paled when compared to her growing bond with Isaac.

"There's David." Isaac pointed to the open front porch, and they hurried over.

David stood on the porch, dazed. "I'm giving the two of them more time together. If I hadn't asked to meet my *daed*, they'd never have gotten together." His face reflected a deep sadness. "They'd have spent the rest of their lives apart and lonely."

"God brought you into their lives," Sovilla told him.

Just like God had brought Isaac into hers. And she needed to guard against anything separating her from Isaac. The person who'd try to do that had driven a wedge between Wilma and Eli. Sovilla vowed to stay alert and fight any more of Lloyd's tricks. She had one advantage Wilma hadn't. Sovilla had a way out of Ohio, thanks to Mrs. Vandenberg.

Sovilla appeared deep in thought, and Isaac didn't want to interrupt her. Emotions flitted across her face. Fierceness replaced sorrow, followed by determination and relief. If only she'd share her mental journey. Isaac longed to be a part of her life—so close she'd never hesitate to confide all her hopes, fears, and dreams.

Wilma and Eli, their faces radiant, emerged from the house. The love shining in Wilma's eyes had softened her and made her almost beautiful. Both of them appeared to be much younger.

Eli placed a hand on David's shoulder. "I'd give anything to have raised you with your *mamm* by my side."

David's eyes welled. "I have wonderful adoptive parents"—his voice grew husky—"but I wish I'd known you both."

Wilma shook her head. "God knew I was too young and selfish. I'm glad he gave you parents who could raise you properly. They did a wonderful *gut* job."

Eli glanced down at her with tenderness. "And you say you aren't kind and generous."

Bewilderment in her eyes, Wilma tilted her head. When she met his adoring gaze, she sucked in a breath.

"Appreciating David's adoptive family when your own heart is breaking." Eli shook his head. "Only a mother who truly loved her child—our child—could be so selfless and giving."

A lump rose in Isaac's throat. What would it be like to be so much in love? Wilma and Eli's relationship stirred a longing in Isaac to have a connection like theirs. He'd only started to realize that his feelings for Sovilla went far beyond attraction. If he truly loved, could he sacrifice the way Wilma had done with David? Or like God had when he gave up Jesus?

Sovilla marveled at the difference in her *aenti*. She'd been transformed by the power of love.

Wilma tilted her head and looked up at Eli with adoration. "Let's go the van so we can share our news with Liesl. I wouldn't be here in Ohio if it weren't for Mrs. Vandenberg."

Her gaze moved to Sovilla. "And my niece started the whole thing by searching for David."

Was that a look of tenderness in Wilma's eyes? Before Sovilla could be sure, her *aenti* slid her walker along the porch, moving so rapidly, Sovilla had to step out of the way, and she bumped into Isaac who stood behind her.

He reached out to steady her, setting Sovilla's pulse thrumming. If only she could sink back into his arms and . . . She jerked herself upright. The last thing she needed was to make the same mistake as Wilma. No matter how difficult, Sovilla would follow the church's rules of no physical contact—that is, if Isaac cared for her the way she cared for him.

"Are you h-heading to the v-van?" He sounded as breathless as she was.

Sovilla nodded but took a few moments to compose herself before following Wilma.

"Well, you certainly look cheerful," Mrs. Vandenberg teased Wilma. Then she raised her eyebrows at Sovilla. "Seems we have an outbreak of happiness today."

"Eli and I have an announcement to make." Wilma glanced up at Eli. "You're sure?" Her voice quavered.

"I've never been more certain of anything in my life," he said. "I'm never letting you out of my sight again."

Wilma giggled. Sovilla couldn't believe it. Her *aenti* giggling like a schoolgirl?

"Eli and I will be getting married. After I join the church, of course. We'll talk to the bishop tomorrow after the service."

David broke into a smile. "I'm so glad for both of you."

"Son." Eli studied David with tenderness. "I'll never forget how you brought us together."

"Now for the hard part." Wilma made a face. "Talking to Lloyd."

Mrs. Vandenberg motioned for everyone to pile into the van. "It's time for a reckoning."

Eli helped Wilma in, set her walker in the back, and then sat beside her. David chose the seat behind them, and with a pleading glance, Isaac invited Sovilla to sit next to him and Snickers.

"Let's stop at that firehouse we passed coming here," Mrs. Vandenberg suggested. "We can get take-out containers of chicken barbecue for everyone. I guess you can't call your *onkel*'s family to let them know we're coming?"

Sovilla shook her head. "Lloyd doesn't have a phone."

"Well then, it'll be a surprise."

Not a happy one, Sovilla suspected.

As they pulled into Lloyd Mast's driveway, Isaac's jaw clenched. At the memory of Sovilla's flight from that house earlier in the day, his insides churned. He didn't want to meet the man who'd scared her.

But he readied himself for a confrontation. His mind echoed Eli's words. *I'm never letting you out of my sight again.* Whatever Isaac had to do to ensure Sovilla went home with him, he'd do it.

Beside him, Sovilla stiffened as the van door opened. She appeared terrified. What kind of a hold did her *onkel* have over her?

Wilma had frightened people at the market, and Sovilla had labeled Lloyd as ten times worse. Isaac pictured a tyrant.

Reaching over, Isaac squeezed Sovilla's hand. "We'll b-be with you."

Her eyes shone with tears. "*Danke.* I've been scared to death of my *onkel* since I was little."

When Isaac whispered, "Let's pray," Sovilla's tense features relaxed.

"I should have thought of that." She bowed her head while Wilma struggled to get out of the van, with Eli's help.

Isaac added his prayers to hers until their turn came to exit. Everyone stayed back to allow Wilma and Eli to reach the porch first.

When Lloyd answered their knock, he focused on Wilma, and his mouth dropped open. "Get off my property," he commanded.

Eli stepped closer to her. "She'll do no such thing. This is her childhood home. She has as much right to be here as you."

Lloyd's gaze flew to Eli's face. "Eli? What are you doing here?"

"Exposing old lies. Time for the truth."

Was that a flicker of fear in Lloyd's eyes? It disappeared too quickly for Isaac to be sure. But when Sovilla's *onkel* lifted his gaze to the man behind Eli, Lloyd's face grew ashen.

"Yes, we brought our son." Wilma's self-satisfied smile threw her brother off balance.

A woman appeared at his side. "Lloyd, why are we keeping everyone waiting on the porch?"

She must be Lloyd's wife and Sovilla's *aenti*.

"Please come in," she said, her tone welcoming.

Isaac motioned for Mrs. Vandenberg and the driver to precede him and Sovilla.

"Who are they?" Lloyd asked, and his wife frowned at him.

Mrs. Vandenberg hobbled over the threshold with her cane. "I'm their driver."

After studying her clothes and unsteady gait, Lloyd looked at her askance.

She pointed her cane at her driver and Isaac, both loaded down with grocery bags filled with take-out boxes. "And they're the delivery boys." She laughed at Lloyd's incredulous expression.

Despite her shuffle, Mrs. Vandenberg sailed past Lloyd, her head high. "Where would you like these?" she asked Lloyd's wife. "We brought enough for everyone."

While Lloyd glowered after Mrs. Vandenberg, Sovilla and Isaac slipped in without him noticing them or Snickers. Lloyd's wife wavered a bit, her gaze fixed on David, Wilma, and Eli, who were heading into the living room.

Then she turned her attention to Mrs. Vandenberg. The smell of chicken barbecue filled the air, and she stared at all the take-out containers. "You didn't have to do that."

"I can't resist supporting charities." Mrs. Vandenberg didn't indicate if she meant the firehouse or the Masts.

"I see." Lloyd's wife beckoned them to follow her. "Right this way. I'm Annie, by the way."

"Nice to meet you, Annie. I'm Liesl Vandenberg."

"Are you really the driver?"

Mrs. Vandenberg chuckled. "No. This is our driver. I guess you could call me the supervisor, or as Wilma often refers to me, the *boss*."

Annie blinked, as if unsure whether to believe her.

Isaac had another name for Mrs. Vandenberg. *Matchmaker*—or *miracle worker*. Sovilla trailed him to the counter holding Snickers's leash.

Despite Lloyd's less than enthusiastic welcome, Isaac's heart filled to bursting. All these people surrounding

Sovilla would keep her safe. Annie appeared kind, so she might be an ally. And Wilma and Mrs. Vandenberg could hold their own.

Annie leaned close to Sovilla and whispered, "Your *onkel* is furious about you leaving without permission."

Sovilla's whole body contracted, and anger coursed through Isaac. No one deserved to intimidate others that way.

"I'm here for you," he said in a low voice after Annie headed to the counter to unpack boxes. "You d-don't have t-to be afraid." He had done well with his first sentence. He only wished he hadn't let his worry affect his second one.

But his words worked. Sovilla's tense shoulders relaxed, and she turned to him with a relieved smile. "You're right. I have you and the others, and we've both asked for God's protection."

If Isaac had his way, he'd stand here all day, staring deep into her eyes, which held mysterious secrets that spoke to his soul.

Isaac's protective stance and expression surrounded Sovilla with warmth and support. God had sent him into her life to remind her to rely on divine help rather than her own strength.

He reached for Snickers's leash, and their hands brushed. Her whole body tingled. If Mrs. Vandenberg hadn't nudged her, Sovilla might still be standing there, mesmerized.

Luckily, Sovilla and Isaac had just jumped apart when Lloyd entered the kitchen.

"What's that animal doing in the kitchen?" he demanded.

"Snickers is a guide dog." Sovilla's voice shook, but

she wouldn't let her *onkel* bully Isaac. "Well, a puppy in training."

"What does he need a guide dog for? He doesn't look blind."

Sovilla gasped. She'd known her *onkel* to be rude, but that had been out of bounds.

"He's not." The stare Mrs. Vandenberg gave Lloyd made it clear she'd found his comment as offensive as Sovilla had. "Isaac's a guide dog trainer, so he needs to keep the dog with him at all times."

Lloyd appeared ready to explode.

Mrs. Vandenberg handed him a take-out box. "Why don't we eat now while the meals are still warm?"

"Good idea." Annie scurried around the kitchen, getting out glasses, iced tea, and milk. "Sovilla," she said, "can you call your *mamm* and sisters? They're quilting in the basement."

Under Lloyd's resentful frown, Sovilla headed for the basement door, and Isaac and Snickers trailed after her. When she opened the basement door, Mamm glanced up. She pressed her hands against her heart to signal her relief over Sovilla's return.

"Supper," Sovilla called, and Mamm and her sisters rushed up the stairs.

Isaac stepped back as Mamm, Lorianne, and Martha Mae enveloped Sovilla in hugs. Oh, how she'd missed their embraces! She welcomed every opportunity to hug them back.

With a quick check over her shoulder for Lloyd, Sovilla introduced Isaac to her family. When her sisters clamored to pet Snickers, Sovilla explained why they couldn't.

Although Isaac had eleven siblings, he seemed overwhelmed by meeting her *mamm* and sisters. Or maybe he was worried about stuttering. He had no need to tense up. He performed each greeting perfectly.

She smiled to encourage him. And once again, their gazes lingered.

"We'd better get to the table before Lloyd gets upset," Martha Mae said.

She and Lorianne skipped off. Isaac followed, but Mamm took Sovilla's elbow to hold her back a few steps.

In a low voice, she said, "You've already gotten over Henry, I see."

"*Jah.*" Since Sovilla had been spending time around Isaac, Henry never entered her mind.

"Mamm, you should know, Wilma's here, and she brought her son."

"How wonderful. I always wondered if she married."

"*Neh*, she's not married."

Her *mamm* blinked rapidly. "I don't understand."

Sovilla's heart sank. Wilma had mentioned Lloyd hadn't given her time to say goodbye to her sister. Maybe Mamm had no idea about Wilma's baby. She gave a brief recap of the story, punctuated by Mamm's gasps.

"Where are Barbie and Sovilla?" Lloyd's irritated voice reached them in the hallway.

"We'd better go." Sovilla said as Mamm wiped away a few tears. "I'll tell you more later." She led her shell-shocked mother into the dining room.

Isaac and the driver had squeezed onto the bench on the opposite side of the table with Sovilla's cousins. Annie slid into place beside Lloyd just before Sovilla and Mamm got to the table.

Isaac's scarlet face made her wonder if her cousins had been teasing him. All three of them chuckled as she sat across from him, and she sent him a sympathetic message with her eyes.

"It's about time," Lloyd said. "The food's probably cold by now."

Annie laid a hand on her take-out box. "Mine's still warm, so everyone else's probably is too." Her fake toothy smile did little to calm Lloyd.

They all bowed their heads for the silent prayer. Wilma shocked Sovilla by lowering her head and shutting her eyes. Her *aenti* praying?

When they lifted their heads, Annie smiled at David. "I didn't get to meet this young man, but I'm guessing you're a relative of Eli's. You look so much like him as a young man."

Sovilla had warned Mamm. She wished she'd thought to do the same for her *aenti*.

"David is my son," Eli said.

All three of Sovilla's cousins had their heads bent over their chicken. At Eli's announcement, their heads popped up.

Annie's brow knitted. "Maybe I misheard. I thought you said *son*." She laughed a little. "You've been a bachelor forever." Then her cheeks reddened, and she stared down at her unopened box.

Wilma set down her plastic fork. "Actually, Annie, what Eli meant is that David is *our* son."

"But that's impossible. I mean . . ." Her voice trailed off.

"I don't appreciate you flaunting your sinfulness at our supper table in front of the *youngie*."

Annie gasped and covered her mouth—whether because Wilma and Eli's behavior had shocked her or her husband's comment had, Sovilla couldn't decide. Perhaps both.

Her cousins had given up all pretense of eating and were staring avidly at Wilma, Eli, and David.

"Pay attention to your meals," Lloyd barked at them. "We should never give sinfulness our attention. Instead of being here, they should be confessing in front of the church."

"I already did so. Have you?" Eli, his voice as stern as a preacher's, pinned Lloyd with a steely glance.

"I have no idea what you're talking about." Lloyd sawed at his chicken leg, snapping his plastic knife in half.

Wilma's eyes narrowed. "We wasted thirty years of our lives because of your lies. And you deprived David of his home and parents."

David started to protest, but Wilma waved for him to be silent. With an understanding nod, David closed his mouth.

"What are they talking about, Lloyd?" Annie sounded close to tears.

Giving up on his knife, Lloyd savagely ripped the leg from the rest of the chicken with his fingers. "I saved your reputation, Wilma. Yours too, Eli. You should be thanking me."

"Thanking you for separating us? For destroying our relationship? For leaving me alone with no place to live?" Wilma's voice rose higher with every word until she was practically shouting.

"Lloyd?" Annie's deadly quiet tone carried more of a lash than Wilma's hysterical one.

"All right, all right. So I fibbed a bit to keep the two of you apart. I did what I thought was best at the time." Lloyd jammed the chicken leg into his mouth and bit down hard.

"All sin is the same in the eyes of God." Everyone turned to stare at Mrs. Vandenberg. "Let him who's without sin cast the first stone."

Lloyd choked on his chicken. Annie pounded on his back, and he coughed so hard tears spurted from his eyes.

Eli gave Lloyd a minute to catch his breath before saying, "Perhaps you can also explain why you left your sister homeless in a strange city when she was only seventeen."

"Seventeen?" Annie's head shot up. "That's when—" A sick look came over her face. "*Neh*, Lloyd. You didn't do this because of my *daed*. Please tell me you didn't."

"Why would you think that?" he blustered.

"You did, didn't you?" she said heavily. "The timing's right. You told me Wilma—"

Lloyd cut her off with a wave of his hand. "There's no need to go into that."

"I think there is." Eli nodded for Annie to continue. "I need to know why you abandoned my sweet, loving girlfriend." His face squinched in pain. "She does too."

Annie pushed away her take-out container. "Lloyd said that Wilma had gone—"

Lloyd tried again to silence her, but Annie ignored him.

"I'm so sorry, Wilma. I didn't know. Lloyd said you'd gone to stay with a great-aunt in Pennsylvania." Placing her hands on the table in front of her, Annie stared down at her work-worn fingers. "My *daed* was very, very strict. He wouldn't have let me marry Lloyd if he thought I'd be around anyone . . ." She lifted a hand.

Tears welled in Sovilla's eyes. She hoped Annie didn't blame herself for Wilma's plight.

"Although I totally disagree with what you did"—Annie swallowed back tears—"I can understand why you wanted to send Wilma away, Lloyd. But not supporting her, that's—that's criminal."

Lloyd lowered his head and shaded his eyes with his hands. "I had no money to send her. Your dad asked me to go into partnership." Lloyd hesitated. "When he told me how much we each needed to buy into the milking business, I told him I had the money, but I didn't."

"You lied?" Eli offered.

"I suppose. I mortgaged the house and took everything out of savings, even sold off furniture. For the next few months, I could barely buy food for Barbie. Many nights, I went hungry so she could eat."

"Don't play the victim, Lloyd. If you hadn't lied, Daed would have worked out a payment plan. He may have been strict, but he was generous."

"I couldn't admit that to him," Lloyd said miserably. "I didn't want him to think I couldn't afford to support you."

"So you sacrificed your sister for me?" Annie reached over and squeezed Wilma's hand. "I wish I'd known. I'm so, so sorry." Then she stood. "If you'll all excuse me. . ." Annie rushed from the table, and nearby, the bedroom door slammed.

Lloyd rose. "I'll be back."

Everyone stared at the two empty places in silence.

Chapter Thirty

Isaac caught Sovilla's eye. This had to be hard for her. Her eyes brimmed with appreciation for him despite the sadness on her face. Her cousins had returned to their meals as if unperturbed. Her sisters looked as if they were fighting back tears.

"I'm so sorry, Mamm and Daed," David said.

"It's not your fault, son." Eli put a hand on his shoulder.

Wilma's shoulders slumped. "Before this, I ached inside because I'd been abandoned, left alone to fend for myself. Now, knowing my brother destroyed my life and happiness for his pride . . ."

"And for love," Eli reminded her. "But what he did was so wrong."

Sovilla's Mamm had her head bowed, and her cheeks were wet. "Wilma, I never knew why you left me. If I'd known, I'd have tried to find you."

"Barbie?" Wilma's voice held a deep tenderness. "You were young. I never even got to say goodbye, and Lloyd forbade me to contact you."

"Why did we listen to him?"

"Because he was our older brother. He took Mamm and Daed's place."

Isaac prayed for healing for all who'd been hurt by this situation, including Lloyd. He had to live with the guilt.

Almost everyone had finished their meals, so Sovilla cleared the table while Barbie went to the kitchen to bring out dessert.

Isaac stood. "I c-can help."

Sovilla's cousin Marvin snickered and repeated Isaac's sentence, but stuttering on every word. "Sounds familiar, don't it?" He poked his brother in the ribs.

Before their teasing could escalate, Barbie set slices of pie in front of them. They'd all settled in to eat their desserts when Lloyd returned.

"Annie won't be coming back to the table. She's not feeling well."

Mrs. Vandenberg's voice cracked across the table like a whip. "Did you not learn anything from the dinner table discussion?"

Lloyd's head jerked back. "What do you mean?"

"Your lying destroyed several lives at this table." She gestured toward Wilma, Eli, and David. Then she included Sovilla.

"I'm sorry," he mumbled. "I didn't mean to hurt them."

"If you'd truly repented, you wouldn't have lied when you just sat down. Is Annie really ill? Or were you saving face because she's upset with you?"

Lloyd bit into his chicken leg, perhaps hoping Mrs. Vandenberg would drop the subject.

Isaac smiled to himself. Lloyd had no idea how persistent Mrs. V could be.

Sovilla met his eyes and pinched her lips together to hold back her giggles. Seeing her struggling to keep her mirth inside made him want to burst out laughing. Her eyes danced as his shoulders shook in silent chuckles.

Maybe he shouldn't find Mrs. Vandenberg's lecture on such a serious topic so hilarious, but she'd made Lloyd uncomfortable and forced him to face his lies.

"Lloyd, you still haven't answered me."

"What was the question?"

Annie returned to the dining room, her eyes red. "I worried about dessert, but I see you already have pie."

"Barbie served us."

"*Danke.*" Annie appeared tired and drained.

Mrs. Vandenberg went after Lloyd again. "Well, Lloyd, Annie's here, so what's the answer? She can decide if you're truthful."

He shrugged and finished chewing. "You can see she's not sick. Why are you making such a big deal about it?"

"Lloyd Mast"—Annie planted her hands on her hips—"is that any way to speak to a guest? And an elderly lady?"

With a loud sigh, Lloyd mumbled an apology.

"I can see you'll have your work cut out for you, Wilma."

Mrs. Vandenberg startled Wilma, and she stopped staring dreamily at Eli. "What? Oh, yes, I'll try to be like you, Liesl, when I move in here on Monday."

Lloyd's fork clattered to his plate. He'd finished his chicken and started on his pie, but his mouth seemed glued shut.

This time, Isaac couldn't help snickering, and Sovilla grinned.

Sovilla's *onkel* glared at Isaac before he faced Wilma. "What did you say?"

"Eli and I will be getting married." Wilma waited a moment to let that sink in. "Because I never joined the church, I'll need to take baptismal classes. I'll stay here to do that."

"Here? As in this house?" Lloyd's eyes seemed about to pop out of his head.

"That's the plan. Sovilla's already taken over my market stand in Pennsylvania, so she can continue to work there."

"Sovilla is not returning to Pennsylvania. She'll be staying here."

Isaac drew in a deep breath, and all three of Sovilla's cousins stared at him mockingly. He had to get out one sentence without stuttering. "Sovilla's old enough"—he gasped for air—"to choose." He'd done it—defended her and completed a sentence.

The joy in Sovilla's eyes added to his triumph.

But Lloyd dashed his hopes. "If Wilma's moving here, I have no idea where *she* plans to sleep, because we still have to make room for Sovilla." He turned to Isaac as he emphasized each word. "She will remain here where I can keep an eye on her."

Isaac had vowed not to let Sovilla out of his sight. He refused to leave Ohio without her. "She's g-going b-back with me."

Sovilla loved that he'd become her champion. She refused to let Lloyd separate them.

"Isaac's right." Wilma shot Lloyd a triumphant glance. "As for where I'm sleeping, I intend to move into the bedroom Barbie's using."

"*Ach*, that'll be much too crowded," Annie protested. "We can't fit another bed in there."

"You won't have to. I'll take Barbie's bed."

Annie's face wrinkled with distress. "But—"

Even Barbie appeared surprised, but she offered, "I can sleep in the basement."

"*Neh*, Mamm, you can have our bed. We'll go downstairs," Martha Mae volunteered.

Lorianne nodded. "Even if I'm scared of the spiders."

"How touching." Lloyd's sarcasm interrupted them. He opened his mouth to say something else, but Wilma cut him off.

"If everyone could be quiet a minute, I'll explain." With a twinkle in her eye, Wilma waggled her eyebrows at Mrs. Vandenberg. "I've learned something about being bossy and directing people's lives from you."

Lloyd started to speak again, but Wilma ignored him and turned back to the others at the table.

"When I went into the hospital," she said, "I put my house in Sovilla's name. She owns it and everything in it."

"In your will, you mean," Sovilla corrected her, then regretted it. Maybe she'd undercut her *aenti*'s opportunity to best Lloyd.

"That's what I told you, but I actually deeded everything to you. I didn't trust certain people at this table not to cheat you out of your inheritance and leave you homeless."

Lloyd pursed his lips and clenched his fingers around his fork.

Wilma faced Eli. "I was positive I was going to die."

His anguished eyes revealed the depth of his love. "I wish I'd been there for you. For that and—and everything else." He lowered his head into his hands. "Thirty wasted years."

All eyes focused on Lloyd. He squirmed. Then he lowered his head and made a show of scraping up the last crumbs of pie on his plate.

"I wish you'd been with me." Wilma's face grew wistful. "But we'll make up for it."

Eli lifted his head. "I'm looking forward to it."

Wilma's happiness radiated from her. "I am too."

Sovilla had been sitting there stunned ever since Wilma's announcement. She owned the house and everything in it? She couldn't accept it. Rightfully, it should be David's. For now, she'd go along with the plan so she could get away from Lloyd and return to Pennsylvania with Isaac. But she'd talk to Wilma in private later. The whole idea thrilled her. But she hated leaving Mamm and her sisters.

"So, Sovilla is all set in Pennsylvania," Mrs. Vandenberg prompted Wilma.

"Right. And I know how much she misses her *mamm* and sisters, so Barbie, why don't you and the girls go back with her? My old farmhouse has five bedrooms."

"What about her quilting?" Lloyd asked. "She can't go. She has commitments here."

"Quilting?" Wilma waved a dismissive hand. "Barbie, you can talk to Mrs. Vandenberg about finding work. Lancaster has many quilt shops, and I'm sure Liesl has plenty of connections."

Mrs. Vandenberg nodded. "I can take care of that. And Sovilla, I assume your sisters can help at the market when they're not in school."

Mamm's delight shone on her face.

Lloyd stood up. "I won't have it." He waved in the direction of Mamm and the girls. "You are all staying here."

"I believe," Mrs. Vandenberg said coolly, "you've been outvoted."

"We'll see about that." He stalked from the room.

Amidst the excited chatter, Sovilla focused on Isaac.

She couldn't believe it. She'd not only be with Isaac and working at the market, but she'd also have her whole family around her. Maybe David would be willing to rent them the house. He already had a place of his own. Could she have asked for anything more?

Only one thing. A relationship with Isaac. And if the signals he was sending her right now were any indication, that might also be a possibility.

Isaac's heart leapt. He'd never been more certain of anything in his life. He wanted to court her. And the looks zinging back and forth between them only confirmed his decision.

"Hey, Isaac." Marvin elbowed him.

Sighing internally, Isaac broke his connection with Sovilla. He needed to be polite. And besides, these were her relatives. If he planned to have a future with Sovilla, they'd be his relatives too.

"*Jah?*" he said after Marvin prodded him a second time.

"Want to toss a baseball with us?"

That meant leaving Sovilla, but she was busy discussing traveling plans with her *mamm*. He'd find time to be alone with her. They had tomorrow and all of Monday while they traveled.

"S-sure. Maybe Sovilla c-can watch S-Snickers." He'd have to feed her and walk her in a half hour or so, though, but that'd give him a little time to play.

"Come," he said to Snickers, who'd stayed under the table by his feet while everyone ate. Lloyd hadn't seemed too keen on dogs, so Isaac had kept her hidden.

Isaac checked with Sovilla, and she agreed. But when she heard his plans, her eyes flashed out a warning. He turned in time to see her three cousins smirking. Isaac had no idea what they had planned. At least he was a skilled pitcher, so he should be able to hold his own in the ball game.

"Let's go." Marvin sounded friendly enough.

"Before we play, we have something to show you," Albert said.

Outside, they moved until they were out of sight of the dining room window. That clued Isaac they were up to something.

"There's something you should know about Sovilla." Marvin flicked his eyes sideways at his brother. "Show him, Roy."

"I d-don't want t-to see it." Isaac stood his ground.

Roy laughed. "I—I—I . . . d-d-don't w-want t-to s-see it."

Had they brought him out here to mock him? Isaac had been teased plenty of times before. He pretended not to notice.

Roy repeated it.

Isaac recalled something Sovilla had told him when they first met. He took a deep breath to help him speak smoothly. "Didn't you"—*another breath*—"stutter when you"—*one more breath*—"were small?"

"Who told you that?" Roy turned belligerent. Then he waved a hand to dismiss it. "Well, I got over it. You still have a problem. You sound like a slow-moving train huffing and puffing."

Isaac tried to pull in air without gasping. "You understood me." That's all that counted.

"Aw, let up on the stuttering stuff, Roy. The guy can't help it," Albert said. "Besides, that's not why we wanted him out here."

"*Jah*, show him the note," Marvin insisted.

"First we should explain." With a grin, Albert clutched his suspenders. "You might be interested in Sovilla, but she's in love with someone else."

Isaac tried not to show their blow had landed. He couldn't bear to think of Sovilla with anyone else.

When Isaac didn't answer, Albert continued. "She wrote her boyfriend a love letter."

Roy waved it in the air. "Bet you're wondering how we got it."

Isaac shrugged. He wanted to ask, but he refused to give them the satisfaction. Maybe if he kept quiet, they'd tell him. They seemed eager to brag.

Marvin took over the story. "When Sovilla moved from Sugarcreek, she wanted to send this letter to Henry." Marvin stretched out Henry's name as if he were a lovesick girl.

Henry? The boyfriend who jilted her? Sovilla had been hurt by him.

"She gave it to her *mamm*." Roy waggled his brows. "But since Barbie didn't have time to drop it off or mail it, we offered."

Marvin grinned. "Instead of this note, we sent old Henry a breakup letter."

They all laughed.

"You what?" Isaac was steaming. They'd been the reason Sovilla's boyfriend had broken up with her?

"So, you want to hear what she wrote?" Roy waved the note in front of Isaac's nose.

"*Neh.*" Whatever Sovilla had written to Henry, she'd intended to be only for Henry's eyes. He'd respect her privacy. Isaac started back toward the house, his heart aching for Sovilla. She'd lost her true love.

Roy pranced after him. In a high, girly voice, he read: "*Dear Henry . . .*"

Isaac's heart clenched. *Dear?* He tried to tune out the rest, but Sovilla's last line delivered a barb that left him bleeding.

If you want me to, I'll find a way to come back to you.

The words played over and over again as he strode across the lawn.

How he wished this note had been sent to him. If he'd received it, he could have never resisted her plea. He'd have come after her to beg her to marry him, and he'd have brought her home with him right away.

Henry probably would have too. Except he'd never received this message.

Roy snickered. "See? She's in love with someone else. You're the leftovers."

Isaac couldn't deny the truth of Roy's words. It hadn't been that long since she'd written this note. If Henry hadn't jilted her, Sovilla never would have been interested in Isaac. In fact, she'd been standoffish when they first met because her heart belonged to Henry.

"Stealing someone's letter like this is cruel." Isaac climbed the porch steps, eager to get away from them and their spitefulness. Like father, like sons.

"Don't worry. Sovilla deserves every prank we've played on her," Albert said.

"*Jah*, she got us in trouble all the time when we were little."

Marvin's sneer struck fear in Isaac's chest. He didn't care what they did to him, but it sounded as if they planned to hurt Sovilla. He'd never let that happen.

As he walked into the house, Isaac sorted through possible choices in his mind. He could pretend he'd never heard about the letter. Henry had found someone else, and Isaac could date Sovilla. His whole being longed to do that.

But would that be right? If he told Sovilla the truth, could she mend her relationship with Henry? Her letter made it clear she loved him. She'd offered to leave everything and come back to him.

Isaac should tell her right away. The sooner he did it, the sooner she could straighten out the letter mix-up, and the less likely Henry would be to fall for the girl he'd just started dating.

But could Isaac tell Sovilla, knowing it would mean he'd lose her forever?

Chapter Thirty-One

Isaac entered the house, his heart weighed down. As he closed the back door, Sovilla's cousins, laughing together, took off in their buggy. Eli, Wilma, and David were still chatting at the table, but Mrs. Vandenberg appeared to be dozing. In the kitchen, Barbie and Annie did the dishes, while Sovilla and her sisters cleaned the dining room.

Watching Sovilla's brisk movements as she swept the floor pierced him. He'd imagined doing chores together in their own home, but now . . . He closed his eyes to block pictures of her working with Henry.

Although he should offer to help, lethargy settled over him. His muscles took on the heaviness of his spirit.

He needed to get Sovilla alone to tell her about the letter. Better to get it over with. A quick, clean break.

Isaac caught her attention and flicked his eyes toward the door, praying she'd get his message.

A tiny nod and smile showed she had. She finished sweeping the crumbs into a dustpan and put away the broom. While she was gone, Isaac rethought using the back door. Anyone in the dining room could see them. If either of them got emotional, he'd rather they do it in private.

"Front porch?" he suggested when she returned.

"*Gut* idea."

The curve of her lips, the gleam in her eye, the suppressed excitement in her walk revealed she expected different news than what he had to give her. Instead of sharing the porch swing and talking of a future together, he'd be hammering a wedge between them.

Isaac opened the door, but before either of them could step foot outside, the bedroom door nearby banged open. It slammed against the wall, making them both jump.

"I caught you." Lloyd emerged from the doorway, his face a mask of fury. "Trying to sneak out?"

Isaac couldn't lie. Although his intentions hadn't been what Lloyd suspected, they had been secretive.

"No answer? Your guilty faces are answer enough."

Hearing the commotion, Eli, Wilma, and David hurried into the hallway. Mrs. Vandenberg followed at a slower pace.

"Close that door," Lloyd commanded. "Neither of you is going anywhere. The last thing we need is more sin." He swiveled toward Wilma with a scowl. "This is all your doing."

Sovilla started to protest, but Lloyd silenced her. "You never got into trouble before you went to stay with Wilma."

"She hasn't done anything wrong." Sovilla's *mamm*'s voice rang out.

"Only because I caught her."

"Perhaps it's time for us to go." Mrs. Vandenberg faced Sovilla. "We'll pick you up for church in the morning. Wilma and David would like to go with Eli."

Brushing past Lloyd, Mrs. Vandenberg straightened her shoulders and tapped her cane down hard with each step.

Wilma clicked along behind her with Eli on one side and David on the other. Isaac trailed behind.

He had one last glimpse of Sovilla's disappointment. Perhaps if she'd heard what he had to say, her expression might be hopeful.

As they returned to the hotel, Isaac held the secret, hot and heavy, inside. The longer he waited, the harder it became. And the more he wanted to forget the letter entirely.

The bubbles of happiness inside Sovilla as she got into the van the next morning popped when Isaac stared morosely out the window. He responded politely to her questions, but he seemed to be lost in thought. After a few attempts at conversation, she left him alone.

Because Isaac didn't seem to want to communicate, Sovilla brought up the concern bothering her. "Wilma, I don't feel right about taking your house away from David."

David turned his head so he could meet her eyes. "I don't want or need it. I have my own home. Please accept and enjoy it."

"Wilma, you might need the money from it," Sovilla persisted.

Eli chuckled. "*Neh*, she won't. We've already talked about that. I've spent thirty years as a bachelor filling my long, lonely hours working two jobs. We have more than enough."

"Seems like you're stuck with the place," Wilma said.

Stuck with it? Neh, she'd received one of the biggest blessings of her life. Not counting Isaac.

She directed her joy and excitement his way, expecting him to reflect it back. Instead, his smile wobbled, and he didn't meet her eyes.

Worry churned in Sovilla's stomach. Ever since she'd gotten into the van, he'd been acting odd. Had she done or said something to hurt or upset him?

Last night, he'd asked to talk to her. After the way they'd been connecting since he'd arrived in Ohio, she'd expected him to ask about courting her. Maybe she'd been wrong. Had he intended to tell her she'd misread their shared smiles, their stolen glances?

As they headed back to the hotel after church, Isaac shoved his hands in his pockets to fight the urge to hold Sovilla's hand. He had no right to do that, especially now that he knew of her love for Henry. He'd wrestled with the situation all last night, but his conscience refused to let him rest until he told her the truth.

He waited until everyone else had left the van. "Could we t-talk?"

"You mean right now?"

Isaac nodded. "I have t-to walk Snickers."

"All right, I'll go with you."

Sorrow filled Isaac. Before her cousins had told him about the letter, he might have taken that as a sign. A sign they belonged together. Now, it meant nothing.

"I'll be in soon," Sovilla said to Wilma and Mrs. Vandenberg.

She was right. He'd only need a few minutes to explain about Henry. Then they'd go their separate ways.

"What did you want to talk about?" Sovilla asked as Snickers headed toward a tiny patch of grass and weeds.

Isaac stayed silent, trying to find the right way to reveal the truth.

Concrete sidewalks and an asphalt parking lot, only a

short distance from a busy highway, didn't provide the ideal setting for this life-changing conversation. But the setting's bleakness reflected the state of his future.

By controlling his breathing and blocking off his heart, he made it through the first statement. "I have to . . . tell you about . . . Henry."

"Henry?" Her face paled. "How do you know about him?"

In halting sentences and stuttering words, Isaac recounted yesterday's meeting with her cousins.

"Henry never got my letter?" Sovilla stared at Isaac as emotions flickered across her face—shock, pain, sadness, regret . . .

He had to look away.

"No wonder he never called. I waited and waited."

Isaac pictured her standing by the phone, longing for a call that never came.

"I thought"—her words were laced with pain—"he didn't call because he'd left me for someone else. If he believed that fake letter, he must have assumed I'd broken up with him."

"*Jah*, he d-did. But now . . ."

She walked along with her head down, her shoulders bowed. "Do you know how much that hurt?"

He certainly did. He was enduring that pain right now.

"It hasn't b-been long. If you explained—"

"*Neh*, too much has happened since then."

"But he might want t-to start over." Or to go back to where they had been. If it were Isaac, he'd leap at the chance to get back together.

"I can't." Sovilla moved ahead of him.

Isaac stayed stuck in place while Snickers nosed at the grass.

"I'm not the same person anymore."

"When you're in l-love, it d-doesn't matter. L-Look at Wilma and Eli." Even after thirty years, they'd connected right away.

"That's what got me thinking. Neither of them found anyone else. Henry and I both moved on so quickly, it couldn't have been true love."

"You m-moved on?" Isaac tried not to show her words had shaken him to the core.

Sovilla kept her back to him. "*Jah.*"

He'd spent a lot of time around her recently and had never noticed her with anyone. Anyone but him. Could she mean—?

Isaac jiggled Snickers's leash to move the puppy forward. He had to see Sovilla's face, but Snickers remained firmly planted.

"Sovilla?" Isaac breathed her name softly, reverently.

She turned when he called her, and their eyes met. Isaac had no doubt now that she'd meant him.

"You know h-how I feel about you, don't you?" he asked.

She shook her head.

Couldn't she tell? Or did she want him to put it into words?

He slipped the loop of Snickers's leash around his wrist so he could take both of her hands in his. This moment was too special and too sacred to make a mistake.

Please, Lord, help me to get this right.

Then, using everything he'd practiced, Isaac poured out his heart. "From the first time . . . I saw you . . . I was attracted."

He couldn't keep his eyes off her, but he'd been drawn to her for other, deeper reasons.

Take in air. "My feelings grew . . . the more time . . . I spent around you." Sovilla's shining eyes encouraged him to continue. "I care about you." Should he use the word *love*? Or was it too soon? "I'd like to . . . court you."

"*Ach*, Isaac, I thought you'd never ask." Her face glowing, she added, "Every word you said came out perfect."

But she hadn't answered. He wanted to hear her say *jah*. He sent the question with his eyes. Sovilla often read his mind. He hoped she'd do it this time.

She squeezed his hands. "I'd like that."

He had one more nagging thought. "What about Henry?"

"Forget Henry," she said. "I have." She went silent for a moment. "I do want to send him a letter."

Isaac's insides roiled. What did she want to say to Henry?

"Henry should know that I didn't write the breakup letter. I don't want him to feel rejected."

"I see." He couldn't keep his concern from his face and voice. "What if he ch-changes his mind?"

"Don't worry. I'll be sure to let him know I'm dating someone else. And I'll wish him and Nancy well."

"That's k-kind of you." But Isaac imagined what he'd do if he received that letter. He'd come after her. Suppose Henry did the same.

"You're frowning."

Isaac's fears constricted his chest so much he could barely breathe. "What if Henry hops on a t-train and comes t-to visit?"

"I'll send him home." Sovilla stopped and gazed off into the distance. "*Neh*, I'd—"

Isaac tensed, waiting for her next words.

"I'd tell him to pray about it and seek God's will." Sovilla ducked her head and glanced up at Isaac through her lashes. "I've been doing that for a while, and all signs seem to point to you."

Isaac had felt God leading him to her too, so all he needed to do was trust the Lord. With God's help, he'd just done the two hardest things in life so far.—giving a speech and asking out the woman he'd fallen for. Surely, he could trust God for all the rest.

Sovilla floated on clouds of happiness the rest of the afternoon. Even learning they'd be going to Lloyd's for supper didn't bring her down.

Mrs. Vandenberg observed the two lovebirds with a self-satisfied smile. Sovilla owed some of her gladness to Mrs. Vandenberg's matchmaking schemes. If it weren't for her, Sovilla wouldn't have spent so much time with Isaac. The two of them owed Mrs. Vandenberg a lot.

"*Danke,*" Sovilla whispered to Mrs. Vandenberg.

"For what?"

"You know." Sovilla couldn't yet put her new relationship into words.

Mrs. Vandenberg's eyes twinkled. "Indeed, I do."

Wilma was too wrapped up in her own relationship to notice the covert glances Isaac and Sovilla exchanged, but when they reached Lloyd's house, her cousins picked up on it right away. They muscled Isaac into a corner.

They may have believed they were talking quietly, but Sovilla could hear.

"So you didn't tell her." Roy's accusation had a threatening undertone.

"I did."

Sovilla's heart swelled with pride at Isaac's calmness

and confidence. Her cousins surrounding him that way had to be intimidating.

"Liar," Marvin said.

"We're going to tell Sovilla," Albert taunted.

"Go ahead." Isaac disentangled himself from the circle.

Sovilla gave Isaac a thumbs-up for holding his own amidst her cousins' bullying. But with Lloyd watching their every move, they went in different directions. Sovilla enjoyed chatting with the women as she helped in the kitchen.

Isaac sat in the dining room with Wilma, Eli, David, and Mrs. Vandenberg. He'd positioned himself so he had the best view of her. As much as it thrilled Sovilla, it proved too distracting. She had to concentrate on pouring milk into the glasses instead of onto the counter.

Good thing they were only setting out sandwich fixings instead of cooking a regular meal. Otherwise, she might have been putting sugar into a casserole instead of salt.

After everyone had gathered around the table and prayed, Wilma plunged into conversation before anyone had taken a bite.

"Because I don't need or want anything from my Lancaster life and I'd rather not relive that painful time of fear, loneliness, and homelessness"—she sent a pointed look in Lloyd's direction—"Eli and I made some plans."

Eli beamed at her.

"I'm announcing them in front of witnesses to be sure nobody tries to change them. I'm sure you understand why, Lloyd." She favored her brother with a fake smile.

He pretended to ignore her dig and her scrutiny as he nonchalantly took a bite of his Trail bologna and Swiss sandwich. But the vein throbbing in his neck and the flush spreading across his cheekbones revealed his agitation.

"I've asked Mrs. Vandenberg to sell my Oldsmobile, since I won't be needing it anymore." Wilma flashed Eli a smile.

"Because it's an antique and in pristine condition," Mrs. Vandenberg said, "it'll be worth a small fortune."

Lloyd's eyes widened.

With another sharp look at her brother, Wilma continued, "The money will be donated to New Beginnings."

Lloyd winced and dug his fork into the heaping mound of potato salad on his plate.

Wilma directed her next comments to Annie. "New Beginnings is a home for teen *mamms*, so I'm sure you understand why I chose them. I've asked Liesl to be sure they set some of it aside for teens leaving the shelter who have no family to provide for them."

Annie nodded, her eyes welling with tears.

Lloyd shoved back his chair. "This potato salad needs more salt." He rushed into the kitchen and banged several cupboard doors.

"And Sovilla, I'd like you to clean out all my closets and dressers. Donate all my *Englisch* clothing and shoes to a *homeless shelter*." She emphasized the last two words and spoke them loudly enough that they'd carry into the kitchen over the noise of slamming doors.

"I'd be happy to." Sovilla pinched her lips together and struggled to hold back tears. When she'd first arrived in Pennsylvania, she'd have done anything to leave and to get away from Wilma. Now, she'd miss her *aenti*.

Isaac sent her a sympathetic glance. Sovilla loved how he could tell when she needed support. She tried to convey her thanks with her eyes. The loving messages passing back and forth between them made Sovilla forget all about eating.

"So, Sovilla," Albert said, breaking the connection between her and Isaac, "whatever happened with your boyfriend? Henry, wasn't it?"

"Why don't you tell me?" Sovilla challenged.

Beside Albert, Roy's smirk faded.

Albert's voice faltered, "Isaac told you?"

"You mean about your plan to break up Henry and me?" Sovilla enjoyed seeing the cousins who'd taunted and teased her throughout childhood looking discomfited.

Annie studied her boys with a frown.

"I have to thank you for sending Henry that fake breakup letter." Sovilla smiled at each of her cousins in turn, making them squirm. "It worked out perfectly, because I found Isaac."

Isaac struggled to hold back a grin, but he wasn't very successful. A huge smile peeked out when she looked his way.

"You did what?" Annie's normally quiet voice shot up several decibels. "I want an explanation."

Heads down, they mumbled a brief reply.

Mamm gasped. "So that's why Henry started dating Nancy? Sovilla, I'm so sorry. If I'd known they couldn't be trusted . . ."

Sovilla longed to point out they'd never been trustworthy as children, so why would they be as adults? Instead, she smiled at Mamm. "It's all right, Mamm. The Lord had a different and much better plan for my life." Sovilla flicked her eyes in Isaac's direction.

Mamm lit up. "He certainly did." She included Isaac in her radiant smile.

"I'm glad it worked out well for you," Annie said. "But what my boys did was terrible." She zeroed in on her husband, who seemed quite focused on scraping the last bit of potato salad from his plate. "Lloyd, you'll speak to them, won't you?"

"What?" His head jerked up, and he stared at his wife with an uncomprehending expression on his face. "Of course, of course," he muttered.

"If your father doesn't, I will." Annie's eyes flashed fire. "I won't have any sons of mine hurting others. This family has been through enough pain."

Judging by Annie's furious look, her sons wouldn't be the only ones to endure a lecture. Sovilla almost felt sorry for her *onkel*. Almost.

Chapter Thirty-Two

Isaac woke on Monday morning filled with joy. Although he couldn't wait to return to Pennsylvania, another state now held a special place in his life. If he hadn't come to Ohio, he might never have discovered the truth about Henry or about Sovilla's feelings. He'd have gone on admiring her from afar.

They'd be leaving at daybreak for breakfast at Annie's. After that, they'd load up Sovilla and her family before heading home. Isaac went out to the van early to reserve the back seat for him and Sovilla. Because it extended across the aisle, there'd be plenty of room for Snickers too.

Isaac slid his suitcase under the seat to allow room for baggage from their additional passengers. Sovilla had been overjoyed her family would be coming with them. After Isaac fed, watered, and walked Snickers, he settled in the van, waiting for everyone else.

David stayed close beside Wilma as she clicked along with her walker, her steps almost jaunty. She'd spent the night at the hotel, while Sovilla had stayed with her *mamm*. Tonight, Wilma would move into that bedroom and prepare to begin her new life with Eli. Given the circumstances, the bishop had arranged for her to take special baptismal classes. Mrs. Vandenberg had already announced her intention to bring a vanload of relatives for the wedding.

When they arrived at Annie's house, Sovilla greeted them as if they'd been gone for months rather than overnight. "I'm so glad to see you."

Her initial welcome included everyone, but then her gaze rested on Isaac. She looked as if she'd like to throw her arms around him and melt into his embrace. Isaac hoped he was the only one who could read her message and the one he returned.

Annie bustled up behind Sovilla. "Breakfast is almost ready." She talked rapidly, and her hands moved nervously. "I apologize Lloyd couldn't be with us. One of our neighbors lost his barn in a fire late last night. Lloyd insisted he needed to speak to Martin and organize the barn raising before it rains."

"At sunrise?" Mrs. Vandenberg pointed out the ridiculous excuse.

Annie shrugged. "*Jah*, well . . ."

No one doubted that Lloyd's eagerness to help his neighbors was only a ploy to miss another uncomfortable meal. But with Wilma staying here, he'd have plenty of chances to face his past.

David carried Wilma's suitcase and *kapp* container upstairs to the bedroom, while Isaac brought down Barbie's things. Behind him, Sovilla and her sisters toted their own luggage.

After Sovilla headed out to the kitchen to help, Isaac and David moved Barbie's quilting supplies out to the van.

They filled a few of the extra seats, but Isaac made sure nobody stowed luggage in the back seat.

By the time David and Isaac finished moving everything and went into the dining room, all the women, except Mrs. Vandenberg, were busy setting dishes on the table. This time, Isaac could enjoy watching Sovilla working. He imagined the two of them preparing meals together and sitting down at the table with her on his left side. And later, their children would gather around the table.

He had no time to dwell on his dreams, because Sovilla's cousins filed into the room, eyes fixed on the ground, looking subdued.

"I'm sorry," each one mumbled in turn to Isaac and Sovilla. Their apologies must have been orchestrated by their *mamm*, because she watched intently from the kitchen.

"I hope you won't do something like that to anyone else," Sovilla said. "I'm just grateful God had a better plan for my life."

Isaac wished he could take her hand and squeeze it. She'd acted so gracious and forgiving.

If her cousins had broken up him and Sovilla, Isaac might have a hard time letting go of his antagonism. This time, however, their interference had given him the most *wunderbar* girl ever.

At the end of his silent prayer, Isaac thanked the Lord for Sovilla.

After they'd finished breakfast, Wilma beckoned to Sovilla. "Could I talk to you for a few minutes before you leave?" When Sovilla nodded, Wilma added, "Alone."

Disappointment clouded Isaac's and Eli's expressions.

"We'll be right back," Wilma assured them.

Sovilla followed her *aenti* upstairs to the bedroom, where Wilma reached for Sovilla's hands. Her *aenti* cleared her throat several times, but her words still came out thick and hoarse.

"First of all, I want to give you these." Wilma pressed keys to the back and front doors into Sovilla's palm.

"I don't feel right taking them. You could take back ownership of the house, and we could pay you rent."

Wilma shook her head. "No, no. I want nothing to do with my Pennsylvania past. You'll be much happier there than I ever was. Besides, you deserve the house and so much more after what I put you through."

When Sovilla tried to protest, her *aenti* interrupted. "I want my sister to have a place to live where she'll be safe from"—Wilma choked on the name—"Lloyd. And I don't want your sisters around his sons."

As much as Sovilla agreed with that, she still felt guilty about accepting the house. "You could still do that if you owned it."

"It's too much trouble. I don't want anything to distract my attention from Eli and our life together." A sweet smile crossed Wilma's face. "If it weren't for you, we'd have never found each other again. And we wouldn't have met David. For that alone, you should have the house."

"But—"

Wilma held up a hand. "Everyone's ready to go, and I still haven't said what I need to. Please let me finish."

Sovilla pressed her fingers to her lips to show she wouldn't interrupt.

Hanging her head, Wilma swallowed several times. "I'm so sorry for the way I treated everyone in Pennsylvania, but especially you. No matter what I did or said, you still treated me with kindness. A kindness I didn't deserve."

Her *aenti* would never say those words if she'd heard some of the uncharitable thoughts Sovilla had harbored.

"I know I shouldn't even ask this. Not after the way I treated you. But I want to make things right between us before you leave. Will you forgive me?"

"Of course." Sovilla had forgiven her *aenti* long ago, once she'd discovered the truth about David. "If you'll forgive me for the resentment I felt toward you."

Wilma lifted her bowed head, and her damp eyes met Sovilla's. "That was more than justified. There's nothing to forgive."

Then Wilma opened her arms, and Sovilla stepped into her very first hug from her *aenti*.

When the two of them returned to the kitchen, with tear-stained cheeks and brilliant smiles, Isaac hurried to Sovilla's side. Eli rushed as eagerly toward his future bride.

Mamm turned from the sink she'd just filled with water. Plates and cups had been piled on all the nearby counters.

Annie shooed everyone from the room. "Leave those dishes, Barbie. I know you need to get on the road. I'll take care of the cleanup later. I do have three fine helpers who'll be happy to assist." She eyed her sons.

They stared at her, their eyes reflecting shock and horror.

But when she pressed them—"Am I right?"—they all fixed their gazes on their shoes and choked out, "*Jah.*"

Sovilla suspected they'd be paying for their prank for quite a while. Perhaps now that Annie was aware of her husband's and sons' actions, she'd work to keep them all in line.

"I'm sorry about how my cousins treated you the other night," Sovilla whispered to Isaac, wishing she could take his hand. "I think they saw how happy we were together and wanted to ruin our relationship."

"Like you said, God had a different, and much better, plan."

Her eyes brimming with tears again, she met Isaac's adoring gaze. "I'm so glad He did."

She still couldn't believe the joy God had given her. It only increased when Isaac helped her to the seat he'd chosen in the back of the van. He settled Snickers on his opposite side and slid in beside her. They'd be able to sit and talk privately during the six-hour trip home. And maybe even secretly hold hands.

Wilma, Eli, and Annie gathered beside the van to say goodbye. Sovilla's cousins hung back.

Both Wilma and Eli fought back tears as they said goodbye to David.

"I'll write often," he promised. "And come to visit whenever I can."

"I'll make sure he does." Mrs. Vandenberg leaned out the passenger window. "I guess I picked the right size van after all, didn't I, Wilma?"

Jah, Mrs. Vandenberg had picked the right van. For Sovilla, cozied close to Isaac, the van was the perfect size.

And Sovilla was grateful for another "van"—Mrs. Van-denberg. This trip wouldn't have been possible without her.

Danke*, Lord, for Mrs. Vandenberg and all she's done. For reuniting Wilma and Eli. For bringing my family to Pennsylvania. And most of all for Isaac.*

As the van started off, heading toward Sovilla's future home and her life with Isaac, her heart overflowed with gratitude to be traveling in this van filled with all of those who were dear to her. A van filled with blessings. A van filled with happiness. A van filled with love.

Epilogue

Sitting across the room during the communion service, Isaac smiled at his wife, who was holding their newborn daughter. It was hard to believe he and Sovilla been married almost two years already. Her eyes met his, and she returned his tender look.

How his love for her had grown since the day he'd asked her about courting! Most days when he thought about her, his heart expanded until his chest ached. And now his love had multiplied to encompass their first child.

Today, the church would be choosing a new minister. After one last adoring glance at Sovilla and the baby, Isaac bowed his head and closed his eyes.

Lord, please direct my heart and mind as we choose the man to serve you.

One by one, the members filed out to walk past the side room where the bishop and two other ministers waited. Each person who passed whispered a name through the crack in the door. Isaac struggled to decide. God had not laid a name on his heart, but his turn had come. He suggested the name of a kind neighbor, one who seemed godly and upright. Then he returned to his seat.

A short while later, the bishop emerged and called out the men who'd been nominated. As he named them, the men moved to the front row. Isaac rejoiced when they named his neighbor.

But his heart seemed the only happy one in the congregation. Men who'd been singled out and their wives, and even their relatives, sat sober or burst out crying.

The bishop studied the sheet in his hand and read off the last name: "Isaac Lantz."

Neh, he must have misheard. He froze in his seat until the bishop located Isaac in the congregation and nodded for him to come forward.

His throat dry, he stood and looked to Sovilla, who wore a serious expression, but she sent him encouragement.

Unlike the others, he walked forward in a daze, his lips pinched together, not making a sound. A sense of inadequacy twisting his insides, Isaac sat beside the other men, all of them older and wiser. Until today, he'd never really understood the groaning and weeping during the selection process. Being a minister was a huge and solemn responsibility. For him, the job came with an extra burden—it required speaking. Would it be right to pray for someone else to be chosen?

But what was he doing up front? Surely there'd been a mistake. Nobody in the congregation would have suggested him. They all knew he stuttered. He'd almost conquered it over the past few years, but he still avoided speaking in public. God would never pick him to deliver messages to the congregation.

Isaac brought his attention back to the bishop, who'd already inserted the slips of paper into the *Ausbunds* in the stack, but only one slip had a verse on it. After Laban shuffled the hymnbooks, each of the nominees chose a book.

Isaac dithered over his choice. He couldn't bring himself to beg God not to give him this responsibility. That didn't feel right. Instead, he sent up a quick prayer.

Lord, you know I'm not worthy to be a minister. Your will be done.

Then he reached out and selected a hymnbook. Taking a deep breath, he ruffled the pages. A slip of paper. With trembling fingers, Isaac withdrew the verse.

Chills washed over him. His eyes burned. He couldn't believe God had chosen him. Not when he had no skill at speaking and he stuttered whenever he was nervous.

Then deep inside, a still, small voice reminded him: "*My grace is sufficient.*"

Although Isaac believed God could do anything, he failed to see how the Lord could use someone so weak and flawed.

The other men, their eyes damp, but relieved, filed past him. Many squeezed his shoulder, and all of them asked God's blessing on him.

Still stunned, Isaac, his stomach churning, made it through the ordination.

Afterward, all he wanted to do was escape, but he forced himself to act normal and prayed nobody noticed his pasted-on calmness or stinging eyes. His brothers gathered around to commiserate.

Andrew slapped him on the back. "I'm sorry, Isaac. Although I agree you'd make a great minister, I know it's the last thing you want to do."

Grateful for his brother's understanding, Isaac managed a halfhearted smile. Ever since Andrew had started dating Ruthie, he'd apologized for his earlier jealousy and nastiness, and Isaac had forgiven his twin. They'd returned to their old camaraderie, and could now read each other's minds again.

Andrew deflected most of the people who sought Isaac out. Although Isaac was grateful for everyone's encouragement, he couldn't wait to talk to Sovilla. What if she didn't want to be a minister's wife?

After what seemed hours and hours, Isaac finally headed out to the buggy. He helped Sovilla in and waited until the horse had started down the road before sharing his worries. "D-do you mind?"

"I do for your sake, not for mine."

Holding the reins in one hand, he reached for her hand. She smiled, shifted the baby to one arm, and entwined her fingers with his.

Her sympathetic glance gave him the courage to say what was on his heart. "I don't think I can do this."

"It won't be easy, but God wouldn't have chosen you if He didn't want you to do it."

"I don't feel worthy. I'm so young. The other men have much more knowledge than I do."

"God doesn't need human knowledge. His strength is made perfect in our weakness."

Isaac marveled at how in tune they were. Sovilla had mentioned the last half of the verse that had come to him during his ordination. "I'm going to need a lot of His strength."

She threaded her fingers with his. "We'll both pray. With God's help, you'll do fine. You've spent a lot of years listening instead of talking. Now it's your turn to speak."

Dread sloshed in Isaac's stomach as he pictured standing

in front of everyone, unable to get his words out. "What if I stutter?"

"People will still listen. They go to church to get a message from God's Word."

Sovilla's words sliced through Isaac's pride. As a minister, he should be focused on the Lord, not himself. "It's *hochmut* to worry about how I sound, to want to be perfect. I shouldn't care so much about how I appear. I should humble myself before God and let him provide the message."

Her brilliant smile reinforced his words.

That didn't stop his nerves from zinging. "Next service, I'll have to read the Scripture passage."

Her lips quirked. "You've had plenty of practice with that."

True. He'd been reading the Bible aloud to his puppies for years. Perhaps all those years of imitating Demosthenes had a greater purpose.

"Maybe if you pretended the people are dogs," she teased, "it would be easier. Oh, and you might want to take the gravel out of your mouth."

Isaac laughed. "What would I do without your helpful advice?" But her joking suggestion had given him an idea. Over the next two weeks, he'd speak to the dogs and Sovilla with and without pebbles.

He also made use of all his sleepless nights. To let Sovilla rest, he paced the floor with his colicky daughter and recited Scripture verses aloud.

Although he missed Sovilla's encouragement each time he read a verse without errors, the nighttime cuddling allowed him to forge a special bond with his little girl. And putting her to sleep to the rhythm and beauty of God's word was a special blessing.

If only he could carry this peacefulness, this closeness, this calmness into the service. But as each day passed, the tension inside increased. And on Sunday morning, when the ministers met before the service, the delicious breakfast he'd choked down earlier curdled in his stomach.

By the time he stood before the congregation, his mouth had dried and no amount of swallowing seemed to wet it. He croaked out the first few words, almost too low for anyone to hear. Then Sovilla's smile buoyed him and reminded him to trust a Higher Power.

Clearing his throat, he started again. He stumbled several times, but people were listening to God's Word and not to his delivery. Mercifully, it was soon over, and Isaac could listen to the sermons and relax . . . at least until two Sundays from now.

Two Sundays later, Sovilla sat on the edge of her seat, holding their sleeping daughter and whispering prayers for God's blessing on her beloved husband before he gave the first, shorter sermon. Isaac had agonized over the past two weeks, because the ministers never decided the sermon topics until Sunday morning before the service.

Several times he broke off from practicing his speech exercises to pepper her with questions: "What if my mind goes blank and I can't think of anything to say?" "What if my mouth goes dry again and I can't get words out?" "What if I start stuttering?"

To each question, Sovilla answered calmly, "Trust the Lord."

Now, as Isaac emerged with the other ministers, her heart was so in tune with his, every cell in Sovilla's body absorbed her husband's nervousness. As if sensing her anxiety, the baby whined. Sovilla needed to heed the advice she'd given Isaac. Cradling her sweet little daughter close, Sovilla prayed.

Please, Lord, calm both our nerves and give Isaac the words to say.

Isaac stood up front, appearing calm on the outside. But Sovilla knew him well enough to note his clenched fists and jaw, the small frown lines that formed between his brows when he faced a problem. And she prayed God's blessing on him.

He opened his mouth, but no words came out. She took a deep breath in unison with him.

Lord, please let sounds, I mean words, come out.

An explosive noise burst from Isaac's lips, and his cheeks reddened. Staring down at the floor, he rocked back and forth on the balls of his feet. Inhaling again, he restarted. He stuttered through the first few words. Finally, he managed a phrase, drew in some air, and completed another. Soon, he established a rhythm. Breath. Phrase. Breath. Phrase. After several sentences, he paused, as if thinking of his next point. Then he returned to his previous pattern.

By the time the sermon ended, Sovilla was as emotionally exhausted and drained as Isaac. She'd inhaled and exhaled every time he did and had stayed connected with him for every word. Now she channeled his relief.

Throughout, he'd glanced up from the floor to fixate on a spot on the far wall, but now he sneaked a look in her direction. She tried to convey how meaningful his message had been and—though she should temper it—her pride in his accomplishment.

The stress lines on his face smoothed, and he stroked his beard. The beard that meant he was married—to her. The beard that always set her heart on fire.

On the way home, Sovilla turned to him. "You did so well up there." Her bright smile and the lovelight shining in her eyes started his heart thumping.

He wanted to take her in his arms, but that would have to wait until they got home. For now, he waved away her praise. "I wish my speech wasn't so jerky."

"That'll come in time. What's most important is the lesson you taught."

As usual, Sovilla focused his attention off himself and his self-criticism. "God gave me the ideas. I couldn't have done it without Him."

"You listened well."

But what about next time? Today he'd only done the first, much shorter talk. In two weeks, he'd face his biggest hurdle—the one-hour sermon.

"You're thinking about the long sermon, aren't you?" As she always did, Sovilla had guessed what worried him.

"*Jah.* I wish we knew ahead of time what the topic will be." Deciding on the sermon topic with the other ministers before each service gave him no time to prepare.

"Trust God for the message."

Her familiar reminder calmed him. The purpose of not planning ahead was to be open to the Lord's leading. "*Danke*, Sovilla."

But when Isaac woke on the day of the service, anxiety gripped him. He reminded himself he'd made it through the first two services. His presentations had not been stellar, but he'd brought God's message to the congregation. He needed to do the same with this longer sermon.

Lord, help me to listen to You rather than my fears.

Sovilla stopped to hug him as she hurried toward the crying baby. "I'll be praying. You can do this."

After she'd fed the baby and him, they cleaned up the kitchen together and prepared for church, which they'd host today. Sovilla, Barbie, and the girls had been working nonstop for the past two weeks, cleaning and baking. They'd left the house spotless and prepared for the after-church meal.

Next door, in the house they'd built onto Wilma's for Sovilla's mamm and sisters, loud laughter resounded through the walls.

"What's going on over there?" Isaac asked his wife.

Sovilla only smiled mysteriously as she pinned on her kapp. "You'll see."

See what? Isaac soon forgot his question as the time for the service neared.

A short while later, Sovilla's sisters breezed in, chattering away. Martha Mae leaned close to Sovilla and whispered, "Does he know?"

Pressing a finger to her lips, Sovilla shook her head.

What secrets were they hiding? Too nervous to ask, Isaac pushed it from his mind. He'd ask after church.

As the men gathered in the barn, Isaac stood apart, praying God would calm his jitters and speak to his heart. After he met with the ministers and bishop to decide the sermon topics, they filed into the living room, where the benches had been set up, and the room around Isaac dissolved into the cloud of worry enveloping him. How would he ever speak on this topic for a whole hour?

Head down, he focused on his clenched hands and begged God for a message.

When his turn to speak came, he stood in front of the congregation, trying to project an air of confidence and surety, but he had no words, no ideas.

He searched the women's section for Sovilla, hoping her loving face would give him some strength and start his words flowing. Instead, he stared in shock at the elderly woman next to Sovilla.

Mrs. Vandenberg?

She smiled at him, her eyes filled with reassurance. Wilma sat beside her. And Annie. His eyes strayed to the other side of the room. Eli. David. Lloyd and his sons, all of them sitting stiffly and looking uncomfortable. Even Jeremiah, the young man in a wheelchair who now had Snickers as his service dog.

When? How?

Sovilla must have arranged all this. His gaze swung to her, and her encouraging smile reminded him he should be speaking.

His face burning, Isaac struggled to remember his topic for the day. He'd been standing here gawking like a fool while everyone in the congregation waited for him to begin.

With another quick petition heavenward, he took a deep breath. God had surrounded him with the love and support of friends and family members. He would speak to them about humility by being honest about his own failings. And about *gelassenheit*, submission to God's will, by yielding to the Lord now and letting Him take over the sermon.

Once he surrendered, Isaac no longer needed Demosthenes or speech therapy techniques. He had the energy and power of the Living God, the Creator of all. He only had to connect with that Source and share God's message with the people gathered here in His name.

Isaac stepped aside and let the heavenly presence flow through him. The Holy Spirit empowered him, filling him with God's love. When he opened his mouth, words flowed from his lips, connecting heart to heart.

When he finished, Isaac bowed his head in silent thanksgiving. He'd learned the secret of preaching without stuttering—complete surrender to the Lord.

Several hours later, after the church members had left following the meal, family and friends gathered in the kitchen. Sovilla put the baby down for her nap and then came to stand beside Isaac.

Wilma had tears in her eyes as she ran her hand over the huge maple table that now replaced the rickety metal one she'd used. "You've done such a wonderful job fixing up the house. Who would have ever thought my house would hold a church service? Or that you'd be a minister?"

"I'm not at all surprised." Mrs. Vandenberg tapped her cane on the floor for emphasis. "I always believed Isaac had messages he needed to share with the world."

"I couldn't have done it without you." Isaac never would have come across Demosthenes on his own.

She waved a hand as if to brush off his comment. "Not me—Divine Guidance. And credit goes to you for your persistence. And to God, of course."

"Without Him, I'd never have been able to preach." Isaac acknowledged the truth.

Sovilla sidled up to him. "You worked hard, and God rewarded your faithfulness."

Lowering his voice so only she could hear, he murmured, "You're one of my greatest rewards."

Jeremiah wheeled closer. "The van will be coming for me soon, but today's message meant so much to me. I can't thank you enough."

Isaac shook Jeremiah's outstretched hand. "I'm glad you could be here."

Snickers whined, and Isaac stared down at the dog he'd spent so much time bonding with. It had been hard to turn Snickers over to the trainers, but knowing she'd be assisting Jeremiah helped Isaac cope. "Can I pet her?"

Jeremiah smiled at Snickers. "She's such a good dog, she deserves a little time off. Go ahead."

Isaac knelt beside Snickers. Oh, how he missed his little companion! But knowing that Snickers had a good home and the chance to help Jeremiah made up for his loss.

Although Isaac still went down to the kennels to take care of the dogs, he hadn't trained another puppy since. His priority these past few years had been Sovilla and then their baby daughter. Working at the market and taking care of all the puppies in the kennel took a lot of time, but now he had his wife's assistance. Soon, though, he and Sovilla, would again become puppy raisers for one special dog.

Heavy footfalls clomped across the kitchen linoleum. Lloyd towered over Isaac, a scowl on his face. Isaac wanted to stand, to puff out his chest, and counteract Lloyd's blustering.

Because he'd just spoken about humility, though, Isaac remained where he was. Surely Isaac could follow the Lord's example. The Savior had bent to wash his disciples' feet. To ease some of his tension, Isaac buried his fingers in Snickers's soft fur.

Annie rushed over and set a hand on Lloyd's arm, but he shook it off.

"I don't appreciate you singling me out with your sermon," Lloyd thundered.

Isaac had spoken more to himself than to the congregation. And he certainly hadn't directed his words to Sovilla's *onkel*.

Annie interrupted her husband before he could say more. "That wasn't Isaac speaking to you. It was God. Perhaps it's time you listened."

Lloyd stared at his wife. Then the hardness and anger in his face turned to woundedness, and his eyes filled with the pain of betrayal. Pivoting, he stalked off, his sons trailing in his wake. The front door slammed behind them.

"I'm sorry, Isaac." Annie wrung her hands. "Lloyd and the boys have come a long way, but they all needed your message today."

"Not my message." Isaac had only been the vessel. He still marveled that God had chosen the one person in the church who stuttered to do this job.

Annie's eyes filled with tears. "At least I know Lloyd listened to the sermon today. Maybe the boys did too. I'm trusting God to keep working in their hearts."

"We'll be praying." Sovilla's heart-stopping smile made Isaac want to wrap her in an embrace. And he would as soon as they were alone.

An hour later, Lloyd returned. "The driver's here. It's time for us to go."

After many hugs and tears, they all headed to the front door, with promises to visit again soon.

As Lloyd reached the porch, he turned. "I'm sorry," he mumbled in a gruff voice, "for everything." He included Sovilla and Isaac along with Barbie and the girls in his glance. Then he looked at Wilma and lowered his head. "And to you too."

It wasn't much of an apology, but for Lloyd, it had been a huge concession. Isaac stood there, dumbfounded. Had the sermon truly touched Lloyd's heart?

"Don't worry," Mrs. Vandenberg assured them as the van left for Ohio. "That's only the beginning of the changes God has in store for him."

Isaac had no doubt she was right. She'd foreseen his need for speech lessons years ago. Mrs. Vandenberg seemed to have a direct connection to God.

Her car glided up to the curb, and they waved her off, certain they'd see her soon. She visited them often and loved to help care for the baby sometimes while he and Sovilla worked at the market, taking turns helping at the auction and the pickle/bakery stand. Wilma had even shared her recipe with Sovilla's *mamm*.

Jeremiah's van pulled up as Mrs. Vandenberg's Bentley drove off, and Isaac said another reluctant goodbye.

"Come and visit Snickers anytime," Jeremiah said. "She'd be glad for the company, and so would I."

"I'll do that." Isaac stared after them with longing as Snickers helped pull Jeremiah's wheelchair up the ramp.

Sovilla slipped her hand in Isaac's. "It's time to train another puppy."

He squeezed her hand gently in reply. Once again, she'd read his mind.

God had blessed him with so many things, including his baby daughter and the most wonderful wife a man could ever have—one who was loving, caring, and wise. And as soon as they shut the door, he took her in his arms to show her all the love overflowing in his heart.